Adiel and the Führer

ELYSE HOFFMAN

ISBN (ebook): 978-1-952742-29-3
ISBN (paperback): 978-1-952742-30-9
ISBN (hardcover): 978-1-952742-31-6

Project 613 Publishing
elysehoffman.com

PROJECT613

To my grandfather David,
my grandmother Shirley,
my mother Lydia,
my father Richard,
my sister Liana,
and to God, Who makes all stories.

BLACK FOX ONE

While *"Adiel and the Führer"* can be enjoyed as a standalone story, it is also a continuation of Elyse Hoffman's previous book, **Black Fox One.** Characters and plot details from **Black Fox One** might be referenced in this book.

You might enjoy this story more if you read **Black Fox One** first.

Thank you, and enjoy!

https://www.amazon.com/Black-Fox-One-Gripping-Resistance-ebook/dp/B0BW15KYVX

ONE

Adiel Goldstein had always wanted a little brother. A little sister would do too. Really, he just wanted a friend.

But his mother Rebecca would sigh sadly every time he requested a brother or a sister, and his father Natan would smirk and say that one Adiel was plenty.

Every birthday, Adiel begged for a sibling, and every year he was rebuffed, given a fancy toy or more paints instead. Which was all well and good, but toys were less fun without anyone to play with, and paints were pointless when there was nobody to paint for.

In a better world, Adiel wouldn't have been so lonely. The village they lived in was small, but there were plenty of children. In a better world, Adiel, ever eager for companionship, would have been swimming in friends.

But Adiel was the only Jewish child in the village. And in the last years of the 1800s, even in a nation as cultured as Germany, being a Jew made him an outcast. At best, he was offered a cold shoulder. At worst, he was driven away with stones and jeers whenever he tried to approach a group of boys his age. Even little children three years his junior had been trained by their parents to spit on the kippa-clad boy when he drew near.

But today...today was the day before Adiel's seventh birthday, and he was hoping beyond hope that today would be the day that he would finally make a friend.

A new family had finally moved into the house next door: the Goldsteins lived in a manor that stretched and stretched so far that it was almost a five-minute walk from the edge of their property to their front door. Beyond the trimmed bushes that surrounded the Goldsteins' estate, however, there was a run-down old ramshackle cottage, a structure that might have once been servants' quarters but had evidently been sold separately. Nobody had lived there before. Nobody wanted to, and the little village so rarely had new people move in.

But today the little house was a home again; home to a pudgy couple that had a golden-haired boy Adiel's age. A child potentially uncorrupted by the ancient hatred permeating the rest of the village.

Adiel's plan was seemingly foolproof, his weapons carefully chosen. First, a drawing, painstakingly painted with all of his best and most colorful paints that showed himself, helpfully labeled "Adiel," and the new blond boy, labeled as "Adiel's Best Friend." Additionally, he had carried out a fair amount of reconnaissance and had deduced that his target loved mud and cars, and so he'd selected his best, shiniest toy car as an offering.

Adiel was ready. His heart was pounding so hard that it felt like it was going to combust, his little hands were so sweaty that he feared he would smudge his beautiful picture, but he was ready. He told his mother that he would be out playing and began his journey.

Eventually, Adiel spotted his target: the apple-cheeked, sunny-haired new boy covered in mud and sporting ripped-up lederhosen. He was kneeling in the dirt and making engine noises as he smashed two hastily constructed wooden cars together.

Adiel knew that he would lose heart if he hesitated, so he made sure his kippa was straight, checked his picture to make sure it was still beautiful, and then marched right up to the boy. The new neighbor looked up with bright, curious blue eyes almost the exact same shade as Adiel's, and the Jewish boy blurted out his practiced introduction in one breath.

"Hi, I'm Adiel and I live next to you, and I like drawing, and tomorrow's my birthday, and I drew you this picture and got you this car, do you wanna be my best friend?"

In the future, when he was old and accomplished enough that childhood memories were less painful, he would laugh, remembering this bungled word-vomit. The way he tried to sell himself like a desperate worker, the way he shoved his painting at the boy like he was offering a resume. The kippa on his head felt like it was scalding his skull, but the neighbor boy only gave it a cursory glance before his eyes fell on the toy car that Adiel offered.

"Okay!" squeaked the neighbor boy, grabbing the car with a smile. "Can I play with the nice car first? I made a track, but if we're gonna have a race, we've gotta make it wider. Oh, and I'm Rupert."

Adiel's little heart soared to new heights. That moment would be bitter in the future because he would know that it ranked among the times he had been happiest. Right up there with the day his wife agreed to marry him, the day she *did* marry him, and the day she would give him a daughter that would be his real best friend.

But right then, six-year-old Adiel, who had never gotten love from anyone except his parents, felt like he wasn't even touching the ground. And it didn't matter that he didn't particularly like playing in the mud, and it didn't matter that his drawing would probably get dirty. He was prepared to kneel down and build an amazing racetrack with his brand-new best friend.

"Rupert!"

But then a woman's voice broke through the birdsong and the happy buzzing in his ears. The joyous moment came crashing down as Rupert's mother emerged from the tiny house, wearing an expression that Adiel knew too well. It was the expression that he saw on the face of nearly every gentile in the village every day.

"Rupert!" the woman said, grabbing her son by the arm and wrenching him to his feet. She pried the toy car from her son's grimy fingers, and though the blond boy argued and whined, she tossed it at the slack-jawed six-year-old Jew's feet.

"We do *not* associate with Christ-killers! Don't you remember what I told you? Jews like him kill good little Christian boys and drink their blood!"

And there, the seed was planted. Perhaps in the past, when Rupert had been warned about the evil of Jewry, he hadn't listened because it was a vague threat, like the threat of cavities if he didn't brush his teeth. But now it was real, solid. Adiel was right there, flesh and blood, and Rupert looked at him with wide-eyed fear.

Adiel barely felt it when the woman spat on him, barely felt the dollop of spit dribble from his forehead down his face. He only vaguely heard her scream, "Go to Hell, Jew!"

But then Rupert giggled, stepped forward, and copied his mother, spitting and echoing her: "Go to Hell, Jew!"

It was then that numb sorrow became white hot fury, like Adiel was a pot that had been boiling too long and needed to explode.

"FINE!" Adiel screamed, and in two swift motions, he ripped the picture in half and kicked dirt right in the ugly, horrible woman's face before turning on his heel and running back to the Goldstein family's grand home.

Adiel was angry. *So* angry. He'd been angry before, but now he felt like something inside of him was straining, near snapping, like his soul was an overburdened horse and its spine was just about to *crack*. He *hated* that lady, and he *hated* Rupert, and he *hated* everyone in this village.

"I hate them!" Adiel screamed as he flew into the house, tears streaming from his face.

"*I hate them!*" he howled as he shoved a table over and sent a vase tumbling to the floor. It shattered. Breaking things helped. It felt like he was letting out the fire, and so he kept at it.

"*I hate them!*"

CRASH!

"*I! Hate! Them!*"

SMASH!

"I HATE THEM!"

Adiel was generally a well-behaved boy, and his parents were indulgent enough that he rarely threw a true tantrum. Not that he wasn't occasionally destructive; he was a six-year-old boy, after all, but his destruction typically served a purpose. When he had been three years old, for instance, he had torn up every pillow in the house so that he could cover himself in feathers and pretend to be the great Ziz Bird Monster of Jewish folklore, an action that had resulted in Natan dubbing his son "little monster."

Natan's epithet had never suited Adiel so well, however: the boy who typically only ever wanted to create set about in a torrent of destruction across his house. Bookshelves were toppled, fine china shattered, vases and decorative statues were hurled to the floor. He screamed and screamed and kept breaking things in a desperate attempt to make the fire in his heart fade.

But then he heard something: sobbing that wasn't his own.

The fire cooled into curiosity, and Adiel stopped himself from tossing a plate into a pile of broken shards. He perked up his ears. A woman was crying upstairs. Adiel realized right then that he must have been horribly loud, and yet his mother hadn't come down to investigate what he was doing.

"Mama...?" he muttered, worry and love quickly taking the place of anger and hate as he scrambled up the staircase. He followed the sound of sobbing all the way into his parents' room, noticing right away that his mother's walk-in closet was slightly open.

He peeked inside without announcing himself. Adiel had been inside the closet on occasion, mostly during bouts of hide-and-seek with his father. During such games, he had often noticed the presence of a large, ancient-looking wooden chest buried behind a few long dresses. Adiel had tried to open it once or twice, but his attempts had been unsuccessful, and he'd given up on the venture.

When Adiel peeked inside now, he realized that his

mother was kneeling before the wide-open chest, looking inside and wailing wildly.

"Mama!" he squeaked, worrying that something inside the mysterious chest was somehow hurting his mother. He knew for a fact that parents weren't supposed to cry. Parents were invincible, and therefore, only a truly monstrous force could possibly make his lovely mother sob.

Becca Goldstein moved so quickly that, to Adiel, it seemed like time itself sped up: one moment she was kneeling before the chest, and then she was slamming the chest shut, locking it, standing up, and tucking the key into her apron.

"Adiel!" Becca cried, quickly wiping her tears away and offering him a wavering smile as she brushed her curly dark brown hair back into place. Adiel acted on his very first instinct, scurrying forward and throwing his arms around her.

"Mama, what happened?" he squeaked, patting himself down and huffing in disappointment when he realized that he didn't have a handkerchief in his pocket to offer her. "Please don't cry!"

"Ah, it's all right, sweetie, it's all right…" Becca muttered, her voice cracking slightly. "Mama was just thinking about sad things."

"Don't do that again, okay?" Adiel begged, squirming and clinging tightly to her apron, casting a frightened look at the chest that had somehow, as though via magic, made his ever-smiling mother cry. Becca let out a small, genuine laugh and ushered her son out of the closet.

"Yes, sir, Adiel, sir," she said, shutting the closet door behind her and then kneeling before him, brushing her thumb under his eye. "Looks like you were crying, too. Why were *you* crying?"

If his mother had been hoping to shift the subject away from whatever had made *her* cry, she was completely successful. A dreadful feeling even worse than fiery hatred welled up in Adiel's chest, like he was being weighed down by a thousand bricks. Guilt. His poor mother was already sad and crying, and he'd wrecked her house even though it wasn't her fault that nobody except her and Papa loved him, and now she'd be even more sad because she'd have to pick everything up, and she'd cry again, and it would be his fault, and...

And that was how they ended up downstairs, with Becca chuckling as she observed the wreckage left behind by her son's tantrum. She held the wailing boy in her arms as he blurted apologies.

"You really did a number on the place!" Becca giggled, carefully tiptoeing over broken shards of pottery and setting her son down in a cozy chair. She knelt down in front of him and offered the corner of her apron as a makeshift tissue. "No wonder Papa calls you little monster! Is this what you two do when I'm not at home?"

"Noooooo," hiccupped Adiel, blowing his nose on the apron. "I'm sorry, Mama! I got angry because the neighbor boy Rupert spat on me and called me a Christ-killer 'cause his mama ruined the friend-plan, and I *hate* her, and I *hate* him, and I *hate* them!"

Briefly, Adiel felt the fire flare again, but it was quenched when his mother shook her head with a gentle, chastising little smile decorating her now-dry face.

"See now, Adiel," Becca said in that voice she used whenever she needed to teach him something very important. "They shouldn't have done that. That was really terrible. And you definitely have a right to feel upset and sad about it. But anger and hate, you shouldn't ever feel anger or hate for anyone, no matter what. You see what happens when you do..."

She gestured to the Goldsteins' ruined home and shattered possessions. "See? You hurt yourself and the people you love first. Hatred, Adiel, it's a fire, and it burns you before it burns them."

Adiel reached up and touched his chest, nodding slowly. She was right, of course; the evidence was all around him. He promised her right then that he would studiously avoid anger and hatred, and if he felt it spark in his soul again, he would extinguish it straight away. He never wanted to be the reason that his mother cried.

Becca happily accepted his apology and helped him get to work cleaning up. Natan Goldstein came home to an almost-clean house, but the investor nonetheless let out a low whistle as he stumbled into the living room and saw broken bits of china littering the floor.

"Hey, little monster, did a storm pass through here?" Natan quipped, tugging on the cuffs of his sweat-soaked shirt. Even though it was a warm spring day, Natan was wearing long-sleeves. Not out of any work-related obligation; Natan was such a talented investor that he probably could have shown up naked to work and they wouldn't have fired him. Adiel didn't know the reason he had never seen his father's bare arms, but he could only assume it was either simple personal preference or, more likely, modesty borne from a birthmark or scar that he wished to conceal.

Not that the almost seven-year-old cared, of course. Adiel would love his father no matter what, and right then, he only cared about Natan's feelings. Adiel ran up to his father, begging him not to cry and promising that he wouldn't get angry ever again. Becca gently explained what had happened.

"You're lucky I just made enough money to replace all this fancy stuff, little monster," chuckled Natan. "Or we'd have to cancel your birthday tomorrow and sell all your gifts."

"Natan!" cried Becca, rolling her eyes.

"We'd have to sell your birthday cake, too. Do we even have any plates left?"

"I left a couple!" Adiel assured Natan, and his father teasingly tugged on one of Adiel's dark brown locks.

"Me and Mama are gonna eat all your cake," Natan joked. "You're gonna have to starve, little monster."

Natan did not, in fact, force Adiel to starve. The next day, they celebrated Adiel's seventh birthday with a big chocolate cake and a smattering of expensive toys. Natan and Becca also offered the boy good news: they would be moving within the week.

Adiel would remember the day before his seventh birthday, the pain of Rupert's rejection, long after they left behind the little village, long after they moved into a majority Jewish neighborhood where he finally made friends, where his neighbors treated him like a human being instead of a byword. He would always remember that day, and he would always remember his mother's counsel against anger and hatred.

Adiel Goldstein would follow his mother's guidance until the end of his life.

TWO

The fact that Professor Adiel Goldstein hadn't punched Leon Engel in his face yet was a tribute to how much he loved and respected his mother.

By no means was the young Nazi the first anti-Semite that Adiel had been forced to teach at the Munich Academy of Fine Arts. Adiel had gone into his profession without any delusion that the enlightened world of academia would be above anti-Semitism. If anything, he had been braced for higher forms of it. Hatred based on figures and purple prose rather than slur-filled guffaws.

Leon Engel might have somehow made it into art school, which was more than could be said of his idol Hitler, but the Brownshirt boy was most certainly the latter, less intellectual breed of anti-Semite. His hateful acts were dreadfully dull and, particularly for a supposed artist, creatively bankrupt.

Case in point: this day in autumn.

"Good morning, students," Adiel sighed as he strolled into his classroom, flashing the bright young artists a brief smile before slamming his bag onto his wide desk and digging through his teaching materials. "Today, we'll be continuing our discussion on Ilya Repin and modeling facial expressions, particularly when using oil. And I can think of no better example than…if I can find it…"

A few students chuckled at Adiel's efforts, and he winked at the ones that he knew meant well. "Oh, laugh at me, you scamps! Next time any of you lose your homework, I'm not showing any sympathy! Ah, here she is!"

Adiel managed to pull one particular rolled-up copy of a famous painting from the bunch. A work of oil realism created by a Russian artist about a Russian moment in history: the moment after the vicious Ivan the Terrible murdered his own eldest son. The once proud Czar cradled the younger man to his chest, his wide, guilt-filled eyes more striking than even the depiction of the wound on the Russian prince's skull.

"*Ivan the Terrible and His Son*," Adiel decreed with a smile. "Painted in…"

Before Adiel could round off the date or say another word about the painting, he turned to pin the print onto the chalkboard only to find himself staring at a message written in familiar tidy handwriting: "Jew, Get Out!" The threat was surrounded by multiple clumsily done swastikas. Hitler would have been quite disappointed in his underling's art skills.

Speaking of which, the guilty party, Leon Engel, started snickering, and several of his Nazi classmates joined in. Adiel, at this point well-versed in the art of quenching the fire of anger, only needed a moment to compose himself before he plastered a smirk onto his face and swiftly erased the hateful screed.

"Very amusing, Herr Engel," he chirped, pinning Repin's art above the dusty remains of the swastikas and turning towards Leon Engel. The young Nazi was sitting in the back of the classroom, dressed in paint-covered slacks and a button-up shirt. Leon's blue-green eyes gleamed with wolf-like viciousness before he scowled in disappointment at his failure to get a real reaction out of his teacher.

"Your swastikas are becoming sloppier, though, and I'm relatively sure that one of them was backwards," Adiel said, earning a round of chuckles from the students that weren't Hitler-loyalists. Leon Engel, whose confidence was morphing into frustration, offered Adiel a murderous glare and pointed furiously at the copy of Repin's work.

"Why are we studying some Slav, anyway?" Leon grunted. "This is a *German* university. We should be studying *German* art."

"We are not studying *some Slav*, Engel," Adiel countered swiftly, lifting up his pointer and gesturing to the painted Czar's face. "We are studying the work of an *artist* who *is Russian*. An artist who can paint eyes better than any German. Find me a German artist who can perfectly capture the eyes of a man who has killed his own child, and I will happily use it as an example. Lord knows, you could stand to study more."

Adiel smirked, and Engel's face became as red as the flag of the communists he brawled with when he should have been studying. It was terribly difficult for Adiel to resist prodding the fuming Nazi more, but the Professor remembered his mother's advice and forced a cool wind to enter his soul. Ignoring Engel was always best anyway. The more attention Engel got, the happier he would be.

The Professor breezed through the rest of the lesson,

keenly aware all the while that several of his students were whispering to each other, one word standing out amongst their snickers and huffs: "Jew, Jew, Jew."

A heavy sigh wracked Adiel's body as he reached up to adjust his kippa. Leon Engel would not know it (and if he'd been told, he wouldn't have believed it) but Adiel Goldstein had worked exceptionally hard, far harder than any German gentile, to become a professor. Despite Leon's almost daily proclamations about the Jews who supposedly ruled Weimar Germany and their propensity towards favoring those of their race, Adiel had never been offered any shortcuts. Quite the opposite, actually.

Adiel's talents had been well-honed over the years, at the encouragement of Natan and Rebecca. He had gone from a decent enough art student to a professor more than worthy of his station, and perhaps worthy of a higher station. Of course, Adiel was lucky enough to be where he was. He'd had to fight tooth and nail against prejudicial policies in order to gain a degree, much less tenure.

Adiel had struggled, but he had prevailed. Of course, in a few months, it wouldn't matter. He would be losing his position anyway. Thanks to Leon Engel's new Messiah. Thanks to one of Adiel's old comrades. Thanks to Hitler.

Technically, of course, it wasn't *entirely* Hitler's fault. Hitler had no power yet.

Yet being the operative word.

Hitler would be running for President in the upcoming 1932 election against the current German President, Paul Von Hindenburg. Though Adiel wasn't entirely sure that a madman who had once tried to overthrow the government in a violent putsch had any chance of gaining office via legitimate means, Natan had declared that there was no future for Jews in Germany even if Hitler didn't win. The mere fact that he *could* win was, in Natan's view, proof enough that Germany was a lost cause.

The Goldsteins' significant wealth would make it easy enough to relocate, and Adiel had learned enough English to get by once they moved to America.

It would be difficult for Adiel to leave behind everything that he had struggled for, but on the other hand, it would be nice to never have to see Leon Engel's face again.

Besides, under no circumstances would Adiel allow his daughter to grow up without her grandfather. She had been torn from more than her fair share of family members.

Briefly, Adiel ripped his eyes from Ilya Repin's *magnum opus* and glanced down at his pocket, at the bulge of his wallet. If he were to take out his wallet and open it, Adiel would be greeted by a picture taken many years ago, the last picture that showed the entire Goldstein family: Adiel, smiling as he laid a hand on his wife Emma's shoulder while their daughter Kaia, then three, stood between her parents and her grandparents, grinning widely.

Little Kaia, now nine, hadn't lost her bright smile despite the fact that her family photos had gotten smaller and smaller throughout the years. First, a horrid bout of polio had stolen her mother. Then, just last year, they had lost Becca to breast cancer. It might have been too much for Adiel himself to bear, but for little Kaia's sake, he would do his best to stay strong and do whatever was best for her, even if that meant moving across the Atlantic Ocean.

It wouldn't be too bad. A new start, a neighborhood full of Jews, and Adiel wouldn't feel any pain about abandoning a homeland that didn't feel much like a home anymore. Any lingering feelings of German patriotism had abandoned Adiel when he'd returned home after four miserable years of fighting for his nation in the trenches during the Great War. He had gone back home with an Iron Cross shining on his breast and hope in his heart that his service would render him an equal among the gentiles.

That hope had been dashed. Adiel was glad that he hadn't actually died for Germany, because Germany had no affection for her Jewish martyrs. He knew many men from synagogue who had gone to war, come back in caskets, and had subsequently had their gravestones desecrated by the Germans they had fought for. Adiel, for his part, was done trying to appeal to a nation that, it seemed, would despise him no matter what he did. Maybe America would be more grateful, and if not, well, at least he wouldn't have to worry about Hitler and his cronies.

The Professor concluded the lesson and wished his students good-day. As the budding artists started to collect their sketchbooks and filed out of the classroom, an intern fought against the stream of students and scurried inside.

"Professor Goldstein," she said. "Your daughter's school called. They need you to come get her early."

"Oh, dear," Adiel sighed with a fondly bitter little smile, rolling up Repin's work and shoving it into his bag. "What did she steal this time?"

"They didn't say, sir. They just said that she's going crazy and breaking things."

"Just…breaking things?" Adiel repeated. That wasn't like Kaia. Kaia usually wasn't one for throwing tantrums or breaking things when she was upset. Kaia was more skillful and careful than that: she prided herself on being a "Lady Thief." Robin Hood and Arsène Lupin were her heroes, and so, rather than engage in wanton and pointless destruction, she preferred to get her revenge on the bullies and adults she despised by stealing their possessions. After that, she would either hold the item for ransom or, if she was sufficiently angry, destroy it.

If Kaia was just thoughtlessly breaking things, something must have gone terribly wrong. Worry made Adiel's heart rate spike. "Call them back," he said. "Tell them I'll be right over, and tell the Dean that I have to step out for an emergency."

"Yes, sir!" The intern scurried out alongside the other students. Adiel paused to make sure he had everything, but as he started to rush out the door, the last remaining student blocked his path.

"If you'll pardon me, Herr Engel," Adiel huffed, fighting to keep his tone professionally polite as the Nazi stood before him, arms crossed, eyes narrowed. "I have a…"

"I got another letter from the Dean," Leon interrupted. the ire in Adiel's heart became moderate amusement.

"Did you?" the Professor said in the bright tone he usually used whenever Kaia said something adorably stupid. Leon bristled.

"Don't give me that tone!" snapped the Brownshirt, throwing his arms to his sides and curling his calloused hands into tight fists. Adiel had been threatened with violence more times than he could keep count of, and so he barely raised an eyebrow at the Stormtrooper's aggressive posturing.

"I think you seem to be under a misconception, Herr Engel," declared the Professor, allowing a slight smile to curl at the edge of his lips. "*I* can give *you* whatever tone I like."

Leon Engel let out an ugly noise, like a pig that had just inhaled a wad of mud. "Just like a Jew to lord their power over us...!"

"I believe you were about to ask for clemency, Engel, and if so, you're doing a very poor job," Adiel said, and right or wrong, he actually *was* quite enjoying the fact that he could lord what little power he had over the young Nazi.

Engel let out a feral noise, but seemed to realize that Adiel was correct, that he was at the Jew's mercy. In a feat of self-control that Becca likely would have admired, Engel took a deep breath and visibly cooled the fire raging inside him.

"I don't expect you to like me, Professor Goldstein," Leon said, his tone calm, almost congenial. "I don't like you. But I have a wife, a child..."

"Don't pull that," Adiel said, perhaps a bit too harshly, but he really was sick of Engel hiding behind his wife and young son. He had allowed the Nazi to manipulate him too many times using that card. *Don't report that to the Dean, Professor Goldstein, I have a son, he's only three...*

Enough was enough. Adiel was through offering sympathy to a man who never learned, never changed, and was never grateful. "There are plenty of fathers more deserving of your seat, Herr Engel."

The fire returned; Engel's calm tone became a vicious bark again. "You're really going to fail me because I'm a National Socialist!"

"No, Herr Engel," replied Adiel brusquely. "I'm going to fail you because you are a failure. And you can try to blame your failures and inadequacies on some mass conspiracy of Jewish Bolshevism all you like, but if I were to fail every anti-Semite that came into my class, I would hardly ever pass a student."

To emphasize his point, Adiel gestured towards the back of the classroom, where Leon typically sat with his fellow Brownshirts. Leon turned scarlet, no doubt knowing full well that among his Nazi friends, he was the only one who was about to fail out.

"You have failed," Adiel continued, "because of *your* actions and nobody else's. If you can realize that and embrace it, rectify it before the midterms, then perhaps you can turn it around. If not, well...then I suppose you'll have something in common with Hitler. You'll both be failed artists."

The Professor smirked, and Leon snarled and stepped forward. "You dirty..."

"Actually," quipped Adiel, unable to stop himself. "You'll be one step above him. *He* didn't even get into art school!"

That did it. Letting out a slew of curses and slurs, Leon Engel lunged at Adiel. His growl of fury became a yelp of surprise when the Professor easily sidestepped the much younger lad, demonstrating a speed that he rarely needed to show off, but which always surprised onlookers whenever he did. Kaia hadn't inherited her quick reflexes from her mother.

Leon tripped and tumbled to the floor, his bag bursting and sending papers and art supplies flying everywhere. Groaning, the young Nazi rolled onto his knees and rubbed his sore side, looking up at the Professor with a quiet inquiry shining in his eyes.

"You know, I served alongside him. Hitler. We were in the same troop. Runners, both of us," Adiel said by way of explanation, letting his gaze wander up to the German flag hanging above the chalkboard. "Both of us received our Iron Crosses from the same Jewish officer, Hugo Gutmann."

"You don't wear an Iron Cross," Leon said, not quite accusingly but verging on it. Adiel rolled his eyes.

"I shouldn't *have* to wear it to get basic human decency," the Professor said, rather politely stopping himself from trampling all over Leon's sketches as he made his way to the classroom door. "I fought for this nation, but it seems that this nation rejects me, nonetheless. So I'll be taking my talents elsewhere soon, and you'll have to find someone else to blame for your failures. Don't worry, there are still plenty of Jews in Germany."

And as he turned and left the classroom, Professor Adiel Goldstein could have sworn that he heard Leon Engel say in a cold, empty tone: "Not for long."

THREE

"Oh, thank God, you're here!"

Adiel was rather surprised and not a little bit disturbed when he arrived at his daughter's school and found her entire homeroom loitering in the lobby. The girls, save Kaia, who was nowhere to be seen, were clustered beneath the trophy cabinet, admiring the shiny awards. The boys, meanwhile, looked absolutely traumatized as they huddled together and kept glancing down the hallway like they expected a bear to come barreling out of one of the classrooms at any moment.

Kaia's teacher, Bruno Arnhoff, was pacing back and forth. When Adiel entered the schoolhouse, he rushed forward and shook Arnhoff's hand.

"What happened, Bruno?" Adiel queried. Herr Arnhoff and he weren't precisely good friends, and Adiel most certainly didn't like the fact that Arnhoff still favored the use of corporal punishment for his students. (Poor little Kaia came home complaining of being spanked more times than Adiel could possibly keep track of.) That being said, strict as Arnhoff was, he was always religious about treating his students equally and showing their parents respect no matter their creed, and so Adiel typically decided to be grateful for small miracles and grant him deference.

Kaia, however, was not so thoughtful, and so Adiel had often been called to the school by an exhausted, frustrated Bruno Arnhoff. Right now, however, the teacher looked like he was about to announce that little Kaia Goldstein had transformed into a werewolf and eaten one of his students. (Adiel did a quick headcount…nope, no missing students except for Kaia, so if she was a werewolf, then she was at least a gentle werewolf.)

"Your daughter has completely lost her wits!" Arnhoff declared, adjusting his loosened tie. "I returned from a bathroom break and found her beating the hell out of every boy in the class. Had to evacuate the students! And now she's just tearing up the classroom and howling like a rabid dog!"

"She *is* rabid! She's a rabid Jew!" yelped one little boy, breaking from the pack of frightened youngsters and showing off a red spot on his wrist. "She *bit* me!"

That accusation might have made Adiel reconsider his dismissal of the notion that his daughter was turning into a werewolf if he didn't recognize the bitten boy. Hannes Berger, Kaia's arch-enemy and most oft-mentioned bully. Suspicion made Adiel give the boy an accusatory scowl.

"Bit you, eh? Just out of nowhere, hm? No provocation whatsoever, *hm?*" Adiel prodded, and every query made Hannes wince and glance warily at Herr Arnhoff.

"I…erm…well…"

Before Hannes could even consider confessing, however, one of the other boys piped up: "There was a spider in her desk and we killed it, and Hannes ripped its legs off. It was a big spider, really creepy, but she just went nuts and called us murderers."

Adiel let out a groan and slapped a hand over his forehead. "Oh *no*," he cried. "Not Bernie."

"Er...Bernie?" repeated Arnhoff, raising a quizzical eyebrow.

"It's her school pet," Adiel said, an explanation that he could tell only raised more questions. Arnhoff knew that little Kaia was odd, but he could hardly fathom exactly *how* odd she was. Kaia had many quirks, but among her oddest was her admiration for the ugliest and most frightening members of the animal kingdom. Creatures that would send the average little girl into hysterics fascinated her: bugs, beetles, snakes, lizards, and spiders in particular.

Kaia had gushed endlessly about Bernie the Desk Spider, who had appeared inside her desk one day. The little spider had either been able to sense that Kaia would be a welcoming host or he was simply very fortunate that of all the students in Arnhoff's class, he'd picked the girl who wouldn't scream and smack him with a textbook. Instead, Kaia went through the trouble of capturing little bugs to "feed" him and crooned at him when she thought that nobody was looking.

Unfortunately, it seemed that her worst bully had discovered her little desk pet. And if he had tortured the poor thing to death right in front of her, well, no wonder Kaia was having a meltdown for the ages.

"I'll pay for whatever she's damaged as per usual," said Adiel, adjusting his tie and waving for Arnhoff to take him to his hysterical daughter. "And I'll take her home early. Let's go."

As Herr Arnhoff turned to lead Adiel down the hall, the Professor looked down at little Hannes Berger. Adiel smirked devilishly. Becca's ghost chastised him, but the Professor couldn't help it: he bent down a little and snapped his teeth at the boy, turning about and readopting a serious expression as the child yelped in fear and skittered down the hall, sobbing like the coward he was.

"What was that?" Arnhoff asked, lifting a brow when he saw the wailing boy flee from the seemingly innocent Professor.

"Not a clue," Adiel said. "Children are strange little things, aren't they?"

"Your daughter being the strangest."

"I pity you for having to put up with thirty of them all day. My students might hate me, but at least they don't…"

As they drew close to Arnhoff's homeroom, Adiel heard a screech that was at once furious and sorrowful. The door opened, but Kaia didn't come out. Instead, Arnhoff's globe, removed from its base and dinged up so badly that it looked like a metaphor for the state of the world after the Great War, rolled into the hall.

Adiel sighed, glancing at Arnhoff and dryly vowing, "I'll pay for that."

"You surely will," Arnhoff said. "Please go calm your spawn, Herr Goldstein."

With a nod and a deep breath, Adiel swerved around the globe and entered the homeroom. The sight of it reminded him of a school he and Corporal Hitler had once been forced to trudge through during the Great War: desks and shredded papers lay hither and thither, broken pencils littered the ground, and the small chalkboard was crooked.

Of course, *this* classroom hadn't been rendered a ruin

by a bomb. The culprit was, in fact, a tiny nine-year-old girl with porcelain skin, rosy-red cheeks, and a short bob of chin-length curly golden hair.

Little Kaia Goldstein was the spitting image of her beautiful mother, and right then, she looked the way Emma had whenever she and Adiel had gotten into a particularly intense political debate. Of course, those debates had been good-natured, and Emma had never ended one by grabbing a paddle and nearly beating her opponent to death. Such could not be said of Kaia right then: she had stolen Herr Arnhoff's discipline paddle and was screaming in rage as she smacked it against the teacher's desk, either trying to break the paddle or the desk. Maybe both.

Sighing once more, Adiel skillfully hopped over broken writing utensils until he was standing behind his enraged daughter. "Kaia…"

If she heard him, she ignored him and kept wildly sob-screaming as she beat the desk.

"Kaia!" Louder, but still gentle. Adiel's gaze flitted to the one desk in the classroom that had been spared Kaia's wrath: Kaia's own desk. On top of that desk was a fat little spider's corpse. It was missing two legs. Poor Bernie.

Kaia continued to ignore her father, and so Adiel knelt down. "Wolfchen!" he shouted, grabbing her by the shoulders, and at last, she stopped assaulting the furniture, evidently only now realizing that her father had arrived.

Kaia turned around to face him. Seeing Adiel seemed to snap the child out of her state of sorrowful derangement. The anger left her face, but her wide, bright blue eyes (the only physical quality she had inherited from her father) continued gushing tears.

"Wolfchen…" Adiel sighed again, gentle, a one-word

assurance that he wasn't mad. He never used her pet-name when he was mad (not that he often got mad at her.) Wolfchen, Little Wolf, a title Adiel had given Kaia when she had been very little and wolves had been her favorite animal. He still remembered how she had sobbed when he'd read her the tale of *Little Red Riding Hood*. She had forced him to rewrite the story so that Little Red shared her treats with the Big No-Longer-Bad Wolf and they both became best friends.

Quite unfortunately, there would be no rewriting the tragic tale of Bernie the Desk Spider, but it seemed that Kaia's tantrum was over at least. She dropped the paddle and wrapped her little arms around Adiel's neck, sobbing as she hugged him tight.

"They killed Bernie," she hiccupped.

"I heard," Adiel said, patting the back of her head.

"They killed him for no reason. They ripped his legs off. They weren't even scared'a him!"

Adiel nodded and squeezed her a little tighter. For as much as she loved the creepy crawlers of the animal kingdom, Kaia was actually quite sympathetic towards children who screamed in terror when they saw a spider. She would try to defend the spider, of course. Safely capture and remove it, then advise the frightened onlooker that almost all spiders were perfectly harmless. But she didn't begrudge those who stomped on spiders out of fear. The boys who crushed bugs for *fun*, however, those arachnid-killers earned her fury.

"I'm sorry, Wolfchen," Adiel sighed, cupping his daughter's face in his hands, wiping away her tears with his thumbs. "But you gave him a really good life, didn't you? He got to eat lots of tasty crickets, right?"

"Y-yeah…" Kaia hiccupped, glancing over at the corpse of her chubby little desk pet.

"And you even avenged him, didn't you? And Zaidy Natan calls *me* a little monster."

Adiel gestured to the completely destroyed classroom, and despite herself, Kaia offered a small giggle. She then seemed to finally realize just how thoroughly she had decimated Arnhoff's domain and bit her lip.

"Am I in real trouble, or just fake trouble?" Kaia asked, and Adiel gave a slightly bitter chuckle.

"Fake trouble," he assured her, embracing her once more before rising to his feet. "I think this particular tantrum was more than justified, but next time, you shouldn't be so blunt. You're a lady thief, remember? Lady thieves get revenge with *class*."

"Right, *class*," the child said, smiling. Relief flooded Adiel's heart when he saw that he had successfully lifted her spirit, which was more important than the hundreds of Marks he was going to have to pay to replace absolutely everything in the classroom.

"Can we give Bernie a funeral?" Kaia begged, and Adiel nodded.

"I was just about to suggest that we go to the park to cheer you up. I'm sure Bernie would enjoy being buried in such a lovely place."

Kaia nodded and scurried over to the single untouched desk, scooping the dead spider into her hands and cradling him beneath her heart.

"Ready?" Adiel asked. Kaia nodded, and her father lightly grabbed her by the ear, gripping gently but feigning viciousness as he "yanked" her out of the classroom.

"…and you won't be eating dinner for a month, young

lady!" Adiel screamed, "dragging" his daughter past Herr Arnhoff, who gave a nod of approval before ducking into his classroom and letting out a frustrated howl when he saw the state of the place. He would feel better later; Kaia likely would have been expelled long ago if the Principal and her teachers were not well aware that her wealthy father would not only replace anything that she broke or stole, but would get them a nicer, more expensive version. Adiel sometimes suspected that the Principal actually loved it when Kaia misbehaved.

"Yes, Papa," Kaia said in a convincingly miserable tone. The two Goldsteins walked past Kaia's classmates, all of whom leapt out of the way, as though they expected Kaia to break from her father's slack hold and maul their faces.

"And I'm throwing away *all* of your toys, every single one!"

"Yes, Papa..." Kaia said. The girl was well-practiced in the art of feigning remorseful misery when she was chastised by a seemingly angry father. Nevertheless, she couldn't help but smirk at the quaking Hannes Berger as she passed him before bowing her head once more as her father dragged her out of the school.

Adiel continued to yell at his daughter until they were far enough away from the schoolhouse that he felt it was safe to drop the charade, releasing her ear and giving her a small embrace. "Good acting, sweetheart," he said.

"Thanks! You too! Bernie needs a coffin," Kaia declared, unfurling her palm and revealing the little spider's corpse, which she had been careful not to crush. Mournfully, the girl touched Bernie's remaining legs, whimpering softly as she closed her hand again to shield her deceased pet from the elements.

Adiel immediately agreed, though if he'd known what a trouble it would be to find a proper coffin for Bernie, he might have suggested a more natural burial. For the next hour, he dragged his daughter across Munich, flitting from store to store, trying to find a coffin that Kaia would agree to bury her beloved spider in. She was outright *offended* when Adiel initially grabbed a matchbox and suggested burying Bernie in it, loudly decreeing that when Adiel died, she would never even dream of burying him in a hunk of garbage.

Eventually, mercifully, they managed to find a proper box: a music box. It played *Toselli's Serenade,* Emma's favorite song. Emma had played that particular tune endlessly for their daughter, leading to Kaia becoming extremely fond of it.

"Now he can listen to music even though he's dead," Kaia proclaimed, and Adiel was too exhausted to consider pointing out that nobody would be able to wind up the music box once it was buried.

"That's a very sweet thought, Wolfchen," he said, throwing a wad of Marks at the shopkeeper without even bothering to ask the price and cursing his own habit of indulgence. Nevertheless, it was hard to be annoyed at the precious little girl; she gently lowered her little spider into the music box and whispered that she would always love him before she shut the lid.

With the coffin secured, the Goldsteins journeyed to the park without incident, despite the kippa perched on Adiel's skull. As they entered the lovely green space, Adiel prayed that his poor little girl wouldn't have to deal with any more heartbreak today.

Autumn was just barely beginning to turn into winter,

and thankfully, the chill in the air meant that the park was relatively deserted. A few couples walked by, and a few teens were loitering hither and thither, but otherwise, it was peaceful. A good day for a funeral.

"Near the water," Kaia said, gesturing to a small, oval-shaped lake in the center of the park. "I wanna bury Bernie near the water."

They approached the still oasis, which, like most of the park, stood quiet. There was a man sitting on the other side of the little lake: blond, bedecked in a blue sweater, brown pants, and long white socks that seemed a bit too warm for the slight chill. While Kaia knelt down and started digging a grave with her bare hands, Adiel watched the stranger across the water, who idly tossed bits of bread to the few ducks that braved the cold waters.

"Done!" Kaia declared, standing up and scurrying to the edge of the lake. She shoved her hands into the water to wash them off and noticed the man on the other side of the lake as she did so. The man seemed to sense eyes upon him, and he lifted his gaze towards the two Jews. Kaia's eyes twinkled, and she gave the man a smile that could have melted a glacier. Adiel offered a hesitantly polite nod, grimacing when the man's eyes flitted to the Professor's kippa and narrowed.

The stranger's eyes shifted to Kaia, and Adiel was a bit surprised when she seemed to look right past the stranger's frosty gaze and offered him a cheerful wave, wringing her hand in the process. The man seemed surprised too: his eyes widened, then he appeared to let out either a huff or a sigh and returned his attention to the ducks, his jaw tight as he tossed more crumbs.

"Papa, can you say Kaddish?" Kaia said, placing

Bernie's musical casket into the little hole and covering it with dirt. "I don't remember all the words, but I remember the *'amein'* parts."

The fact that Adiel knew the prayer for the dead so well at this point was an unfortunate side effect of having been forced to memorize it twice, once for his wife and then for his mother. It would be easy to do it for Bernie, though: he wouldn't be holding in sobs as he prayed.

Folding his hands in front of him, Adiel started. *"Yit-gadal v'yitkadash sh'mei raba…"*

"Amein!" Kaia cried, copying her father's pose.

"B'alma di v'ra chir'utei v'yamlich malchutei b'hayeichon u-v'yomeichon, uv'hayei d'chol beit yisrael, ba-agala u-vi-z'man kariv, v'imru…"

"Amein!"

"Y'hei sh'mei raba…"

"Tearing up the park, Jews? What sort of weird ass ritual is this?"

Adiel was barely able to remember his mother's counsel as frustration morphed into an almost overwhelming bout of fury. He turned his head and found himself facing a small gaggle of young men in wrinkled brown uniforms.

SA troopers. Leon Engel's comrades. Hitler's rowdy street fighters who roamed every German city, battling communists and assaulting Jews. Seeing the familiar uniforms made Adiel feel a horrific wave of nausea. He had to take in a deep breath and look down at his sweet child to keep the fire of hatred away from his heart.

"Not now, please," the Professor said, though he knew that such a plea was pointless. The Nazis circled the two Jews like a pack of wolves ready to savage a duo of helpless hares. Adiel reached out and grabbed Kaia by the shoulder, hoping that the SA troopers would be humane enough to refrain from hurting a little girl. He could bear a beating, but if they touched Kaia…

"We're having a funeral," Kaia squeaked, severity etched onto her young face. Living in Munich for most of her childhood meant that she was too familiar with Nazis. Nevertheless, she spoke in a soft tone, as though to plead for the better part of the Stormtroopers' souls to win out.

"A funeral for what, a rat?" laughed one Brownshirt, kneeling before the fresh grave and prodding at the mount of dirt.

"It's Bernie," Kaia explained gently. "He's a spider."

"Aha!" snickered the Nazi. "I was close!"

"He was a nice spider…" Kaia said, gloomy and yet hopeful, starting to step forward as though to engage the SA trooper in a conversation about why spiders were actually lovely creatures.

"Kaia, come on," Adiel mumbled, trying to pull her back and usher her away from the Brownshirts. "Let's get going…"

"Hey, what's the rush, Jew?" snapped another SA trooper, leaping into Adiel's path before he could hope to escape the confrontation.

"We don't want any trouble," Adiel muttered through gritted teeth only to be shoved back by the sneering SA man.

"Trouble's all Jews are good for!" one Nazi snapped, kicking at Bernie's fresh grave.

"Hey, stop, stop it! He's supposed to be resting in peace!"

Kaia tore away from her father and leapt upon the Brownshirt cadet, grabbing his arm and desperately attempting to wrench him away from the spider's grave. The SA officer cackled cruelly.

"This one has a fire in her!" he said. He grabbed Kaia by her golden locks and wrenched her off his arm. The SA trooper roughly pulled on Kaia's hair, eliciting a yelp of pain from the girl.

Anger. The sort that made his blood boil, the sort that made every atom in Adiel's body feel like it was on fire. Though his mother's voice echoed in his ears, almost desperately reminding him that *it burns you before it burns them*, he was unable to stop himself.

"Don't touch her, you piece of shit!" Adiel barked, running at the SA officer. Adiel might have made it to the Nazi holding his child if he were a slightly younger man, but swift as he was, he was no longer a soldier in his prime darting through no man's land.

His speed was more than enough to dodge a furious Leon Engel, but he was surrounded by a gaggle of guarded, jumpy anti-Semites. The Nazis grabbed Adiel and shoved his face into the moist ground. The Professor's kippa flew off his skull. He felt a bolt of pain as two Stormtroopers pinned him down, pressing all of their weight down on him.

"Papa!" shrieked Kaia, wriggling in a desperate attempt to escape the SA trooper's grasp.

"Language, Jew!" teased the Stormtrooper, giving Kaia's hair another rough tug as though to emphasize his point.

"Jews are so crude, aren't they?" another Brownshirt cackled, shoving Adiel's face deeper into the dirt and dead leaves. "No wonder they all turned out so shitty if this is how they're raised."

"Look at the little one, though!" sneered the SA trooper that had grabbed Kaia, giving her tangled locks yet another particularly vicious tug. "Look at the hair! She doesn't look like that big nosed Jew!"

He gestured to the dark-haired Adiel, who snarled and writhed, but couldn't hope to throw off the weight of two SA men.

"What do you think, boys?" the Brownshirt holding Kaia sneered. "This one must be a mongrel!"

"She's *definitely* a mongrel!" hooted another Nazi. He pressed his weight down harshly on Adiel, and the Professor felt his ribs nearly buckle. "Which means this damn Jew's been touching *our* women!"

"Ow, ow!" Kaia shrieked, wriggling about like a fish dangling from a hook. "You're really hurting my hair, let go! You're gonna pull my head off!"

"Quiet, you little shit!" snapped the Nazi holding her, drawing a dagger from his side and waving it in front of the terrified Jewish girl's nose.

"Stop it!" cried Adiel, half pleading, half demanding. His heart was burning, burning so much that it felt like fire was about to rise up from his chest and erupt from his mouth like a dragon's breath. "Put her down! She's only a little girl!"

"A little Jew!" scoffed one of the Nazis, grasping Adiel by his hair and slamming his face against the ground.

"Little Jews like this one are the worst of the worst. Half-breeds polluting our blood," sneered the SA man holding Kaia, bringing the blade terrifyingly close to the little girl's bright blue eyes.

"Little blonde, blue-eyed Jews like you are worse than Jews like him." The Nazi gestured to Adiel with the blade before waving it under Kaia's nose. "Your type, you fool us. You look human. It'd be better if we could just cut off your hair and pluck out your eyes…"

"*Enough.*"

"Jesus fucking Christ!" The SA man that had been holding Kaia yelped in shock and dropped the child and the knife, whirling about to face the source of the command.

The man that had been feeding the ducks across the water had traversed the park and appeared behind the SA leader, a feat of surprising stealth given his height. Adiel craned his neck to try and get a better look at the man who had interrupted the Nazis' fun. It was difficult to do so when his vision was spinning, but he managed.

The stranger was easily three inches taller than any of the SA attackers. There was an imposing aura about him. He held himself with a soldierly bearing that indicated a long military career, significantly longer than Adiel's compulsory service.

He almost looked like the perfect Aryan that Hitler and his cronies brayed on about, with his golden blond hair that was gelled and brushed to German perfection and blue eyes that had a wolflike harshness to them. However, his nose was a bit too long, his hips a bit too wide, and he emanated a distinct air of discomfort despite his proper posture, as though he was an injured lion braced for a rival to attack him at any moment. When the stranger spoke, his voice was oddly high-pitched.

"You lot are harming the reputation of the Führer," the stranger said. "The National Socialist Party is a *political* party. Attacking small children reflects poorly on the movement."

"These are Jews," blurted one SA trooper, shivering slightly when the stranger turned his harsh gaze upon him.

"I heard," declared the stranger, and his gaze briefly flitted to Adiel. The stranger lifted a brow when he beheld Adiel's face, regarding the Professor with a strange look, as though something about the fallen Jewish man was familiar to him in a way that he simply couldn't place.

"Nevertheless," the stranger continued, his eyes shifting to the SA trooper that had been pulling on Kaia's hair. "This pointless barbarism will not serve the Cause."

"And just who the fuck are *you*," the SA man sputtered, stooping down to retrieve his dagger, "to tell *us* what the Cause demands?!"

The stranger smiled at the Brownshirt's query, as though he had been hoping that one of the Stormtroopers would ask that. It was a wolflike smile—no, *catlike*. He rolled his shoulders, and the defensiveness of his soldierly stance gave way to arrogant confidence.

"Lieutenant Reinhard Heydrich of the SS, the head of the intelligence division, Himmler's employee."

It felt as though the stranger's introduction stole the souls of the Stormtroopers. They all blanched practically in unison. The name, *Heydrich*, was vaguely familiar to Adiel. He could have sworn he'd heard it whispered when he passed by the Nazi Party's Brown House Headquarters, or perhaps it had been blurted by Leon Engel. Yes, Engel! He had bragged about kicking down the door of a Bolshevik meet-up alongside a promising new SS man. "The Blond Beast, Heydrich," Engel had said. "He really knows how to fight."

"I...I...Lieutenant Heydrich..." stuttered the SA man that had been holding Kaia.

Kaia, for her part, had by now risen to her feet, her gaze fixed upon Heydrich. She looked at the Blond Beast with quizzical admiration. Heydrich's eyes flitted down to the girl. She gave him a dazzling smile, and Adiel could have sworn that he saw the Blond Beast wince. Heydrich gazed at the little girl with something almost akin to disgust. Not the typical anti-Semitic brand of disgust one would expect of a member of Hitler's elite, no. It was the expression of a father that had just hit his child's kitten with his car.

"Ah, I'm very sorry, Lieutenant..." The SA leader spoke, drawing Heydrich's attention back to the party of idiots and away from the beaming Jewish girl. The Brownshirt doffed his cap at the Blond Beast. "We, uh, we didn't recognize you..."

"Clearly," Heydrich drawled, his expression becoming icy once more. "Now, are you going to leave on your own, or should I get your names and tell Ernst Röhm that you're wasting your time harassing little girls when there are Bolsheviks to deal with?"

"We...ah...we'll leave. Let's go, boys."

It was a small miracle that the SA men didn't trip into the oasis filled with squawking ducks in their haste to get away from the Lieutenant. The Brownshirts who had been holding Adiel released him and then, either by accident or on purpose, one of them stepped on the Professor's leg as he followed his comrades out of the park. Adiel let out a yelp of pain that drew Kaia's attention away from Heydrich.

"Are you okay, Papa?" she queried, and the Professor gritted his teeth and tried to ignore the throbbing pain in his spine and femur, offering her a small smile.

"Takes more than a bunch of morons to bring down your papa," Adiel declared with significantly more confidence than he actually felt, but it seemed to work since his daughter gave him a bright smile.

"Oh! Your kippa! Here!" Kaia turned away from Adiel and scurried to grab his skullcap, but as she plucked it from the dirt, she realized that Lieutenant Heydrich was marching towards the park exit. Clearly, he had hoped to slip away before either Goldstein could drag him into a conversation. No such luck.

"Kaia!" Adiel hissed. He tried to grab his daughter as he shakily rose to his feet, but the girl was already bolting towards the retreating SS man.

"Hey!" Kaia squeaked, and she was polite enough not to grab Heydrich's hand or tug on his pant leg to get his attention, but she stopped so close to the Nazi that she practically bumped into his leg. Heydrich didn't turn towards her.

"Thank you!" the child chirped. "That was really…"

"Don't talk to me, Jew." Heydrich's tone was cold, but there was a forcefulness to it, like he was struggling to do something that typically came as second nature to him. Kaia winced and shrunk back, clutching at her father's kippa and bobbing her head. Heydrich stalked out of the park, and despite his biting remark, Kaia still watched him with a twinkle in her eyes.

"He was nice," she declared when he was gone. Adiel took his kippa from her hand. The Professor didn't want to ruin his daughter's good spirit, and so he didn't tell her that doing something good for an awful reason didn't make someone nice.

"Let's go home," Adiel suggested, putting his kippa

back on his head and glancing up at the red-spotted sky. "It's getting late. Don't want to be in the streets after dark."

"Uh huh...are you okay to walk home?" the child queried, hastily scurrying to Bernie's partially disturbed grave and reburying the little spider properly. Adiel chuckled and knelt down, turning and offering her his back.

"Yes, and I'll prove it! Hop on, you little miscreant! You, doubting my strength, just how old do you think I am?!"

Kaia had never been able to resist a piggyback ride and was keenly aware that despite her father's insistence that he would always be able to carry her, she was getting bigger, and he was getting older. She crawled onto Adiel's back and pretended not to hear his subtle grunt of struggle as he carried her out of the park.

"Wish we still had the car..." Kaia sighed. "Then we could have stayed longer."

The Goldsteins had more than enough money for a car. Once, they had possessed several. But Jews with cars were tantalizing targets. Adiel and Natan had agreed that it wasn't worth the bother when their windows got smashed every other week.

Adiel had really liked the cars. Especially the Mercedes. He hated thinking of everything that he couldn't have because desirable possessions made his life even more dangerous.

Adiel decided to be optimistic lest his dourness infect his child like a disease. "In America, they all have cars. We can get away with it in America. Everything will be much easier once we're there."

"Hm..." Kaia's arms tightened around Adiel's neck, and when she spoke, her voice was so quiet that if her face weren't right next to his ear, he would have never heard her. "There aren't any Nazis in America, right?"

Well. There were Klansmen. Adiel didn't know much about the Klan except that they were like the Nazis, which didn't bode well. Little comfort it would be to Kaia if she got beaten up by men in white hoods rather than men in brown shirts.

Still, optimism. Hope and all that. "There are lots of Jews there," Adiel said, hoping that Kaia was still too young to realize that he hadn't answered the question. "We'll be in a Jewish neighborhood. Nobody will bully you at school for being a Jew. Everyone there will be a Jew. You'll make lots of friends."

Kaia's grip loosened in a gloomy manner that Adiel knew too well, and he tightened his hold on her legs. "Wolfchen?"

"I don't even have any friends at synagogue," Kaia muttered morosely. "I don't think anyone likes me. Even if I wasn't Jewish…"

"I like you! Zaidy Natan likes you!" Adiel said. "That's two people who know you very well. People who don't like you? They just don't know you very well or they'd love you a lot."

"Do you think I'm strange, Papa?" Kaia asked.

"Oh, most definitely!" Adiel declared cheerfully. "But you know, all the best artists are strange. I was very strange when I was your age."

"You're not very strange now, though, Papa."

"How dare you! I'm very offended! As I said: great artists are strange. Strange is a compliment. 'Normal' is the same thing as boring, and it's far worse to be boring!"

"Well," muttered Kaia fondly. "You're not boring, so you're strange."

"Thank you, Kaia. And you are the least boring girl in the world, so you're also the strangest."

Kaia offered Adiel a sweet giggle that made his heart swell with affection. Losing his position at the Academy would be more than worth it if it meant that little Kaia would be able to go to the park without having to worry about Nazis ever again. At least Klansmen would stand out more. Easier to spot in public. Besides, the Klan would probably avoid going to the park on warm days. Those sheets couldn't have been comfortable in summer heat.

"Is Hitler gonna be President?" Kaia's query pulled Adiel from his ruminations on whether or not the Klan had some sort of summer uniform, maybe a swimsuit set. He was going to inquire why she felt the need to ask such a thing, but then his eyes flitted to his left and his question was answered. The wall of one dilapidated building was covered from top to bottom in Nazi posters.

A familiar face was peppered across the posters. A dark mop of hair, steely blue eyes, and a moustache that would have made for a fantastic bullseye if Adiel didn't respect his mother and still played darts. Hitler's visage was familiar, and not simply in the way that it was familiar to everyone across Germany.

Adiel still remembered being huddled in a trench in no man's land, being castigated for his race by the other soldiers, and being welcomed by a very different Hitler. A Hitler with a handlebar moustache and a relatively liberal attitude, one that was keenly aware that his comrades regarded him as an outcast too. The strange artist who preferred to sit by himself with Fuchsl, the little British hound he'd rescued from the battlefield. Adiel still remembered how Corporal Hitler had cried when a railway attendant had stolen his dog.

"Maybe," the Professor answered. "It won't be our business after we move."

He braced himself because Kaia never asked one question where fifty were available.

"Zaidy said that you and Hitler were in the same troop. You mentioned that a few times."

"You have an admirable memory, darling," Adiel chuckled even though a bitter taste rose in his throat. He had gone an entire childhood without one gentile friend and for a moment, when the man who loved art as much as he had slapped his shoulder and said *don't mind the fools, a German is a German regardless of religion,* Adiel had thought he'd finally found one in Hitler.

Hitler had been a twenty-something back then, and perhaps Adiel had hoped that the sickness of anti-Semitism had passed him over permanently.

"You said he was nice before," Kaia squeaked, and Adiel gave a small grunt. *Nice* was perhaps inaccurate. Hitler had never spared a *nice* word for Adiel—merely offering to treat him like a human instead of a rat that had crawled into the trench and somehow donned a German uniform was not *nice*. It was *baseline.*

Corporal Hitler had been *decent,* but always when they sat beside one another, engaging in a friendly rivalry of sorts as Adiel attempted to draw buildings and Hitler tried to draw people, Adiel had sensed a brand of toxicity.

Corporal Hitler had never offered Adiel a kind word or admitted defeat when his art was inferior, at most proclaiming with a twitch of his lip that Adiel's art was *fine* before launching into a long critique of it. And if Adiel had tried to offer critiques of his own, then Hitler the Man Who Was Convinced He Had Nothing To Learn would grumble and flee to Fuchsl, all but covering his ears so that he couldn't hear a single disparaging word.

Of course, Kaia wouldn't understand all that.

"He *was*," Adiel answered. They passed the many Hitler faces, and the Professor felt like his old comrade's eyes followed him and his daughter as they did.

"But not anymore." Kaia sounded rather gloomy. "He knew you were Jewish, though."

She knew her father too well to assume that he would ever hide a part of himself, much less such an important part. "He did."

"So…"

Kaia's question went unspoken: *Why is he Hitler the Crazy Man Whose Soldiers Keep Attacking Us instead of Hitler the Old Comrade who comes by for tea—not coffee, because he never liked coffee in the trenches—every Sunday?*

It would have been a good question, and one that Adiel could have never hoped to answer. He recalled that Corporal Hitler had been quite proud of his race and would get extremely offended whenever someone pointed out his odd accent or called him *Austrian* instead of *German*.

("You know, I'd have been promoted by now," Hitler the Eternally Bitter had once complained to Adiel. "But Austrians aren't allowed to rank higher than Corporal in the German army." It would have been quite ironic if Adiel had responded with: *Yes, how terrible, it's so awful to be judged by your ethnicity, to be held back because of something you can't help.*)

Corporal Hitler hadn't hated Adiel back then, because Corporal Hitler was agnostic and therefore couldn't have cared less if Adiel Goldstein was a "Christ-Killer." ("I remember I wanted to be a pastor when I was a child, though," Hitler the Man Who Never Stopped Wanting To Talk About Himself noted once. "I remember I used to drape an apron over my shoulders and stand on a stool. Made my sister listen to me preach." Adiel had been dearly tempted to say that Hitler would have made a great pastor because he clearly loved listening to the sound of his own voice, but that would have been hypocritical, so he had just laughed and nodded while Corporal Hitler launched into a rant about how indulgences were hogwash.) Hitler had, back then, thought that Jews were merely adherents to a religion and not a distinct racial group, and so he hadn't cared about them one way or another.

But now he thought they were a race. And so hatred had weaseled its way into yet another potential friend, just like Little Rupert so many years ago.

"He changed his mind, I suppose," Adiel said, which made him smirk because he remembered that Hitler the Man Who Thought He Was Always Right would have rather put a bullet in his skull than confess that he had changed his mind about anything.

"Then maybe he could change his mind again," Kaia suggested, her voice bright as she craned her neck to catch a glimpse at the wall of Hitlers. "Then we wouldn't have to move. Maybe you could write to him?"

Adiel might have chuckled at her innocence if the notion weren't something he had ruefully pondered more than once. When the Great War had ended and the two artists had gone their separate ways—Adiel with relief that the war was over and delirious excitement after he managed to snatch a kiss from the beautiful nurse that would become Kaia's mother, Hitler the Warmonger with a dreary moroseness that bordered on suicidal depression— they had promised to write one another.

For a while, they had, Hitler the Narcissist scrawling three-page long letters about himself and his opinions while Adiel studiously tried to avoid mentioning his successes in love and career, keenly aware that his old comrade wouldn't take such bragging, however gently delivered, with grace.

Then Hitler had stopped writing, and Adiel had worried that the despondent young man had done something stupid. Then he'd heard about the Nazi Party and its new orator, and he'd learned that his fear had been well-founded, but not in the way he'd thought.

"You don't want to move, Wolfchen?" Adiel said because he really didn't want to tell his daughter any of that. He felt the child squirm.

"I don't know English yet," Kaia sighed. "And we'll have to leave Mama and Bubbe Becca."

Leave their graves was what she meant, and remembering the carefully carved headstones that had been defaced with swastikas more times than Adiel would ever admit to Kaia made the Professor's heart sink.

"Bodies are bodies, my darling," Adiel assured her gently. "Their souls are in the World to Come. They'll be able to see you even when you're in America."

"I know...still...I wish we didn't *have* to move."

"Me too, Wolfchen." Even if he didn't love Germany, Adiel wished he could.

"Didn't Mama fix Hitler's eyes?" Kaia queried, and Adiel chuckled. Emma the Nurse who had become Emma, Wife of Adiel, Mother of the World's Most Adorable Little Girl, had done her best for both Adiel and

Hitler when they'd both been laid up near the end of the war.

Both had very nearly lost their eyes to mustard gas. In Hitler's case, his handlebar moustache had prevented his gas mask from creating a perfect seal. (Evidently, this was the reason behind Hitler's blatant theft of Charlie Chaplin's toothbrush moustache, but Hitler the Soldier had once said that he had utilized the style in the past only to abandon it because *I didn't feel like it suited me.* Palpable irony there.)

Adiel's gas mask hadn't sealed because one of his comrades had thought that it would be tremendously funny to cut the straps. Watching Jews choke to death on poison was evidently amusing for some people.

"Your mama was a nurse, Wolfchen," Adiel corrected. "She didn't do surgery. I'm sure she cleaned his bedpans once or twice, though."

"Mama said you were her favorite patient, and Hitler was her least favorite."

"I was her *most handsome patient*, and as a matter of fact, I am *still* her most handsome patient."

That was what Emma had told him anyway, though she had also noted that when Hitler shaved his moustache off, Adiel and he looked nearly identical. She had assured Adiel that he was much more handsome than the Austrian, however. Probably because Hitler, who had been hysterically angry once he'd learned that Germany had surrendered, had worn an ugly expression for the duration of his stay in the hospital while Adiel had been happy to be alive and even happier to be tended to by a lovely lady.

Emma must have thought that Adiel was extremely handsome, however, since she had gone and married him despite their many, many differences. Despite the fact that her communist, atheist parents had threatened to disown her if she married a rich, religious Jew like Adiel. She had done so anyway, and her parents had never met their granddaughter.

Their loss.

"Papa, you're...oh!"

Adiel's heart leapt into his chest as Kaia suddenly released him and fell to the ground with the grace of a feline. Paternal protectiveness always made him forget that she could land on her feet just fine.

"Wolfchen!" Adiel said, and before he could even turn around, the girl was already scurrying towards one particular storefront and squishing her face against the window. He couldn't see her smile, but he could *feel it* as he ran to stand beside her.

"Puppies!" Kaia chirped, and indeed, the pet shop that they tended to pass by on their way home had restocked its cutest inventory. Pups of every breed tousled in a display case that was perhaps a touch too small for all of them. The puppies chewed on a thoroughly destroyed rope toy, nipped at one another's ears, batted at balls with their paws, and nibbled at the bits of dog food strewn about their cage.

It wasn't unusual for Kaia to stop and gawk at these dogs, but Adiel glanced down and realized that his daughter's eyes were not performing their typical frantic dance as she looked from cute puppy to cute puppy, drinking in all of their adorable antics. Her pupils were still, pinned upon one dog that was sitting by the glass, wagging its tail and staring at the little girl with tender chestnut eyes. The puppy was some sort of mutt, maybe a shepherd mix. It was brown with a black blotch on its belly. A black blotch that looked an awful lot like a spider.

Oh, dear. Adiel hardened his heart and readied his tongue with a slew of assorted refusals, prepared for each and every one of her arguments.

One damn look was all it took to break him. One brutal big-eyed look with a little wobble of her bottom lip. Natan was right: Adiel was indulgent. But Kaia had gone through a uniquely awful day, and after what she had said about her lack of friends, this was the least he could do to alleviate her loneliness. Adiel knew too well the horrid pain that was friendlessness and hated that his precious girl was feeling the same thing. If Becca hadn't been terrified of dogs, then he was sure that she would have bought six-year-old Adiel Goldstein a puppy to soothe the ache.

"You'll walk it," Adiel commanded. "One piss stain on my nice carpet and it's living in the backyard. You'll also feed it…"

"And water it!" Kaia squeaked. "I promise, swear to God and Moses and everyone!"

Adiel cast a cursory glance at the door to make sure that the store didn't forbid Jews from entering and nodded. "This is your birthday gift and *all* of your Hannukah presents. For the year. For *two* years."

"Yes, yes! Thank you, Papa! You're the best!"

"I certainly am," Adiel said, opening the door and grunting as Kaia spared him an affectionate hug, planting a kiss on his arm before scurrying into the shop with an almost frenzied pace, as though she was afraid that her father would come to his senses if she tarried.

The dog was half-off because of its odd markings, and the shopkeeper was friendly even towards the kippa-clad man. "Those Nazi shits keep disturbing the poor animals every time they march by," she said. "Smashed my window last week. They can go to Hell."

Adiel was happy to give her his money, and even bought bowls, a leash, a few cans of food, and some toys that the slobbering mutt would no doubt destroy in a day.

"He loves you, sweetie," the shopkeeper said when she removed the dog from the display case and handed him to Kaia. The puppy wriggled and whined and tried to lick the girl's tears of happiness off her face. "I think he was waiting for you!"

"His name's Bernie! Bernie the Second!" Kaia decided, proudly slipping the new leash around the mutt's neck. Bernie the Second was sniffing Adiel's foot. The Professor smiled. He had always liked dogs, and dogs had always liked him in return. Hitler's little British mutt Fuchsl had been particularly fond of the Jewish man, much to Hitler's bristling jealousy. Maybe Corporal Hitler had started hating Jews because his dog had liked a Jew more than he'd liked him. Could be. Probably not. His hatred was probably awakened by something more complex than that.

It would be nice to have a dog of his own. Well, to have a dog in the house, since this dog was clearly going to be Kaia's even if her vows to take care of all his needs inevitably fell through and Adiel ended up picking up the mutt's poop. Wouldn't be too bad. He'd wanted a dog all his life anyway, so he wasn't being *too* ridiculously indulgent.

Adiel kept trying to tell himself that even as Kaia asked him to buy the damn mutt a split elk antler that cost more than some Germans probably made in a week, and he bought it like the stupid, indulgent father that he was.

It occurred to Adiel as he was leaving the pet shop that Natan was either going to be mad or, worse, *amused*. Smug like he was whenever Adiel shoved another silver spoon into Kaia's mouth.

It was worth it, though. Kaia was skipping, stooping down to kiss the puppy (who, judging from his bouncy gait, had clearly realized that he had won the lottery, getting purchased by a duo of wealthy Jews instead of some dog fighting ring.) When she grew older, she would remember this as the worst day ever which had turned into the best. That would be worth a few stained carpets and a lifted brow from Natan.

The Goldsteins reached their gated abode, situated in a faraway suburb of Munich that was a hassle to walk to but worth it for the space and security. Adiel unlocked the wrought-iron front gate and welcomed Kaia and Bernie in before shutting and locking it behind him. They hadn't had anyone break into their home yet, but there was a first time for everything, and Adiel would rather be safe than sorry. The doors and windows of the Goldstein household would always be locked, and he couldn't imagine that habit changing even once they'd moved to America.

"Papa, we're home!" Adiel cried as he entered through the hefty double doors and cast a brief glance about their house, savoring what he was sure would be the last time the beautiful manor was spic-and-span. Adiel was something of a neat freak, a trait he had inherited from his father, which meant that the manor didn't have a single stain on its carpets or a dusty corner on any of its many shelves. Bernie was almost certainly going to be doing his darndest to make the perfectly clean Goldstein home filthy.

"I'm sorry!" Adiel cried as Bernie bolted towards the largest living room.

"Sorry about what, son? Did—*oh.*"

Adiel entered just as Natan, who had been sitting in his favorite cozy chair and reading one of Becca's books about Jewish folklore, found himself staring down at the little dog. The old man raked a hand through his silver hair and narrowed his dark blue eyes at the pup before raising his gaze towards his son and granddaughter.

Adiel smiled guiltily. Kaia, cheerfully.

"He's Bernie the Second!" Kaia squeaked, dumping Bernie's toys onto the ground, and said dog licked at Natan's polished shoes.

"Is he now?" sighed Natan, giving Adiel a look that was at once fond and chastising, the same look he had given his son when Adiel was a ten-year-old getting on his mother's nerves. "Well, I suppose now we all have to figure out how to bring a dog to America."

"I'll carry him in my lap!" Kaia volunteered.

"Not if he grows to be bigger than you, you won't!" Natan quipped, watching as the puppy started sniffing the air, no doubt catching a whiff of the Sabbath meal cooking. Bernie started waddling towards the kitchen. Adiel chuckled and patted Kaia's head.

"Wolfchen, go set the table for *Shabbat*," he commanded. "We'll have dinner soon."

"Okay, Papa! And a spot for Bernie too, right?"

"He can have some of your chicken. I suppose everybody is getting spoiled today."

Kaia grabbed Bernie's new dog bowl and scurried to the kitchen, nearly tripping over the small pile of chew toys on the floor. Adiel, left alone with his father, flashed Natan a wide smile.

"She had a bad day," the Professor said in the sort of tone that he had used when he was a little boy reciting a well-worn excuse. Natan groaned, smacking his own forehead with Becca's fairytale book.

"I give up," sighed Natan, tossing the book aside and throwing up his hands. "I give up! You can't say no to that girl! When we get to New York, she'll ask for the Statue of Liberty and the next thing I know, it'll be in our backyard!"

"I don't spoil her *that* much," Adiel lied, eliciting a raucous laugh from his father. "Anyway, I've always thought that she should have a dog. Wish we'd had one when I was a boy."

"You know your mother was terrified of them, rest her soul, especially the big ones. What kind of dog is Bernie?"

"Mix of some sort. I think he's got some German shepherd in him, though."

"Ah! Your mother's least favorite type! Forgive me, Becca, I've let the little monster bring an enemy into the house." Natan's gaze flitted up to a wall decorated with family photos, his dark blue eyes falling upon a portrait of Becca smiling cheerfully.

"Oh, it's not like we can't afford him," sighed Adiel, sparing a smile at his mother's picture before turning his attention back to his father. "And I'm sure getting him to America will be perfectly simple. We'll just put him in a crate. By the way, I was going to ask if you wanted to leave early. You could take Kaia, and I could finish off the semester and then join the two of you in New York."

"I'm not packed yet, and I don't think Kaia would like it if we were separated on Hannukah. Why? Something happen today?"

Natan would worry if Adiel offered too many details, and so he simply shrugged. "Bumped into some Brownshirts at the park, had a little incident, but we're fine."

"*Fine*...right..." Natan's eyes flitted to Adiel's rumpled, dirt-stained suit before he shook his head. "As long as we keep our heads down, I know we'll be okay until January. Don't worry about it. Finish up the semester."

"Papa, the table's ready!" Kaia cried. "Can Bernie sit next to me?"

"I thought *I* got to sit next to you!" cried Adiel with false umbrage, helping his father to his feet and walking with him into the dining room. Kaia was placing Bernie the Second's bowl near her seat.

"I'm being replaced already!" Adiel yelped. "You, dog!"

The Professor knelt before the mutt, who was sniffing his empty bowl, and held up two fists. "Stick 'em up, little pup! If I have to fight for Kaia's attention, you're in for a brawl!"

The dog turned his chestnut eyes towards Adiel, wagged his tail, and jumped back, clearly mistaking the Professor's jovial threat as some sort of human offer for a game of chase.

"Papa, don't!" Kaia giggled, grabbing her father's arm and yanking him to the other side of the table. "You've gotta Iron Cross, he's just a puppy!"

"He'll grow into a real wolf, Wolfchen, you'll see! And then *he* won't go easy on me!"

"He shouldn't! You're bullying the poor creature already!" Natan said, taking his seat at the head of the table and testing the lighter to make sure it would be ready for *Shabbat*. "Kaia, get your butt in the chair or *I'm* going to light the candles."

"Ah ah, that's my job, I'm the lady of the house!" Kaia clambered onto her chair, making sure that Bernie's new bowl was positioned beside her and pouting when the little dog instead trotted over to where Adiel sat on the other side of Natan. The puppy pawed at the Professor's ankles.

"No, dog, you're barking up the wrong master," chuckled Adiel, pointing to his daughter. "If you want a sucker who'll give you food, run to her."

"As though you're not a sucker!" cackled Natan. "Between the two of you, this dog will be a thousand pounds! You'll *both* be feeding him entire chickens! Kaia, speaking of chicken, let's start so we can eat."

Once upon a time, it had been Rebecca's task to lead the Friday night prayers. She had done so with grace and ease, and the remaining Goldsteins had never been able to replace her bright aura despite their best efforts.

Kaia was well-versed in the first prayer of the night, the prayer over the Sabbath candles, and she managed all right even though Adiel was always terrified that she'd burn her hand on melting wax. Adiel led a good chunk of the little service, being the one who knew the prayers by heart and spoke Hebrew with the least hesitancy. Finally, Natan finished them off with a prayer over the *challah* before cutting the sweet bread and declaring that they had thanked God enough for their lives, bounty, and the Sabbath. It was time to eat.

Some Jews, Jews even more religious than the Goldsteins, hired a trusted gentile to cook, clean and light fires on *Shabbat*, interpreting the divine dictate against working on the Sabbath to mean that everything besides eating, drinking, and breathing was forbidden. The Goldsteins were not so strict, which was good. Adiel didn't know a gentile that he would trust to be his *Shabbos goy*. (Idly, and with not a small amount of disgust, he realized that if Hitler the Maniac had become Hitler the Family Friend, then he would have been the only one that Adiel would have ever even considered for the post.)

Additionally, it was good because Natan was a fantastic cook, as good a cook as he was an investor. Natan had joked more than once that if he weren't so good at picking stocks, he would have been a chef instead. Of course, Kaia ended up giving Bernie half of her chicken, and the little mutt even managed to convince Adiel to slip him some table scraps.

Good food, good company, a good end to an otherwise bad day. Adiel allowed the tension within him to ease away and enjoyed basking in the presence of his family. To Hell with the rest of the world. Germany could hate him as much as it wanted. As long as he had little Kaia's giggle, and as long as he could share a glass of wine with his father, he was happy.

Dinner ended with a heaping helping of chocolate cake for the Goldsteins, which Bernie tried to partake in even though he was so stuffed from the chicken that in order to continue begging, he was reduced to lying down on Adiel's shoes and whimpering.

With the meal complete, the Sabbath had officially commenced. It was time for a well-deserved, religiously mandated rest. Of course, rest didn't mean sitting around and doing nothing. Natan ushered little Kaia back into the sitting room while Adiel followed, finishing off his wine and settling on the couch while his father sat the child down at the family's grand piano.

"English-piano lesson time, darling," Natan said, sitting beside his granddaughter. Both Becca and Emma had been quite good at playing piano, a skillset that neither Adiel nor Natan had ever grasped as well. Natan was better than

Adiel at the instrument, but in lieu of trying to replace Becca as Kaia's piano teacher, he'd decided to come up with a unique new curriculum; in preparation for their move to America, he'd found several American songs and was teaching Kaia how to play them while, in the process, improving her English.

"Which one is this, sweetie?" Natan asked, somewhat clumsily playing the first few notes of Kaia's favorite jazz tune.

"*Anything Goes!*" Kaia chirped eagerly.

"Can you sing it?" Natan requested, and Kaia swayed from side to side and confidently began to comply.

"*Times have changed, and we've often rewound the cock...*"

Adiel nearly spat his wine all over the pristine carpet and felt his lungs burn as laughter overtook him.

"No, no, darling!" Natan yelped, shaking his head and turning crimson. "*Clock*, it's *clock*. Cock is something...ah... very different..."

"Different how? What's it mean?" Kaia queried, of course. Natan looked like he was about to have a heart attack.

"Ah...it means...ah..."

"Rooster, Wolfchen, it means rooster," Adiel cut in just in time, saving the day with his quick remembrance of English and its many synonyms. Natan shot his son a look of pure affection and then quickly played another song, distracting the girl before she could ask any more questions about "roosters."

While Natan's clumsy piano playing and Kaia's slightly hoarse English singing echoed about the warm, grand abode, Bernie finally managed to drag himself out of the kitchen. The dog wagged his tail happily as he settled down at Adiel's feet.

"Stuffed?" Adiel whispered, leaning down and scratching the little mutt behind his ears. "That's fine. I want you to grow into a big, strong dog. Next time someone messes with Kaia, you bite their face off, got it?"

The dog clearly didn't, but he nonetheless leaned against the Professor, panting happily. Adiel glanced at the puppy that would, hopefully, one day grow into a great and loyal wolf-sized dog. He then looked at his daughter. It was easy not to notice since Kaia's brilliant smile and dancing blue eyes obscured her little flaws, but Adiel saw redness near the edge of her hairline, a minor injury brought about by the Brownshirts' attack.

"You *will* protect her, won't you, boy?" Adiel whispered, dread building in his chest like he was reading a book that he knew ended in tragedy.

"You'll be her friend," Adiel said, all but commanding the little dog that was starting to snooze. "She deserves a real friend, someone to protect her."

FOUR

The hours after Saturday morning *Shabbat* services gave way to a free afternoon. Kaia had bellyached quite a bit about leaving Bernie behind for synagogue, and perhaps with good reason. They returned to the house and found no less than three piss stains on the nice carpet. Adiel decided to be happy that the dog hadn't done worse. Sabbath blessings.

Once the Goldsteins had changed out of their Saturday wear, cleaned the carpet, and taken Bernie for a well-deserved walk, the rest of the day was reserved for family playtime. The Goldsteins' grand abode offered Kaia and Bernie plenty of space for games. They started in the vast, slightly overgrown yard, with Adiel and Natan teaming up to catch them. Bernie didn't seem to understand the idea of tag and kept running towards Adiel.

"Bernie's terrible at tag!" Kaia observed, fighting to catch her breath after Natan captured her and tickled her until her already rosy cheeks were the shade of two tomatoes. Adiel knelt before the dog, who rolled onto his back and panted happily as the Professor scratched the spider-shaped splotch on his chest.

"Maybe he'd be better at hide-and-seek," suggested Adiel. "He *is* a dog, after all. Maybe he already has your scent. I'll distract him: run into the house quickly and hide, let's see if he can find you!"

"If he's got German shepherd blood, he'll find her right away!" laughed Natan, collapsing into a lawn chair and taking a swig from a glass that was now more melted ice than lemonade. Nevertheless, he waved for Kaia to go and hide.

Kaia's eyes brightened at the notion of testing the tracking mettle of her new pet, and while Adiel wrestled with the dog, crooning and offering loud compliments, she slipped out of the backyard and into the manor.

The Goldstein abode was practically designed for hide-and-seek, offering guest rooms galore, almost all of them barely used save for the rare occasions where Adiel hosted a party for the congregation or Natan felt the need to entertain one of his work acquaintances. When Kaia and Adiel played, it always took him quite a while to find her. There were endless closets to search, dozens of beds to hide under.

Kaia realized right away that Bernie's keen sense of smell would give him an advantage, but she didn't want to make the game too easy. Perhaps if she could hide in either Adiel or Natan's room, the game would be more difficult as their scent would cover hers.

It was a risky move: Adiel and Natan typically checked their own rooms first and always noticed when their things had been moved, but if the dog would be in charge of seeking, then it could work in her favor this time. Adiel would likely follow the hound.

Kaia ducked into Natan's room simply because it was nearest: her grandfather had evacuated the master bedroom that he had once shared with Becca after her death, leaving it barren and bringing most of their shared possessions into a smaller room. She crept inside, smiling up at a picture of Becca holding a pouty-faced three-year-old Adiel in her lap.

Kaia loved her grandfather enough to respect his privacy, and so she rarely entered his room, but the game was afoot and there was no room for politeness in war. Nevertheless, she did want to minimize the amount of mess she made, so she decided not to go near the bed. Instead, her gaze found the closet and she slipped in, giggling as she crouched down and waited.

Seconds ticked by, and the limited patience of a nine-year-old began to wear down. Kaia shifted about her hiding spot, curiosity making her hesitance to mess with her grandfather's possessions wane as she poked about the closet. It was a spacious walk-in sort of closet, though rather packed, and not just with clothes. A few boxes were stacked high in one corner. A green dress poked out of one. Becca's. Kaia remembered that her grandmother had worn it during one of her birthdays when they had all gone to the zoo and stared at the snakes.

Kaia glanced away, her bright blue eyes flitting about the dark space again until one particular box caught her eye. Half-hidden beneath a small pile of coats was a trunk, much older than anything else her wealthy family owned. She crawled close and examined the rusted lock.

Adiel was partial to cowboy books (Kaia suspected that his eagerness to move to America was in no small part because he was eager to see the fantastical land where his heroes lived.) Kaia, on the other hand, was fond of pirates. Tales of dashing thieves finding treasure hidden in the strangest places. This chest, which seemed to have tumbled straight out of one of her favorite bedtime stories, was therefore completely irresistible. Politeness be damned! She *had* to see what was inside.

Kaia reached into her pocket and pulled out a seemingly innocuous little tool: a bobby pin. She always made sure to have one with her for devious purposes. Usually to escape the classroom during detention when her teacher locked her in, or to break into the Principal's office and lay a tack on his chair.

Kaia was well-practiced, but not quite to the level where she could pick a lock with her eyes closed. Squinting in the scant light of the walk-in closet, she focused intently, so much so that she didn't hear the patter of paws, the heavy pants of a puppy with a mission, or the shuffling of feet approaching her hideout.

She did, however, hear the *click* as she undid the lock.

"Yes!" she squeaked, but her victorious euphoria was short-lived as the closet door flew open.

"Aha!" Adiel cried, and Bernie barreled towards her, leaping upon the girl and licking her face until her cheeks felt raw.

"Tried to fool the mutt by covering up your scent with Zaidy's coats, eh?" chuckled Adiel, strolling into the closet and standing above the girl as her dog assaulted her with kisses. "Well, Bernie's more skilled than I thought. Maybe he can help me find that old silk handkerchief...oh."

Adiel's eyes landed on the old trunk and widened as an old memory struck him: anger gnawing at his guts, fury and sorrow abandoning his soul as he wandered into his mother's closet and found her sobbing beside the mysterious chest whose contents he had never beheld.

His daughter had opened it. Adiel knelt down and couldn't contain a chuckle when he saw the bobby pin still lodged in the undone lock.

"Aren't you just a little secret agent!" he chuckled, pulling the bobby pin from the keyhole and turning towards his daughter, who was hugging Bernie. Kaia, who could always tell when her father was feigning a chastising tone to disguise his pride, beamed at the Professor.

"I'm a lady thief," Kaia proclaimed. "A lady pirate."

"Oooh, so you were going to plunder from Zaidy, eh? And on *Shabbat!*"

"I was just curious! I only would'a plundered it if it was gold, and then I would'a spent the gold on more toys for Bernie the Second."

Bernie the Second, whom Adiel was beginning to believe could somehow actually understand German, craned his neck all the way back and licked Kaia's nose.

"Ah, steal from the rich and give to the spoiled dogs. I'm the little monster, but you're the little bandit. Do I even want to know where you learned how to pick locks?" Adiel queried, holding up the bent bobby pin.

"You know Simon Berkovits?" Kaia replied, leaning her face against Bernie's neck.

"From…Hebrew school? Isn't he the one that got in trouble for eating a moth in front of the girls?"

Kaia giggled. "It was a dragonfly. He also eats glue. I dunno how *he* knows, but I caught him breaking into the Rabbi's study after services one day. I asked him to teach me, and he said he would if I gave him a kiss. So I said yes, and he taught me, and I gave him a kiss, but then he called me a prostitute 'cause prostitutes do kisses for trade, and I punched him in the face. He didn't want anyone to know he got punched by a girl, though, so he blamed Yehuda Glick and that's why they got into that fight that one time."

"Ah." The fraught politics of the playground. Sometimes, it almost made Adiel glad that he had been an outcast for a significant chunk of his childhood.

"Don't say prostitute," Adiel said, tossing the bobby pin aside and ruffling his daughter's already untidy curls. "It's a bad word."

"I know it's a bad word, that's why I punched him!"

"Don't punch people, that isn't what lady thieves do. Next time just steal his allowance. *Class*, remember?"

"Ah, right, *class!*" Kaia agreed with a flourish of her hand, giggling when Bernie interpreted her motion as an invitation to play more. The dog leapt off her lap, crouching down and wiggling his rump.

"Chase him, Wolfchen!" Adiel commanded. "I'll clean up in here. Don't want Zaidy Natan to think less of you."

"Okay, we'll get snacks! Bernie, to the kitchen!"

With that declaration, the girl chased the puppy out of Natan's room, shutting the door behind her and leaving Adiel standing in the closet. He turned on the light and knelt in front of the trunk.

Loyalty and the commandment which obligated him to respect his parents made Adiel hesitate for a moment before he decided that sating his burning curiosity would be worth a Heavenly finger-wagging when he met his Maker. He opened the chest, coughing and rubbing his eyes as a minimum of twenty years' worth of dust flew into his face.

Once his vision cleared, he peeked inside. The chest was filled with books and film reels. One leather book caught Adiel's eye right away: a photo album labelled "*Libman*" in faded gothic script.

Mama's maiden name, I guess, Adiel assumed, plucking it off the pile and setting it in his lap. Adiel was a curious soul by nature, and therefore he had always wondered about his family background. Curiosity, however, could not overcome his love for his parents. He had seen how they had winced when he'd asked about their childhoods. He remembered how his father had warned him against drinking because *you've got a family history of drunkenness.* He recalled how, when he'd inquired about his grandparents, Becca's eyes had filled with tears and Natan had quietly muttered that they weren't around anymore.

Adiel had dropped the subject quickly, not wanting to bring them any more pain. The absence of pictures hadn't been too odd either: pictures were a luxury in the 1800s, and if his parents' childhoods were fraught, he could see why neither of them would want to waste money and energy maintaining bad memories.

Evidently, however, they *had p*ossessed pictures but had simply kept them locked up. Adiel opened to the first page, smiling as a black-and-white picture of a girl with curly pigtails greeted him. "*Becca, 8.*"

"Damn good picture, Mama." Adiel sighed sadly, and it really was: shockingly high quality for a picture that must have been taken during the mid-1800s. Adiel was more familiar with painted art than photographic art, but it did make him raise an eyebrow. Then again, perhaps Becca's family had been wealthy.

Adiel turned the page and his breath caught in his throat. A crystal-clear image of a family Passover celebration. Becca, aged nine, sat between two younger girls.

Aunts? Adiel had never realized that he had aunts before. Five and three, the youngest cradled in the arms of a woman with curly dark hair and a weary smile. Adiel's grandmother. He ran his thumb along the image of her oddly hollow cheeks. She looked like his mother. A pang in his chest made him feel robbed. Why hadn't he known her as well as Kaia had known Becca?

His eyes glided to the man of the house, his grandfather. Adiel chuckled and rubbed his chin when he beheld his grandfather's impressive beard, which barely concealed a hopeful smile. Adiel had thought of growing out his own facial hair as a boy, but Natan had advised against it. *You never see me with a beard for a reason, little monster. We don't have the genes for it.*

Well! Apparently, Adiel had *half* the genes for it! Maybe he would grow it out once they moved to America and he didn't have to worry about looking too much like a stereotypical religious Jew. Maybe. Probably not. He couldn't imagine the labor it would take to maintain such a magnificent chest-length beard. Would he need to use some type of beard shampoo? He shook his head. No, certainly not worth the effort.

For a few moments, Adiel stared at the family he had never gotten to know, saving up questions to ask his father. He hadn't thought of grandparents or aunts as an adult. He'd been focused on his career, then Emma, then Kaia, then losing Emma. But he was a forty-two-year-old man now, certainly more than mature enough to deal with whatever familial drama his poor mother had been burdened with. *Besides,* he thought bitterly, *she's not around to feel embarrassed about it, whatever it is.*

He turned the page hoping for more answers, but instead only received questions.

The next page showed his mother again, ten years old, posing with her two sisters in front of what must have been their cozy childhood home.

Their house, a two-story tall abode, stood on a street that was covered in swastika banners.

What?

Adiel's smile tapered into a confused frown as he leaned down and peered closely at the picture. He knew that photographs could be altered—he had heard of Joseph Stalin editing former comrades out of pictures, literally erasing them from memory. Even if this level of forgery had been possible, however, there would have been no need for it. Why in the name of Heaven would Natan deface his wife's childhood pictures in such a way?

A glance at the handwritten label beneath the photo invited even more confusion. *"Becca, Rahal, Leah, 1936."*

What? What? What?

Frantically, Adiel began to flip through the album, trying to find an explanation and only uncovering more impossible pictures. Natan as a boy sitting beside little Becca on a fountain. *"Best friends forever!"* the label read. Adiel remembered that on the few occasions where Natan and Becca had spoken of their past, they had mentioned that they had been neighbors as children.

They *hadn't* mentioned that the street they had lived on was Adolf Hitler Street, that it had been guarded by demonic men bedecked in black tunics and swastika armbands.

The next page. Natan and Becca's families gathered together for Purim. Natan was dressed as Mordechai, Becca as Esther. The date was 1938. Their faces, once bright with only a hint of trepidation, were becoming notably wearier, more frightened.

More pages, more impossible dates. Leah's birthday, 1939, and after that year, fewer pictures, as though his parents' families didn't want to immortalize the awful events that followed.

Adiel turned the page. His parents, now teenagers, stood arm-in-arm in a room far too filthy and miserable to be a synagogue. His mother was dressed in a frayed white gown with a six-pointed star sewn onto her breast. *"Jude"* it said in ugly gothic letters, and every guest at her and Natan's wedding wore the same patch.

Another page. His parents, worn down, horribly thin, but nevertheless smiling at the cameraman. Their clothes were ruddy, their matching *Jude* stars tattered. In his mother's arms was a baby. Adiel had seen pictures of his mother, vibrant and healthy, holding him when he was a child. He had enough baby pictures of himself to know that the child in this picture was not him. The label confirmed as much.

"Natan, Becca, Avi, 1942."

Avi? Adiel turned the page to find a picture of the same little boy, now about two, sitting by himself and staring at the camera with big, bewildered brown eyes. Baby Avi...his brother? The brother that he had always wanted. Little Avi had the anxious expression of a mouse that was well aware it lived next to a cat.

Adiel turned the page, but the rest of the album was blank. Unleashing a shuddering breath, he tossed it aside and peeked into the trunk again. His eyes flitted to a pile of film reels piled high on one end of the trunk. The one on top caught his eye: *"The Great Dictator."*

His gaze shifted to the other side of the chest, hoping to procure another album to give him more answers, or at least more questions.

Instead, he found a pile of books. Books about a war that had not yet happened, a genocide not yet committed, a man who didn't exist yet.

Adiel grabbed the first hardback, his hand trembling as he beheld the cover. An image of a rigid battalion of men in black uniforms saluting a familiar figure with a mop of dark hair and a toothbrush moustache. The title screamed in a gothic font just like that of the star sewn onto his mother's breast: *The Third Reich, A Modern History.*

Adiel opened to the first page, and it took all of his self-control to stop himself from vomiting all over the precious, prophetic book before him.

Since the death of Adolf Hitler and the fall of his so-called Thousand-Year Reich, experts and historians have plumbed the depths of the Nazi psyche to determine what caused the great slaughter of our time...

"Wнат is this?"

Natan knew that there was something wrong by his son's tone alone: cold, distant. Adiel had been angry before, but during those times he was anything but restrained. Always a whirlwind of emotion; usually sorrow, sometimes anger before he remembered Becca's counsel and doused that particular fire.

Only shock so awful that it dulled his senses could bring

about an icy mood in Adiel. Natan took one last sip of his lemonade and turned to his son.

When he saw what Adiel was holding, Natan nearly choked on his drink. A book. An old book, except it wasn't old. It was beyond new.

Natan began to cough. Despite his confusion and mistrust, Adiel stepped forward, his eyes wide with concern.

"Papa...?!"

"I'm...fine, I'm..." Natan took a moment to catch his breath, ramming his fist on his chest to suppress the cough and make sure that the lemonade went down the right tube. "Where's Kaia?"

"Inside...getting a snack...are you...?"

"I'm fine...I can breathe...I've been through worse, I just don't want her to hear, she won't..." Natan sunk into his lawn chair and shook his head. "How did you...?"

"Kaia knows how to pick locks. She hid in your closet, found it, got curious."

"She didn't see anything, did she?" Natan yelped, and Adiel shook his head, grinding his teeth together. The Professor had always been a fast reader, and so he had been able to skim through the four-hundred-page book quickly and get a general gist of what it said. What it *predicted*.

The pictures, however...he would rather experience the agonies outlined for his people's future than let innocent little Kaia see the horrific images that the book held. Piles of corpses. Children starved, tortured, and used as guinea-pigs for sick experiments. Women being shot while holding babies in their arms. Sneering beasts beating Jews in the streets. Crimes yet to be committed. A pogrom reserved for the future.

"Good, good...I had hoped...I didn't want you to ever

see…" Natan hiccupped, his cheeks turning red. A feeling of dread filled Adiel's stomach. He had seen his father shed tears maybe thrice in his life—Natan had cried when Becca had passed, and he'd cried tears of joy when he held his granddaughter for the first time, but that was it. Both Natan and Becca had been plagued by nightmares, but they had always been keen to appear fearless before their boy.

But now…now Natan was gasping for air as sobs wracked his body.

"Papa," Adiel muttered softly, in a tone that he hoped would tell Natan that this grand and insane lie did not diminish the Professor's love for his father. "Please, breathe!"

Natan laughed. An ugly, bitter sound, nothing like the good-hearted chortle that he normally offered Adiel.

"You…little…oh!" the old man cried. "Why did you have to find it? It's all useless now. I should have gotten rid of it all after she passed, but I couldn't…it all meant so much to her…"

"Papa, are you…some sort of time traveler?"

Another laugh and a nod were his answers. Adiel dug his nails into the hardback. It was all so insane, and yet it made sense.

"That's how you've been able to make all your money," the Professor realized, and Natan, who was evidently not the brilliant investor that he had always portrayed himself as, shrugged.

"Hindsight, haha!" the old man jested.

"You predicted hyperinflation before it happened," Adiel said, glancing back at their massive manor. "That's how you knew to make sure we had our assets in tangible goods and foreign currency."

"I guess it's cheating, but…I think we all deserved to live well. You saw the album."

Adiel bit his lip, felt the impulsive urge to pace like he typically did when he was stressed, but stayed still and nodded.

"Then you know…you know what we went through," Natan whispered, and now his bitter chuckle was gone, replaced by a low, dark tone. The tone that he had used when vaguely declaring that his parents were no longer around. "Besides, living well, giving you a good life, that was its own good deed."

"You never told me…"

"Haha! Didn't want to, and even if I did, you would have thought I was crazy unless I showed you…and I did *not* want to show you…"

"You went through this," Adiel muttered, glancing down at the hardback in his hand, thinking of the unimaginable horrors it had described, and realizing that his beloved parents had experienced all of it. His gentle mother, branded with a yellow star and treated like a parasite instead of the lovely woman she was. His father, enslaved, and…

For the first time in Adiel Goldstein's life, Natan rolled up his sleeves. On his left forearm, faded from time, was a blue tattoo, a number sewn permanently onto his flesh. Adiel felt a wave of emotions wash over him: anger, quickly suppressed because now he knew why his mother had feared the mere concept of hatred so much. Then, pity, affection, admiration, and disgust.

"Papa…I'm so, *so* sorry…" Adiel said, and he might have dropped the damned book and run to embrace his father if Natan had not started laughing.

"I *knew* you would say that!" the old man cried, grasping at the number on his arm, tears streaming down his face. "I knew it…you'd say it, and you'd really mean it…damn it all…"

"You were trying to stop this," Adiel assumed, his eyes flitting from his father's arm to the book in his arms. Natan nodded grimly.

"And we failed." Natan's tone was morosely resigned.

"But it was a one-way trip," Adiel guessed, and Natan offered a small nod.

"These books are the future, then," Adiel muttered. "But…there's something that doesn't make sense."

Adiel quickly opened the book to one particular dog-eared section, a one-page picture of the future Führer of the seemingly inevitable Reich. Cold, familiar blue eyes glared at Adiel, and he almost hesitated to show the image to his father lest he trigger unspeakable memories. Curiosity, however, won out, and he turned the picture of Hitler towards Natan.

"This man," Adiel said. "The Führer. It's Hitler, but it's…different. It's him, but the book keeps calling him *Adolf* Hitler. But that…that's *Edmund* Hitler."

There was silence for a moment. Natan bit his lip as though he wanted desperately to say nothing before he seemed to finally decide that he couldn't keep secrets anymore.

"No, Adiel…" Natan muttered. "That isn't Edmund Hitler. Son…that man, Adolf Hitler, that's you."

FIVE

1955

"I think it was this way."

"Becca…"

"I promise it's real, Natan! A real demon!"

Natan Libman grunted in response. The blue number sewn onto his arm prickled as he gripped his wife's hand and let her lead him deeper and deeper into the woods that surrounded their little home.

Natan loved his wife dearly, but they didn't agree on anything. Not about magic: Becca had believed in fairytales long past the point where it was understandable. Natan didn't even believe in angels, much less demons and Ziz monsters and every other ridiculous imaginary being that Becca insisted was real.

They didn't agree about how to tackle their shared status as Holocaust survivors, either. Natan was a living fire. If Becca hadn't survived Auschwitz alongside him, then he might have sought out the mysterious Avenging Angel vigilante who butchered SS men and joined him in his vicious crusade. Natan felt nothing short of utter and complete hatred for Germany and her people, the people who had betrayed him and taken his parents, his sisters, his house, his dignity, everything but his beautiful wife.

He lived a peaceful life for Becca and only for her. If he hadn't had her, he would have made it his mission to find every SS man and give him the slowest, most painful death that he could conceive. An eye for an eye.

Becca, on the other hand, didn't have a spark of hatred in her soul. While Natan was filled with anger towards his tormentors, Becca was possessed by an obsessive spirit of curiosity. She simply couldn't comprehend how her neighbors and friends had seemingly been transformed into ruthless monsters, and the question of *why* had led to her becoming something of an amateur historian. Becca had filled their little cabin with books and films about the Final Solution and the Nazis. She spent hours watching old newsreels of Hitler's speeches.

It all made Natan nauseous, but for some reason, it helped her. Perhaps it made her feel like she was doing something. Perhaps she thought that if she looked hard enough and learned every detail about the men who had destroyed her life, then she could figure out *why*, and that would somehow make the world better. If she could just learn what had made Adolf Hitler the Failed Artist into Adolf Hitler the Irredeemable Monster, then she could somehow be at peace.

"Becca, it's seriously getting dark!"

"Just a little further, I promise! I swear to God!"

Above all, the Libmans didn't agree about the existence of God. Rebecca clung to the faith of her ancestors, but

Natan had decided that God didn't exist the day a Nazi had torn his son out of his wife's arms and slammed the baby's skull against the train car that had delivered them all to Auschwitz-Birkenau.

Monsters like the ones in Becca's folklore books might have been entirely imaginary, but Natan knew that demons were real. They just looked human.

That was what he believed, at least, until his wife finally led him into the clearing that she had discovered while wandering the woods earlier that day.

"What the fuck…" That was all Natan could possibly say as he saw the thing his wife had found. At first, he thought that it looked somewhat like a griffin, but when he dared to emerge from the bushes and draw ever so slightly closer, he found that he had never seen anything like the beast. It was the size of a lion, covered in black feathers, and possessed a pronged tail and bat-like wings that sprouted from its arched back. It pawed at the ground with great hooves, and its two heads, one distinctly feline and the other goat-like, opened both of their maws in unison and let out a single unearthly howl.

"You see it too?" Becca asked, and when Natan could only dully nod, she let out a hoot of delight. "You can! I knew I wasn't crazy! Now come and help me!"

"Help…what? *Becca!*"

Before Natan could even think to grab Becca and stop her from doing something utterly and completely insane, his wife ran towards the demon's pronged tail. The creature, surprisingly, made no move to bite her. Rather, it gave her a pitiable glance with both of its heads, like a cat desperate to be let in out of the rain.

Becca knelt down, and Natan only then realized why

the demon was screeching. One of its hooved legs was caught in a strange sort of bear trap: a silver maw with golden Hebraic letters painted on its teeth attached to a chain that kept it and the beast grounded.

"The person who owned the house must have left this!" Becca said, and Natan could only nod slowly. The Goldsteins hadn't exactly procured their abode via legal means, but that was only because the German legal system had utterly failed them. They had tried to reclaim their childhood homes from the Germans that had stolen them after the Libmans and the Blums had been deported by the Nazis, but it was all for naught. The German judge overseeing their case had sneered in their faces and said *everyone suffered during the war*, damning the couple to homelessness.

Becca, ever the bright spirit, had decided to make the most of their situation by stealing a tent from an American GI and setting off on the long camping trip that she had always wanted to go on with her husband. They had wandered the woods of Europe for a while, having a surprisingly decent time when they weren't stumbling upon unburied mass graves or shot-down airplanes.

Eventually, however, they had found a small, cozy cabin in the middle of the forest. A cabin with a *mezuzah*, broken windows, a menorah resting above the fireplace, and a bookshelf full of tomes about Judaic mysticism.

Becca had, of course, been delighted and had insisted that they wait for the occupant to return, but though they had waited and waited, the cottage's owner had never shown up. Perhaps the Nazis had tracked him down and butchered him with all the rest, or maybe he had simply fled when things had gotten bad, leaving behind his little home and most of his possessions. Either way, Natan and

Becca had decided not to let the place go to waste. They had lived in the little house without incident for almost a decade now, only occasionally venturing into town for supplies.

The demon must have only recently stumbled into the trap, and now it seemed that Natan's wonderful, stupid wife was determined to free the disgusting beast.

"Here, it's heavy! Hold down the latch on the other side!"

"Becca, it's a *monster!*"

"It's in pain!" Becca retorted, almost crying herself, her squeal melding with the creature's howls of agony. Natan could tell that there would be no dragging her away from the beast so long as it was trapped. Becca had never been able to listen to the sounds of an animal in pain. Even in Auschwitz, even the snarling hounds that she had come to fear after one of them mauled her sister to death. If one of those vicious German shepherds would yelp in pain when their masters struck them for showing weakness, Becca would still wince.

Natan ran to her side, and again he was surprised by the beast's self-control: it continued to cry out in pain but didn't writhe or kick at the two Jews. In fact, the demon regarded the Libmans with a strangely intelligent glimmer in both sets of its eyes, as though it knew that they were trying to help and felt grateful.

"Push down on the button when I say," Becca instructed before reciting some sort of Hebrew incantation. The glowing letters on the trap flickered out, and when Becca commanded him to release the beast, Natan did so.

"Becca, get down!" he cried once the monster was free, wrapping an arm around her shoulders and gripping the handle of the Luger he always carried with him, a weapon that he had stolen from a dead SS officer at the end of the war. The little gun probably wouldn't do much good against a beast that large, but at the very least Natan could distract it and let his wife escape.

But it seemed that freedom did not diminish the creature's strangely human sense of gratitude. It leapt away from the trap and the Libmans, then briefly turned its two heads towards the Jews.

And Natan, who was already convinced that he had gone insane alongside his wife, could nonetheless not believe his eyes when the beast nodded both its heads before launching itself into the air and vanishing in a flash of red light.

"I CAN'T BELIEVE IT…"

"Natan, is your brain broken? You haven't said anything except 'I can't believe it' for the past hour."

It took the Libmans well over an hour to get home after they released the creature, partially because the trap had been far away from their little cabin, and partially because Natan had needed time just to clear his mind enough to stand and walk.

The monster hadn't laid a hoof on them, but Natan nonetheless felt like he'd been struck by some sort of demonic curse that had robbed him of his sanity. His brain buzzed, his knees felt weak, and reality itself no longer felt real. Every step that he took alongside his beaming wife as they trudged back towards their house felt like it should have been the step that led to him finally waking up with a horrid hangover.

Every step, however, confirmed that Becca had been…

"Right! I was right!"

"I can't believe it…"

"You can't believe that I was right about something?" Becca gave her husband's arm a teasing slap, and despite his stunned state, Natan couldn't help but smile when she then wound her arm through his.

"I think it's amazing!" Becca declared. "The books, the fairytales…not just fairytales, huh? And he wasn't a demon like from the Christian stories, he was just a scared animal! No harm done, and now we know there's magic in the world! Isn't that great?"

"There's definitely magic in the world," Natan concurred somewhat gloomily, glancing down at the ugly blue number on his wife's arm. Demons were nothing. Becca's ability to smile like Auschwitz had never existed, that was real magic.

Night had fully fallen by the time they reached their little home. Fireflies danced about, bugs nipped at the Libmans' exposed arms, and Natan, dazed, wanted nothing more than to collapse onto his bed and wake up in a reality that was sensible.

"Ah. Welcome home, you two."

But of course, nothing could ever be that simple.

There was a man in their home, sitting in Natan's cozy chair. A man with onyx black hair neatly combed and parted, a simple upturned handlebar moustache, and dark red eyes that twinkled with mischief. He wore a three-piece suit, and when he rose to his feet, he revealed an imposing height, easily over six-foot-six.

Becca squeaked and leapt behind her husband. "We're sorry!" she cried. "We didn't mean to steal your home, we were just…"

"My home?" the man said, his voice deep and yet velveteen soft. He glanced about the cozy little living space and unleashed a chuckle that Natan felt echo about his ears. "Oh…this is not my home. I'm here because of you two. Natan and Rebecca Libman."

The stranger stepped forward, and Natan drew the gun from his side.

"Hey, friend, step back," Natan warned. "Don't make me do anything we'll regret."

"Dear, dear…" Dark red eyes flitted not to the gun Natan had pointed right at the stranger's breast, but at the number sewn onto the Jew's outstretched arm. "Now, that's a new one. Reminds me of that time…"

The stranger took another step forward. Natan felt Becca's hands on his shoulders, squeezing.

"One more step, friend, and I *will* shoot!" Natan warned, his heart pounding like a drum. He was lucky. He knew so many Jews at Auschwitz that had only survived by killing their fellows: by helping the Nazis shepherd women and children into the gas chambers, by stealing food from weaker bunkmates, by any means necessary. Auschwitz made men into animals, but Natan, son of a talented chef, had managed to gain a post in the kitchens that had given him the ability to steal food for himself and a few fellow prisoners. Natan had not only survived; he had survived with his conscience intact, without blood on his hands.

As much as he had fantasized about making the monsters who had killed his family pay, Natan was not a violent man. He hated the idea of shooting someone who

80

wasn't a Nazi, who was perhaps simply confused and insane.

But the cabin was small, and if the stranger got any closer, he could grab the gun, shoot Natan, and then Becca would be at his mercy. Natan couldn't let that happen.

The stranger looked at Natan, glanced at the gun, sneered like the Jew was a child trying to rob a bank with a toy pistol, and then took a step forward.

BANG!

Becca shrieked. The smell of smoke filled the cabin as Natan pulled the trigger and a bullet struck the stranger in the chest.

But the stranger didn't fall. He didn't gag. He didn't cry. He didn't even bleed. He let out a curious hum and looked down at the gaping hole in his chest.

"Quaint," the stranger said, and with a wave of his hand and a scarlet glow in his eyes, the wound was fixed, his clothes were fixed. It was like Natan had never even shot him.

Natan dropped the utterly useless gun and grabbed his wife, dragging her close and bracing himself for a magical assault. The man—no, he wasn't a man, he was something else—the *demon* looked at the Libmans and tilted his head to the side, like a wolf confronted with an unknown sort of prey.

But the demonic intruder did not attack. Instead, he offered a formal bow, smiling at the two Jews.

"Forgive me for intruding, Israelites," the stranger said. "I'm not known for my patience."

He lifted his scarlet eyes, and the corners of his lips curled as he declared, "I am Asmodeus."

"The Demon King?" Becca wrenched herself from

Natan's arms and stepped forward. Natan tried to grab her and pull her back, but she was already walking up to the creature, her eyes glistening.

"Correct, dear lady," Asmodeus said, standing up straight, the top of his head almost hitting their roof. "A pleasure to make your acquaintance."

He offered Rebecca his hand, and the damn woman almost shook it before Natan grabbed her wrist and pulled her back.

"Becca!" he hissed. "Don't shake hands with the Devil!"

"He's not the Devil, Natan, didn't you ever read the Talmud?" Rebecca sighed even though she knew full well that Natan *hadn't*. "Demons can be evil, but they can also be good. More often, they're just...hedonistic. *Mischievous.*"

"Guilty as charged!" Asmodeus concurred, his scarlet eyes flitting to the number on Natan's arm. "Unlike Adam's children, demons do not strike for no reason. Certainly, we do not harm friends."

"We're not friends," snapped Natan, and Asmodeus chuckled, reaching out and prodding Natan's cheek like he was an adorably unruly toddler.

"Oh, but you are!" the Demon King declared. "Both of you! I was beginning to get very worried about my poor boy Mazik."

"Mazik..." muttered Natan, rubbing his cheek and shaking his head. "Wait, that goat...cat...thing..."

"My son," Asmodeus confirmed. Natan decided that it probably wouldn't be a good idea to say he didn't see the resemblance.

The Demon King strolled over to the mantlepiece, eying the rusted menorah. His scarlet eyes fell upon a faded picture of their murdered baby, Little Avi, one of only two pictures that Natan and Rebecca had managed to capture of their son. They were lucky. Mountains of family albums had been incinerated in Auschwitz, leaving the few survivors without even a single photo of their loved ones. Natan remembered sitting beside a woman in the court-house when he and Becca had been trying to get their house back and seeing the stranger break down when she confessed that she didn't remember what her children had looked like.

Asmodeus leaned down, staring into the two-year-old's befuddled eyes, and it was strange to see a demon regard the picture with empathetic graveness. Natan's shoulders relaxed. The Demon King looked upon Avi with more kindness than any Nazi in the Terezin Ghetto ever had.

"You both, of course, know what it's like to lose your son," the Demon King said, turning to the Libmans and smiling again, this time a softer, more human smile. "So you can imagine my relief when my boy came home after I'd begun to fear the worst. To lose a child is the most terrible feeling in the world, and to think you've lost them and have them returned? You, sadly, can only imagine."

Becca's gaze wandered to her son's visage and her lip wobbled. Natan clutched at his pounding heart.

"Or, at least, it *was* only imaginable," the Demon King declared. "But you have gained my favor, and therefore, I offer you a boon: an eye for an eye, a life for a life, and if you wish, a son for a son."

"W-what?" Rebecca whispered, and Natan's pounding heartbeat became frantic, and yet less painful. For the first time since he had reunited with Becca after Auschwitz was liberated, he felt the barest trace of hope bloom in his soul.

"As the stories have no doubt told you, my dear,"

Asmodeus said, glancing at Becca and gesturing to the bookshelf stocked with tomes of Jewish folklore. "I have power, and I offer this power for your purposes. You may have one life, any life you wish. If vengeance is your goal, then I can claim the life of an enemy in the most painful way imaginable."

Asmodeus' scarlet eyes glistened with glee for a moment, and his handsome face barely concealed his demonic spirit. His pupils found little Avi's image again, however, and his features softened once more as he gestured to the boy. "Or," Asmodeus continued, "I can steal a soul from the Heavens or the depths of Hell, whomever you desire, and bring them back to life."

Becca covered her mouth with her hands and unleashed a shuddering breath. Natan, who had learned to see the worst in humanity and therefore knew better than to immediately throw his lot in with anyone, much less a literal monster, scowled at the Demon King.

"What's the catch?" Natan asked in a tone that was perhaps a bit too aggressive for a helpless man speaking to an all-powerful demon. Asmodeus regarded Natan like he was a puppy that had just snarled at a lion: an amused curl of his lip matched with condescending exasperation in his eyes.

"I think you misunderstand: I'm not doing this out of the goodness of my heart, nor am I the Devil looking to steal your soul—not sure what I'd do with the damned thing anyway." Asmodeus strolled over to the frayed cozy chair and plopped down once more, lighting the fireplace with a snap of his fingers and a flicker of light in his wine-colored eyes.

"At the moment, I'm in your debt," Asmodeus said,

folding his hands in his lap. "I don't like to owe a debt. That's all there is to it. Just tell me what you want, and then I'll be on my happy way."

The Demon King was beginning to sound rather annoyed, like he was a worn-out teacher hosting an after-school club against his will. The little seed of hope in Natan's soul began to blossom into an oak. A miracle, a true miracle brought about by a demon of all things.

"We want our son back," Natan declared quickly, almost desperately, afraid that the demon would change his mind and embrace his bestial nature if the Libmans took too long to make their wish. He heard Becca make a small noise of discomfort behind him. The Demon King chuckled.

"The enthusiasm is...appreciated. However, you alone didn't save my son. You worked *together* to free him, and so you *both* must agree on what you want."

Natan nodded, turning to his wife, assuming that she would agree to their mutual wish.

His heart almost stopped when he saw Becca's face: blanched white and paired with wide, pleading eyes. Asmodeus let out a low whistle.

"Ah, damn, I always hate it when Lilith gives me *that* look," chuckled Asmodeus, the gaze of a wife who was bracing herself to ruin her husband's life evidently being universal amongst demons and humans alike.

With a grunt of defeat, Natan drew close to his wife, hesitating to turn his back on the Demon King even as Asmodeus casually grabbed a book of Jewish folklore off the shelf and started thumbing through it with a nostalgic smile.

"Becca," Natan hissed, grabbing his wife by the shoulders. "You know more about this shit than me. Should we take the deal?"

"We should, but…" She bit down on her knuckles so hard that he worried she might draw blood, exhaled sharply, and then declared in a muffled, anxious tone: "We shouldn't ask for Avi."

"W-what?! Becca, why…?"

"It's not fair, don't you get it?" Becca gasped, tears forming in her dark eyes as she threw down her arms. "What about all the others?! Leah, Rahel, your sisters and little Elijah…"

Name after name brought pang after pang, and Natan realized what she was saying. The Demon King had offered only *one* life, and it would no doubt be foolish to ask for more. Being demanding would only provoke the Demon King into refusing to give them back even one person. Still, Natan remembered his nephew's cheerful laugh, his sisters' bright smiles, his parents, Becca's parents. He missed them all terribly, but not more than he missed his child. If he could only have one, it would be Avi.

"Darling, darling, I know," Natan said, and his grip on her shoulders became gentler, more comforting. "But if we can only save one person…"

"Maybe we can save them all," Becca whispered. "It isn't *fair* to only save one, to save our baby and let all the millions of others stay dead! It's not fair for them, or for the survivors like us, but maybe…maybe there's something we *can* do."

She pulled him close and whispered her plan in his ear. If Natan hadn't been completely in love with the damn woman, he would have divorced her right then on the grounds that she was clearly insane. As it were, he heard the determination in her voice, and the sapling of hope grew taller. It was a long shot, but if it worked, they could save millions. Natan's sisters, his parents, Avi, everyone he had ever loved, every speck of ash that had fallen on him in Auschwitz.

"Ask him," Natan said, and Becca stepped forward, offering the Demon King a curtsy that made Asmodeus' scarlet eyes sparkle with amused affection.

"You've decided on your wish, my dear girl?" he said.

"If it's possible," Becca replied.

"Ask, my dear. The impossible is a trifle for Lord Asmodeus."

Becca straightened up, folded her hands over her chest, and declared, "We want the life of Adolf Hitler."

The Demon King's eyes twinkled again, and he let out a chuckle.

"Unless you mean a *different* Adolf Hitler, that's going to be quite impossible...that is, unless you want me to bring him *back* from the dead. I can't imagine *why* you'd want such a thing."

"No," Becca said, shaking her head. "We want you to take his life completely. Make it so that he was never born, or so that he died as a baby, so that he never grew up to be Adolf Hitler the Great Dictator."

Natan almost chuckled at his wife, who was so in love with that stupid Charlie Chaplin film that she felt the need to reference it even during such a precarious negotiation. Asmodeus, however, had stopped smirking. He stroked his chin and hummed thoughtfully.

"Quite the request, quite the request," the Demon King mumbled. "Hardly simple, but very clever. I remember why I was always fond of your people. You remind me a little of

King Solomon, though of course he was more *forceful* when asking for magical favors."

Asmodeus lifted up the book of folktales and tossed it onto the coffee table. Becca squirmed. Natan curled and uncurled his fists.

"Is it possible? Our request?" Natan finally asked after a few agonizing moments of demonic pondering passed. He was fully prepared to demand his son's soul if the Demon King declared that Adolf Hitler's life couldn't be offered.

"It is," Asmodeus said slowly, in a manner that made Natan instantly know that a *but* he wouldn't like was incoming.

"But..."

There we go.

"Time is finicky. It is the domain of the highest angels, and demons are not permitted to directly meddle with it. I myself could not go back in time. The angels have already seen to that. They can't very well allow an immortal creature such as myself to romp around in the past...it would be far too much fun."

Becca's shoulders sagged. Natan glanced at Avi's picture and let his disappointment dissipate.

"However..."

Becca's eyes brightened. *Oh, dear...*

"Just as I can steal one soul from the Heavens, I could also steal the Book of Time from the Archangels for less than a second," Asmodeus proclaimed, rising to his feet and strolling towards a coo-coo clock that hung on the wall. "And while I could not send *myself* back in time, I could send the two of you back..."

The Demon King reached out and pressed one finger against the minute arm of the clock, casually turning it the other way. "Of course, it would need to be quick. I would steal the Book, send you two back, and then…well, then we would never have this conversation. I would be able to send you to the past, but it would be completely impossible to bring you back to this time no matter what. I would send you back to a time shortly before Hitler was born, you would kill him, and then you would have to live out the rest of your lives in the past."

"Wouldn't that…cause trouble? There would be two of us running around," Becca said.

"Two very different versions. You would be significantly older than your younger selves. It's a rather novel idea, but it *should* work if it's what you truly want. I made a vow to give you whatever life you wish, and if you want Adolf Hitler's life, this is the only way to get it."

Natan didn't precisely relish the idea of reliving the 1930s, but he had lost everything once for no reason and had survived. He was more than willing to give up what little he had for a chance at saving everyone that he had ever loved. A brief glance at Becca, whose eyes were flaring with determination, proved that she felt the same. Both Libmans nodded.

"We'll do it," Natan said.

"Uhm…can we bring some things back with us?" Becca queried, her eyes flitting to the picture of her son, then to a photo album resting on top of one bookshelf.

"You won't be going back nude: pack whatever you want, though I don't recommend taking anything too large, or anything that would raise eyebrows in 1889," the Demon King said, sitting down and waving for the Libmans to get ready to go.

Natan packed practically: clothes, shoes, his gun, knives,

what little fineries they had. Everything they would need to kill a baby and then start a new life in an old time period. Becca, meanwhile, took a trunk and filled it with every book and film reel about the Third Reich that she had.

"Becca, we're changing all that, why are you packing it?" Natan asked, and Becca lifted her gaze and offered a slightly sad smile.

"Better to have it and not need it than need it and not have it," she said, and Natan chuckled bitterly. Becca's father, a merchant by trade, had lived by that motto. Natan wondered if he and his wife could somehow go and see their respective parents after they killed Baby Hitler. That would be odd, and perhaps a bad idea if it somehow led to him and Becca never being born. It would likely be best to wait until later, after the Libmans and Blums were already established.

"Ready?" Asmodeus said once Becca stuck Avi's picture in the family album, set the album on top of the pile of books, and shut the trunk.

"Wait, if we're going back in time and don't want to draw any eyes, we need to get rid of..." Becca turned her forearm towards the Demon King, showing off her Auschwitz brand. Asmodeus once more offered a somewhat soft smile and nodded once.

"Easily done," the Demon King declared, and with a snap of his fingers and yet another flash of light in his eyes, Becca's arm was wrapped in a crimson aura. When the aura dissipated, it took the tattoo with it. It was like she had never spent a day in Auschwitz. Becca beamed at her unmarked flesh and let out a small giggle of delight before bowing to the Demon King.

"Thank you!" she chirped, and Asmodeus offered her a

wink that might have concerned Natan if the Demon King's character was actually demonic. Asmodeus then turned his gaze to Natan, nodding his head, a silent instruction for Natan to lift up his arm and have his turn.

"No," Natan said, slapping a hand over his tattoo. The Demon King raised an eyebrow.

"No?"

"I'm keeping mine," Natan proclaimed, glancing uneasily at Becca, hoping that she would know that he was speaking exclusively for himself and didn't disparage her for removing her number. She smiled gently and nodded once.

"That's your right, Herr Libman," Asmodeus said with a shrug. "But might I ask why?"

"Because I earned it," Natan declared. Perhaps the Nazis had meant for the tattoo to be a symbol of dehumanization, but Natan Libman was a living man who bore the mark of a prisoner of Auschwitz. It was a battle scar to him, and to remove it would be to remove proof that he had survived the worst things that Hitler had thrown at him.

Besides, it would be nice and ironic when he strangled Baby Hitler using an arm branded with an Auschwitz number.

"All right, you two are ready to go," Asmodeus declared. "Now, I will ask one thing: when you go back in time, be sure to return to the woods and disable the trap my poor son traipsed into so that he'll never be captured. In this way, we'll both be spared agony, and we'll be even. Deal?"

"Of course," Natan said, and Becca bobbed her head.

"Swear to God!" she chirped, and it seemed that the Demon King took a vow to the Most Holy more seriously than Natan. Asmodeus showed off a confident smile and nodded.

"Hold one another close and keep a grasp on the things that you wish to bring back," the Demon King instructed. "This is going to happen very quickly."

"Thank you so much, Lord Asmodeus," Becca declared, and when she reached out to shake Asmodeus' hand this time, Natan made no move to stop her. Asmodeus chuckled, shaking her hand jovially.

"Think nothing of it, my dear," he declared. "You've earned it, both of you."

The Demon King released Becca's hand and glanced at Natan. The Jewish man, still wary but nonetheless realizing that the monster had shown him and his wife more respect than most humans had during the war, grasped Asmodeus' hand and shook it once. A strange feeling shot through Natan, like he had leapt from a great height. The Demon King's flesh was oddly warm, but not quite to the point where it hurt to touch.

"Good luck, both of you," the Demon King said, and everything else happened so fast that Natan could barely comprehend it all. The Demon King vanished in a flash of red light, reappeared holding some sort of silver book, said something in a booming voice, and then, there was a hectic, suffocating sensation like he was drowning in rushing rapids.

Then, they were in the middle of the woods over half a century in the past, and their quest began.

———✡———

Braunau Am Inn,
1889

"ARE YOU SURE ABOUT THIS?"

"Yes."

"Becca..."

"Natan, you'll never pass as a nurse."

True enough, though Natan would probably blend in a bit better if he were to traipse through the bar that took up the first level of the building that was Adolf Hitler's birthplace.

The Hitlers had rented a room on the second story, and perhaps Adolf's alcoholic father had chosen the building specifically because it provided easy access to a bar, the *Stag.* Natan couldn't imagine that the noise or the smells emanating from the *Stag* were good for a baby's health. The scent of booze and piss was intense even from the alleyway across from the *Stag* building, where Natan and his wife were hidden, and the sound of drunken men shouting and cursing was making his ears ache despite the distance.

Natan glanced at his watch. 10 PM. Adolf Hitler had been born three-and-a-half hours ago. The midwives had left. Nobody would question another nurse popping in to check on the newborn.

Getting to Baby Hitler wouldn't be an issue for sweet, innocent-looking Becca. Natan, however, was worried that his wife wouldn't be able to use the knife in her medical bag to slit the little dictator's throat. Becca was undoubtedly stronger than she looked, but Natan hated the idea of making his wife dirty her hands, even with blood as filthy as Adolf Hitler's.

"It doesn't have to be tonight," Natan said. "I'm sure

we'll get another opportunity if you want me to do it. We have time. We're stuck here either way."

"I can do it," Becca declared firmly, gripping the bag and adjusting her smock. "I've got the sleeping pills for Klara."

The Libmans had both agreed that Klara Hitler, despite her reputation for raising a future mass murderer, didn't deserve to die. A tub of sleeping pills would render her helpless. As for Hitler's father…

"He's there," Natan whispered, spotting one pathetic figure sitting by the window of the *Stag* bar. A face he had seen in Becca's history books: seemingly older than his fifty-two years, weary, red from drunkenness, sporting a greying moustache that made him look a bit like a walrus. Alois Hitler was hunched over a half-empty mug of beer, muttering something to a fellow beside him. Natan didn't want Becca to have to deal with the brutish man, and fortunately, it seemed that the Führer's father wouldn't be leaving the bar for a while.

And if he *did*, well, he'd likely be too plastered to stop any attempted infanticide either way.

"All right," Becca whispered. "I'm going in. I love you."

"Stay safe…I can't…" Natan grabbed his wife's pristine arm and hesitated to speak his feelings lest he seem weak and needy. He couldn't lose her. He couldn't bear to be trapped in this time period, surrounded by loved ones and yet entirely alone.

Becca silenced him by kissing his lips. She whispered another promise to return and ran towards the *Stag* bar before Natan could hope to change his mind and insist on going in her stead.

Thirty minutes he stood there, the late-night April

breeze nipping at his skin, watching as Alois Hitler finished off his beer and immediately ordered something else, likely something much stronger. Every laugh from the men in the bar made Natan wince as he kept mistaking the cheerful drunken cries as yelps of outrage directed at his wife. He braced himself for a scream, a shout, *something*.

But after a half-hour of agonizing *nothing*, Becca came rushing out. Nobody paid her any mind as she made a brisk exit. Anyone sober enough to even notice her must have merely assumed that the nurse was desperately needed elsewhere. Becca was thus able to rush back into the alley and meet her husband without any interference.

"Let's go!" she commanded, and Natan didn't need to be told twice. The Libmans made haste, escaping from the alley and winding their way through the streets of Braunau Am Inn, crossing a bridge and finally finding a small, wooded park that would allow them a modicum of privacy.

"Did you get him?" Natan gasped once he and Becca managed to catch their breaths, and Becca nodded, falling to her knees. She opened her bag, revealing a bundle of baby blankets. At first, Natan thought that his wife had been wise enough to take the body with her for a secretive disposal.

But then the little bundle wriggled and let out a sob.

"Becca, you did *not*..." Natan gasped as his wife reached into the doctor's bag and pulled Adolf Hitler, not even a full day old, into her arms.

"Deep sleeper you are," Becca mumbled, letting the murderer of their child nestle against her breast. The same breast she had tried to feed Avi with in Terezin when they were starving. Natan remembered holding her when she sobbed because she was too malnourished to produce enough milk. If not for the kind intervention of another woman whose baby had perished, Avi might have starved before he could even make it to Auschwitz.

"I guess you *did* sleep through D-Day," Becca muttered, sounding rather amused. "Guess those drunks wouldn't have heard you either way."

"*Becca!*" Natan snarled, and he had never in all of his years been more tempted to be an abusive monster to his wife. To hit her until her stupid, *stupid* brain kicked back into gear and she dropped the little monster to the ground and crushed his skull.

"I couldn't do it, Natan…"

"Clearly! Then you should have sent me——!"

"You don't understand!" Becca yelped, tightening her grip on the little demon. Adolf Hitler crooned and trembled in the cold night wind, nestling against the Jewish woman, making Natan feel like he'd swallowed a razor blade.

"Natan, his father's been drinking all day!" Becca whispered, staring down at Hitler with a sorrowful mist in her eyes. "He was shouting at Klara *while* she was giving birth! She was so grateful to take the pills so she could sleep for a moment, but she was worried he'd come back and be upset if he couldn't wake her…"

"Becca, don't tell me you're *sympathizing* with the little shit!" snarled Natan. "You and I had shitty childhoods too, all thanks to *him!*"

"I'm not…I'm not *excusing* what he did, I'm just saying that I can see how he'd become a monster in that home," Becca said. "But he doesn't have to grow up in that home anymore. *We're* here."

Natan felt a brick fall into the pit of his chest. He *might* have been willing to entertain the notion of finding the richest, most loving family in Germany and dumping Baby Hitler on their doorstep. Hope for the best, follow him around with a shotgun and blow his head off if he showed any sign that he was destined to become the worst.

"Becca, don't you dare even *suggest...*"

"His life is ours. We can do what we want. I want to...I *need* to try..."

"Rebecca Libman, you are fucking insane!" Natan shouted, and if anger hadn't been burning his skull like an inferno, he might have been worried that his screech would draw unwanted attention despite the fact that the park was utterly deserted.

Hitler started crying. Somehow, that made it worse even though Natan had always wanted to hear Hitler cry.

"Shhh, shhh," Becca whispered, bouncing the little demon the same way she had bounced Avi. Pity twisted Natan's guts: her maternal instincts, cut criminally short by a peon of the baby in her arms, must have been driving her mad. It had been foolish of him to even think that a woman whose baby had been torn from her arms and killed right in front of her could ever kill a baby, even Baby Hitler.

"I will *not* do this, Becca," Natan snarled. "I will *not* replace Avi."

"It's not about replacing..."

"I won't replace Avi with *Adolf Hitler!* I can't believe you'd even *suggest* such a thing! He killed our baby, *my* baby! He killed our families, and you want to give him a chance?! He doesn't deserve a chance! He doesn't deserve *us* as his parents!"

He certainly didn't deserve Becca as a mother. She had only entertained the notion of adopting the kidnapped dictator, and yet she was already clutching him protectively close, giving her husband a stern stare even as her body trembled.

"I want to do this. This is what *I* want," Becca declared in the sort of tone that she had used when they were little and Natan wouldn't play house with her. "If you don't want to be part of it, then fine. Go do what you want."

"B-Becca!" That hurt. He and Becca had always been together. The only time that they had been separated was at Auschwitz, and even then, he had snatched tender moments with his wife when he'd delivered meals to the doctors' offices where she had been kept as a guinea pig.

Now Hitler was threatening to truly tear them apart.

"It's up to you," Becca whispered. "If you want..."

"I *want* to beat that little shitstain's head in!" Natan cried, desperation lacing his tone as he tried to think of a way to keep his wife and be rid of the little monster. Hitler was really screaming now, his wails echoing about the park.

Becca faced her husband, and *that look*. He had seen it before, but not directed at him. It was the look she had given a Nazi guard in Terezin that had offered her a loaf of bread for sex. It was death in a stare.

"Fine," she said, her tone colder than the nights at Auschwitz. "Then do it."

Natan lifted a brow. A small part of him that was stupid enough to assume his wife would fold so easily expected her to offer the baby to him.

She didn't. She held Hitler close.

"Becca..."

"What's wrong? Go on. You're bigger and stronger," she spat, and every word struck him like a knife to the breast. "You're *right*, so it's *fine*. Just rip him out of my arms and kill him. I'm too weak to stop you. You can and you want to, so *why not*, huh? *Why not?!*"

Now she was crying, crying and shouting and clutching little Adolf Hitler as tightly and tenderly as she had Avi on that horrible first day in Auschwitz. Natan felt ill at the notion of making her relive that moment. His knees buckled, and he knelt before her.

"Becca, Becca, my love..." Natan said, and he was afraid to reach out to her lest she think that he really was going to rip the little dictator from her arms. "I'm sorry, don't cry, I won't..."

He scowled at the baby, who sobbed practically in unison with the woman who was being entirely too merciful. Adolf Hitler shrieked in terror, knowing that people were shouting but being too young to know why, too young to know why he *deserved* it.

"Fine!" conceded Natan. "Fine, if this is so important to you, we'll do it. But if I even *think* he's on the path to become a monster, I'll strangle him myself. Got it?"

Becca, perhaps knowing better than to argue when she had managed to make her husband bend so much, looked up and nodded, wiping her tears on Hitler's little tuft of dark hair.

"Okay...okay..."

"Stand up...let's go," Natan sighed. "We're stuck here now. We have to make the most of it."

A LIFE FOR A LIFE. A SON FOR A SON.

What a joke, Natan thought bitterly as he stood in the

nursery, watching his wife offer a fussy six-month-old Adolf Hitler a fresh bottle. Adolf Hitler had been a petulant, demanding man and it seemed that this was more nature than nurture. Avi had been much hungrier than Adolf, and yet he had never cried so much.

"Calm down, Adiel, come on, be nice for Mama," crooned Becca, and Natan scoffed. Right. Not Adolf, or Hitler, or demon, or little monster, or son-of-a-bitch, or disgusting creature that needed to be stepped on. *Adiel.*

("That's rather on-the-nose," Natan had said when Becca had decided on the name, but she had rejected all of his even more on-the-nose suggestions—Haman, Amalek, Rameses—and had muttered something about Adiel meaning jewel or some other such nonsense. Close as it was to Adolf, it was still a better name than the monster deserved.)

Adiel Goldstein. The damned demon would always be Hitler, but Becca had warned Natan that if he didn't start calling the boy *Adiel* now, he would be liable to slip up later, when Hitler was old enough to ask questions.

Adolf Hitler finally took the bottle, gazing up at the woman who was far too good and merciful to be his mother with wide, gleaming blue eyes. Adolf Hitler was healthy as could be—well-fed and well-loved.

Bitterly, Natan glanced about the nursery, which was handsomely furnished and filled with every baby toy on the market. It had been too easy for Natan to become an investor, and a skilled one at that. An outsider would have been forgiven for seeing Natan Libman-now-Goldstein's astonishing success and assuming that he really was a member of an international Jewish financing conspiracy. Really, though, he just had the benefit of hindsight, which meant that, trapped as they were, they wanted for nothing.

And neither did Adolf Hitler. Avi had nearly starved in the Terezin Ghetto. Adolf Hitler never felt the pangs of hunger. Avi hadn't had a single toy. Adolf Hitler had chests full of them, every sort of rattle and stuffed animal. Avi died, and Baby Hitler was nestled in Becca's arms, crooning happily as he finished his meal.

It wasn't fair. It made Natan want to break his vow and smash the baby's skull in. That would be fair. An eye for an eye.

But doing that would also break Becca.

"You look exhausted," Natan said. "Take a nap. I'll look after the little monster."

"Please stop calling him that," Becca sighed, earning only a non-committed hum from her husband. Natan hated to call the dictator by the name that he didn't deserve, and anything more vicious than "little monster" riled Becca up, so it was his go-to epithet.

"He can't understand what I'm saying," Natan pointed out.

"He *will*."

"Then I'll come up with something."

"It won't do any good to steal him from one awful father just to give him another one."

Well. Natan felt a pang of umbrage at that. He was a good father. If he were a bad father, he would have been more lenient towards his son's murderer.

"Are you going to take a break or what?" Natan asked, aiming for a fondly teasing tone but coming off a touch too aggravated. Becca gave him *that look*, the one that she sported whenever she desperately wanted to trust him even though she *couldn't*, before exhaustion won out over suspicion.

"Ten minutes so I can go to the bathroom and clean the bottle," she said. "Just let him sit, you don't have to hold him."

Good. Natan still wasn't sure if he would ever be able to hold the little monster without killing him. It would be too easy. *Oh dear, I dropped Baby Hitler and then accidentally stepped on him six times! Clumsy me!*

Rebecca was too smart to fall for that, of course, so Natan likely wouldn't have tried it even if she shoved the little dictator into his arms. Luckily, she respected him enough to instead set the baby on the plush carpet, smiling at her husband and promising to be back soon.

Grunting, Natan knelt down in front of the baby: standing up when Adolf Hitler was practically begging to be punted like a genocidal football was dangerous and too tempting, so he sat in front of the little monster.

Adolf Hitler wasn't quite at the age where he knew how to crawl, but he was old enough to have some sort of instinctual awareness that he could move without Becca's help. The baby swayed a bit, steadying himself with his little hands and staring up at Natan with worshipful curiosity.

Natan scowled as harshly as he could, but Baby Hitler must have thought that he was pulling a funny face because he had the gall to giggle.

"Laugh it up, you little shit," hissed Natan, keeping his tone quiet lest Rebecca somehow hear him lambasting the potential Führer.

Adolf Hitler squeaked something incomprehensible in

that tiny, adorable voice that would one day become a deep, hypnotic bark.

"Fuck you, too," Natan said, and he somewhat recognized that he was being incredibly immature. The child probably hadn't been saying *go to hell, you filthy Jew* in its Baby Hitler language.

Still, Natan wasn't going to be permitted to tell Hitler exactly what he thought of him to his face when the child was old enough to know what his "father" was actually saying. And it felt good to say it to Hitler's face even if this helpless baby wasn't a moustache-clad beast. Even if he would *never* be a moustache-clad beast.

He was still Adolf Hitler. No matter what. Nothing could change that.

A tiny yelp and a *thud* yanked Natan from his hateful ruminations and drew his eyes back to the baby. Hitler had tried, with all the boldness of the man who had invaded the Soviet Union, to crawl. And like usual, he had overestimated his abilities and flopped onto his belly. Surprisingly, Adolf Hitler didn't cry. He merely lay face down, crooning as though the floor was an absolutely fascinating piece of art.

The universe was teasing Natan. Gift-wrapping him a plausible excuse. *No, really, Rebecca, I took my eyes off of him for one second and he fell down and died of whatever kills babies that are left on their stomach! Hardly my fault!*

Natan wouldn't even have to do anything, really. Just sit back and watch as the little dictator suffered a death far kinder than he deserved.

But Becca would probably chastise him. And then she would cry. And Natan couldn't break her heart when for some insane reason raising her son's murderer was melding it back together.

"I hate you," Natan said, his voice pure venom as he flipped the baby onto his back, barely able to see Adolf Hitler's cherubic little features through the tears in his eyes. "I *hate* you."

ADOLF HITLER'S FIRST WORD WAS "MAMA." THIS WAS NOT shocking.

Adolf Hitler's second word was "blue," though it came out more as "brew." Also not shocking since Becca had made Natan paint the little monster's room cerulean.

Adolf Hitler's third word was "Papa." Natan smiled and encouraged him even though he wanted to wring the little bastard's throat and scream right in his face. *I'm not your Papa. You don't get to call me that. There's only one boy who can call me that and you killed him, you killed him, it's your fault…*

Adolf Hitler's fourth word was his false name, or an attempt at it. He tried for "Adiel." He managed "Adi." It sounded more like "Avi."

Adolf Hitler was lucky that Natan Libman-now-Goldstein loved Becca more than he hated the little monster.

HITLER WAS THREE. TOO OLD FOR NATAN TO TELL HIM how much he deserved to be dead, how much his "Papa" hated him. Now he was old enough to remember things, and so Natan was obliged to slap a devoted-father mask onto his face and play nice with Avi's killer. He was glad for his work. He could be gone most of the day and only had to smile and hug the little monster for a few agonizing moments in the afternoon.

Distinctly, he wondered if Hitler the Führer had ever felt like this when he lied. Hitler had lied quite often, after all, and Natan had never thought that disguising one's true feelings could be this painful. It felt like there was a creature inside of him, clawing at his guts and fighting to crawl out of his throat.

Natan hoped that it had been this painful for the Führer. He hoped every moment that Adolf Hitler had pretended to be anything less than the Devil in human form had torn him to shreds.

Regardless, if Natan had hoped to avoid dealing with Adolf Hitler altogether, he was going to have his work cut out for him. Becca was becoming increasingly insistent that Natan spend "father-son" time with Hitler, sometimes simply shoving a thoroughly unwilling Natan into the nursery and proclaiming that she was going shopping and would be back in half an hour.

"Don't kill each other," she said in a tone that was somehow both teasing and perfectly serious.

Fortunately, three-year-old Adolf Hitler didn't demand tickles or ask to play hide-and-seek. He had spread several papers and safe paints that Becca had bought him on a small desk and was quite focused on his masterpiece. His bright blue eyes possessed an intensity that was far too reminiscent of his older self. His rosy cheeks were smudged with green paint (green, evidently, was Hitler's favorite color) and his untidy dark locks hung slightly in his face. The three-year-old stuck out his tongue and stabbed at his paper with a brush.

He would have looked very cute if he weren't Adolf Hitler.

Grinding his teeth so harshly that he worried he might need dentures before he was forty, Natan glanced about the small nursery. Adolf Hitler's artistic habit had bloomed early, and the blue-painted walls were all but completely covered in his drawings.

As an adult, Adolf Hitler had been relatively talented at drawing houses and buildings but had failed to get into art school because he simply couldn't paint living beings. Three-year-old Hitler, however, had a clear preference for painting creatures. Animals, people, and especially his family. Half of the paintings on the walls were family portraits with arrows pointing to the smiling stick-figures. *Me, Mama,* and on a figure with the biggest smile of all, *Papa.*

The realization struck Natan, not for the first time but particularly fiercely, that he had been Adolf Hitler's father longer than he'd been Avi's. That thought made him want to set the house on fire.

"Papa!"

A squeak that was too cheerful for Natan to ever mistake it as the woeful, timid voice of Avi Libman. He looked at Adolf Hitler, who was beaming with the pride of a Nazi that had just crushed a Jewish child's skull, blue eyes glistening as he held up his completed *magnum opus.*

"I drew'd a...the kitties from the store," Adolf Hitler said, pointing towards one carefully drawn tabby. "Papa kitty."

His finger traveled to a black cat, almost smudging the not-yet-dry paint. "Mama kitty."

Vaguely, he waved his hand to indicate the little blobs of various shades with crooked triangle ears and curly wisps of paint for tails. "And the baby kitties."

Adolf Hitler looked up, brimming with anticipation. Natan would have dearly liked to spit on the stupid boy and his stupid kitten painting because *Avi should be painting kittens and you should be rotting in a ditch*, but rule number two of Becca's Rules For Raising Adolf Hitler To Not Be A Genocidal Manic had been: "Encourage him to be an artist."

Rule number one had been "don't beat him," which was admittedly an impulse that was becoming less and less strong in Natan. Adolf Hitler still deserved to have his skull cracked open, but Natan would prefer it if somebody with less compunctions about beating a three-year-old to death could do it. For some reason, the idea of killing Baby Hitler was easier than the idea of killing a three-year-old Hitler.

Frankly, Natan had never liked babies very much even at the best of times. Babies were misshapen, smelly, loud mounds of flesh and potential. He was sure that he would have even hated baby Avi if paternal instinct hadn't made the stinky little fellow so lovable.

Perhaps a brainwashed Nazi could cheerfully crush a toddler's skull, but Natan knew that he couldn't, and not merely because doing so would make him feel too much like that Auschwitz guard. A baby cried, but a three-year-old could be betrayed. A baby sobbed, but a three-year-old could look at him with wide, stupid eyes not yet possessed by hatred and choke out a plea. *Papa, please, don't, I love you, don't...*

"Do you like it, Papa?"

Natan shivered and plastered a smile onto his face that anyone smarter than a three-year-old inbred potential dictator would have realized was bitterly false. *Remember rule two,* he thought.

"It's amazing, the best drawing I've ever seen," Natan said, and fortunately, while three-year-old Hitler was now too old to be directly insulted, he was still young and dumb enough that he didn't recognize sarcasm. "You're an amazing artist. Someday, when you're older, your work will be in every museum in the world, and everyone will just *love you.* "

Those last two words almost emerged as a bark, a quieter version of the tone that the guards at Auschwitz had used when they yelled, *"Get moving, Jews!"* Adolf Hitler seemed to mistake this for resolute emphasis because his little jaw went slack and his blue eyes glowed.

"Really?!" Hitler chirped. There was an innocent genuineness to his tiny voice that made Natan's trampled paternal instincts flare against his will. Anger at the little bastard for being so damn manipulative so damn early consumed him for a moment before Hitler tilted his head sideways, leaned forward, and looked up at Natan with a worshipful trust that was very much unlike Avi.

Avi had been born during the Holocaust and had possessed the keen sense that his parents were as helpless as he. That they couldn't save him even if they wanted to so, *so* badly. Natan had always sensed that little Avi Libman hadn't trusted his parents for that reason, unlike Adolf Hitler, who trusted them completely.

"Yes, I mean that. You're a great artist," Natan said, more softly than he intended. "You should keep painting."

Hitler smiled the smile of a dictator that had just stolen

Austria. "Okay, yeah!" he said. "I'm gonna paint more kitties...Mama, Mama took me to the pet place...and the kitties, I liked 'em, but they made me go sneeze..."

The toddler prattled on as he was wont to do—Hitler was a prattler, which was not in and of itself surprising, though Natan had been aggravated by just how quickly that particular trait had surfaced. On and on Hitler went, pausing to collect his jumbled thoughts as he babbled about puppies and kitties and the nice lady at the pet store who told them *Happy Hannukah* and not *Merry Christmas*.

Adiel was just beginning to realize that he and his "family" were different from their neighbors.

Natan watched his worst enemy with a growing sense of unease.

It would have been easier to kill him when he was a baby. As a baby, he was little more than a malformed Hitler-in-waiting. Now, however much he was Hitler, he was also Adiel, who liked painting kittens even though they made him sneeze.

Now he was a *person* instead of a *thing*, and Natan might have hated him, but he knew well that the Nazi who had crushed Avi's skull had been able to do so with a sneer and a laugh because to him, Avi had been a *thing* and not a *person*.

ADOLF HITLER WAS A TROUBLEMAKER. THIS WAS PERHAPS not entirely because he was Adolf Hitler but more because he was an almost four-year-old boy. Natan remembered his nephew Eli well enough to know that little boys, be they Jew or Hitler Himself, were wont to unleash their bottomless energy in strange, stupid, annoying ways.

It really should have aggravated Natan more than it did when Hitler, for example, ripped open all of their very expensive down pillows (more expensive than anything sweet Avi had ever been allowed to lie upon, which was still not fair, but Natan was beginning to think less about his poor son whenever Hitler did anything that Avi hadn't been allowed to do.) That alone should have gotten a rise out of him even though money wasn't really a concern.

Of course, Hitler didn't just destroy things for no reason. No, he had to go and make it *artistic*.

"What *exactly* are you doing, little monster?" Natan asked, the epithet that had once been spat with absolute poison falling from his lips a bit more gently as he gazed upon the child.

Adolf Hitler stood before him, barely recognizable as a human being: he had stripped himself down to only his underwear and painted his body blue and green. Natan was actually rather impressed by the fact that the boy had literally managed to paint himself from head to toe: his face, his back, his damn eyelids! Even his hair was painted, though it was hard to tell since his dark brown locks hid the blue paint.

As for the pillows, well, it appeared that Adiel had found a use for the down feathers: he'd stuck them all over his body. In his painted hair, on his chest, and on every inch of both his arms.

The feather-and-paint-clad future dictator climbed onto a cozy chair, balancing precariously on the armrest as he stretched out his bird-like arms and proclaimed, "I'm a Ziz! Squawk!"

Ah. Right. Becca had started telling Adiel stories based on Jewish folklore, perhaps preparing him for the future when (*if*) they ever chose to tell him about Asmodeus and their real identities. Adiel had, for one reason or another, really fallen in love with the Ziz beast, a bird that was so tall that its neck reached the Heavens. He had taken to drawing the monster constantly, and now, it seemed, he'd gone one step further and decided to *become* the mythical bird.

Watching little Adolf Hitler squeal with glee as he leapt off the chair and pretended to fly probably should have filled Natan with jealous rage on behalf of Avi. Avi hadn't gotten a chance to give in to his childish imagination with such messy, reckless abandon. Avi hadn't gotten to dress as mythical monsters, but this real monster did.

However, even though the boy insisted right then that he *was* a monster, Natan had never seen a creature that looked less monstrous than the paint-covered Adiel Goldstein.

"Hey, little monster," Natan said, suddenly grabbing the boy. "Here, you're not flying right."

Natan tossed the child into the air several times, and while he told himself that he was just playing the part, following Becca's rules, he would have been lying if he proclaimed that hearing little Adiel's squeals of glee and pleas for "Again! Again!" didn't stir something in him.

Adolf Hitler was being stubborn again. This was not unusual. Hitler was wont to be fussy for a variety of reasons. *I want chocolate, I want playtime, I want Poland.* Admittedly, four-year-old Hitler hadn't asked for that last one yet, but it was only a matter of time.

This time, his fussiness was borne from something else entirely.

"I wanna cap like Papa! I wanna God cap!" Hitler cried, slapping his tiny hands over his skull, like he was embarrassed by his bare hair. The little dictator's eyes flitted to the kippa perched on Natan's head, which the time-traveler wore more out of spite towards the spirit of anti-Semitism than genuine religiousness.

Becca was trying to pull Hitler out the door for a family walk. Hitler was inflexible. He dug in his heels and pouted in a manner that was far too adorable for a future mass murderer.

Well. A *potential* future mass murderer.

Then again, an anti-Semitic mass murderer would never be so eager, so determined, to wear a kippa.

So…

Natan went to a drawer and retrieved a spare skullcap. "This one?" he said, kneeling before the toddler and offering the kippa. The boy's pout morphed into a smile.

"Yeah, so we can…so it's like yours!" Adiel chirped, happily plopping the kippa onto his skull and then pointing to his false father's head-covering.

The realization struck Natan right then that Adiel's tantrum had not merely been borne from childishness, but from a familiar desire. The desire that had gripped little Natan Libman when he had been a boy, when he would follow his father into the kitchen and pretend to be a chef just like him. A son's urge to become the man that his beloved father was.

Adolf Hitler had shared many things with his biological

father. Looks, temperament, but according to Becca, Adolf had hated Alois Hitler so much that he'd gone out of his way to be his opposite. While Alois Hitler had been a civil servant, Adolf Hitler had aspired to a career in the arts. While Alois Hitler had been proudly Austrian, Adolf had been a German nationalist. Alois had smoked and drank, and Adolf had refused to touch tobacco or alcohol.

Adolf Hitler almost certainly hadn't wanted to dress like Alois Hitler, but Adiel Goldstein wanted to dress like Natan.

Adolf Hitler loved him. That was an odd thought, and not nearly as foul as it should have been.

"Let's go, little monster," Natan said. "Listen to your mama next time, and don't be mean. You'll make Mama sad."

"Nah ah, no! Sorry, Mama!" Adiel yelped, squeezing Becca's hand and sporting a look of terrified guilt. Because while Adolf Hitler had been all too happy to break Becca's heart a million times over, Adiel Goldstein was absolutely horrified at the mere idea of making her *sad*.

"You're forgiven, sweetie!" Becca assured the boy, taking his hand and offering her arm to her husband. "Appeaser," she whispered in Natan's ear with a testing lilt in her tone.

Shut up, he almost said, but instead he shrugged like it didn't matter, and they all left for a relaxing family outing.

ADOLF HITLER EXPERIENCED TRUE, VIOLENT ANTI-SEMITISM for the first time during his first day of school.

They lived in a village with no Jews on purpose, because

Becca and Natan had agreed that Hitler needed to taste what it was to be a Jew. Becca believed that Adolf Hitler had some smidgen of empathy left in his soul and thought that if he experienced the ancient hatred, he would never even consider inflicting that agony onto another person. Natan, initially, had merely wanted to see Hitler feel everything he and his loved ones had felt.

Be careful what you wish for, Natan thought when he entered his house and realized that something was wrong. The boy hadn't run to greet him with a hug and a "Papa's home!" like he always did. Natan walked into the living room and found the child on the couch, hugging Becca and wailing wildly, sporting a nasty cut on his forehead and a bruise on his arm.

Seeing Adolf Hitler in pain should have made Natan absolutely giddy. But seeing little Adiel Goldstein sob made his chest writhe.

"Hey, little monster, what's wrong?" Natan asked, setting his briefcase on the ground and kneeling in front of the boy. Adiel wrenched himself from his mother's embrace and threw his arms around Natan's neck, squeezing tight.

The boy explained what had happened. Or at least he *tried* to. He was barely comprehensible since he was sobbing so much, and Becca needed to fill in the gaps in his testimony. Apparently, Adiel's first day of school had been awful. He had eagerly skipped up to a group of boys and offered to draw pictures for them. The boys had broken Adiel's pencils, torn up his art, beat him up, and sneered that he was going to burn in Hell when he died because he didn't worship Jesus.

Adolf Hitler most certainly deserved all of that. He

deserved worse. Experiencing the brutality of anti-Semitism, that was fair, an eye for an eye.

But Adiel Goldstein hadn't done anything to deserve such horrible bullying. And so Natan could hardly help himself when he patted the crying child's back and muttered the same comforting words that his own father had espoused when he himself had first experienced the ancient hatred. "I'm sorry you had to go through that, son. Don't be too sad. It'll be alright."

Natan's father had said that. *It'll be alright.* That had been a horrible, horrible falsehood ultimately, but at least Natan could utter it while knowing for certain that the Holocaust wouldn't ever occur.

Adiel's sobs tapered into little hiccups as he took comfort from his father's words.

"I'm not gonna go to Hell, right, Papa?" Adiel squeaked. "Right?"

Adiel pulled back, gazing up at his father with innocent, trusting terror. Out of the corner of his eye, Natan saw Becca wince.

The answer came easily: "No, don't worry. You won't ever go to Hell."

Natan was surprised by how much he was certain of that.

NATAN WOULD HAVE NEVER BEEN ABLE TO PRECISELY PLACE when his feelings towards the stolen boy shifted from *hate* to *tolerate* to *like* and then *love*. It wasn't a single moment, but a slow creep, like aging. Something he simply recognized and accepted one day.

He supposed it started when he stopped mentally calling the boy *Hitler* and started calling him *Adiel*. When Adiel became a boy who certainly was *not* Hitler, even if he *was* in the most technical sense.

Maybe it was against Natan's will to a certain extent. He imagined that any man forced to act as a father to any child, no matter how terrible that child was, would eventually start to love it. As a means of self-defense, of self-preservation, like a kidnapped woman who forced herself to fall in love with her abductor so that she could still pretend to be in control.

Sigmund Freud would have no doubt had a field day with Natan Libman-now-Goldstein, but screw him. Natan had never believed in the mumbo-jumbo science of psychology anyway. He felt how he felt, and that was that. Adiel adored him, and he liked being Adiel's father.

Adolf Hitler had grown up with a lovely mother and a terrible father, and the latter had no doubt been a contributing factor towards young Adolf's eventual monstrousness. Not that Alois Hitler was *responsible* for the Holocaust, of course. Adolf Hitler was hardly a precious little baby who just needed love.

Still, the smallest thing made a world of difference. Natan surely would have been a different person if he had been an SS officer's son instead of a Jewish chef's loyal child. Maybe he would have been a Nazi guard. Maybe he would have bribed Rebecca for sex instead of falling in love with her. Maybe he would have crushed a Jewish baby's skull.

It wasn't out of the question. Just as Adiel would have

been Hitler if things were different, Natan had come frighteningly close to strangling a baby to death with his own two hands. And yes, that baby had been Hitler, but that nameless Auschwitz guard had looked at Avi and seen little more than an unsalvageable demon. A beast to be crushed when it was a whelp rather than offered a chance to live and grow into a monster.

Both Natan and Becca had started their quest intending to destroy a monster. Natan would have never thought that Becca could have won him over, but her method was simply superior to the one he had favored that night in Austria. Love, it seemed, could kill a demon just as thoroughly as hatred.

Eventually, after one particularly terrible incident of anti-Semitism, Natan and Becca agreed that it was time to move away from their little village and find a new home. A home with a synagogue. A home with other Jews.

Even though Natan had accepted that Adiel Goldstein and Adolf Hitler were two entirely different people, he would have been lying if he'd proclaimed that he wasn't at least a little nervous about the concept of the boy meeting other Jews. True, Adiel always wore his kippa. True, he loved Jewish fairytales. True, he claimed to be a Jew. True, certainly, he loved his Jewish parents.

Nevertheless, there was always the risk that something would go horribly wrong. Maybe Adiel would throw off the mantle of *Jew*. Maybe he would adopt a *different* worldview.

This fear was quashed when Natan returned from work

shortly after their move and was greeted by an absolutely ecstatic Adiel Goldstein. The boy was practically dancing as he described his first day at school: he had nervously approached his new classmates, remembering how terribly his past offers for friendship had gone. He'd shown off a picture he'd drawn of the Ziz monster.

They had loved it. One boy had asked him to draw a Leviathan, and then another boy had asked Adiel to draw his dog who had died recently, and then a girl had come over and asked him to draw her, offering him a kiss as a reward.

"They like me, and they called me an artist, and I'm gonna draw everyone a picture, and nobody was mean!" cried Adiel breathlessly, and it looked like he was about to cry from sheer happiness.

From that day on, Adiel Goldstein was the most popular boy in the Jewish school. He drew self-portraits and pet portraits for every one of his fellow students, then drew some for the teachers, which they hung above their desks. Perhaps once upon a time, Natan would have regarded the boy's natural charisma with suspicion, but in this case, Adiel exclusively used it for good. During Purim plays, he would help the other children memorize their lines. (It was probably a little concerning that Adiel more often than not was handed the role of Haman, but that was mostly because he was very comfortable yelling on stage, and the villainous role required such boldness.)

Adiel keenly remembered his days as an outcast, and therefore he always invited the shy boys to join in his playground games. He was always the first to raise his hand in class, sparing other students the responsibility to answer while never tattling on them when they passed notes behind his back. In every way, Adiel Goldstein became the benevolent Führer of the Jewish school.

"I am *so* glad we moved to a neighborhood with more Jews," Becca sighed one day when Adiel left to play with his gaggle of friends. "It's made Adiel completely blossom! He loves it—loves his classmates, his teachers, I don't think I've ever met a little boy who loves school this much!"

"He's popular, and he gets good grades too," Natan noted, glancing at Adiel's latest report card that hung on a wall and featured perfect marks. "Damn smart kid. I thought you said he failed out of school back when he was…"

Natan pressed a finger under his nose, his little gesture for Adolf Hitler. Becca snickered.

"He did," she confirmed. "I don't think that's because he was stupid, though. Actually, back when he was Adenoid…" That was her preferred euphemism for the non-existent Führer. She couldn't help but borrow from Chaplin. "He did very well in school for a while, up until his brother died. That's when he started to really go off the rails."

"Brother?" Natan repeated, raising an eyebrow. "Didn't you say his brothers all died as babies?"

"Gustav and Otto died as babies, but Adolf had a younger brother, Edmund. They were apparently really close, but Edmund died of measles when Adolf was eleven. Apparently, that was the first thing that started to make him go…" She circled her finger near her ear. "He started doing real bad in school after that. Personality apparently changed, too. When he was really little, he was a lot more like…well, Adiel. Cheerful, you know, even with his father being the way he was. When Edmund died, though, that's when he really started to change for the worse. But, well, Adiel doesn't have to worry about that!"

"No," Natan concurred with a casual shrug, and he didn't think of Adolf Hitler's younger brother again for many, many years.

Adolf Hitler had been rejected from the Academy because Adolf Hitler was an arrogant fool who thought he never needed to improve.

Adiel Goldstein was rejected because he was a Jew.

This time around, his attempt to get into art school was enthusiastically encouraged by his parents. Not simply based on Rule Number Two, but because Adiel Goldstein's many years of drawing pictures for every person he knew meant that he had become a genuinely talented artist, far more talented than Adolf Hitler. Becca had told him to be an artist. Natan had said that he would support his son no matter what but had also pushed him down a more practical path.

"Artists starve, but art *professors* get tenure," Natan had pointed out. "Besides, you love to hear yourself talk."

Adiel had laughed and agreed—as a child, he had always gotten excited for oral reports, after all. Besides, unlike high-school dropout Adolf Hitler, Adiel Goldstein had perfect grades and a stellar portfolio. Getting into university should have been easy.

Should have. Instead, Adiel returned to his parents with tears pouring from his eyes, announcing that the recruiter hadn't even glanced at his marks or his portfolio but had merely sneered that they already had too many seats taken up by *his type.*

It was, of course, woefully ironic. Or it *would have* been woefully ironic if Adiel Goldstein was Adolf Hitler.

Quite fortunately, while rejection from the Academy had sent Adolf Hitler into a spiral of hopelessness and homelessness, Adiel Goldstein had loving parents to turn to.

"Thanks, Mama," the young man said as Becca offered him a mug of hot cocoa like she had whenever he'd needed comfort as a child. He managed to smile for her before turning his gaze to his father. Ideally, a boy would look to his mother for warmth and his father for words of wisdom, a gentle push up the hill.

"It isn't *fair*, Papa!" Adiel hiccupped, and for the briefest moment, those bright blue eyes flared in a manner that was distinctly familiar and distinctly frightening. A reminder that for as much as nurture had changed Adolf Hitler into Adiel Goldstein, there was a natural Hitler inside of him that could never be fully extinguished. "I *hate* them, I—!"

But then the fire was swiftly quenched as Adiel's eyes flitted to his mother and he remembered himself. "Sorry, Mama."

"Atta boy," Becca said, patting his shoulder.

"You have every right to be upset, of course, but you shouldn't give up just yet," Natan said, setting his tone to paternal-advice mode, a mode he had adopted from his own father but was able to utilize with more confidence given his foresight.

"Think of this as a race," Natan suggested. "The asshole referee keeps putting extra hurdles in front of you. The goal is to make you give up, or at least make you lose to every other racer who doesn't have as many hurdles, but you shouldn't just give in. That's what the referee wants, after all. But it's not hopeless. There are Jews who make it in, and I'd bet they're less talented than you."

"Natan!" chastised Becca, but Adiel brightened and wiped his eyes.

"Right, Papa," he said, setting his hot chocolate mug down on the side table.

"We can reapply, reapply to every university if we have to. Move if it becomes really necessary. You've got our support either way, so those assholes with the hurdles don't stand a chance."

That earned Natan a dazzling smile from Becca and a hug from Adiel. One natural quality that Adiel Goldstein had inherited from his predecessor was strength of will. The words of encouragement from his father were all he needed to keep pushing.

Adiel had the benefit of not being a high-school dropout, unlike his alternate self, and so eventually, he leapt over the extra hurdles and got into university. He worked ruthlessly, with all the determination of a man that had once conquered Europe, and before the Goldsteins knew it, Adiel was pursuing a doctorate.

But his education had to be paused, because shortly before he could finish his PhD, WWI began.

IN FAIRNESS, THEY DID TRY TO STOP IT. NATAN CALLED THE police and left an anonymous tip that if and when Black Hand assassins attempted to murder Archduke Franz Ferdinand, they should make sure that the Archduke's car didn't go near Schiller's delicatessen when fleeing.

Of course, Natan was told that the guards would be on the lookout. They lied, and so the Great War began, regardless. Ah, well. Natan supposed that two people could only stop so many World Wars.

He was worried, however, for his adopted son. Adolf Hitler might have had unusually good luck on the battlefield, but there was no guarantee that Adiel Goldstein would fare so well.

Adiel was optimistic, at least. No amount of begging and pleading could convince him to try and weasel his way out of mandatory service.

"All my friends are signing up: drafters don't even need to ask for them!" Adiel chuckled when Natan brought up the possibility of an extended vacation outside of Europe. "This is a great opportunity! Nobody will be able to say anything against us anymore if we fight alongside them for Germany!"

Natan, of course, knew that wasn't true. He knew that Jews bearing Iron Crosses would have been herded into Auschwitz alongside their children and grandchildren. He knew that the entire First World War would be an utterly pointless venture that would cost millions of lives. He knew that there would be no glory awaiting the martyrs.

But he didn't know whether or not his new son would survive like his predecessor. And on the off chance he *did* fall in battle (and Natan prayed to God he wouldn't, which was, of course, rather ironic in its own way), Natan would prefer that his son perished thinking that his death was meaningful, that it would advance the acceptance of Jews everywhere.

And so Natan didn't reveal their true identities. He and Becca kissed Adiel goodbye as he and his old childhood friends gleefully marched off to a war that would last a grueling four years.

And it *was* a grueling four years, even for the Goldsteins left alone in their luxurious manor. Natan spent every moment of the Great War worrying about his son's safety.

Fortunately, Adiel was extremely good about writing to them. The mailman practically delivered a letter every day. Some were longer and more detailed than others, some were worryingly smudged with blood. But it was one seemingly innocuous letter that nearly made Natan's heart stop when he read it. Amongst a page filled with complaints about his comrades rejecting him because of his proud proclamation of his Jewish faith, Adiel had written about one particular soldier.

Still, it isn't all bad! There is, as a matter of fact, a decent gentile here. One year younger than me, an Austrian (don't tell him I said that, he insists he's German) by the name of Edmund Hitler. He's a fellow artist. I've attached one of his sketches. Please offer only kind words for my sake!

A coincidence. A horrible coincidence. That was what Becca said when Natan handed her the letter with trembling hands.

"W-well, I suppose they had Edmund early, you know, Klara and Alois, after we took…Adiel, that's all, that's all…" she stuttered, hastily running upstairs to their closet, unlocking her trunk, and yanking out one particular book. Natan laid Adiel's note on the table, taking the drawing that Edmund Hitler had made and separating it from their adopted son's note. It was a pencil sketch of a house with a chimney spewing smoke.

Natan felt his tattoo burn as Becca opened her book and flipped to one page that featured a drawing that Adolf Hitler had sketched during the Great War.

The drawings were identical.

"It's a coincidence..." Becca whispered, her hands shaking, her breath coming in short gasps. "Just a coincidence."

ADIEL RETURNED SAFE AND SOUND: SHELL-SHOCKED, certainly, and mourning the childhood friends who had been lost in the pointless slaughter. Nevertheless, he was cheerful as could be when he introduced his parents to a nurse that had tended to him when he was injured. Emma Ritter.

No matter how much his parents tried to interrogate him about his "friend" Edmund Hitler, Adiel would simply chuckle, say that they were going to write to each other, and then go back to swooning over his new girlfriend.

Natan and Becca clung to the illusion that it was all a horrible coincidence for as long as they could, but soon, a familiar political party arose, led by a familiar face with a slightly different name. While Adiel Goldstein recovered from the war, finished his PhD, and spent long afternoons wooing Emma Ritter, his brother, his replacement, was readying himself to lead Germany into oblivion.

"I don't understand...I don't *get* it..." Becca sobbed when they read an article about Edmund Hitler's activities that perfectly matched her history books.

"It's almost like the timeline corrected itself," Natan

whispered, pulling her close. "Like someone or something realized we'd messed with how things were supposed to go…"

"No, no, that's not…unless you're saying God *wanted* the Holocaust to happen…"

Wanted. Needed. Maybe it wasn't even God, but some force even more depraved than a Demon King.

It didn't matter. Either way, their mission to kill Hitler was a successful failure. They had destroyed Adolf completely, but Hitler, it seemed, went beyond one man. Perhaps he really was a monstrous force more than a singular human being. But it didn't matter. Where once they had been confident that this future would be better than the one they had left, now they were keenly aware that they were completely and utterly helpless.

"It didn't work, it didn't work…" Becca sobbed. "We didn't change anything, we didn't…"

"Mama, Papa, I…oh! Mama!"

"Frau Goldstein, are you all right?"

Adiel and Emma returned right then, arm-in-arm. It was a wonder that Adiel didn't lose his kneecaps in his haste to kneel in front of his mother: he all but slid from the doorway to her side, grasping her hand and gazing upon her with wide, worried eyes.

Natan and Becca's eyes flitted briefly from Emma, who kept her distance but offered the two of them a comforting smile, to the man who might have been in the headlines if not for their intervention.

"Just…worried, you know…" Becca said, offering a small laugh that was as genuine as it was sorrowful. She no doubt realized that they *had* changed something for the better. Not the course of history itself, but the young man in front of them.

"Oh, about the Nazis?" Adiel sighed, glancing warily at the papers and shaking his head when he saw his old comrade's name. "Don't worry about it, Mama, they're just a bunch of nutcases."

"Fascist bastards," Emma concurred, shaking her head. "They don't stand a chance."

"Besides, you have me and Papa here to protect you."

"*Ahem!*"

"Ah, and Emma too, I *definitely* wouldn't want to cross her. You should have seen how she talked to Hitler when he was laid up with me!"

Becca's spirit was lifted as she talked with Adiel and his girlfriend. Not completely, of course, for they had ultimately failed and now had to live with the knowledge that Auschwitz was inevitable. But Adiel Goldstein was living proof that even if they couldn't change history, they could change some things, save some souls.

And so they got to work. Saved their money. Readied themselves for the day that they would have to start buying their own people's lives. They first sought to save their families, which was so ridiculously easy that it almost hurt. Natan Goldstein only needed to visit his father's restaurant, pretend to eat his cooking for the first time, and act as a stranger who fell in love with the chef's skill. He became the Libman family's primary investor and close personal friend. From there, it was easy enough to get into contact with Becca's father, a skilled merchant, and become his boss too.

When the time came, it would be easy to convince the Libmans and the Blums to move to America, to start a new business there with their extended families, all generously paid for by their wonderful investor.

Herr Libman was so grateful that he vowed that if and when he had a son, he would name him after Natan Goldstein. Most Jews didn't name the living after the living, thinking it to be bad luck, but Herr Libman was a skeptic by nature who didn't believe in silly superstitions or anything fanciful.

Besides, he had always liked the name Natan.

EMMA RITTER WAS JEWISH IN THE MOST TECHNICAL SENSE, in the way that would only matter to Edmund Hitler in about a decade. A blood Jew. A Jew who believed in what they saw with their eyes and read in textbooks, who didn't put too much weight on the laws of the Torah. Adiel, meanwhile, was a loyal Jew in every sense: he kept kosher, always wore his kippa outside no matter the danger it brought, and prayed thrice a day to a God that he was utterly convinced existed.

Their political views were also quite different: Emma was from a family of Jews who were not only staunch atheists, but rabid communists. Emma wasn't quite as extreme as them—from her description, her father was so ardent that even Stalin likely would have told him to take it down a notch—but she most certainly admired Marx and his ideals. Adiel, meanwhile, didn't care much for politics in general (thanks to his parents), but given that he was the loyal son of a stockbroker, he most certainly leaned towards being a capitalist.

Emma Ritter would have been a terrible match for Adolf Hitler. Hitler the Narcissist who exclusively liked to hear himself speak and asked for only praise and never argument would have despised the mouthy nurse.

Adiel Goldstein, who loved to talk *to* people and not simply *at* them, who liked to hear other voices as much as his own, was a good match for her. (Older, certainly, by about ten years, but Natan supposed some things couldn't be changed. Some tastes were genetic. Thankfully, not the genocidal ones, apparently.) Adiel liked to debate with her, to hear her opinions, and when she was particularly passionate about a subject, he liked to prod her with questions and make her reconsider her most firmly held beliefs.

Sometimes, he actually managed to change her mind. While before Emma had only been mildly curious about the religion of her ancestors, Adiel managed to talk her into embracing her roots and joining him for synagogue services. She enjoyed it. She also loved Becca's fairytale books. Quite soon, she had stopped calling herself agnostic and was proclaiming that she was a Jew.

Sometimes, however, Adiel lost. And sometimes he lost *badly*. Sometimes, he said something to offend her; making fun of any communist leader was the best way to make her cry, and whenever that happened, he would run to his father for advice.

"I just said that Lenin's a brute."

"He *is*."

"She even *agreed* that he's a brute! But she *didn't like my tone*!"

Adiel rolled his eyes, downed his brandy, and shook his head. (Adolf Hitler had been a teetotaler, perhaps because of his drunken father. Natan had warned Adiel that he should watch his alcohol consumption since he had a family history of drunkenness, but Adiel was able to enjoy an occasional drink without much issue.)

"Well, son, your first mistake was having an argument with a woman in the first place, much less a woman you like!" chuckled Natan, which earned a snort from the younger man.

"I *like* arguing with her. I can't imagine being with a woman who agrees with me about everything, it would be horribly boring…"

Eva Braun had no doubt agreed with Adolf Hitler about everything. That was why he had married her. Loyal and brainless, the exact opposite of Emma Ritter. Natan wondered if Adolf Hitler had liked Eva so much because she had been so *boring*.

"Still, I just wish she wouldn't get so upset!" Adiel continued. "When I say anything against communism or socialism or any of those Soviet maniacs, she immediately acts like I've just kicked a homeless person. She can never just approach things calmly, it's all so *personal* to her."

"You *do* love her, though."

"I do! But it's just that every argument becomes *emotional*."

"Becca can be the same way. You should have heard some of our arguments once we had to talk about more complicated things than backyard games. That's typical, you know—women can be emotional sometimes," sighed Natan. "Sometimes it's frustrating, but sometimes…"

He stared at Adiel, the man who would have been dead by his very hands if not for Becca's emotions. Just as she had a million times in the past, she had cried, and therefore he had lost the argument. Natan would always shiver slightly when he thought of what might have happened if he'd won on that cold April night.

"Sometimes, that womanly instinct is important. A world run by men would be cruel and heartless…"

"The world's already ruled by men, Papa!" noted Adiel. "And it *is* cruel and heartless sometimes! Maybe women should get their chance. They couldn't possibly do worse."

Oh, good Lord. Not enough that Becca had transformed Adolf Hitler into a devout Jew, now she'd gone and made the man a feminist too.

"Tell Emma that," Natan said with a smirk, pouring his son another drink. "She'll forgive you for your slight right away."

"She'll think I'm bullshitting, I'm sure," Adiel sighed, and Natan shook his head.

"Ah, son, you're not a very good liar."

Natan had heard once or twice that the childless Adolf Hitler had been infertile. Such was not the case for Adiel—soon after he and Emma were married, Adiel came to his father with anxious joy, proclaiming that his new wife was pregnant.

"How do you feel?" Natan asked, pouring his stolen child a drink. Decades of parenting his former tormentor had still not dulled the small twinge of amusement that he felt whenever Adiel achieved some sort of ironic milestone, and parenthood…well, Natan previously would have never celebrated the birth of a new Hitler.

Of course, this child wouldn't be a Hitler, so he still *wasn't*.

"Nervous!" Adiel answered with a chuckle. "And excited! I've wanted a child forever, but…"

Adiel heaved a sigh and ran a finger along the edge of his glass. "I don't know…every time I think that I'm happy and this is what I want, there's a little feeling inside like I don't actually want to do this. Once it happens, it's done, and there's no going back. Did…you get the same feeling when you had me, Papa?"

Natan almost swallowed his own tongue. He despised thinking of those early days before he was convinced that Adolf Hitler was dead, and Adiel Goldstein deserved to be loved genuinely and not merely as a means to an end. When he remembered the absolute hatred he'd felt for the little boy he now saw as his own, it made him feel like the weight of the world was pressing down on his gut. One small movement, one different choice, that was all it would have taken, and he would have never known just how much he would love being Adiel Goldstein's father.

Natan had certainly not felt what Adiel was feeling, not mere *uncertainty*, but he couldn't possibly tell his son that he had once hated him, much less *why*.

"Yes, I did," Natan whispered. "That feeling won't go away for a while, not until they're a real person. Mothers, they love easily, right away. Fathers, it takes more, but it's worth it once you see the little person and know they're yours."

"Do you think I'll be a good father?" Adiel asked softly, with the same desperate little edge that his voice had possessed when he was a child asking Natan if he liked his drawings. Adolf Hitler, the brute, the monster, Adolf Hitler the most hateful human to ever exist would have been a dreadful father.

Adiel wasn't Hitler, and Natan knew that his son would have nothing but love to give to his child, and so he answered, "Yes. Absolutely. Maybe even the best."

"So, sweetheart, are you hoping for a boy or a girl?"

"Haha! Well, don't tell anyone, Mama, or I'll be laughed out of synagogue, but I'd prefer a girl."

"Really?" Natan let his voice become high-pitched with surprise. Adiel nodded.

"Boys are loud, and noisy, and messy," Adiel explained, downing a sip of peppermint tea and chuckling. "I've heard the horror stories you two told, and from what I gather, I was relatively tame as a child! I don't have the patience to chase a little monster of my own around the place."

"Careful, Adiel," Becca cautioned cheerfully, pouring herself some more tea. "You'll get your wish, but she'll be a tomboy, completely untamable. That's always how it goes."

"Haha! Right you are, Mama. With any luck, it'll be a girl that takes after her mother in looks and character."

"Oh, I don't know..." hummed Natan, dumping some more sugar cubes into his mug and winking at Becca. "You weren't *too* awful. A boy might not be so bad."

A boy might not have been bad, but Natan would have been lying if he declared that he didn't feel a slight twinge of relief when Adiel got his wish and his baby was a girl.

KAIA GOLDSTEIN WAS NOT A TOMBOY. KAIA GOLDSTEIN WAS not a girly girl. Kaia Goldstein was impossible to put into any one box. Utterly strange, utterly undefinable, utterly precious. Even though she wasn't Natan's blood, she was still his beloved granddaughter, and he cried when she was born because he had once been convinced that he would never see a son give him a grandchild.

Little Kaia liked music, especially when her mother played piano. She didn't really care what she wore so long as it was comfortable, so she would don pants just as happily as she would skirts and dresses. She wasn't very interested in dolls, but equally didn't relish the idea of rolling about in the dirt. She loved all of God's most awful creatures: snakes, spiders, and wolves.

She was Jewish, and happily so. She loved hearing her grandmother's folktales. In particular, she loved the Leviathan, and she learned to swim specifically so that she could breach the water with a growl and pretend to be a little sea monster. During Passover, she would hop around the house pretending to be a frog from the Second Plague.

She was a kleptomaniac practically from birth, and the Goldsteins were always having to search her room for little trinkets she had stolen.

She pitied the wolf in *Little Red Riding Hood*. She cried when he died because he was just hungry, and she wouldn't stop crying until Adiel rewrote the story so that Little Red shared her goodies with the beast. Somehow, even though Kaia wasn't Becca's biological grandchild, she had inherited her spirit.

Adolf Hitler would have almost certainly hated Kaia Goldstein even if she weren't a Jew, but she was Adiel Goldstein's sun, moon, and stars.

THEY KNEW, OF COURSE, THAT THE CAREFREE DAYS WOULD end. They didn't expect them to end so soon.

Emma passed from polio. Perhaps that, too, had been inevitable. Perhaps she had gone the same way in that other timeline. Either way, it might have destroyed Adiel if he hadn't had little Kaia as his anchor.

Natan and Becca did as well as they could, although balancing taking care of Kaia and comforting Adiel with making preparations to move themselves, their families, and as many Jews as possible far away from the future Reich was difficult. Nevertheless, they managed. Emma's absence stung them all, especially Adiel, but they all focused on Kaia, on making her happy. For a while, they managed a cheerful, comfortable existence despite the shadow looming in the future.

But of course, eventually, that cheerful, comfortable existence was interrupted.

Adolf Hitler's mother died of breast cancer. This was one thing that he had in common with Adiel Goldstein.

Adolf Hitler's family doctor, Eduard Bloch, had once declared that when Klara Hitler had been dying, Adolf Hitler had utterly devoted himself to her care. Dr. Bloch had never seen a son who adored his mother so much. Adiel Goldstein most certainly didn't love his own mother any less than Adolf Hitler had loved his, but he had Kaia to worry about. The girl had seen too much death already, and so, ultimately, it was Natan that took care of Becca during her last days.

Which was good, in a way. Because Becca couldn't have possibly shared her earnest final thoughts with her stolen son.

"Everything's going to be alright," Natan assured her, gripping her hand. "Our parents are safe. We're going to save a lot of people…"

"I know, but we still failed," Becca sobbed, her voice small and weak, chills wracking her body. "I'm so sorry."

"No…no, don't say that," Natan said, throwing an arm around his precious wife. "We didn't fail, don't you see? We *didn't* fail. I'm glad. I'm glad we did what we did. I'm happy…"

He pointed to a picture hanging on a nearby wall of the Goldstein family: much odder, of course, than their son could have possibly realized, but a blessing in its own regard.

"We saved them, and we saved *him*," Natan said, holding his wife close so she could hear the steadiness of his heartbeat, so she could know that he meant it when he whispered, "A life for a life. It was a good deal."

SIX

A memory: Adiel Goldstein and the man who was supposed to be him, Corporal Hitler, lying next to one another in the hospital, blind and shaved.

Emma, whom Adiel had then only known by her lovely voice, had glanced at the two soldiers and asked, "Are you brothers, by any chance? You look like identical twins."

Edmund Hitler had sputtered and denied it with utmost umbrage. Adiel Goldstein had chuckled and said *no relation*.

They had both been wrong.

"I DID THIS..."

Adiel spoke for the first time in nearly twenty minutes, since he had broken into a fit of crying worse than when he'd lost Emma. His strong voice was punctuated by sobs that tore from his throat in ugly gasps.

He would have given absolutely anything short of his daughter for all of it to be a lie. If Natan had started laughing and proclaimed that this was actually the cruelest and most elaborate practical joke in world history, Adiel would have been utterly ecstatic. He wouldn't have even been mad. Anything would be better than knowing that he was the monster scowling at him from the open book laid out in the grass.

Adiel knelt before the book, glancing back and forth between Adolf Hitler's vicious visage—*his* vicious visage, utterly unrecognizable because of the distinctive moustache and the overwhelming hate pouring from his other self's every pore—and a picture of his handiwork. A train car full of emaciated corpses. Little children Kaia's age, old women like Becca, old men like his father. How many of his friends from synagogue, his schoolmates, were in that single train car? How many Libmans and Blums and Ritters?

Adiel couldn't even begin to describe what he was feeling. Horror, yes, but so much worse than that. Guilt, too, was part of the suffocating concoction he felt at once pressing down upon him like the foot of an elephant and clawing at his guts like a parasite.

Adiel had thought that he knew himself quite well, and while he had never thought of himself as a *great* man, he had always assumed that he was at least a *good* man. A good man, or at the very least an *average* man destined to be remembered as a loving father and a talented artist. But in reality, he was beyond evil. If he was capable of committing every awful, horrific sin he had read about to his own people, his own parents, his own wife…

Emma! Good God, what did I do to her?! Adiel thought, and

he nearly vomited right then, but instead he just sobbed harshly.

"I did this…"

"No, you did not!" Natan's voice, hoarse from his long tale, was nevertheless strong as he made this declaration. The old man rose to his feet, sapphire eyes flaring, and he stepped towards his kneeling son.

Adiel winced and covered his face. The sight of the number *he* had sown onto his own father's arm made his eyes burn. He wished that his father would slap his face right then. Natan had been entirely right: Adiel hadn't deserved any of the mercy and love he'd been shown by his parents, his *victims*.

"Adiel, look at me!" Natan said, putting his hands on the Professor's shoulders. Adiel desperately didn't want to, but he had been trained from the day he had been stolen to respect his parents, and right then, when he realized that he was entirely in his father's debt, he wasn't about to become recalcitrant. He looked up, meeting Natan's steely gaze.

"Don't make the same mistake as me. *Don't*," Natan said, shaking his head, reaching out, and shutting the open book. "You are *not* him. It doesn't matter if you have the same DNA, even if you have the same soul, it doesn't matter because *you're not him*."

"But…"

"*Stop*. You know…I think our mistake from the beginning was that we gave him too much credit."

"'*Him*'…" repeated Adiel, barely suppressing a hiccup, his eyes flitting to the closed book, to the swastika banners decorating the back cover. "You mean *me*…"

"No, I mean *him*," Natan said, squeezing Adiel's shoulder tightly. "But that was our mistake, you know. We thought that it was *just* his fault, that he was *special.* We thought removing him from the equation would fix everything. But we were wrong. There wasn't anything in *his soul* that made him *different.* So either way, it's pointless to let this weigh you down so much...here."

Natan offered the hysterical Adiel Goldstein a handkerchief and helped him to his feet like he was a teenage boy recovering from heartbreak again.

"Come on," Natan said, pausing to grab the book before ushering his son out of the garden. "Let's head inside. To your room. We don't want Kaia to come out and see us like this."

UNFORTUNATELY, NATAN WAS TOO LATE: KAIA HAD ALREADY seen and heard everything. Lady thieves, after all, were masters of subterfuge and spying, and so she had stayed crouched behind a rosebush the entire time, her hands wrapped around Bernie's snout to keep him quiet, her heart palpitating.

Perhaps a typical child would have reacted poorly to discovering that they were the spawn of a potential mass murderer. Kaia, however, was not a typical child.

"Time travel..." she gasped, her eyes twinkling. "Wow!"

She released Bernie and petted the dog with one hand whilst stroking her chin with the other. Adults, *ugh.* The problem with them, all of them, even the ones she loved, was that they were ever so pessimistic. One little so-called failure and they threw in the towel. One spider bit them and they dismissed the entire arachnid class as being irredeemably awful.

Her father was sad, hopeless, and it seemed that her grandfather had already given up on changing anything. Silly! After all, her father had been evil in that other timeline, but now he was great! And so it wouldn't be too hard, surely, to make everyone else good too, especially her uncle! She would force the fates to rewrite history just as she had forced her father to rewrite *Little Red Riding Hood*.

Strategy, of course, would be key. Just as she didn't pick up a spider without knowing it down to its phenotype, she would need to learn about her targets, approach with as much sneakiness as sweetness, and then—*bam!* She would strike their hearts, and then all would be well. She would have an uncle, and Zaidy Natan and Papa would feel better too!

"C'mon, Bernie!" Kaia whispered, and the mutt followed the girl into the manor. She scurried up the stairs with a purpose, slowing and quieting her pace when she strode past Adiel's room and heard him sobbing inside. Poor Papa! She really wanted to run in and give him a big hug, assure him that he was still a great papa and didn't have to feel bad about something he hadn't even done, but first things first: she needed to get to the books before her well-meaning and condescending family moved them.

Kaia crept into Natan's bedroom and was grateful to see that her father had left the trunk open, its contents spilled about the closet floor. If Kaia had actually bothered to go through every single book, she might have become bothered enough to pause her mission. Hearing about all the awful things that had happened in another time period was one thing, but seeing pictures…

Fortunately (or perhaps unfortunately), one book that was lying on the ground immediately caught her eye. A familiar face, a familiar scowl.

"Oh! Hey, you!" she cried, picking up the book and leaping onto Natan's bed, where she was swiftly followed by Bernie. Kaia was an ardent reader of history books and biological tomes about spiders and snakes, and therefore, she sped through the crisply written biography. She only needed to get to chapter three before she slammed the book shut and smiled widely.

"All right, Bernie, I've got it!" she proclaimed, petting the snoozing dog on the head. "Stage One of saving the world for good this time!"

"WHAT ARE WE GOING TO DO?"

When Adiel finally gained enough control over himself that he stopped sobbing and was able to eke out a small, hoarse question, this was what he asked. Natan offered his son the last of his clean handkerchiefs and heaved a sigh.

"The only thing we *can* do," the older man said, tracing the numbers sewn onto his flesh, "is continue on with the plan that me and your mother made. Rescue as many Jews as we can, move to America..."

"I can't do that, Papa!" Adiel yelped, tossing the handkerchief aside and gripping his bedcovering so harshly that his knuckles turned white. "I can't just abandon..."

"We won't be *abandoning* people, son," Natan assured him, setting a hand on the Professor's shoulder. "We're going to save as many as we can, but the universe has made it *very* clear that there's nothing we can do to actually *stop* it from happening. We can make some changes for the better, but we can't stop history from playing out..."

"That can't be true, Papa! What about free will?" Adiel argued, gesturing towards a copy of the Torah that rested on his nightstand, the one he read from every single day. "The human soul's capacity to choose between the *yetzer hara* and the *yetzer hatov*, between the good and evil inclinations. I know you don't fully believe in it all, Papa, but *I do!* In that other timeline, I made a *choice* and everything that happened was *my* fault, not the fault of some ethereal puppet-master!"

"I don't disagree, son," sighed Natan. "But I think the choice was made, and whatever plan the forces-that-be have written out calls for it now. Calls for *this*..." Natan held up his tattoo-emblazoned arm. "We tried, son..."

"But maybe it's not too late!" Adiel insisted frantically, leaping to his feet and beginning his old nervous habit of pacing back and forth across the pristine carpet of his room. "If something happened to Edmund Hitler *now*, I doubt another identical Hitler would just drop out of the clouds to replace him! Maybe there's still something we can do to stop it, maybe..."

"Adiel, Adiel!" Natan cried, leaping into the path of his son's pacing and grabbing his shoulders. Adiel unleashed a shuddering gasp.

"I can't...I can't just do *nothing* when it's my fault this started! It's not fair!" the Professor cried.

"We're not going to do *nothing*, son."

"But it's not enough, it's *not*, we have to try and save them all or...or..."

"*Adiel.*" The paternal scold made Adiel cease resisting as Natan forced him to sit down on his bed.

"Listen to me: the point of the matter is that you're just one man," Natan said. "And you can't tear yourself apart over the fact that you can't stop someone else's actions, even if they were yours once upon a time. Maybe we can do more, *maybe*, but Adiel: think of Kaia. You don't want to do anything stupid that will put her at risk, right?"

"N-No…"

"Then whatever we do, we do it intelligently, slowly. We help as many people as we can without doing anything foolish. You're not in a good headspace right now, so you need to calm yourself. You won't do anyone any good if you act hysterically out of some misplaced sense of guilt."

"I…just…" His father was, at once, right and wrong. It wouldn't do for Adiel to act hasty right now, but at the same time, he simply couldn't stand the thought of continuing on and pretending like he was a good person who didn't need to seek absolution at all.

Somehow, someway, he needed to find true redemption by stopping his sin from being carried out a second time. His eyes flitted to his father's arm, and he found himself quietly vowing that he would either make it so that Natan Goldstein was the only Jew in the world branded with such a number, or he'd die trying. He was going to see to it that Auschwitz was never built, and he wasn't going to let any divine roadmap stand in his way.

"There, much better," Natan said, mistaking Adiel's quiet determination for resignation.

"Papa, I'm sorry," Adiel said for about the millionth time, shivering as he glanced from Natan's tattoo to his face, this time preparing a true, well-worded apology free of ugly sobs. "I have no idea what I was thinking in that other life. I can't fathom ever hurting you or Mama. I wish she was still here so I could actually apologize to her…"

"As I've said, you don't have anything to apologize for," Natan replied, waving his arm dismissively and glancing at a family picture propped up on a nearby dresser. "And your mother would have just been sad to see *you* so upset. She did love you, you know, really and genuinely, much faster than I did."

"I know…"

Natan stared at Becca's frozen visage for a moment before saying, in a nearly frightened voice, "You know I love you too, right?"

"Unjustifiably," replied Adiel, unable to repress a small smile when Natan let out a soft laugh.

"Good. I was worried, you know. I had sort of hoped that you would never find out about it at all, but on the off chance you did, I had no idea how you'd react. I was expecting you to be at least a *little* angry…"

"I'm not," Adiel assured him, offering a quizzical look. "What in Heaven's name would I be angry about?"

"The lifetime of lies, the kidnapping, the fact that I almost killed you," Natan answered, ticking off three fingers. Adiel fiercely shook his head.

"How in God's name could *I* be mad at *you* for wanting to kill me after what *I* put you through?" Adiel cried. "You were too good to me. And angry about the 'kidnapping'? You *saved* me, saved my life, saved my soul, and gave me a chance. I've always been grateful to you and Mama for being good parents, but I didn't realize how much I owed you. Thank you, for everything."

Quickly, the two shared an embrace, Adiel squeezing

his adoptive father tight, Natan taking a moment to suppress a small sob of his own before he once again pushed his son back towards his bed. "Take a nap or something, clear your head. I'm going to put away the books and move them before Kaia gets any ideas."

Adiel agreed and bade a weary, early goodnight to Natan as the old man exited.

Even though he felt exhausted down to his last atom, Adiel found himself unable to actually sleep. He lay on his bed, staring up at his ceiling, his body numb, his brain buzzing.

It was all, of course, quite a bit to learn in one day. Learning that he was adopted, that alone might have thrown him into a tizzy. Learning that he was adopted by two time travelers, one of whom had justifiably tried to kill him because he was destined to become the worst man in world history?

The negative emotions were starting to shift into an intense feeling of fortune. Adiel Goldstein was, by far, the luckiest man in existence. Lucky to be alive, of course. Lucky to have a good life, he had always known that. More than anything, he was lucky that he wasn't Adolf Hitler. Once upon a time, Adiel had imagined that the worst fate imaginable would be something physical. Being burned alive or keelhauled like the landlubbers in Kaia's pirate stories. But no. He would rather be chucked into a pyre than exist for one second as that horrible, irredeemable monster.

"I'm not him," Adiel whispered. "I'm *not* him." He kept at that, repeating the dictum until he mostly accepted it. His father was right. He wasn't Adolf Hitler. Adolf Hitler the anti-Semite likely would have thought that being Adiel Goldstein was the cruelest fate imaginable.

Well, too bad for you, Adolf, thought Adiel, and he almost smiled. In a way, Natan had done worse than kill Adolf Hitler. Adolf Hitler would have surely chosen death over becoming a Jew. Thankfully, he hadn't had a choice.

But Adiel did, and while the thought of his alternate self foaming at the mouth in fury at Adiel Goldstein's mere existence did temporarily lift his spirit, an awful sensation of what he could only describe as survivor's guilt continued to eat away at him.

Certainly, his existence wasn't bad in and of itself: ruining Adolf Hitler's soul, that alone made continuing to live his life as a Jew worthwhile. Raising Kaia, of course, was a *mitzvah* (and that would have certainly made Adolf Hitler blow a gasket: not only *being* a Jew but having a Jewish child.) Nevertheless, continuing on as a Jew wasn't nearly enough. There had to be *something* he could do.

Even if he couldn't save everyone, he had to save as many as possible. It was already so unfair that his life and soul had been spared while millions of Jews would inevitably die and millions of Germans would be brainwashed by his replacement. Made into monsters…

"Papa!"

Adiel grunted in pain as his daughter, who had slipped into the room without him noticing while he'd been ruminating about his past and future, suddenly leapt upon him. The girl apologized for nearly crushing her father's spleen and shifted her weight so that she was sitting beside him instead of on top of him.

Seeing sweet little Kaia momentarily made nausea rise up in Adiel's chest as he thought of the pictures of the little children like her that he had mercilessly slaughtered as Adolf Hitler, but Kaia smiled brightly, and he found that he couldn't possibly remain dour.

"Kaia, sweetie, sorry," Adiel said, sitting up and patting her head, noticing that she had a book tucked under her arm. No doubt she was here to demand a bedtime story. "Papa's not feeling well..."

"Because you're Hitler, I know!" Kaia chirped in the sort of tone that might have been appropriate if she were proclaiming that her father had a headache or the flu.

Adiel felt as though a boa constrictor had crushed his throat. For a moment, he couldn't breathe, and when he finally managed to make a noise, all he could say was, "W-what?"

"I heard you and Zaidy Natan talking about how he's a time traveler, and how he saved you, and...Papa...?"

Kaia's bright smile morphed into a concerned frown as Adiel began to shake. Sobs started to crawl up his throat once more. Before Adiel could even consider fully breaking down, however, Kaia lunged forward, engulfing him in a hug with one arm while the other cradled the hardback.

"Hey, Papa, don't cry, c'mon, it's okay. You're still the best."

"Kaia..." Adiel hiccupped, but before he could return her embrace, she pulled back and gave him another enthusiastic smile.

"You don't have to worry!" Kaia assured him. "I did some snooping, and now I've gotta great idea, and we're all gonna save Europe together and actually stop the war!"

It didn't surprise Adiel at all that sweet little Kaia would regard the news of her father's true identity and the seemingly undefeatable rise of Nazism with a can-do attitude.

"We?" he repeated, somewhat curious as to how she thought that she and her family could save the world.

Kaia showed him the cover of the book under her arm, and Adiel's heart nearly stopped.

"Yeah! You, me, and him!" the child cried cheerfully. The book was not, in fact, about pirates or spiders or Jewish fairytales. It was one of Becca's books from the trunk. An SS officer was featured on the cover, bedecked in a black uniform and scowling viciously at the camera. Light colored hair, light-colored eyes, a merciless gaze, the perfect National Socialist.

"See, it's the man from the park!" Kaia announced proudly, and indeed it was. The title of the biography said it all. *The Man with the Iron Heart: A Biography of Reinhard Heydrich.* Adiel had been too occupied by everything else to focus much on Heydrich's monstrous future when he had been perusing his mother's books earlier, but he had read one blurb about the Blond Beast.

The man who had, for whatever reason, good or ill, chosen to stop the Brownshirt attack in the park would, in the future, be the man who masterminded the Final Solution. The Head of the Gestapo, the chief of the mobile-killing *Einsatzgruppen* units, the man who would come up with the idea for the awful yellow stars that Rebecca and Natan had been forced to wear. Reinhard Heydrich was destined to become Hitler's most devious underling. The worst of the worst.

"Kaia, did you *read* that?" Adiel gasped, reaching out to snatch the book from the girl only to be rebuffed when she hugged it to her chest.

"Yeah, a bit!" Kaia said with innocent enthusiasm, as though it really was nothing but a book of fairytales. She lifted the hardback above her head. "And we're gonna get him to help us!"

"K-Kaia, he's…"

"Not a Nazi yet, not really! Look!"

Kaia opened to one particular chapter and shoved the book into Adiel's arms, eagerly pointing to a paragraph that she had circled (in pink crayon with little hearts, no less.) Adiel had read far too much about Nazis today, but nevertheless, he obeyed and swiftly skimmed the section.

After his meeting with Heinrich Himmler on June 30th of 1931, Reinhard Heydrich would become the chief of the fledgling SS intelligence wing. Nevertheless, Heydrich would remain lukewarm towards Nazi ideology for some time. As late as 1932, he would continue to express his doubts about the Nazi Cause and Adolf Hitler.

There were a few more paragraphs after that which explained why Heydrich would join the SS if he wasn't even a Nazi. Apparently, desperation for a job, a familial connection, and the political persuasion of his fiancée Lina Von Osten had convinced him to give the Nazis a chance. At the moment, however, Reinhard Heydrich had been an SS man for less than six months, and if the biography was to be believed, he was not yet the murderously loyal National Socialist that he would one day become.

Not *yet*. After all, unlike Adiel, who was only his counterpart in the most technical sense, the slightly doubtful Heydrich of today *was* the murderous Heydrich of tomorrow. A caterpillar and a moth might have appeared different, but at the end of the day, they were one and the same.

But Kaia, of course, didn't see it that way. "So, see?" she chirped with utmost ardor. "We can talk to him and show him what's gonna happen!"

"Kaia…"

"And since he's not a real bad guy yet, he'll get shocked! Like if you turn up the heat on a frog too fast when it's in a pan!"

"*Kaia…*"

"Pot, right, sorry, not pan. And actually, that story wasn't super true because I think when I read about it, they actually took the frog's brain out before they boiled him, so that's why he didn't jump out. Anyway, since Herr Reinhard's already in the SS, he could help us, kinda like a double-agent—!"

"*Kaia, he's a monster!*" Adiel didn't intend to yell at his daughter, but he knew that when she went off on a fantastical line of thought, a firm burst of reality was the only thing that would stop her. And if he didn't stop her, she would no doubt march right into the Brown House and invite Reinhard Heydrich over for tea and soul-searching.

The girl winced, as she tended to whenever Adiel *actually* shouted, but recovered quickly. Holding up the biography, Kaia proclaimed, "Not yet he's not. He's just like you. Soooo…"

Kaia twirled her hands as though to physically demonstrate the logical conclusion before she declared, "We should try to make him better just like Zaidy made you better."

Any thought of arguing further faded as nausea and shame struck Adiel. It was a stupid idea. Stupid and naïve and entirely too optimistic, as stupid and naïve and entirely too optimistic as the idea of sparing baby Adolf Hitler, hoping that nurture would overcome a seemingly monstrous nature.

Kaia might not have been Becca's biological descendant, but she was undoubtedly her granddaughter.

"What's your idea, Wolfchen?" he sighed. Adiel Goldstein was not Adolf Hitler, but his daughter had doubtless
inherited some sort of Hitlerian charisma because even as
indulgent as he was, Adiel would have never agreed to her
insane plan if she didn't absolutely *sell it.*

SEVEN

"Reinhard, is everything all right?"

Everything was most certainly not all right for SS Lieutenant Reinhard Heydrich. His last street fight had ended with him being punched quite painfully in the ribcage and his side was still sore. Richard Hildebrandt hadn't been willing to relinquish his typewriter for the entire day, which meant that Reinhard's already rough schedule was going to get even more distressing since he would have to handwrite all of his reports. His future mother-in-law, whom he usually got along with, had sent him a stern letter asking for interest (*interest!*) on the debt that he had already repaid her while living hand-to-mouth.

All that, and Reinhard's landlady had begged him to pick up one specific brand of wine from one specific store on his way back home from work. His landlady was nice, and motherly, and she knew damn well that he wouldn't say no to her. Which meant that Reinhard wouldn't even have time to head down to the park and stare at the water before it froze, stealing away his ability to nostalgically reflect on his lost days in the Navy.

So if he were weak enough to want sympathy or pity, Reinhard would have answered *no*. But he wasn't weak, and he didn't desire pity, and so he looked up at Dieter Amsel, a fellow SS officer, and declared, "I'm fine."

"Right..." Amsel smoothed back his greying blond hair and gave the younger man a small smile that was amusedly paternal, like Reinhard was a teenage boy who was studiously avoiding the subject of an ill-forged crush rather than the chief of the SS intelligence division who was suffering through a shitty life. "Well, either way, you know you were supposed to leave the office an hour ago."

Don't try to parent me, Reinhard wanted to say, because he knew his own schedule perfectly well and didn't need to be reminded. *Don't try to be my friend*, he almost said, because even though he was more than willing to go horseback riding with Dieter every once in a blue moon for his own enjoyment and the purpose of learning what he could about his underling (knowledge was power, after all), Reinhard had never had a friend in the Navy, and he didn't intend on making any in the SS.

Reinhard decided not to be rude, however, and so he held up a cigar box full of index cards and said, "I have a few more things to get done."

"You're about to regret your dedication to the Cause," Dieter warned with a chuckle. "Himmler's here."

Reinhard let the mask fall for a moment, his neutral expression becoming a scowl. "Why?"

"Something about the Führer, I think," Dieter replied, and he uttered the title of the Nazi Party's leader in the same affectionate, adoring tone that Reinhard's mother used when speaking the name of Jesus Christ. The sort of tone that she had beaten Reinhard for *not* using.

"Is he finally back in Munich?" asked Reinhard, and Dieter shook his head.

"Doubtful, but Himmler did look happy. Might be good news. Just, eh, brace yourself, you know, good news from him can be..."

Dieter heard footsteps approaching, heavy and yet light, the footsteps of a man too small and sickly to be donning military boots. To complete his thought, Dieter gritted his teeth and twirled his finger in a circular motion, a gesture that was perhaps too subtle to represent the unique quirkiness of the Head of the SS.

Himmler knocked, a pedantically polite little gesture that Reinhard Heydrich certainly wouldn't indulge in if and when he became as powerful as his boss. "Enter!" Reinhard cried, standing up and readying himself to salute.

Heinrich Himmler entered, bearing a smile and a sopping umbrella that dribbled droplets onto the nice, clean floor of the nearly empty little office. Himmler looked shorter than he was. His posture was that of a gerbil that was perpetually tormented by the family cat: shoulders slumped, elbows tucked, grey-blue eyes flitting nervously hither and thither behind a pair of pince-nez glasses rendered misty from the rain.

"Sorry, sorry!" yelped Himmler with a self-effacing grin as he leaned the umbrella against the wall, whipped off his SS cap, and ran a black-gloved hand through his tidy brown locks. "It's storming something fierce out there!"

"Odin must be angry, *Reichsführer!*" chuckled Dieter. *Reichsführer* was not Heinrich Himmler's official title, but it was what he liked to be called, and Heaven help you if you called him *Obergruppenführer* instead.

"*Thor*, Amsel, *Thor*! Read the damn *Poetic Edda* before you try to impress me!" chuckled Himmler, waving his wrist in a dismissively jesting way, making it clear that Dieter's attempt at referencing the *Reichsführer's* fascination with the Norse pantheon was appreciated despite his cluelessness. "How are you, by the way, Amsel? Your weekend off went well?"

Himmler, perhaps kindly, perhaps stupidly, liked to think of the SS as one big family. He always maintained a fatherly attitude towards his underlings and kept track of their families and activities. Amsel, who had been away over the weekend to visit his teenage son, grinned.

"Quite well! Jonas was happy to see me, though I don't think he was very happy that I took him away from his girl-friend for a few hours, haha!"

Himmler chuckled and muttered something about boys being boys while Reinhard suppressed a knowing little smirk. Himmler knew that Dieter left his son with his neighbors, the Kellers, every time he traveled to Munich to work for the SS. What he *didn't* know, and what Dieter himself almost certainly didn't know, was that the Kellers were blood Jews.

No doubt Dieter would have hesitated to let his neighbors babysit if he knew that they were Jews. No doubt he would have been less amused by his son's crush on the Kellers' eldest daughter if he'd been aware that she was a Jewess. If Himmler knew that one of his more promising cadets was cavorting with Jews, he certainly wouldn't have greeted that news with gentle, paternal humor. Himmler might have tried to be congenial, nice, fatherly, but when it came to the Jews, he had no patience or kindness whatsoever.

Reinhard, for his part, really wasn't entirely sure what he thought of the Jews as a people. He recalled being play-mates with one or two as a child. He was relatively sure that his aunt was at least half-Jewish, and she seemed nice enough. When he was younger, Reinhard himself had been mistaken for a Jew—because of his large nose, because he had played violin and that was evidently considered a Jewish trait in some circles—and he had hated being *called* a Jew because he hated being *treated* like a Jew.

He didn't like the religious sort, the strange Jewish-Jews who kept kosher and maintained long beards and spoke Yiddish. The normal ones, though, the *assimilated* ones... well, Reinhard really didn't care very much either way. If having a job in the SS meant nodding along while Himmler talked about how Jews poisoned the wells and ate babies, fine. Reinhard didn't hate Jews, but he didn't like them either.

Besides, it would probably be in everyone's best interest if Hitler got his way and the Jews were gently removed from German society. Less friction, less trouble. If Himmler and Hitler were right and the Jews really were a distinct racial group, then it would be better, of course, for them to be among themselves. Germans with Germans, Jews with Jews, perfectly reasonable.

Of course, the Jewish Question was more complex than that, as Dieter's situation demonstrated. Reinhard was completely certain that Amsel didn't know his old friends were blood Jews. From what Reinhard could tell, it seemed that even the Kellers themselves didn't know just how Jewish they were. The father had been baptized as a baby;

the mother was a runaway from an insular Orthodox community. Both of them were ardent National Socialists.

It was perhaps a little ironic that a family of Jews almost certainly loved Hitler far more than Reinhard Heydrich the perfect Aryan did. If Reinhard were a true fanatic, as fanatically anti-Semitic as Himmler, he likely would have already gotten Dieter kicked out of the Party for associating with filthy Jews.

But Reinhard didn't care very much, and besides, as Head of the SD, he knew that damaging information was powerful. Only he knew about the Kellers' blood background. For now. And it would stay that way until Reinhard decided that the information needed to be used. Until *Dieter* needed to be used.

And so he remained silent and let Dieter ignorantly blabber on about his Jewish friends while Himmler listened with a smile. When their conversation finished, Himmler's gaze flitted to Reinhard. The *Reichsführer* lifted up a palm and greeted the Nazi Lieutenant with a friendly, "Heil."

"Heil!" Reinhard replied with practiced zealousness, and it took quite a bit of self-control to stop himself from wincing at the awkward squeak of his own voice when he tried entirely too hard to sound like the greeting was second nature. It truly wasn't, not yet: even after months in the SS, the little quirks and intricacies still hadn't solidified. He still had to stop himself from saluting in naval fashion, and every once in a while he called Himmler "Herr *Reichsführer*" instead of merely "*Reichsführer.*"

Then again, of course, Reinhard hadn't been in the SS for more than six months, and most of those months had consisted of loitering around Hamburg, waiting to be summoned to Munich, occasionally brawling with Reds.

"Glad I caught you working late," Himmler said. "Wanted to run by and tell you that I have excellent news: you have a new assignment, and a special one at that. I mentioned you to the Führer the other day, spoke very highly of you..."

Himmler paused, either for dramatic effect or to silently demand gratitude for deigning to mention a soldier as new as Reinhard Heydrich when speaking to the almighty Edmund Hitler. Reinhard nodded once, all but bowing his head, barely resisting the urge to bristle at the indignity. He had been tantalizingly close to becoming an Admiral in the Navy. It really should have been *him* offering lowly lieutenants scraps.

Himmler seemed satisfied, nonetheless, as he continued. "The Führer will be returning to Munich on New Year's, but he doesn't wish to spend the night at his apartment because of...well, you know..."

Himmler offered a rather tense expression, like that of a man who had just made a joke about the dreadfulness of marriage in the middle of a wedding ceremony. Dieter shifted his weight from leg to leg. They all knew better than to say the name of Geli Raubal, the Führer's niece (and possibly, if the rumors were to believed, much more than that, though Reinhard decided that even if he found evidence of such an arrangement, he'd ignore it for the sake of his own sanity.) The young girl had shot herself in September, sending the Führer into a fit of nearly suicidal sorrow himself. It wasn't entirely surprising that Hitler wasn't eager to return to the scene of her death so soon.

"At any rate!" Himmler said with a slightly nervous lilt in his otherwise cheerful tone. "It's a bit early to work out the exact details, and we don't want anything too concrete too early or else we'll just be giving the Jew-Reds time to plant a bomb or an assassin, but I just wanted to let you know that he chose you to be in charge of security for his return to Munich! It's a great honor!"

It was, actually. A phenomenal opportunity. A step closer to a real prestige, higher rank, the honor that Reinhard had lost when he had been ousted from the Navy. Reinhard offered a true smile and another salute, this time almost managing actual enthusiasm. "I won't disappoint, *Reichsführer.*"

"I'm sure you won't!" chuckled the *Reichsführer.* "At any rate, how is your fiancée?"

"Lina's doing well, sir." Lina Von Osten, Reinhard's fiancée, partially his undoing and partially his salvation. Reinhard had been kicked out of the Navy because he had chosen, on something of a whim, to propose to her after a courtship of mere days.

That decision had led to trouble. An ex-girlfriend of his had filed a complaint, alleging that Reinhard had promised to marry *her* at some point (which he might have in an attempt to get in her pants, but he frankly couldn't remember if he had pulled that particular card on her or not.) *That* complaint, along with Reinhard's arrogant defense of his ungentlemanly behavior before the naval Honor Court, had gotten him kicked out of the Navy.

But Lina, herself a National Socialist, had also pushed Reinhard into getting a job in the SS. He owed her his current post, for he would have never considered joining the ranks of a political party that he frankly didn't like very much if not for her.

"You two are still getting married soon, yes?" Himmler said. "Before the ceremony, I'd like to see her. I was reading about this very interesting old practice from our ancestors, a sort of fertility ceremony…"

No, no, no, no, thought Reinhard, all enthusiasm for the SS and the Nazi Party vanishing on the spot. If only he were stupid enough to be a communist. Surely none of *their* leaders cared so much about the fertility of their underlings' wives.

"I'll think about it, sir," Reinhard said, emphasizing the formal *sir* and speaking in the tone of a woman offering to *think about* a date that she would absolutely *not* be going on.

"Certainly do! And you should participate as well!"

Communism was looking better and better. Yes, the entire country would probably starve to death, but at least Reinhard wouldn't have to do…whatever Himmler wanted him to do.

"Don't insult him, *Reichsführer,*" chimed in Dieter, no doubt thinking that he was saving the day even as he only made things so, *so* much worse. "He doesn't need a fertility ceremony, I'm sure!"

Himmler laughed. Reinhard decided that he was already dead and in Hell. His punishment was going to be reliving this moment over and over for all eternity.

"I have to get going, have errands to run," Reinhard said, eager to leave before his boss and underling drove him into a state of psychosis. He was lucky that he'd practiced *tact.* Reinhard wouldn't have gotten kicked out of the Navy if he'd managed to smile and escape instead of effectively calling his ex-girlfriend a whore in front of the Honor Court.

"Go ahead and take my umbrella!" Himmler offered. "It's really coming down now, and I'm heading right home."

"Thank you, sir!" Reinhard said, not forgetting his desire to get as far away from Himmler as physically possible, but nevertheless offering a small, genuine nod of gratitude as he grabbed the umbrella.

Reinhard rushed out of his office. (Which wasn't really *his* office, it was a shared office. He wasn't quite important enough to have his own office. Not yet anyway. Maybe Hitler's visit would change that.) It was an arduous journey to the particular shop that sold the particular wine that his landlady wanted, but Reinhard had never been one for giving up, and so he traveled through Munich, battling the rain, until at last he emerged from the shop, victorious. Now he just needed to get home without getting mugged.

With the bottle tucked under one arm, Reinhard stood at the bend of a quiet street, holding the umbrella above his head and leaning forward every once in a while to see if the streetcar was approaching. He people-watched for a moment, but quickly found that the prevalence of umbrellas shadowing faces as civilians ducked into restaurants and apartments to escape the rain made the activity dull.

"Hiya!"

A lifetime of his Catholic mother's spare-the-rod style parenting had trained Reinhard to hold in curses even when surprised, and so he didn't swear even as a squeaky voice startled him something fierce. When he turned to his side and saw the small speaker, his surprise became a nauseous feeling that he couldn't entirely define.

It was a little girl. Her father had sent her out without an umbrella: her blonde locks were soaked, her red-and-white checkered dress was dripping, and her bright blue eyes were obscured by the drizzle.

Reinhard was a man with a photographic memory, and immediately, he recognized the child. The little Jewish girl from the park. His eyes flitted here and there to be sure that there were no other SS men skittering about, and then he looked at the smiling girl, forcing a withering glare onto his face.

"You left before I could talk to you the other day," the child chirped before Reinhard could even hope to get a word out. "Hiya, I'm Kaia!"

"I told you not to talk to me, Jew," Reinhard snapped, tightening his hold on the umbrella and glancing away from the girl. He forced himself to focus on a nearby bookshop. The owner had neglectfully left a rack filled with half-off copies of *Mein Kampf* outside, and the paperbacks were all getting destroyed by the downpour. Reinhard really needed to force himself to actually finish that damn book since Hitler was his Führer now and for the foreseeable future.

"Oh…" was all the girl said in reply, and it was the most pitiable, pathetic little "oh" that Reinhard had ever heard in his life. More akin to the disappointed squeak of a puppy that had been denied table scraps than the sort of sound a human child was supposed to make.

Reinhard gritted his teeth. *Do not look, do not look,* he commanded himself, attempting to focus on the disintegrating prints of Hitler's face plastered on the soaked copies of the Führer's autobiographies.

It wasn't as though he *wanted* to be cruel to the child: Reinhard considered himself to be an honorable officer. He had been trained to be polite and protective towards apple-cheeked little girls. Nevertheless, if people saw him speaking to a Jewess, it could end badly, with him in the position that Dieter unwittingly occupied.

163

And even if it *didn't*, well, Reinhard needed to start acting like a Nazi if he was going to be one. Being nice to a little Jewess, even for just a moment, would be an eternal hurdle. If his job demanded that he move against the Jews at some point in the future, it would be all the harder to do so if he was plagued by the memory of a pleasant conversation with an adorable Jewish child. Better to sour such an encounter right off the bat.

The girl, however, wasn't going to make that task easy for him. She started to hum a little tune, sorrowful and yet, despite her lack of skill, oddly pleasant for something that she was clearly making up on the fly.

Do not, do not, do not, Reinhard commanded himself over and over, gritting his teeth and trying desperately to steel his soul. It felt like another force of nature had claimed control of his eyeballs, however, and he glanced at the shivering, pathetic little girl.

She sneezed.

Goddamn piece of—!

With a huff of exertion that didn't suit the subtle, small movement, Reinhard shifted his arm so that the umbrella was shielding the girl. He felt heavy droplets hammer at his SS visor cap, which fortunately kept the rain from getting in his eyes.

The girl almost immediately realized that she was no longer being battered by droplets. She looked up, and when she saw the black-gloved hand clutching the umbrella, she turned her gaze to Reinhard again, her eyes round and wide and shining in a way that made him feel oddly nauseous.

She smiled—easily the widest smile he'd ever seen on any child's face, he was sure that he could have offered to buy her a candy store and he would have gotten a more subtle smile. Reinhard expected a "thank you" or something to that effect, but instead the girl—Kaia, that was her name—proclaimed in a singsong voice, "I was right!"

"What?" Reinhard said with a scowl, but Kaia merely hummed happily and rocked on her heels, grinning like she had a phenomenal secret that she wouldn't be sharing. He waited for her to break down, but she kept her lips sealed.

"You'll catch your death out here," Reinhard declared. "Where is your father?"

Kaia offered a noncommittal shrug and an "I dunno" that was quiet and muffled by the thrum of raindrops and the distant chuff of the approaching streetcar. Reinhard huffed and tried to remember how much money he had on him.

"You shouldn't be wandering the streets alone in times like these," he muttered, tilting the umbrella back over himself and whipping out his wallet, counting the few bills he had tucked inside before stashing it back in his pocket and shifting the umbrella over the girl again. Kaia wore an expression that was half a grateful smile, half an affronted scowl.

"I'm tough!" she insisted, earning a snort from the Chief of the SD.

"That came across at the park," Reinhard retorted with a smirk. "Where do you live?"

Kaia told him—now fully pouting as she did so and punctuating her address with a proclamation that she *was* tough, but she'd merely been outnumbered the other day.

"Do you have money for the tram?" Reinhard queried, noticing that the girl wasn't carrying a purse.

"Nah ah."

"Then how exactly were you planning on getting home?"

"I was gonna grab onto the outside!" Kaia announced, like that was something completely normal to do.

"That is—" Illegal, dangerous, and the exact sort of thing that Reinhard would have done, so he wasn't one to talk. Reinhard sighed and recalled his wallet's scant weight. He could afford it if he pinched. She didn't live too far away, and he really didn't relish the idea of opening up the newspaper tomorrow and reading her obituary when it would only be a minor headache to make sure that she made it home unharmed.

"If I take you home, can your father repay me for your fare?" Reinhard queried, intending on paying either way, but hoping to gain a promise for compensation, none-theless. Kaia beamed.

"Oh! Yeah, he could!" she assured the Lieutenant with a nod, bouncing on her soaked-shoe clad feet as the streetcar drew near. "And if he's not home, my grandpa can pay you back, and if *he* can't, you can have some of my worldly possessions!"

Reinhard was unable to hold in a snort of amusement even as he bit down on his tongue. "Worldly possessions?" he repeated, nodding at the attendant as the streetcar came to a halt in front of them and he waved for the girl to hop inside.

"Like jewelry!" Kaia explained, skittering to the back of the nearly empty car and plopping down on one polished seat, whipping her head back and forth like a puppy and banishing some water from her curly golden hair. "I don't really like jewelry, but adults always get it for me for my birthdays, so I have some bracelets and stuff you could have as payback if you want! Papa says jewelry's better than money sometimes because it's always valuable, but I still don't like it because it's heavy and itchy. I just like to use it for pirate treasure when I'm playin'..."

Oh, dear. Reinhard really needed to consider bringing earplugs to work, if not to get through a conversation with Himmler then just in case he ended up chaperoning a chatty little girl.

Nevertheless, it was actually somewhat nice. Reinhard didn't particularly like children, but he didn't *dislike* them either, and there was something rather charming about listening to the girl's sweet little voice as she blabbered on and on about how she liked to play pirate games with her family. Not precisely *engaging,* but endearing; it was like watching a little kitten bat at a boring piece of string and enjoying how something so innocuous made the creature so happy.

"Hey! You should sit down!" Kaia chirped as Reinhard grabbed onto one of the straps and waited as a few more people hopped onto the streetcar and took seats at the front of the vehicle. "Ya don't have to sit next to me, but there are lots of seats!"

She gestured about the nearly empty compartment. Reinhard shook his head and plopped his soaked umbrella onto one wooden chair, keeping the wine bottle safely tucked against his black coat.

"Thank you," Reinhard said, clinging tighter to the strap as the streetcar started moving, grateful that the black gloves of his uniform prevented the leather strap from digging into his delicate palm. "But I've been sitting all day long. I'd rather stand."

"Oh, right!" the girl squeaked, kicking her legs and

looking up at Reinhard with vivacious curiosity shining in her blue eyes. She really was a very cute child. And she didn't look like a Jewess at all. If he hadn't seen her father, Reinhard would have assumed that she was merely a little German girl. Maybe she was. One of the SA troopers had suggested that she was a half-breed. Perhaps her mother was German. If anyone caught Reinhard escorting Kaia home, he'd have to play that card. *Of course I didn't know she was a Jewess, just look at her.*

"You said you were in the 'SS' intelligence division at the park, and the others acted like they knew who you were, like you were important," Kaia said. "So are you like a secret agent, or a spy, or a detective?"

Reinhard chuckled and felt his chest swell a bit with pride. "Yes, a little bit of everything," he said. Calling himself a secret-agent-spy-detective was perhaps a bit of an overstatement for the work he did, which mostly consisted of trying to figure out the deep secrets of friends and foes alike and filing all of those clandestine affairs in cigar boxes after begging Hildebrandt for an hour at the typewriter. But...well, he *was* technically an intelligence officer. And he was proud of his work even if he still wasn't sure about the company it made him keep.

"So, what *do* you do all day?" Kaia asked, turning her whole body so that she was facing him and resting her cheek on the backrest of the streetcar chair like she was readying herself for a long story.

Smirking and perhaps taking a bit too much joy in teasing a nine-year-old, Reinhard replied, "Classified."

"Okay," Kaia sighed, though she didn't sound happy about being denied a real answer. "But the SS isn't like the SA? How are they different?"

There were many differences. Numbers for one thing; the SA outnumbered the fledgling SS ten-to-one. The SS had fewer ruffians and homosexuals too. The SS was supposed to be the elite of the elite, the best Nordic stock, the smartest and fittest, those worthy of personally guarding Edmund Hitler.

It was also supposed to be the home of the most ideologically devoted Nazis. *Supposed* to. Himmler clearly wasn't doing a good job of enforcing that standard since Reinhard Heydrich, who still hadn't read *Mein Kampf* and was fully willing to eat a few Marks to make sure a little Jewess got home safe, was one of its top members. Beggars couldn't be choosers, though. Reinhard was still good at his job, and Himmler had promised him that he would "grow into" the rest, whatever the Hell *that* meant.

"We're smarter," Reinhard answered. "And we're not as violent, and we have better uniforms."

He only half meant that last part as a joke, but the girl offered a very cute little giggle, nonetheless. "You've got the black uniform with the little red thing?" Kaia said, gesturing towards Reinhard's arm, no doubt trying to reference the red swastika armband that his jacket concealed. "It kinda reminds me of Latrodectus."

"Lat...what?"

"The black widow spider! Well, that's Latrodectus Hesperus, they're the most famous ones, and I really like them because I like the color. Red's my favorite color..."

Reinhard learned, as the streetcar chugged along, that the girl had an odd interest in arachnids. Apparently her dog was named after a spider that had lived in her desk, and apparently spiders in general were terribly misunderstood and delightful creatures. Kaia rounded off her favorites, listing their scientific names with a practiced flair and babbling on about how she still wasn't sure if she liked trapdoor type spiders more than the traditional sorts that spun intricate webs.

Reinhard was not himself much of a conversationalist. He was a good listener, if not necessarily an enthusiastic one. He could listen to and remember almost anything that someone told him, but that didn't mean he would enjoy doing so. It generally depended on who he was listening to and what he was listening to them about. His fiancée could talk about Hitler or farming from dawn til dusk and he would listen happily. On the other hand, he could barely tolerate being in the same room as Himmler when the *Reichsführer* went on about his odd obsessions (if Reinhard had to hear the term "our ancestors" one more time...)

The child was ridiculously easy to listen to even when she talked about such an odd, inane topic. Perhaps it was her voice: Reinhard had always been particular about voices, being the son of a musician and possessing an acute ear. His own voice was terrible: squeaky like that of a teenage boy, by no means befitting a man of his stature. He hated it, which was likely why he hated talking in general.

The girl had a good voice. Not excellent—Reinhard could tell that if she sang, she'd likely sound a bit like a dehydrated mouse—but it was still a nice voice laced with a brand of contagious mirthfulness that demanded amused attention. They almost missed their stop because Kaia was so busy talking about the difference between brown and black widows, and Reinhard was too busy marveling at how thoroughly he was enjoying her company.

"Oh! Here we are!" the girl squeaked, leaping up and reminding him to grab his umbrella. Reinhard nodded and followed her out, opening the umbrella and setting off down the street towards the girl's house.

Kaia had stopped talking about spiders. As she trotted at his side, occasionally pausing to kick at a particularly deep puddle, she started humming a song that Reinhard knew and hated. *Toselli's Serenade.*

Immediately, Reinhard's good mood dissolved, and a fire erupted in the pit of his stomach. A familiar memory took hold: a memory of humiliation and helplessness. When Reinhard had been a cadet in the Navy, he'd been at the mercy of a fat little Polish drill sergeant who had delighted in lording his power over his underlings, particularly Reinhard. The sergeant, who had been fond of *Toselli's Serenade*, would wake Reinhard up at an ungodly hour practically every night and force him to perform the song like Reinhard was some sort of servant instead of a soldier.

It had been a demeaning, horrid experience, and Reinhard had never been able to play or even listen to *Toselli's Serenade* without recalling the dreadful sensation of being treated like a subject.

Reinhard didn't intend on saying anything, but the girl, seemingly able to sense the shift in the air between them, looked up. He must have been grimacing because she stopped humming.

"Are you okay?" Kaia queried in an almost maternal tone which at once amused and aggravated him. Reinhard almost said "fine" like he would have under normal circumstances, but something about the girl's genuine gaze wrenched the truth from his throat.

"I don't like that song," he said. He saw curiosity glisten in those great blue eyes of hers, and he prepared a rebuke for the inevitable *why*. *None of your business*. Or maybe, *I just don't*.

"Oh, sorry. Mama liked that song, so I listen to it a lot, so I sometimes hum it without thinking. Sorry. If I hum it, you can just tell me not to."

Reinhard felt a small flood of gratitude that was tempered by the realization that Kaia had spoken of her mother in the past tense. Curiosity fought with the urge to be polite to the girl who hadn't pressed him for more answers than he was willing to give, but curiosity won out. "Your mother?"

"Yeah, she was a nurse. She liked that song a lot. I don't remember her much because she died when I was little, but I remember that because she sang it and played it on the piano."

"Ah..." Reinhard should have asked, *Was she a Jew?* Instead, he muttered, "My condolences."

"It's okay!" Kaia said in the forced sort of voice that made it clear it wasn't okay, but she was too used to the state of affairs to be truly troubled. "I live with my papa and my grandpa, and my grandpa teaches me piano now."

"Ah, really?" Reinhard said. Thank God, a different topic, and one that he was abundantly familiar with. "What do you play?"

"Well, my grandpa mostly teaches me American songs and has me sing them so I can learn English 'cause we're gonna move to America soon."

"*Ah, English. And how well can you speak English?*" Reinhard was unable to suppress a smile of prideful amusement when he switched to English, making her stop in her tracks and gawk at him in amazement. Perhaps impressing a nine-year-old was nothing to be proud of, but Reinhard would have been lying if he'd said he didn't enjoy the way his little talents made her jaw drop like he'd announced that he had the ability to fly.

"Wow!" squeaked Kaia. "Okay, I understood 'English' and 'how much'...uh...you were saying, 'How much English do you know?'"

"Very good," Reinhard said with a nod, and just as gaining her admiration was oddly fulfilling, there was something pleasant about the way she drank in his praise.

The rest of their trek to the Goldstein household was spent with Reinhard testing the extent of Kaia's English, nearly shouting phrases over the drum of the rain. When they finally reached the wrought-iron front gate, Reinhard was struck by an ache in his chest, a hollow sensation similar to what he had felt when he had been denied affection as a child. It would have been nice to go inside, perhaps say hello to her father and grandfather. Maybe they could have invited him in for a drink and laughed about the rain, and Reinhard could have praised Kaia's English skills and then tested out the Goldsteins' piano, which judging from the size of their manor must have surely been a beauty.

That would have been nice, but there was an SS uniform hidden under Reinhard's long coat. It would be better for both him and the girl if she went to America and he never saw her again.

"Okay, so, I'll wait here, then?" Reinhard said as Kaia took out a small key and opened the gate. The girl opened her mouth to answer, but before she could, a different voice, a deep and *familiar* male voice, spoke.

"Reinhard Heydrich."

Reinhard turned on the heel of his jackboot and found

himself facing a man. Clean-shaven with a mop of dark hair, a broad nose, and striking bright blue eyes weighed down by bags that hadn't been present when the SA men had beaten him in the park.

"Irresponsible," Reinhard accused, wrapping the cold mantle of an SS man about himself and regarding Kaia's father with an icy expression. "Be grateful. You shouldn't allow a young girl to wander by herself. You owe me..."

"No, *listen*," the Jewish man said, and Reinhard nearly did a double-take at his tone, his *voice*. Commanding and forceful and so *familiar...*

Click!

Reinhard whirled about and discovered that Kaia had slipped behind the safety of her house's wrought-iron gate and locked it behind her.

"Listen to him," she said, and her own voice had adopted her father's forcefulness, albeit a forcefulness that was tinged with a plea. She backed away from the gate like she was at the zoo and had traipsed a bit too close to the lion's enclosure for comfort. "Listen to what he has to say, and I'll give you your wallet back."

What? Hastily, Reinhard reached into his back pocket only to find it empty. When he looked up again, he saw that the girl was holding up a familiar thin leather wallet.

Goddamn little Jew piece of—!

Angry as Reinhard was—and he was certainly angry, his anti-Semitism and his admiration for Hitler both skyrocketed simultaneously—he was also rather impressed. He'd been pick-pocketed before, but always in crowds, and he had always been able to tell when it happened. Kaia had skillful sticky fingers. Reinhard might have liked her if he hadn't hated her so much right then.

Yet while there was a familiar glimmer of pride in Kaia's eyes, the same glint that Reinhard glimpsed in his own reflection whenever he won a fencing match, there was also a genuine gloominess. It was clear that Kaia didn't want to keep the Nazi's meager money. She nudged her head towards her father. Scowling and huffing, Reinhard relented.

"Talk fast, Jew," he spat. Herr Goldstein rolled his shoulders.

"You didn't hurt Kaia," the Jewish man muttered.

"No, though maybe I should have!" Reinhard snapped, casting a brief scowl at the thieving little girl, who flashed an apologetic smile that made the Nazi Lieutenant's gut roil. That was an *I know you only sort of mean that* smile. Damn her, she could read him well for someone who hadn't known him for more than an hour.

Heaving a defeated sigh, Reinhard clarified, "I just didn't want her to get killed."

"You didn't..." Goldstein said, and there was a strange lilt in his tone, somewhere between surprised and disbelieving. Reinhard bristled.

"I'm not some thug who beats up little girls!" he snapped. "Even if those little girls are thieving Jews!"

Again, Reinhard looked at Kaia. She smiled even wider, as though "thieving Jew" was a compliment.

"You're a Lieutenant in the SS." Goldstein spoke again, drawing Reinhard's attention back to him. Reinhard huffed and found himself adjusting the trench coat that concealed his night-black SS uniform.

"Which means I have no problem beating *you*, but..."

"You used to be in the Navy."

Reinhard raised an eyebrow, then sneered. "Correct, which means that…"

"You've told everyone that you were kicked out for political reasons, but that's a lie. You weren't a National Socialist when you were in the Navy. You're barely one now. You just wanted to keep wearing a uniform, *any* uniform. Your fiancée was a Nazi and begged you to join the SS. And you wanted to make her proud because she stood by you even after you were dishonorably discharged from the Navy."

"What?" snapped Reinhard, anger coursing through his body. Goldstein was no longer slouching. The Jew stood up straight, scowling, his striking blue eyes glowing through the drizzle.

"You were booted from the Navy, and not because of politics. You slept with a girl, promised you'd marry her, then you met your fiancée Lina. The first girl, you broke up with her by sending her you and Lina's engagement announcement. She had a breakdown, and unlucky for you, her father was friends with one of the naval higher-ups."

Rain drummed against the umbrella in tune with the steadily quickening heartbeat of Reinhard Heydrich. Kaia let out a curious little noise, no doubt wondering what the significance of sleeping with someone was.

"You…" Reinhard hissed, stepping towards Goldstein, trying to mask his shock and fear with anger. It wasn't hard. "You've been spying on me!"

Goldstein shook his head, teetering a bit, like he wanted to match Heydrich's step forward with a cautious step backwards. Instead, however, the Jew took a shuddering breath and planted his feet in a deep puddle.

"You got the job from Himmler," Goldstein continued.

"He thought you were an intelligence officer. You were actually a signals officer in the Navy. He had you sit for twenty minutes and sketch out a plan for how to form an intelligence unit for the SS. You had no clue what you were doing, so you made shit up based on British spy novels. Himmler, though, he was even more clueless than you. He was impressed and hired you on the spot."

Reinhard felt his face drain of all color. His humiliating naval background was one thing, any intrepid sleuth or someone that had been present at the Honor Court hearing would have known those details, but unless Goldstein had been listening in on his conversations with his fiancée...

"That's...have you been speaking to my...?"

"Fiancée? Lina? You met her at a ball in Kiel. You proposed to her three days after you met. She said yes because you played the violin so well."

Faintly, over the sound of his own frantic heartbeat and the pitter-patter of rain on the umbrella he was holding in a steadily slackening grip, Reinhard heard Kaia let out a little "Aw!" If he weren't so terrified and enraged, he might have found her little show of support for his impulsive romantic choices cute.

"I know a lot about you that's impossible to know," Goldstein said.

"Because you're some sort of...spy or..." Reinhard stepped forward again. Goldstein winced, but didn't move back.

"Spy," Goldstein said slowly, shaking his head. "A spy couldn't know all of this; you must realize that. Would a spy know that you're the middle child, and you always resented your older sister and younger brother because your relatives and family members would gush over them and ignore you?"

Bam. Bam. Bam. He could feel his heart leaping into his throat. "Shut up."

"Would a spy know that when you were a child, you once climbed onto a schoolhouse rooftop…I guess that was either for attention or just to see if you could…"

Crash! The wine bottle shattered against the pavement as it fell from Reinhard's grasp. Rain swept the broken glass and blood-colored liquid into a drain. "Shut up!"

Reinhard dropped the umbrella, and a stray gust of wind dragged it away from the confrontation. The screech of its prongs scratching at the pavement made his ears ring.

"Would a spy," Goldstein continued, bravely, *stupidly,* "know that your mother used to beat you until you couldn't sit, and your father was too busy writing his operas to pay you any mind?"

"Shut…!"

"And once, when she slapped you across the face, you looked her right in the eye and said, 'What about the other cheek?' And she beat you so hard…*unk!*"

Kaia let out a little shriek as Reinhard closed the distance between himself and the Jew speaking impossible truths, unveiling memories he had buried long ago, and grabbed him by the collar, nearly lifting him off the pavement.

Goldstein coughed, gagged, and then, barely audibly, he looked the soaked SS man right in the eyes and said, "You're going to name your firstborn child Klaus, your second born Heider, and your daughter is going to be named Silke."

Shock struck Reinhard worse than any bolt of lightning,

banishing anger. There was impossible, and then there was that. A spy could unearth quite a bit, but a conversation he hadn't even had with his fiancée yet—*if we have a girl, I want her to be named Silke*—that breached the realm of sense.

Goldstein put a gloved hand on Reinhard's trembling arm, speaking in a strangely strong tone for a man being choked, "I'll explain. Let me."

"Please!" Kaia's sweet little voice cut in, reassuring as it was pleading. Reinhard nodded slowly, set Goldstein on the ground, and forced an icy mask onto his face.

"Explain," Reinhard commanded, doing his best to sound strong even as he could already feel everything slipping from his grasp.

After that curt "explain," Reinhard Heydrich didn't say another word for two hours. He said nothing even as Adiel told the impossible story of his parents and the deal with their Demon King, even as he informed the Nazi Lieutenant quite soberly that their timeline wasn't the way it was supposed to be and that *he* was supposed to be Heydrich's Führer.

Heydrich said nothing. He sneered, he smirked, he rolled his eyes, but he was silent.

Then Adiel showed him the books. Heydrich's smirk morphed into a scowl and his eyes became hard.

While Adiel watched, the heft of the gun hidden beneath his layers of rain-soaked clothes reminding him of its presence, Reinhard Heydrich read. While Kaia played a quiet game of tug-o-war with Bernie the Second, Reinhard

Heydrich perused his own biography. While Natan snoozed upstairs, Reinhard Heydrich's eyes roamed the pictures of train cars full of emaciated corpses and twins sewn together by Josef Mengele.

As Reinhard read, his eyes flitting from a picture of his future self scowling at the cameraman to an image of one of his underlings gunning down a woman with a baby in her arms, he didn't say a word or make a sound, but his every twitch spoke volumes. The tightening of his jaw, the way his gaze morphed from restrained anger into horror, the fact that he began to sway as though he was about to vomit on the Goldsteins' carpet.

The gun in Adiel's belt felt less heavy as he became steadily more convinced that Heydrich wasn't about to toss the Holocaust book aside and cackle gleefully about his future genocidal endeavors.

Finally, slowly, Reinhard Heydrich stopped his skimming and set the last book aside. When he spoke, his high-pitched voice was halting in a familiar way: it was the restrained tone Adiel had used when he'd told Kaia that she didn't have a mother anymore, the tone of someone desperate to sound strong even when their soul was being ripped to shreds.

"This is impossible," Reinhard said, crossing his arms over his chest and shaking his head.

"Believe me," sighed Adiel, removing his hand from his side, now completely convinced that Kaia had been right about the Blond Beast. "I was going to say the same thing…"

"No, *this* is impossible!" Heydrich shouted so loud that Adiel feared he might awaken Natan, who would no doubt be rather upset if he found one of his tormentors having a mental breakdown in his living room.

"Trust me, I know how you're feeling," Adiel said, but Heydrich shook his head and grabbed one book from the pile. He tore it open to a splash page that featured four pictures. Hitler, smirking; the monster Heydrich holding a death warrant pinched between long fingers; a snapshot of a decimated Czech village; an illustration from a Holocaust survivor showing SS men tossing babies into a pyre at Auschwitz.

"No, you don't!" Heydrich cried, all but losing his grip on the book as his entire body quaked. "You're living a different life entirely! I'm still myself! But you're telling me that I'm going to be this 'Hangman of Prague' in less than ten years!"

"A lot can change in ten years," Adiel said, averting his eyes from the gruesome imagery and his own utterly unrecognizable face.

"Yes, but not me, not *that* much!" Reinhard insisted, throwing the book down to the floor. It landed on its spine, which Heydrich must have bent since it flew open and showed off the same splash page "I have no compunctions about killing communists and criminals, but I would *never* slaughter innocent children!"

Reinhard placed harsh, desperate emphasis on the world *never*, glancing down at the image of the Reinhard Heydrich that now, it seemed, would never be: the cold-eyed Butcher of Prague killing thousands of innocent children with the flourish of a pen.

"Never," Adiel repeated, folding his arms tightly over his chest and glancing at Adolf Hitler's visage.

"*Never.*" Reinhard proclaimed, and then, in a voice that

trembled, he said, "I'm not a child murderer, I am *not*. Maybe I'm not a good person, but I'm not…"

He looked down at his demonic doppelgänger, then at the image of Nazis tossing children into roaring pits of fire, and then Heydrich glanced at Kaia. Adiel knew exactly what he was thinking. Kaia looked up with wide, worried eyes. Reinhard winced as though her gaze was a slap right in his face, collapsing back into the chair and clutching his stomach.

"Are you gonna be sick?" Kaia cried, letting Bernie win their game and running to grab the garbage can. Reinhard shook his head even as his face turned green.

"I am *not*…" he insisted weakly, turning away from Kaia as she ignored his insistence that he wasn't about to throw up and left the garbage can at his feet. Heydrich's eyes were fixed upon his future self. "I'm not *that*, I am *not*, I will *not*…"

"Herr Reinhard, maybe you should——" Kaia started to say. Reinhard let out an odd strangled sound.

"'Herr Reinhard'?" the Blond Beast repeated. Adiel chuckled somberly.

"She, ah, she does that. She hates using last names," Adiel said. That was one of his daughter's more peculiar little quirks: when he had asked why she despised using last names, Kaia had simply declared that calling people by their surname made them *feel scary*. Her teacher had tried to beat proper etiquette into her many times, but he had eventually given up and allowed a compromise by saying that she should at least call him *Herr* Bruno.

"Ah…" Reinhard looked at the girl. "Would you mind getting me a cup of water?"

A transparent attempt to get her out of the room, and Kaia realized it immediately. Sighing, she nodded.

"All right, but…you shouldn't feel sick about this 'cause you're not gonna do it now, right?" Kaia gestured to the books.

Reinhard shook his head emphatically. It was a wonder he didn't accidentally break his own neck. "I will *not*."

"So…there!" Kaia declared with a smile, like that was the end of it, before turning on her heel and running to get their strange guest a drink. Bernie, who had already memorized the route to the kitchen, followed at her heels.

The second she was gone, Reinhard let out a slew of curses that cemented his status as a former sailor. "Shit, fuck, piss, *fuck*, *shit*, *shit*, *shit!*"

Reinhard leapt to his feet and kicked the book he'd dropped, denting the hardback but not shutting it. Mass murderer Reinhard Heydrich scowled at his past, softer self. Younger, better Reinhard let out a sound of utter frustration at his inability to easily banish his wicked doppelgänger. He collapsed back onto the chair, taking in deep breaths as though he was breaching the ocean's surface after nearly drowning.

"Why did you show me this?!" Reinhard cried, covering his face with his hands, his tone at once accusatory and sorrowful. Adiel bit his lip, fought his urge to nervously pace, and glanced at the kitchen.

"Desperation, mostly," he confessed. "It was my daughter's idea. She got it in her head after you helped us at the park that there was good in you, that you weren't an irredeemable piece of shit *yet*, and if we got to you early…"

Adiel sighed heavily and looked down at the Hangman-Heydrich of 1942. "I suppose she was right. Guess it makes sense: I imagine Himmler didn't include 'commit mass murder' in the job description when he hired you…"

The Professor hoped that a little bit of dark humor would calm Reinhard down, but the Blond Beast merely gave him a rather frosty look and said, "He did not."

"Well…" Adiel muttered, tugging on his collar. "The books said you were a late-bloomer Nazi. I was just hoping to shock you into agreeing to help me. I can't do this by myself…"

"Do what?" Reinhard's icy gaze melted into one of almost desperate eagerness, as though the mere concept of doing something, *anything*, was his one lifeline.

"Stop this," Adiel said, gesturing to the pile of books. "Prevent this from ever happening."

"Didn't your parents already try that?" Reinhard said, now sounding rather frustrated, like he had hoped that Adiel would have a more concrete plan. "And it didn't *work*."

"Yes, but we can't just do *nothing!*" Adiel argued, smacking his fist into an open palm like his own hand was a podium. "You're in a position to really help us. We can save millions of people. We have the knowledge, you have the access…"

"Access to Hitler, you mean," Heydrich said.

"More access than me." Adiel sighed. "And either way, you're smart enough to start a genocide, you *must* be smart enough to stop it."

Heydrich gave a small nod, and Adiel had to stop himself from letting an amused smile grace his face when he saw a determined fire flare in Reinhard's lake-blue eyes. It seemed that Heydrich could not refuse a challenge, *any* challenge.

"Think of it as redemption," Adiel continued, his gaze falling upon Adolf Hitler's frozen visage. "I…listen, even if we're different, you and me, it's still…that still would have been me. I understand the feeling. Maybe this is stupid. Maybe I should just count my blessings. Maybe you just want to quit the SS and wash your hands of it, but they'll replace you, and…"

Adiel took in a sharp breath, let his hands fall to his sides, and in a voice that he hoped was as resonating and convincing as the one he had possessed in his previous life, he declared, "We know too much. We can't just stand by and do nothing when *we* were the ones who did it the first time. Knowing that this is in your soul somewhere, that you *could* do this, that you *did* even if you *didn't*…I get it. But we can fix it, *really* fix it. It should be easy. All we need to do is stop Hitler from becoming Chancellor."

"No!" Heydrich suddenly leapt out of his chair, shouting the single word in the frantically commanding tone of an officer watching a new recruit chuck a live grenade at his own men. Adiel raised an eyebrow.

"No?" he repeated, but before Heydrich could explain himself, Kaia came skipping into the room with a tea-tray in her arms and a satisfied Bernie at her heels. She must have been utilizing her time in the kitchen to give the dog treats. Or maybe whole chickens.

"Hiya!" the girl chirped. "Are you two done talking without me? I made tea so it'd take me a little longer. It's peppermint."

"Ugh…" Reinhard groaned, wrinkling his nose and rubbing his temple as though the smell gave him a headache. "I'm going to need something stronger."

"Brandy?" offered Adiel, gesturing towards the dining

room. "Or is there something else that'll help you think of a way to save Europe?"

"Brandy's fine." From the near desperation in Reinhard's voice, it sounded as though brandy would be far more than just *fine*. Indeed, when Adiel sat Heydrich down at their table (he sat across from the Blond Beast, which meant that Kaia got to sit at the head of the table for once, which absolutely delighted her), the Nazi Lieutenant all but inhaled the bottle.

"From reading these books," Adiel said, stealing the peppermint tea that Kaia had prepared, "it seems like the easiest way to prevent this tragedy would be to stop Hitler from becoming Chancellor."

"That's a terrible idea," Reinhard interrupted. "Hitler *needs* to become the Führer."

From Heydrich, and particularly in these circumstances, Adiel might have considered that declaration concerning, but Reinhard almost spat out that statement. Like it was truly a necessity and not a desire.

"Heydrich," Adiel said. "Once Hitler becomes Führer, it'll be too late. At least forty-two people tried to assassinate me—to assassinate *Adolf Hitler*, and all of them failed."

"Assassinate...?" squeaked Kaia softly. Heydrich shook his head and slammed his brandy onto the counter.

"You seem to believe that Hitler is the *only* bloodthirsty, genocidal madman in Europe," Reinhard said. "Stalin is still alive, and from the looks of it, he won't be dying of natural causes anytime soon. If we completely remove Hitler from the equation, then what? At best, we'll have a weak Germany. At worst? A communist Germany. Either way, Stalin will steamroll us, and then? Then there's no telling what the future holds."

Reinhard jabbed his thumb in the direction of the sitting room where Becca's books remained. "Give Stalin a decade of uncontested rule over Europe and he could very well make Hitler look like a helpless kitten. Another world war could start anyway if France and the UK fight him. Maybe a worse war. And do you think the Jews will fare well under Stalin? Do you think *anyone* would fare well under Stalin?"

Of course not. Rebecca's books primarily focused on the Holocaust, but a few chapters had mentioned Joseph Stalin and his crimes, how far he was willing to go for his impossible communist utopia. Next year, the Holodomor would begin, plunging Ukraine into a man-made famine that would kill millions. Natan had been right about one thing: Adolf Hitler wasn't special. There were plenty of monsters like him in the world. One of them already had power, and he was already well past the point of no return.

"I...you're right," Adiel whispered, combing a hand through his dark hair and clutching at the pant leg of his thigh. "You're right. So what *do* we do?"

"There's a question...hm..." Heydrich leaned back, drumming long spider-leg-like fingers on the tabletop. Adiel could see why Kaia seemed to have taken an instant liking to the Blond Beast: he seemed like some strange combination of a snake and a spider.

"I don't suppose you could set another trap for the Demon King's son, then free him again and earn another boon?" suggested the Nazi Lieutenant, and it only somewhat sounded like he was joking. Adiel let out a snort and shook his head.

"Papa said he and Mama already destroyed the trap years ago, when I was a baby," Adiel declared. "Even if he hadn't, I don't think it would be a great idea to try and trick the Demon King."

"No," Reinhard concurred. "With our luck, that would only make things worse. I suppose we'll have to do this the hard way, then. No magic. Hm…well…I'm going to have access to Edmund Hitler. I'm in charge of the security for his return to Munich. If we're going to pull something…"

"I don't know if this will be of any help," Adiel interrupted. "But me and Edmund Hitler were in the same unit during the Great War. We were sort of friends, and we were pen pals for a while before he stopped writing."

"Small world."

"Do you think maybe that could be useful? Perhaps I could try to get back into contact with him, maybe you could arrange something…?"

"Why don't we just talk to him on New Year's?" Kaia piped up, evidently tired of sitting and listening so politely. "Herr Reinhard could sneak us in, and we can show him the books, and then we could change his mind!"

A sweet suggestion that earned a sneer from the Blond Beast.

"Incredible idea," said Reinhard, his voice absolutely oozing sarcasm. "While we're at it, why don't we stroll up to the Kremlin and give Stalin a hug? That'll fix all of our problems."

Kaia, who wasn't stupid but also wasn't often the victim of sarcasm, gaped hopefully at Heydrich. "You really think that'll work?"

"No, I do not think that will work!"

"Heydrich!" snapped Adiel, but the rebuke didn't even fully escape his lips when the potential Hangman of Prague seemed to realize that he'd outright *screamed* at the child. Reinhard slapped a hand over his mouth.

"I'm sorry!" he said. Kaia hadn't even winced, though perhaps that was because she was used to getting screamed at by everyone except her family. She smiled brightly and waved a dismissive hand.

"It's okay!" she declared. "Well, maybe Stalin's too evil right now, but we definitely need to try and talk to my uncle! Except I guess we shouldn't show him the books or let anyone get them or else they'll know the future, and if they know the future and they don't change their minds…"

"Yes, you're right!" Reinhard said hastily, cutting her off before her ramble could really get going. "Under no circumstances can anything we say in this house leave it, and you must keep those books locked up. Kaia…"

Reinhard turned his chair towards her and leaned down a bit so that he was nearly at eye-level with the child. This time when he spoke, his tone was gentle, the sort that he would no doubt offer to Silke Heydrich in a few years.

"I appreciate that you…thought I wasn't *too evil* to tell me about all of this," he said quietly. "Nevertheless, don't tell anyone else, all right?"

"I'm not stupid!" Kaia said, before smiling, winking, and pressing a finger to her lips. "It's *classified*."

That must have been some sort of inside joke that the two of them had come up with while Adiel had been trailing them because it wrenched a small, genuine chuckle from the beleaguered Blond Beast.

"Classified indeed," Reinhard said before turning back to Adiel. "Well…I suppose it's up to us. We'll need to brainstorm something. There has to be some way we could stop this without making everything worse. Some way to optimize…"

"Adiel, did I hear scre—?!"

Natan had always been something of a heavy sleeper, and so Adiel had hoped that his father wouldn't hear Reinhard's outburst. No such luck as the time traveler came strolling into the dining room only to freeze as he found himself face-to-face with the man who had killed his family.

There was a horrible, *horrible* silence for a moment as it seemed that time itself froze. Both the Blond Beast and the Auschwitz survivor stared at one another, all but mirroring each-others' expression of terror.

It was, unsurprisingly, Kaia that broke the silence. "Hiya, Zaidy! Don't worry, he's not evil right now!"

"Kaia!"

"I'll just—"

"Upstairs!"

"I'll leave—"

"Right now!"

"We'll talk later!"

Then the stillness was broken by a whirlwind of motion as Reinhard bolted from the house, Natan grabbed Kaia and dragged her upstairs, Kaia whined and squirmed and blurted something about giving Heydrich his wallet back, and Bernie ran around barking. In the blink of an eye, Adiel found himself sitting alone at the table, dread building in his stomach like he was a little boy again, waiting for his father to come home and decide his fate after a day of misbehaving.

Eventually, Natan came back downstairs, somewhat concerningly carrying a knife that Adiel knew he kept by his bedside in case of emergencies.

"I've got the gun," Adiel sighed, and Natan glanced about as though he thought Heydrich might be hiding behind the furniture, ready to spring out and continue his genocidal tasks at any second.

"Should have used it," Natan hissed, unleashing a small sigh of relief when he realized that the Blond Beast had left the premises. He sat at his usual spot and tossed the knife onto the table.

"Papa," Adiel said. "I know it sounds utterly insane, but Kaia..."

"Kaia!" Natan slammed a fist on the table, nearly sending the cups and silverware flying. "I have no idea what you were doing, but I can't believe you would even consider letting that damn *monster* anywhere near her!"

"Papa, remember how I told you we had a run-in with the SA at the park?"

Natan brusquely nodded, and Adiel hastily recounted the attack at the park, the intervention of Reinhard Heydrich, the information provided in the biography that had convinced Kaia that the Blond Beast was approachable...

"...and ultimately, she was right," Adiel concluded. "He's agreed to help us."

"Help?! Adiel, this is *Reinhard Heydrich* we're talking about!" snapped Natan. "I don't know how much you managed to read the other day, but he's the Head of the Gestapo! He's a lying, manipulative son-of-a-bitch! How do you know he's not going to run right to his bosses and send them after us?!"

"I just..."

Natan likely wouldn't believe him if he described Reinhard's near-breakdown. The old man hadn't talked too much about Heydrich, but he had mentioned that the Libmans and the Blums had been interred in the abominable Terezin Ghetto just outside Prague. It had been Heydrich, ultimately, that had starved Natan's father to death and killed his mother. One of Natan's sisters had even been executed as a reprisal for Heydrich's assassination.

Natan would not be working with Reinhard Heydrich. He had only been willing to accept Adiel Goldstein because he had finally become convinced that Adiel was not Hitler.

But though Adiel was not Hitler, he still had Hitlerian charisma, and so he summoned it and declared in a strong voice, "Listen: I need you to trust me. Heydrich isn't a decent human being by any means, but he's also not a Nazi at the moment, and we just delivered a sledgehammer to his face. He didn't join the SS to kill children."

"Maybe, but…"

"He would have, but he won't now. Just like I won't now."

"Adiel, that's *different*…"

"Yes, but not by much. An entirely different childhood will of course create an entirely different person, but even a slightly altered choice later down the path can be the difference between a monster and a decent person. You gave me a chance, and today, in my eyes, Heydrich proved himself worthy of the same. It's entirely unfair to grant me leniency and give him none, Papa. Remember: he hasn't done anything yet. In his mind, he's an honorable naval cadet that just realized he's joined a murderous cult. The brainwashing hasn't had time to work yet, and so he's willing to help us."

Natan's anger slowly seemed to dribble out of his body. "Adiel…"

"I'm not asking you to get involved in this. You've done more than enough. But he and I have an obligation…"

"You don't—!"

"At the very least, I have an obligation to *try*. And I have an obligation towards him as well: it was my fault he became a monster in your timeline. He was following *my* orders."

"He never had to! He made a choice!"

"True, but who's at fault when a hitman kills someone: the hitman, or the man who hires him? In the eyes of God, both are equally guilty."

"Ah! Why did I ever send you to yeshiva?!" snapped Natan, tracing the numbers on his skin with his index finger.

"Because you believed in me. Please believe in me now," Adiel said, reaching out and putting a hand on his father's arm. He felt Natan stiffen, then relax in resignation.

"Fine, *fine*…if it has a chance of saving more people, fine…I suppose I'm not one to chastise you for working with demons," sighed Natan before his sapphire eyes flashed. "But I don't want Kaia going anywhere near that monster! I don't care what he's like right now! If he puts a single finger on her…!"

Natan's gaze flitted down to the knife, and Adiel patted his father's arm. "Kaia won't get involved in any of this," he promised. "I'll make sure she stays away from him."

And hardly had that vow left his lips when Adiel regretted it, for he knew Kaia well enough to know that she wouldn't quietly retreat from all of this excitement.

EIGHT

"Reinhard, is everything all right?"

Everything was most certainly not all right for Reinhard Heydrich. His landlady had been disappointed that he hadn't gotten her the wine last night, he had forgotten to take his wallet back from Kaia, and he was apparently an insane child murderer.

Was. Could be. Would be. There was an insane child murderer lurking somewhere in his soul like a parasite waiting to conquer the entire organism, and knowing that meant that Reinhard now hated the feeling of his own skin. Hands that had once easily been able to flourish a signature felt heavy and clumsy now that he knew he had (could have, would have) used them to butcher one-and-a-half million children.

(That was an incomprehensibly large number. Six million was equally hard to fathom. Even one would have shocked him. One little Kaia Goldstein was one too many.)

Reinhard felt sick down to his last molecule: really, the fact that Kaia had taken his wallet probably didn't even matter anymore since he doubted he was ever going to eat anything again. He hadn't even been able to down a drop of coffee, which meant that he had a blistering headache in addition to everything else. He probably should have stayed home, called in sick, but he had hated taking sick days in the Navy and he wouldn't take one now. Not when it was so important that he be allowed near Hitler. If he lost that job now…

So he had gone to work, and walking into the Brown House had been an indescribable experience. Not quite like walking into a lion's den, no: lions didn't hide their true nature behind friendly smiles and vows of camaraderie. A lion ate you, he didn't turn you into a cannibal.

So when Dieter strolled over to Reinhard Heydrich's desk and found the typically pristine Nazi Lieutenant looking worse for wear (Reinhard might have assumed that he looked like a walking corpse, but he had seen walking corpses last night and by no means did he come close), it was only natural that he showed concern.

"I'm fine," lied Reinhard, and Dieter winced at the Blond Beast's tone: viciously angry like a viper. It could hardly be helped. Just yesterday, he had regarded Dieter as a friendly enough fellow, and the men around him as annoyingly stupid at worst. But now Reinhard knew that every man in the Brown House was evil, including himself.

"Are…you sure?" Dieter said, glancing nervously to and fro, making sure that the men who worked at the desks beside Heydrich had run off to their breaks before he leaned close and muttered. "Er, not to offend, but you sort of look like you got hit by a car."

"I'm fine, I just got up on the wrong side of the bed,"

Reinhard insisted, sitting back and raking his hands through his hair.

"You look like you *fell* off the wrong side of the bed," Dieter sighed. "Did you get stuck in the rain last night or something? You should just ask Himmler to head home early if you're sick, he won't mind."

No. Of course not. Himmler would be more than willing to give perfect, blond, blue-eyed Reinhard Heydrich a day off because Himmler was oh-so *nice*. Fatherly, really. If the child slaves in Himmler's camps got sick, though, well, good, that would just thin their numbers.

(Reinhard himself would apparently say those exact words later. "Start an epidemic," he would advise the Nazis overseeing the Warsaw Ghetto in less than a decade, just like that, because the Reinhard Heydrich of less than a decade would rather see babies choke on their own blood than waste a bullet on them.)

Reinhard was about to argue once again that he felt fine, absolutely *fine*, but right then another SS man shouted: "Hey, Heydrich, your niece is here to see you!"

Reinhard had no niece. Not yet. He gritted his teeth, somewhat afraid that if little Kaia was invited in, the lions prowling about the Brown House would sniff her out and savage her. Even so, refusing to let her in would only increase suspicion and thereby put the little girl in even more danger.

"Kaia, come here!" Reinhard cried, and Kaia came skipping towards his desk, pausing to brightly greet every SS man that flashed the adorable blonde a welcoming smile. Dieter, who couldn't even sniff out Jewish blood in his longtime friends much less a strange child, knelt down when she stopped beside him.

"Reinhard, I didn't know you had a niece!" Dieter chuckled, pinching the girl's cheek. "How do you do, Fräulein? I'm Dieter Amsel. I work with your uncle."

"Hiya, Herr Dieter!" the girl said brightly, pulling her face away and rubbing her cheek with her hand.

"Aha, actually, it's Herr *Amsel*!" Dieter said, standing up and straightening out his uniform. At least he wasn't so far gone that he was about to insist that a nine-year-old refer to him by rank. Not *yet*.

Kaia shrugged carelessly and turned her attention towards Reinhard, flashing him that carefree, optimistic smile of hers. Maybe she *could* convince Stalin to change his ways after all. If they could export that smile to the Kremlin…

"You forgot your wallet at Papa's house, Uncle," she said, plopping Reinhard's wallet onto his desk. He grunted and took it slowly, tucking it into his pocket and giving her a chastising scowl.

"You should be in school, Kaia," he said, earning a chuckle from Dieter, who of course couldn't understand what he meant to say: *you, a Jew, shouldn't be here.*

"Uh huh!" Kaia squeaked. "I'm playin' hooky."

Blunt. Reinhard's malaise fractured, and he gave a small snort. Dieter's eyes brightened when he saw that the girl was so effortlessly able to improve the Blond Beast's mood.

"Run along home to play hooky, then," Reinhard said. "Remember what I said about things being *classified*."

"*Classified*, right," Kaia said, winking and pressing her finger to her lips. She turned on her heel and it seemed that she was about to obey and exit the Brown House…

"Reinhard!"

Shit, shit, shit, shit, shit!

Heinrich Himmler came strolling in, bedecked in his ill-fitting uniform. He stopped in front of Reinhard's desk and flashed his underling a friendly smile.

Reinhard had learned quite a bit about himself yesterday, and it said something about how awful he was that learning the day and circumstances of his own death had practically been a relief. The worst days of the Holocaust began in the summer of 1942, but the monstrous Reinhard Heydrich of the not-too-distant future hadn't lived to see his glorious genocide arrive at its apex. Adiel—no, *Adolf*—had given his most loyal underling a gift in the form of occupied Czechoslovakia, where Hangman-Heydrich had ruled with a brutality that had earned him the epithet of the "Butcher of Prague."

That brutality, however, had also earned him the deserved ire of the Czech resistance, and two brave agents, Jan Kubiš and Jozef Gabčík, had embarked on a suicide mission to take him down. Together, they had ambushed Reinhard Heydrich at a bend in the street on his route to Prague Castle, and together they had mortally injured him. Reinhard Heydrich the Butcher of Prague had died, slowly, deservedly, and hopefully painfully.

(Perhaps it was a tad odd that Reinhard supported his own killers, but perhaps not. Surely a dog, if it knew that it was destined to become rabid, would similarly empathize with the person who put it out of the world's misery.)

At any rate, Reinhard Heydrich was supposed to die in Prague, though not before he outlined exactly what he wanted the Holocaust to become. And Himmler, good friend that he was, had executed Hangman-Heydrich's plans perfectly, even naming the most terrible stages of the genocide in his honor. "Operation Reinhard" it was called, when thousands of children were gassed to death. Himmler had—*Would? No, I refuse*—Himmler, in that seemingly unstoppable timeline, had apparently visited Auschwitz and watched one such gassing.

It was hard, borderline impossible, to see Himmler smile without imagining that same smile decorating his face as he stepped away from a concrete room full of choking children. Himmler would whip out his handkerchief like he often did, mop his brow, and then smile a little and think, *There, Reinhard, we did it all just like you wanted. You would be proud.*

And the worst part, of course, was that Reinhard *would have* been proud.

"Oh!"

Himmler's grey-blue eyes only lingered on Reinhard for a fraction of a second before they shifted to the brightest spot in the room: smiling little Kaia Goldstein. Of course, Himmler wouldn't suspect that the blonde, blue-eyed cherub was a Jewess. Of course not. Which meant she was just an innocent little girl and not a rat that needed to be poisoned.

The wastebasket was temping. Reinhard would have liked to vomit right then, but doing so would have been too suspicious because there was nothing going on that should have made him sick. Just Himmler, smiling that Auschwitz smile as he knelt in front of the little Jewish girl and ruffled her hair.

"And who is this?" Himmler crooned, his typically friendly voice taking on a pitch of genuine delight.

"That's Reinhard's niece, sir," Dieter the Snitch proclaimed, and for a moment Himmler's smile faltered.

He knew the Heydrich family tree from top to bottom. The *Reichsführer* always checked to make sure there were no undesirable elements in his recruits, not a drop of Jewish blood. He knew that Reinhard had no niece.

"The daughter of a close friend," Reinhard demurred quickly, and thankfully, he was so dog-tired that there was no way for nervousness to wriggle into his tone. "She just calls me 'uncle.'"

"I'm Kaia!" piped up the Jewish girl. Only a child that loved snakes and spiders could have smiled so brightly at a man like Heinrich Himmler when she must have known who he was. Only a child who loved God's most disgusting creatures wouldn't have even winced when Himmler grabbed her little hand and planted a kiss on her knuckles.

"I didn't know we'd have such a lovely guest at the Brown House! I wish I'd brought flowers!" Himmler laughed. "It's very nice to meet you, Kaia! Any particular reason you've come to visit?"

"Uncle Reinhard forgot his wallet at my house, so I brought it to him."

"Aren't you a sweetheart!" Himmler crooned, lifting his gaze to Reinhard and frowning when he saw that his underling was practically green.

"I see my umbrella didn't save you, eh?" the *Reichsführer* chuckled, rising to his feet and ruffling little Kaia's perfectly Aryan curls as he did so. Reinhard grunted.

"Wind took it away. Sorry," he said, his mouth tasting sour as he apologized to a man who was at least partially responsible for turning him into a monster in that other timeline. *You'll grow into it*, Himmler had said once, and Reinhard would have never realized what that really meant. Not until it was too late.

"Ah, it was cheap anyway!" Himmler said. "Are you feeling alright, though?"

"Don't try to convince him to take a sick day, *Reichs-führer*," Dieter chuckled. "I think you have a better chance of turning the Führer into a Bolshevik."

"I'm not sick," Reinhard insisted. "Just forgot my coffee this morning."

"Ah, and you don't wanna touch the stuff we have here," Himmler snickered, jabbing a black-gloved thumb towards the doorway. "Understandable. I'm relatively sure some spy has poisoned it."

Thoughts of poison made a fresh wave of nausea wash over Reinhard. Right at that moment, of course, little Kaia's stomach let out a wolf-like snarl that drew Himmler's attention to her.

"Oh, dear! Looks like someone else skipped breakfast!" Himmler laughed, and Kaia nodded.

"Tell you what," the *Reichsführer* said, gesturing towards the window. "I can't possibly allow a young lady to starve…" *Unless she's a Jewess.* "And I don't think Reinhard's going to be getting a lot done in his present condition. Reinhard, Kaia, there's this darling little cafe a block away. I'll treat the both of you and myself. I skipped coffee and breakfast as well!"

No. No. No. NO.

"Yeah, sure!" said Kaia. That bend in Prague was looking better by the second. Maybe if Reinhard painted a target on his own back and went there carrying a sign that said, *"FUTURE CZECH KILLER,"* one of the Slavs would take initiative and put him out of his misery a decade early.

At any rate, Reinhard wasn't about to let Kaia go to brunch alone with a potential war criminal, so he let Dieter take over his work and tagged along. Barely had he sat down at a small table outside the cafe when he realized the irony of his cautiousness. Heaven forbid the little girl go off alone with *one* future war criminal, better make it *two* just to be safe.

"So, Kaia," Himmler said once the odd trio had been served their coffee and pastries. "What are you learning about in school right now?"

An innocuous question coming from the man who would one day proclaim that the children of lesser races should be forbidden from learning how to read, a talent that wouldn't serve their German masters. Kaia shrugged.

"Uhm, history stuff, some science. We learned about the Vikings last week, and that was fun 'cause they're kinda like Norse pirates!"

Maybe it was a coincidence, or maybe Kaia was simply uniquely talented at charming Nazis—if Reinhard had been told that she'd been created in a lab for the purpose, he would have believed it. Himmler's eyes twinkled at the mention of Vikings, his own personal obsession, and for the next ten minutes Reinhard sat, watching his untouched coffee go cold as the Head of the SS and the little Jewish girl talked about the ancient Nords.

"...and I read once that 'Viking' even means 'pirate raider.'"

"It does indeed!" Himmler said, finishing off his coffee. "You're very smart, Kaia. You must do very well in school."

"Uhhh...I do okay," the girl who was playing hooky proclaimed, sinking down a bit in her chair. "I don't really like school, though. The teachers are strict, and the other kids make fun of me all the time."

"Oh no!" squeaked Himmler, because of course the

thought of a precious little Aryan girl being bullied would offend sensitive Heinrich Himmler's soul. The *Reichsführer* leaned close to the child, spared a wink at Reinhard, and then said, "Well, let me tell you a secret, Kaia: the same thing happened to me when I was your age. My teachers were dreadful towards me, and my classmates were even worse. But, well, as you can see…"

Himmler leaned back and threw out his arms as though to gesture to his entire being. "Here I am! You'll come out on top just as I did, and that'll be your revenge. I can't imagine why anyone would make fun of a sweet thing like you. What do they tease you about?"

"Well, I had a spider living in my desk, and he was my school pet, and they killed him!" Kaia said, stabbing at her strudel with her fork, scowling down at the pastry. Himmler lifted a brow and shivered as though he could feel Kaia's little spider friend skittering up his spine.

"A…spider?" he said. "Well, erm, that is a bit of an unorthodox…pet."

"Spiders are good!" Kaia argued, looking up with a determined flash in her bright blue eyes that quite suddenly resembled Edmund's in their magnetism. "They're neat, and sometimes they're fuzzy, and they're artist bugs! I love their webs! And y'know…even if you think they're scary, almost all of them are completely harmless to humans. Most aren't poisonous, and they're actually good animals because they eat flies!"

"That's…hm…a very interesting perspective," Himmler said, fiddling with the ear-chain attached to his pince-nez glasses, his little nervous habit. "Although, myself, well, in the heat of the moment when I spot one in my house, I tend to err on the side of caution and squish it."

"You really shouldn't...even if you're scared..." Kaia mumbled, and Reinhard wondered if she was truly talking about spiders anymore. She was clever, despite her naïve trust in people's better nature. Either way, her lesson was clearly falling on deaf ears.

"Maybe not," Himmler said with a chuckle. "But better safe than sorry! Either way, you certainly don't deserve to be teased so cruelly, whatever your preference in pets. Maybe you could have your uncle teach those bullies a lesson, assuming he doesn't keel over. Reinhard, are you all right?"

"Peachy," lied Reinhard, pushing his coffee away and barely resisting the urge to projectile vomit right in Himmler's face.

"He's tired 'cause he had to take me home last night 'cause the streets are dangerous," Kaia said, and Himmler nodded, adopting an expression of gentle, paternal concern, like he was a schoolteacher offering an important life lesson.

"They are. You shouldn't walk in the dark without a man to protect you," he said. "Too many Bolsheviks and Jews crawling around right now that would love to get their mitts on a pretty thing like you. Don't trust anyone except your parents and the SS. And don't worry: Hitler will be President soon, and then the streets will be safe for girls like you."

Reinhard was about to choke on all the excess irony floating between the three of them. Kaia was evidently immune to it as she merely let out a small hum and finished off her strudel.

"This is really good, can I have more?" she asked.

"They *do* make good strudel here, but not as good as my

wife makes!" Himmler said fondly. "She uses apples from our farm. Very fresh. Next time I can convince her to make some, I'll drop them by the office and trust Reinhard to share with you. Tell you what: one more strudel on me, then I have to get running if I want to make my next meeting."

Himmler ordered the girl another strudel and chatted with her about his wife and daughter. Eventually, the *Reichsführer* stood up and declared that he had duties to attend to.

"Don't rush back to the office, Reinhard," Himmler said, slapping his underling's shoulder, sending a shiver through the exhausted Blond Beast's body. "Be sure to take care of Fräulein...ah! Forgive me, Kaia, I forgot to ask your surname!"

Don't be stupid enough to stay Goldstein, Reinhard prayed, and fortunately, Kaia was not so foolish. She smiled a bit cheekily and proclaimed, "It's Schicklgruber!"

For a moment, Reinhard was worried that particular surname—a surname that had belonged to the Führer's father before Alois abandoned it in favor of the decidedly more marketable *Hitler*—would be familiar to Himmler. Fortunately, the *Reichsführer* hadn't investigated his Messiah's family history that thoroughly, and so he merely nodded.

"Fräulein Schicklgruber, then!"

"You can just call me Kaia!" the child offered, and Himmler patted her head.

"It was lovely to meet you, Kaia! Stop by the Brown House whenever you like, even if your uncle isn't there. Reinhard, take care of her, all right? That's an order."

The only order Himmler would ever give to protect a Jew. Reinhard nodded and gave a firm, "Yes, sir."

"Bye!" Kaia squeaked, waving energetically as Himmler

plopped his SS cap back on his head and strolled off to continue his work creating the Third Reich.

"Schicklgruber?" Reinhard said once Himmler was long gone, glancing at the girl and at last letting the slightest of amused smiles pull at the edge of his lip. "Really?"

"What?" Kaia squeaked, pausing as she stabbed her strudel with her cream-covered fork. "I thought it was clever! Are you sure you don't want anything? It's on Himmler."

"He's gone, child," Reinhard pointed out, shaking his head when she pushed her plate of pastry towards him. "You'd have to pay."

"Nah ah." A familiar devilish gleam came to the girl's eyes. She reached into her pocket and pulled out a brown wallet stitched with the initials "HH."

"You did *not*," Reinhard said as the thieving little Jewess plucked a few Marks from Heinrich Himmler's pilfered wallet.

Kaia grinned, proud as a Viking with a ship full of stolen treasures, and proclaimed, "Revenge!"

Reinhard hated his voice, but more than that, he despised his laugh. It sounded more like a bleat than a laugh. He had been teased mercilessly by his naval comrades, called "Billy Goat Heydrich," because he had dared to laugh in their presence. He studiously avoided making himself laugh because of this, particularly in front of other people.

Reinhard couldn't help himself right then: he slapped one gloved hand over his mouth and laughed harder than he probably had in three years. It wasn't a good laugh— worse than usual, actually. Half a guffaw and half a hiccup with a bit of a choke mixed in because guilt was gnawing at him for daring to laugh after what he'd seen yesterday.

Kaia didn't laugh back, either at him or with him. She did smile widely, though, as though snatching a laugh from the Blond Beast was an accomplishment greater than stealing from Heinrich Himmler.

"ALL RIGHT, STUDENTS, HAVE A GOOD DAY AND REMEMBER: your midterm portfolios are due next week, and the exam is on the same day. The exam will just cover some of the readings on the great artists and their techniques, but the portfolio is the main bulk of your grade. If you can only focus on one thing because you're lazy, focus on the portfolio. Looking at you, Engel."

Over the din of students packing up their books and items, Adiel heard Engel mutter something to a fellow Stormtrooper about Jews.

Adiel sighed heavily, remembering his mother—Becca was still his mother, always would be, and he owed her more than his life, so he dearly wanted to adhere to her values. She would have wanted him to be like Kaia, to assume the best of Engel and his comrades, to say, *Maybe if I showed them the books, they'd be horrified like Heydrich. They'd change on the spot and help us. Engel's bad, but surely he wouldn't want to kill children.*

Then again, it was equally easy to envision Engel studying the books and grinning with pride. Heydrich was one thing: true, he was destined to become the Hangman of Prague, but they had gotten to him before he was anything resembling a true believer. According to Engel himself, he was from a long line of anti-Semites. Reinhard hadn't even been willing to die for the Nazi Cause yet, much less murder for them. Engel, meanwhile, had boasted of his willingness to take a bullet for Adiel's replacement.

"Professor Goldstein."

Adiel looked up and offered a small smile to one female student. Elfriede Lahner, one of his favorites. A sweet girl who was too afraid of retribution to erase the swastikas Leon drew on the chalkboard herself, but always offered the Professor words of comfort.

"I hope you're feeling better, sir," Elfriede said. "I was really worried when you didn't show up to class yesterday."

Her eyes darted briefly, but not too subtly, towards the Stormtrooper boys in the back of the classroom. Engel was fighting to put a tattered notebook into a thoroughly over-stuffed bag. Adiel gave Elfriede a smile and shook his head.

"I'm fine," he lied with a nervous laugh. "Just felt a little under the weather, but I'm glad to be back."

He really was. Right after he'd discovered the truth, Adiel had taken Monday off. He had wanted to prepare for Operation Tame the Blond Beast, and he had also hated the idea of going to class, looking at the faces of his students, innocent and hateful alike, and imagining the awful fate he had consigned them to in his former life.

What had happened to poor Elfriede? Or Max, who sometimes left an apple on his desk when he was sure that Leon and his goons weren't looking? Had they escaped? Succumbed to the poisonous swill of Nazism and turned on their Jewish teachers and classmates? Were they raped and killed by the Soviets that Adolf Hitler had prodded into ravishing the Reich after he decimated the East?

Adiel hadn't wanted to see them, any of them, convinced as he was that the guilt would rip him in two if he did. But strangely, now that he had returned, he felt better about it. It was nice to pretend that things were normal, that he was just a normal Jewish professor and nothing less.

Besides, sitting in his house and staring at Adolf Hitler's crimes would do him no good: better to keep living. He needed to find a way to vanquish his replacement so that he could continue on with his life unburdened. Nothing would have made Adolf Hitler angrier than knowing that he was destined to not only live and die happily as a Jew, but would ultimately foil his own wicked schemes.

Redemption was, in its own way, the best revenge.

"Hey, Papa!"

Elfriede smiled and bade the Professor farewell, wishing him good health and stepping aside, letting Kaia skip up to his desk. Adiel chuckled and pinched his daughter's ruddy cheek.

"Hello, Wolfchen!" he said. "You certainly got here quick. I'm going to guess you didn't go to school."

"Couldn't have focused anyway!" Kaia proclaimed. Fair enough. Adiel kissed the top of her head, drawing her close out of instinctual protectiveness when Engel finally zipped up his bag and stomped past, casting a withering glare at the Professor as he did so. Engel evidently didn't want to say anything nasty in front of such a young child because he kept silent and simply exited. Small virtues. Maybe he wasn't utterly irredeemable.

"Well, if you weren't in school, then I'm going to guess you were with *our mutual friend*," Adiel said, nervously glancing at the few students who hadn't filed out yet.

"Uh huh. He brought me here. He's waiting outside to make sure you can walk me home, and then he said he'd meet us at the house. He doesn't wanna be seen with you 'cause you're too Jewish. Err...that's what he said, I think he meant because of the kippa."

"Ah, right!" Adiel said, feeling a wave of giddiness as he brushed his fingers against the kippa on his head. Adolf Hitler had no doubt endlessly catastrophized about his seemingly Jewish features: the broad nose obscured by his toothbrush moustache, the dark hair, the shorter stature. Adiel had been indifferent to these physical traits all his life, but now he treasured every seemingly Semitic feature he happened to possess. The more Jewish he was, the less connection he had to that awful other life.

"Let's get going, Wolfchen," Adiel declared happily, grasping her hand and leading her out of the classroom, drinking in every disdainful look from the Academy's anti-Semites with utmost gusto. Every scowl from a Nazi was one more assurance that he wasn't Adolf Hitler.

REINHARD HAD NEVER BEEN "INTO" ART THE WAY THAT some people were. He could understand the fascination to a certain extent since he was "into" music in a way that Adiel surely wouldn't comprehend, but a song was a song. You listened to it and appreciated it while it played. He wasn't sure how anyone could gawk at even a beautiful piece of art for hours on end.

So he was only able to glance at a small, covered installation of student-made statues situated in front of the

Munich Academy of Fine Arts for about five seconds before he got bored, found a wall by the grand staircase, and had a smoke. Reinhard realized that he probably looked a little conspicuous, but as long as he didn't actually interact with Kaia or her father when they exited, he would probably be just fine.

The Blond Beast got a few looks from the students and professors who skittered down the steps and saw the Nazi loitering in the shadows: some admiring, some frightened, but fortunately they all left him alone. Reinhard saw Kaia and her father exit the building, Kaia skipping, Adiel keeping his head down. Briefly, he and the Professor locked eyes. Reinhard dropped his cigarette and stomped it out, waiting, giving the Goldsteins a generous head-start.

"Lieutenant Heydrich?"

An unfamiliar voice. Reinhard turned to see a young man in paint-covered slacks and a white button-up. Blond hair, blue-green eyes, not remarkable. He looked like every other SS man.

The student must have seen Reinhard's quizzical look because he laughed. "Ah, sorry, you probably don't remember me. I'm SA Private Leon Engel. We beat up some commie shits together when they met in that underground beer hall…"

"Oh. Sorry, I forget faces easily." That was a lie if there was one: Reinhard Heydrich never forgot anything. His photographic memory had served him well in school, as a naval cadet, and no doubt it would have become extremely useful once he became a genocidal maniac.

Reinhard studied the young man's features; he did somewhat remember him. A Brownshirt, yes, someone who had fought alongside him during street battles. He recalled the vicious grin that Engel had sported when he'd decked a Bolshevik with Semitic features right in the jaw.

Reinhard decided not to judge Engel too harshly. He had no idea what sort of man Leon was destined to become, after all. Maybe he would have learned the error of his ways and saved a school full of Jewish children from the bloodthirsty Butcher of Prague. Anything was possible. Better to be polite until he could get to the Goldstein household and look him up in Frau Goldstein's books. Leon offered his hand, and Reinhard gave it a firm shake.

"What brings you here, sir?" queried Leon, pointing towards the building behind him and declaring with a bitter chuckle, "This place won't offer much by way of beauty, I'm afraid. It's crawling with Jews right now."

"So I've heard," Reinhard said, hoping that Engel would mistake his tiredness for anti-Semitic disdain. "I was just passing by. Glanced at the statues and needed a smoke. I have to get back to work soon, I just need to clear my head sometimes."

"Right, I can imagine!" chortled Leon. "I have to get moving myself, can't leave the missus for too long with the little one."

"Ah...how old?" asked Reinhard, because making fathers talk about their children was the easiest way to distract them. Asking Himmler about his daughter Gudrun was the only way to make him shut up about ancient Germans.

"Three, and he's still a crazy little boy, haha! He takes after me. Ah...I'll let you go, but can I ask really quick: is the SS hiring? I know I'm only an art student, but I've done well in the SA. I'd like to, ah, maybe look for something more permanent in the Party, though. A real career."

"Ah...hm...I'm not sure about that," Reinhard blurted. "Himmler, he's very...strict about hiring, and our department is very small right now. I don't even have my own typewriter."

"Haha! My, they need to treat you better, sir!" Leon chuckled, but there was a shadow behind his eyes that was familiar to Reinhard: the same shadow that he'd seen in his own reflection when he'd been kicked out of the Navy.

"I can get by without a typewriter," Leon said. "And I have a clean family lineage going back to the 1700s. And my wife is clean too, we just checked her ancestry..."

"Err, listen, you'd have to take it up with Himmler," Reinhard said, desperately not wanting to induct a potentially blameless man into the murderous cult he himself had stumbled into, but also not wanting to appear suspicious by actively dissuading him. "My department might expand in the future, but not now."

"Right! I'll give him a call. Thanks anyway, sir! I'll be heading home. Ah, Sieg Heil!"

Leon gave a loyal fascist salute. Reinhard realized right then that he hadn't given the salute at all since he'd found out about his future.

"Sieg Heil," he said, hastily lifting up his arm. Reinhard hated the fact that he was certain he would be using that salute for the rest of his life.

NINE

"Ah, there you are!"

"Apologies. A gentleman held me up. Wanted to ask about joining the SS."

"By any chance was his name Leon Engel?"

"Good guess."

"Ha! He's anything but a gentleman. Don't let yourself get held up by him again, all right? Kaia was worried when she realized that you weren't following us."

"She was worried about me?" snorted Reinhard as Adiel opened the wrought-iron gate and let the Nazi Lieutenant onto the Goldstein property.

"She likes you," said Adiel with a shrug, and there was an unsaid *I'm not sure why* that hung in the air between the former Führer and his ex-minion.

Reinhard hummed. Briefly, he considered telling Adiel about little Kaia's encounter with Heinrich Himmler and her visit to the Brown House, but he decided against saying anything. The little loudmouth would likely tell her father if she felt safe to do so, and if not, well, Reinhard didn't want to be the reason she got a beating. It was against his nature to share information unless it was absolutely necessary anyway, and since he, Head of the SD, was the only person who would have had the motive or the means to investigate little Kaia "Schicklgruber," he decided there was no reason to snitch.

"Where is she?" Reinhard asked as Adiel let him into the manor and led him into a large sitting room. Reinhard stole a glance at the Goldsteins' piano, which was, as he'd suspected, a gorgeous instrument that probably cost more than the Nazi Lieutenant would make in three years.

Or at least more than he would make until he started ripping gold teeth from the mouths of old ladies.

"She really wanted to help us brainstorm," chuckled Adiel, gesturing to an easel set up near a long coffee table piled high with Becca's books. Reinhard almost let out a laugh: Kaia had set up the easel like some kind of office presentation. At the top of the canvas, in her untidy script, she'd painted:

PLANS TO SAVE THE WORLD!

OPTION 1: TALK TO UNCLE EDMUND AND MAKE HIM BETTER!

Beside that extremely naïve suggestion, Kaia had drawn a smiley face and a heart.

It was so cute that Reinhard might have died of diabetes right then if he didn't recognize that it was also sad. The poor little outcast girl had lost her mother and her grandmother, and now she learned about a living family member and wanted so badly to save him even though he wanted nothing more than to kill her.

"I didn't want her looking in the books again, and neither did Papa," Adiel explained, plopping down on the couch. "Luckily, my mother packed this movie she liked from the future, *The Great Dictator*. Papa and Kaia are watching it right now. 'Research.' Should keep her out of our hair for a little bit. Ah, you can hang your coat over there. I haven't gotten too far reading the books, haven't had any brilliant ideas myself."

Reinhard nodded, whipping off his coat. Hardly had he stepped towards the coatrack when his eyes darted down and he nearly winced. He was still bedecked in his slightly rumpled SS uniform, swastika armband and all. Reinhard suddenly became acutely aware of all the Jewish trappings surrounding him: the menorah resting above the piano, the shelves laden with books deciphering the Torah, the paintings of Hebrew calligraphy decorating the walls. It felt as though every piece of Judaica was a set of his future victims' eyes staring, rebuking.

"The, ah, the uniform, should I—?" Reinhard asked, turning to Adiel and gesturing towards the offending outfit. Maybe taking it off would be best, at least the armband, but then again maybe Adiel wouldn't want him to leave it lying around. Heaven forbid he forget it like he'd forgotten his wallet. Reinhard could all but see Kaia thinking that it would be hilarious to put it on and goose-step right into the Brown House to return it to him.

"Ah, don't worry about it," said Adiel, grabbing a hefty book. "Do whatever makes you comfortable."

Comfortable. Reinhard hadn't been *comfortable* since he'd first learned exactly how awful he truly was. He would have been most *comfortable* never learning about any of this, continuing on with his murderous destiny, dying in Prague slowly and painfully thinking that he was a good person.

Too late for that. He sat on a floral couch across from Adiel and got to reading.

Not much to Reinhard's taste, reading—good as he was with files and as much as he liked the occasional spy novel, reading had never been something he liked to do. It was too quiet an activity for the ever-active Reinhard Heydrich, and he quickly found himself glancing up at his compatriot, who, for his part, was obviously able to not only focus well, but read at an admirable speed.

"Find anything interesting yet?" Reinhard queried when Adiel's grim but determined expression melted into a harsh scowl that looked too much like the face Edmund Hitler had pulled for the cover of *Mein Kampf.*

"You said you bumped into Leon Engel earlier," Adiel said, and it was obvious that he was barely suppressing his anger. "Look."

The Professor slid his book towards Reinhard, pointing to one particular blurb in the upper right-hand corner, a mini-biography that the book had chosen to highlight.

Unsurprisingly, there was Leon Engel, ten years older and dressed in an SS uniform. (Grey instead of black. Was Himmler going to change it at some point?) Engel stood rigidly a few feet behind Adolf Hitler while the Führer greeted some guests at his Berghof home. (Reinhard stole a glance at Adiel. It really was amazing how little he looked like his other self, maybe because of the absence of the toothbrush moustache. Maybe Hitler was nothing more than a moustache and a hateful scowl.)

The blurb mentioned a few biographical details: date of birth, a few facts about Leon Engel's future career as one of Hitler's bodyguards, but the last paragraph was clearly what had bothered the Professor.

"Unbeknownst to Leon Engel, however, his own wife was a member of the famous resistance movement, the Black Foxes, whose primary mission was to rescue Jews. Anniska Engel (1913-1941), also known as Black Fox 25, was working undercover to smuggle Jewish families to safety.

"However, tragedy would strike when her thirteen-year-old son Norman Engel (1928-1944) would discover her activities and report them to the infamous SD Special Agent Jonas Amsel, aka "The Fox Hunter" (1917-1942). Amsel immediately arrested Anniska Engel. In order to prove his loyalty to the Führer, Leon Engel personally executed his wife. It is unknown if Engel asked for this task, or if it was demanded by his superiors."

Startling, especially because the name of the arresting officer immediately leapt out to Reinhard: Jonas Amsel, Dieter's fourteen-year-old son who, if Dieter's affectionate diatribes were anything to go by, was absolutely head-over-heels for the eldest daughter of the Jewish Keller family. Reinhard would have to read more about the Amsels later, but for now, he looked up at the Professor, who was grasping at the fabric of his pants and grinding his teeth together.

"Awful," Reinhard concurred. "Though I'm not sure we're in a position to judge him, you and I."

"He always talks about her," Adiel said, his voice halting. "Anniska, his wife. Tries to use her to guilt-trip me into giving him better grades, and I almost fell for it. He talked about her the way I talked about Emma."

"Emma...oh..." Reinhard's gaze shifted to one picture above Adiel's head, to a smiling woman who was unmistakably Kaia's mother. "Your wife."

"He always says he loves her, but clearly he doesn't because why would he...?" Adiel gestured to the books.

"Things change, like you said," Reinhard noted. "Not to defend him, but I'm sure if you walked up to him right now and told him he's going to shoot his own wife, he'd say, 'I'd never do that.' But if you'd walked up to me a week ago and told me that I was going to murder a million children, I'd have said the same thing."

"Right..." whispered Adiel, his shoulders slackening, craning his neck to steal a glance at his wife's portrait. "I'd never hurt my wife...I like to think that, anyway. But God knows what I did to her when I was Adolf."

"'Let he who is without sin cast the first stone,'" Reinhard quoted with not a small amount of bitterness. He had hoped that he would never have to dredge up those Bible verses his mother had beaten into him again, but it made Adiel chuckle at least.

"Right. Can't be a hypocrite," the Professor agreed. "I have plenty of other reasons to hate the little shit anyway. It's still disturbing, though...not even Leon, but his son. Norman. It says the boy was only thirteen when he betrayed his own mother. Why would any child do such a thing? Not to say 'I'd never' again, Heaven knows I certainly hurt my own mother as Adolf, but..."

"Maybe she was an awful mother?" Reinhard suggested. "Besides that: brainwashing, propaganda. Children can be easily influenced."

KAIA HAD SEEN CHARLIE CHAPLIN FILMS BEFORE: THE American Tramp was a comedic delight who could never fail to make her laugh. All of the Chaplin films she had seen before had been silent, so it was rather nice to actually hear his voice even though she could only somewhat follow along with the English.

"Bubbe Becca brought this movie from the future?" she squeaked when her grandfather set it up for her, and Natan laughed.

"Some GI screened it for us when the war ended, sweetie. Personally, I thought it was a little offensive because it's a comedy. I didn't think anything about the war could be funny. But it made your grandmother laugh so hard, harder than I'd seen her laugh since we were deported. She loved it so much that the GI gave it to her as a gift. You'll like it. Becca absolutely loved the ending speech."

The plot of *The Great Dictator* was easy enough to decipher even though Kaia couldn't understand every word of it: two stories destined to intersect. Charlie Chaplin played Adenoid Hynkel, a parody of her father's alternate self. At the same time, Chaplin also played a gentle Jewish barber that, by pure coincidence, looked just like the ridiculous warmonger. The Barber reminded her quite a bit of her father.

Natan, who had evidently seen *The Great Dictator* one too many times, fell asleep around the scene where Adenoid danced with a giant balloon-globe, leaving Kaia sitting at his feet in their little private theater, petting Bernie as the pup happily chewed on an antler.

Eventually, the kind Jewish Barber was sent to a concentration camp—which was, in the film, not nearly as horrifying as what her grandfather had described, but maybe Chaplin simply hadn't fathomed how terrible the camps could be. Either way, the Jewish Barber managed to escape the camp, and coincidentally enough, he did so right as the

Great Dictator himself was out hunting. The Nazi guards mistook their own leader for the fugitive Jew and arrested him while the Jewish Barber, having donned a Nazi uniform during his escape, was confused for the Führer and sent to speak to Hynkel's fascist forces.

Kaia could see why her grandmother had loved the ending so much. Pretending to be the Great Dictator, the gentle Jewish Barber announced that he'd had a change of heart and called for peace, liberty, and love between all the races of Europe. His speech resounded across the continent, and the bloody war was over before it could truly begin.

Natan, fortunately, was a deep sleeper, and so he didn't wake up even as the movie ended and Kaia leapt to her feet.

"Eureka!" the child squeaked in delight. "Bernie, I've got a eureka! I know what to do!"

"You've got a very contemplative look on your face. Think of anything?"

"Hm? Oh. No. Nothing yet. Sorry, I got a little distracted."

"Distracted?" repeated Adiel, who, after spending two hours reading about his own gruesome crimes, was more than eager for a distraction of his own. Heydrich, who hadn't flipped the page of the hardback he was reading for almost five minutes, sighed and turned the book towards Adiel.

Heydrich had found another picture of his alternate

self, but this one was significantly less sinister. The Hangman, bedecked in civilian garb, sat flanked by Heider and Klaus Heydrich, smiling tenderly as he held baby Silke in his arms.

"That's my daughter," Reinhard said, his tone oddly dull. "And my sons."

"Silke, Klaus, Heider," Adiel said with a nod, offering the Lieutenant a small smile. "Good thing you picked a unique girl's name, or you wouldn't have believed me."

"She's...cute," Reinhard muttered, turning the book back towards himself and staring down at his baby daughter's image with an odd expression, like that of a hound seeing a car for the first time. "They're all cute. Hm...this is what I imagined, you know. Being normal, but..."

Reinhard pursed his lips tightly and paused for a moment, his eyes flitting from his daughter to his other self. "It's odd...that I was...*normal*. It feels like if I did every horrible thing that I did in these books, then it must be because I went mad or something, because I wasn't really *myself* anymore. Not *normal*. But..."

Heydrich shook his head. "I guess not. I guess some normal people just aren't normal. Or maybe nobody's really normal..."

"What you said before, about me not understanding what you're going through..." Adiel said in his most empathetic tone, glancing at the menorah perched on a nearby shelf. "You were sort of right. I'm glad I'm as different as I am. I think it makes all of this easier to deal with."

"I didn't intend that as an insult," Reinhard muttered. "I envy you. Even though I don't want to be a Jew, I *do* wish I was so different that none of this was so..."

"Papa! Herr Reinhard! I've got it!"

Reinhard slammed the book shut and shoved the most graphic tomes aside. Adiel leapt to his feet and attempted to intercept Kaia as she dashed into the sitting room and made for the "Plans to Save the World" canvas, pencil in hand and Bernie bouncing at her heels.

"Kaia, where is Zaidy?" queried Adiel, sighing in amused frustration as the girl easily out-maneuvered him, ducking under his legs and scurrying to the board. While she stood on her tiptoes and wrote something out, Bernie held Heydrich hostage by lying down on the Nazi's boots and offering him a big, slobbering smile. Reinhard didn't look particularly amused and made no move to pet the mutt. Evidently, Reinhard Heydrich was not much of a dog person.

"Zaidy's sleeping, hush!" Kaia commanded. "I've gotta eureka! There we go!"

She tossed the pencil onto the coffee table and stepped back, proudly gesturing to her addendum. *OPTION 2: OPERATION CHAPLIN!*

"Chaplin?" Reinhard said. He had surrendered to the hound and was scratching Bernie behind his ears. Kaia launched into a detailed and, to the naked ear, exceptionally odd summary of the Charlie Chaplin comedy she'd been watching with her grandfather. She spoke excitedly of the Prince-and-Pauper-esque escapades that apparently culminated in a mix-up between a kind Jew and a wicked dictator which brought about world peace.

"So you see," Kaia proclaimed, turning to the list, grabbing the pencil, and adding a little drawing: her father's smiling face on one side, then Edmund Hitler's scowling visage on the other, then two arrows cross-crossing between them.

"You said before that Mama thought you two were twins, and you look so much the same!" the girl said. "We should make you grow a moustache like Uncle Edmund, and then we can sneak in during New Year's with Herr Reinhard's help. We'll knock Edmund out, kidnap him, and you can take his place and pretend to be him! Then, while you make sure there's no war, we can talk to Uncle Edmund while he's our hostage and make him better, and then we can let him go and you guys can swap back once he's good!"

A jumbled, naïve, adorable plan that was childish and *entirely* Kaia. Adiel chuckled and knelt before his daughter, patting her head. "Kaia, that's..."

"That's it."

Reinhard's voice and the sound of the Nazi rising to his feet made Adiel glance at his partner-in-preventing-crime with a raised eyebrow. The Blond Beast ushered Bernie towards Kaia and stood above Adiel, gesturing for him to stand. Adiel did so, and Heydrich leaned uncomfortably close, making the Professor squirm as the Blond Beast's wolf-blue eyes burrowed directly into him.

Reinhard let out a disappointed little huff and stepped back. "It *could* work," he said. "You definitely look exactly like him, a dead ringer if you grew a moustache, but there's something missing."

"Missing?" repeated Adiel, and Reinhard stroked his chin and shook his head as though he was a musician that couldn't think up the right lyrics.

"Or...well, I don't even know if I'd say it's *missing*, but you don't have the right...*aura*."

"'Cause Papa's too nice to be Hitler?" piped up Kaia, and that earned a small chuckle from the Blond Beast.

"Precisely, actually," Reinhard replied.

"I know Hitler. I served with him," Adiel said. "I might not *be* him, but I know what he's *like*."

"Then why don't you just pretend, Papa?" Kaia suggested, practically bouncing with enthusiasm. "Like acting! Like Chaplin! You're a good actor anyway when you pretend to be mad at me! Herr Reinhard can train you to act like Uncle Edmund, and we have all the books to tell us everything he should know, so you can study, and no one will know the difference!"

Adiel nodded at his daughter, but kept his gaze trained on Heydrich: it seemed astounding that the cool-headed Lieutenant was even considering a plan that was, on its surface, so childish. But then again, if they wanted to stop Hitler without stopping Hitler, Kaia's plan was likely the best one they had so far.

Still, Adiel caught a few hints of anxiousness from Heydrich: a shift of his shoulders, a gaze that flitted from Adiel to Kaia, something resembling guilt flashing in his lake-blue eyes.

"Child," Heydrich said at last, his voice oddly gentle as he squatted down so that he wasn't positively towering over her. "It's a good plan, but we need to think about it. Also…"

He gestured towards Bernie, who wasn't so much wagging his tail as wagging his entire body while he tried to lick Heydrich's face. "Your dog is harassing me. Could you take him somewhere else?"

Transparent as before. Kaia let out a frustrated sigh and grabbed Bernie's collar. "Fiiiine! Just tell me when you want me to go away! You don't have to make up an excuse!"

"Forgive me, *kleine*, you're just too smart," Heydrich

said, and it sounded like he was barely suppressing a chuckle as the girl dragged her squirming hound back down into the theater, leaving the two adults to ponder her scheme.

"You think her plan is crazy enough to work?" Adiel said once he was absolutely certain that the girl was out of earshot, smiling as he glanced at his daughter's rather impressive sketch of his face. Heydrich's jaw was tight, and his posture became as rigid as it was in so many pictures of his iron-hearted alternate self.

"Yes, with some obvious edits," Reinhard said, and his voice was strangely detached. "First, you'd need a significant amount of training to impersonate the Führer. Additionally, kidnapping Edmund Hitler won't work. We'd have to kill him. Disfigure his face, maybe have you shoot him in the head if you could."

"Look, I'm not thrilled about the idea of killing someone, but I've shot at people for less. I don't care," Adiel said, plopping down in a cozy chair and crossing his arms over his chest. That wasn't quite a lie, though it wasn't the full truth either. Adiel didn't relish the idea of shooting someone he had once considered a friend, much less someone who was not only his brother, but a victim in a way. It should have been *him* in Edmund's shoes: miserable and hate-filled, the target of righteous assassins. It felt wrong in a way, like he'd cheated at life itself.

"If saving Europe means manning up and killing my brother, I'll do it myself," Adiel declared despite these misgivings. "I don't need you to—"

"That's not the main problem," Reinhard interrupted, heaving a sigh and glancing down at Becca's books. "This plan of Kaia's might be our best option, but do you realize what it will mean for you?"

There was a sinisterness to Heydrich's query, like he was asking Adiel what type of coffin he would like to be buried in. The Professor shook his head.

"Adiel Goldstein would need to die," Heydrich declared. "You would need to take Hitler's life; become the man you were supposed to be. Your life would be over. Maybe in ten years when Europe is at peace, we could fake your death or something along those lines, but that's unlikely. There's every chance you would have to live the rest of your life as Hitler. Die as Hitler."

Heydrich's gaze shifted to the wall, to the cheerful Goldstein family pictures, to an image of Kaia grinning happily as she embraced her father during a day at the zoo. "You would likely never be able to see your daughter again. *Ever.* If your cover was blown, it could mean the destruction of Europe. You couldn't take the chance, even to see her, not even once."

Those words felt like a thousand hot needles puncturing every inch of Adiel's brain. Everything else would have been a torment. Living the life that Natan and Becca had saved him from, even a gentler version. Becoming Hitler when his one comfort was that he *wasn't* Hitler, that he was so different that even Heydrich thought he would need *training* to pass as him.

Adiel could have gritted his teeth and dealt with all of that for the sake of redemption, but the mere idea that he would never hold his daughter again, that he wouldn't see her graduate school or meet her husband or give her away on her wedding day...

"I can't do that!" Adiel gasped, grasping at his chest. It

already felt like Kaia was a part of his heart manifest, and giving her up would be no better than ripping his heart in two. "I *can't*...she's my daughter, you can't possibly expect..."

Heydrich's gaze became frosty, frighteningly similar to that of his genocidal counterpart. "I see," he drawled. "So, what you said about redemption was nonsense. *I* should give up everything, my entire life, *I* should suffer, but not *you*..."

"Look! You don't have children yet! You don't understand what you're asking of me!" Adiel cried, leaping from his chair, both fists clenched at his sides. Heydrich stepped back, and there was a brief, hopeful glint in his eyes.

"There," the Blond Beast said. "You can pass as him just fine."

"And I'm willing to!" Adiel insisted. "Look...it's not that I'm not willing to make sacrifices for this. If it costs me my life, fine, but I can't...I can't keep going in life without being able to see or know what my daughter's doing. I *can't* do that! I'd rather be dead!"

"Fine, but would you rather see *twelve million people* dead?!" Heydrich barked. It was a little odd to hear him *shout* when he seemed like such an icy person in general. Fiery anger didn't suit him, but it seemed that Adiel's hesitancy was aggravating an already irate Blond Beast.

Reinhard took a step forward, gesturing towards the books and snapping, "One-and-a-half million children! Does *that* sound fair? Especially when at the end of the day, this is *your* fault, *Adolf!*"

"*Don't call me that! Do* **not** *call me that!*"

Reinhard's shout was nothing compared to Adiel's: the Professor didn't tend to scream, but when he did right then, his deep voice echoed about the Goldstein manor. His blue eyes flashed with a strange sort of power before filling with tears. The momentary lapse made guilt tear through the Professor, and he glanced at a picture of his mother, mentally apologizing to her spirit before he collapsed back into his chair, covering his face with his hands.

"I am not him…I'm *not* him…" Adiel insisted, and even he didn't know if he was speaking to Heydrich or the universe itself.

"Adiel." Reinhard placed emphasis on the Professor's true name as he spoke. "I'm sorry, but I'm also right. Whether or not it's your fault is actually immaterial: you need to think beyond yourself as an individual. I'm going to leave. Just…act natural and think about it for a few days. But decide quickly. The New Year is coming soon."

Heydrich was a swift man: by the time Adiel found the strength to lift up his head, the Blond Beast was already gone with his coat and death's-head cap. Left alone, Adiel could only glance between his family photos and his former sins, desire and guilt battling in his chest as he pondered whether or not to become Hitler again.

TEN

Adiel went to sleep in his warm room, in a cozy, soft bed. He awoke sore, dazed, kneeling on a cold floor with chains restraining his wrists. He blinked to clear his blurry vision and found that his hands were bound before him. His pajamas had been replaced with striped, black-and white-prisoner apparel. There was a number sewn onto his breast.

"Ah. Welcome back."

A voice, not quite strange but not quite familiar either, like the voice of a teacher from his youth. Adiel looked up and realized that he was chained and kneeling in the midst of a strangely ornate circular room.

The walls were blindingly white and blank save for a glass display case hanging on the farthest wall which seemed to contain a grey garment, a sackcloth. The roof seemed nonexistent, taken up instead by what appeared to be a nighttime sky. The ground...Adiel shifted his weight and looked down. It felt...strange. Like he was kneeling on water made semi-solid: not ice, and yet just as fragile. He hesitated to move very much lest the black waters beneath somehow break forth and take him. Pillars of darkness erupted from the floor, forming eight columns that stretched into the night-sky ceiling.

In the center of the room was a grand desk that seemed to be fashioned from black diamonds. A silver eye with a flame for a pupil was carved onto the front of the desk, and it felt as though the insignia was moving, living, *watching*.

Flanking the desk were two small figures: children, it seemed, and yet there was something distinctly inhuman to them. Their apparel was strange: both wore identical red cloaks and hoods, black boots, and curved mirror masks that covered their faces completely. They stood rigidly, hands behind their backs, wooden swords at their sides, staring not at him, but right past him.

Sitting at the grand desk, drumming black-gloved fingers on the onyx surface, was a man in apparel equally strange as that of the tiny guards. The man was bedecked in a black cloak and hood with an upside-down yellow triangle emblazoned on his chest. He wore a mirror mask just like those of the red-cloaked guards. Though his eyes were covered, he must have been able to see nonetheless as he kept his gaze fixed upon a piece of sun-gold paper laid out on his desk. Beside the document he was studying was a folded-up napkin that reminded Adiel of the type he would see at fancy dinners, the ones that would contain every sort of fork, spoon, and knife.

"What's going on?" The query, reasonable enough, vaulted from Adiel's lips without his will. The black-cloaked figure before him made a noise like the sort his mother would make (*Becca, like Becca, Becca was his mother, nobody else*) when she caught him doing something naughty as a boy and he denied it: amused disapproval.

"You were found guilty," said the black-cloaked figure in the strangely familiar voice—a stranger? No, a prosecutor. Adiel knew that somehow, even though he wasn't supposed to.

The Prosecutor leaned forward, lacing gloved fingers together and tilting his masked face sideways. "Tell me...what do you think should be done with the wicked? With evil souls? Should they be shown mercy, or should they be punished for their crimes?"

Adiel gritted his teeth. The Prosecutor leaned back, his posture shifting into one of resignation as he laid his hands flat on his black-diamond desk.

"I think," the Prosecutor said, his amused tone morphing into one of utter bitterness, "your answer would be obvious given what you did with your life."

"There's been a mistake. I'm a good person."

Adiel found himself uttering those words without thought, without commanding his vocal cords, as though his body wasn't his. The Prosecutor threw back his head and let out a single laugh that sent ripples across the ground and made Adiel's ears burn.

"I think even you would be truly shocked to know how many times a day I hear those words," the Prosecutor said, grabbing a pen and hastily scrawling something onto the paper in front of him. "God makes no mistakes...*none*. He gave you free will, and He never took it from you even when you abused it, even when you used your free will to torment others. But now..."

The Prosecutor looked up and let the pen fall from his

fingers. "Now your actions will have consequences. You went too far, and now you've been disowned by God. Now you belong to me. So I ask again: what do you think should happen to a man like you?"

And once more, words vaulted from Adiel's throat, desperate and in a commanding tone that *wasn't him* but was familiar, too familiar. "I'm a good man! I did nothing wrong! I was trying to save my nation, to save the entire world from—!"

"*Enough.*" The Prosecutor rose to his feet, his single command making the black water beneath them tremble.

"Your opinion no longer matters," the Prosecutor said, and with a casual flick of his wrist, he unrolled the folded-up napkin, revealing a small array of silver tools. Scalpels and scissors shimmered.

"Your will no longer matters," the Prosecutor continued. "You were given free will by a lenient, loving God and you abused it. Now...now you will have a different God."

The eye on the desk suddenly shut. The Prosecutor picked up a small pair of scissors. He opened them and they glowed crimson.

"This will hurt, but believe me, it's better than the alternative…" the Prosecutor said. He lifted up his face, and the reflection that looked back at Adiel from the angel's mask was *not him, not him, not him.*

"After all, as we say: **Hell is Mercy.**"

Then, there was pain, pain like nothing he had ever experienced. Not even shooting himself in the head. *(No, he hadn't done that, that was Adolf, he was Adiel, Adiel, Adiel…)*

"Adiel!"

And then Adiel was in his soft bed, in his pajamas, flailing as Natan burst into his room.

"Adiel, are you all right?" Natan cried as his stolen son struggled for a moment to remember where he was and *who* he was.

"I-I-I…!" Adiel stuttered, feeling a wave of relief crash over him when he ran a hand along his sweat-soaked but still unshaven face. He was Adiel, still.

"Papa, we'll save you!"

In bolted Kaia with Bernie at her heels. The dog immediately leapt upon the bed and lapped the sweat from Adiel's face while Kaia, wearing her little tin helmet, brandished a wooden sword that reminded Adiel a bit too much of the ones carried by the red-cloaked guards in his dream.

"Oh…nothing…" Kaia mumbled as her gaze swept her father's room. She dropped her sword and joined Bernie on Adiel's bed. Natan chuckled and combed his hands through his silver locks.

"You scared me, son," he said. "You really screamed loud. I thought you were being attacked. Bad dream?"

"Bad and strange…" muttered Adiel, his eyes flitting to his father's arm, to the blue number he (*no, not he, Adolf had done that, and he was Adiel*) had emblazoned onto the man. Eager to look away from his father-victim, he glanced down at Kaia, who had removed her helmet and was fiddling with it, a thoughtful frown marring her adorable face.

"Hey, Bernie, move over! Kaia's cuter than you," Adiel said, pushing the puppy aside and gathering the girl into his lap. Kaia giggled and Bernie, not one to be deterred, nudged the helmet out of her hands and leaned against her. She hugged the dog tight and settled against her father's chest.

"What about you, silly thing?" Adiel chuckled, nudging

his head towards her helmet. "Thought I was being attacked by burglars? Came in to protect me?"

"No..." Kaia muttered, her bright blue eyes flitting to and fro, lingering on shadows like they had when she was very little and would insist that strange creatures were lurking in the darkness. "Actually...I've been worried about the Demon King."

"Ah," Adiel said, glancing at Natan. The old man shook his head and sat at the foot of the bed, putting a comforting hand on his granddaughter's knee.

"Don't worry, sweetheart," Natan declared. "Asmodeus liked us. Even though he was a demon, he wasn't completely evil. He even said he doesn't like to hurt people who don't bother him. Your grandma told me all about him, and you read about him in her books, right?"

"Yeah..."

"Then you know that he isn't going to come and hurt you."

"I'm not worried about me, I keep worrying about Papa," Kaia confessed, clinging to the front pocket of Adiel's pajama shirt and aggressively nestling against him. "Even if it's silly, I keep thinking he's gonna come and take Papa away 'cause we did the deal wrong."

Kaia craned her neck back so that she could look at Adiel's face, her great blue eyes shining with a sort of fear that he hadn't seen in them since the day before Becca had passed away. "I don't want that," the child declared. "I wanna have Papa forever."

The feelings from the dream briefly flooded Adiel's soul: the horrific sensation of being someone else, someone with a burning heart and a head full of lies. Reinhard's accusatory arguments echoed in his ears.

Adiel squeezed his daughter tight and rested his cheek in her curly hair.

"Don't worry. Papa's not going anywhere," he assured her, and he hated that he didn't know whether or not he was lying.

"AND YOU'RE ABSOLUTELY CERTAIN WE HAVE TO POSTPONE *again?*"

"Lina, my darling, I don't want to disappoint you..." Reinhard squeezed the phone tight, fighting to keep a nervous stutter from entering his voice as he spoke to his fiancée.

"It's not that I'm impatient, Reinhard...well, I *am* impatient. *Von Osten* sounds fancy, but *Heydrich* is just a better surname!"

Reinhard laughed, and this time he utterly failed to suppress his nervousness. He wondered if she had enjoyed having that last name at the end of the other timeline, when *Heydrich* was not merely an honorable SS upstart that had charmed her into marrying him with his bluntness and his violin skills. Maybe when *Heydrich* was synonymous with genocide, Lina would prefer her maiden name.

"Reinhard, it's fine, really," Lina said, her voice becoming gentler. Reinhard loosened his death-grip on the phone. It would have been unmanly to talk to her about his insecurities, but she already knew them from experience. In the days after he had been kicked out of the Navy, Reinhard had been utterly terrified that Lina would leave him. She would have had every right to do so, after all: he had nothing to offer as a disgraced, penniless ex-naval officer that she barely knew.

Any other woman would have left him, but Lina hadn't. She had loved him enough to stand by him. Reinhard would always be grateful for that, no matter what the future held.

Really, it was a bit stupid that he was panicking this much about merely pushing back the day of their wedding, which had already been pushed back from November and should have taken place on the 26th of December. Lina was generally a very forgiving woman.

Lina almost certainly *wouldn't* have been so forgiving, however, if Reinhard had called her up and told the full truth. *Sorry, darling, but I need to delay the wedding because me and a Jew who was going to be Hitler in another timeline need to find a way to kill your favorite politician before he takes over Europe and I become a baby-killer. Does January 12th sound good to you?*

No. *That* probably would have made her decide that they should start seeing other people.

Fortunately, Reinhard's excuse actually made Lina quite excited: he claimed that he simply couldn't have a wedding in December when he had been offered an all-important assignment to arrange the Führer's New Year's security.

"Consider this a great opportunity: I'll have a chance to meet Hitler face-to-face. I might be decent at multi-tasking, but for this, I need to be completely focused. Besides, when we marry, I want to *only* be thinking of you."

"Aw!" Lina giggled, and Reinhard smirked. *Too easy.*

"You *are* right, actually, Reini," Lina said. "I'd feel terrible if something happened to the Führer while you were busy worrying about my silly feelings. Obviously, your work comes first. It's too important."

"Of course," Reinhard said, his smile wilting. He could only hope that Adiel would make up his mind, choose to be selfless, choose to make sure that something horrible happened to the Führer.

"Focus on your work! We'll plan something nice for January when I have your full attention," Lina said. "And don't feel bad. Your success is my success, after all! If you do well, it's like I did well!"

"Right..." Reinhard could not help but let a lilt of sadness enter his voice. It was true what she said: he never would have joined the Nazi Party, much less the SS, if not for Lina. He had always thought that the Nazis were absolute clowns, but Lina had seen Hitler speak once and had become politically enthralled. When Reinhard had been kicked out of the Navy and his godmother's son, who happened to work with Himmler in the SS, had suggested he join the fledgling paramilitary unit, Lina had pushed. When Himmler had tried to cancel their interview, Lina had literally forced Reinhard to pack his bags and had all but shoved him onto the train against his will, insisting that he go anyway and convince Himmler to hire him.

And he had. Because he hadn't wanted to be a worthless failure who didn't deserve her.

Lina was proud of herself for that. She always had been. She was proud of him, and proud of herself for pushing him.

Reinhard wondered what she would say if she saw the ultimate fruits of her labor. She'd hate him, of course. Maybe she'd insist that the books were lies and claim that her beloved Reinhard would *never* do such a thing.

Maybe she would approve. Reinhard dismissed that idea before it was even fully formed. No. Lina was a more ardent Nazi than he right then, but she wouldn't marry a baby-killer. Never.

Never. He hated how worthless that word was now.

"Reinhard, darling, are you all right?" Lina's worried voice yanked him from his morbid, terrible thoughts.

"I'm fine," Reinhard lied. If he continued to be this good at lying, he would surpass Joseph Goebbels in no time. "Just tired. Moving offices right now, should probably go make sure Amsel didn't mess anything up. I'll call you again later and we can set the new date, all right?"

"All right! Will it be okay if I come up for Christmas, though? I really wanted to celebrate with you."

"I think so. We could get you a hotel if my landlady isn't willing to let us live in sin for the night. Himmler's throwing a Christmas party—sorry, *Yule* party. You might want to stay where you are if he forces me to go."

"Haha! I'll endure it to spend Christmas—sorry, *Yule*—with you. Himmler is so odd sometimes."

"You have no idea..." Reinhard sighed. "Listen, I love you, all right?"

"I would hope so, we're going to get married one of these days!"

"One of these days," Reinhard concurred. "Hope to see you soon, *schatzi.*"

Reinhard hung up and shuffled into the other room. Viktoria Edrich, Reinhard's elderly landlady, was knitting a sweater. Once he walked into the small sitting area, she greeted him with a warm smile.

"Apologies, Herr Heydrich, I didn't mean to snoop..." the old lady started to say, and Reinhard shook his head.

"You're fine, Frau Edrich: I don't mind *you* snooping on me, it's everyone else I'm worried about."

"Certainly, that's why you're renting out the other room, correct?"

"Yes, ma'am," Reinhard said, perking up his ears and listening to the sound of Dieter barking orders at a few SS men who were setting up Reinhard's new office, a single room right beside his apartment, ostensibly rented because the Blond Beast feared that the Brown House was a breeding ground for leaks and spies.

Reinhard had thought of moving out of the Brown House and into a more private, secure space a few times before Adiel had ever showed him his potential future. That newfound knowledge had pushed him to act on his little idea, and Viktoria, a longtime National Socialist, had been more than happy to let him rent the space cheaply since he was supposedly doing it for the Cause she valued so highly.

Really, of course, Reinhard was doing it because it lessened the chance of some SS upstart discovering his link to the Goldsteins. Plus, this way he could avoid the lion's den.

"Did I hear you say you were going to be in charge of guarding the Führer when he returns to Munich?" Viktoria queried. Reinhard nodded, and Viktoria set her half-done sweater aside.

"How exciting!" she said, clapping her hands together. "Do your best to protect our blessed Hitler. He is such a good man, such a kind man. I remember when he came to retrieve the Blood-Banner after I'd been hiding it..."

And off she went speaking about Hitler the lovely, caring, sweet-as-honey human being who had trusted her to watch over the Nazi Blood-Banner, a swastika flag splattered with blood shed during the disastrous Munich Putsch of 1923. A flag that would, in the not-too-distant-future, become a holy symbol for the Molech-like cult of Nazism.

Reinhard, ever the good listener, listened particularly carefully to Viktoria's tale. Hitler may have been little more than a moustache and a scowl, but he wasn't all tirades and threats: he could be charming, genial, *nice*. There was a reason he was able to convince a nation to descend into barbarism, and Adiel would need to be able to impersonate Hitler at his best as well as his worst if he chose the path of true redemption.

"Ah, well, you don't want to hear an old lady's stories!" Viktoria laughed when she'd finished her tale. "Go on, go see your new office! Hopefully, the peace and quiet will let you be more efficient when you make plans for dear Hitler."

"Hopefully," Reinhard agreed, a little smirk working its way onto his face. He scurried up the stairs, nearly bumping into a few SS men as he did so. The office was small, with a tiny desk, a few wobbly chairs, and a swastika flag hanging on the wall beside a picture that Himmler had gifted him. (A picture of Himmler himself. Reinhard looked forward to chucking *that* onto a bonfire one of these days.) Sparse, but at least he had an actual filing cabinet. More importantly, he could be alone.

"Looks good?" Dieter said as he plopped one more cigar box full of index cards into the lovely, blessed filing cabinet. It didn't look nearly as good as the sprawling office that Reinhard knew he would have in the future, when he earned chandeliers and oaken desks through his hard, genocidal labor, but it looked better than what he had at the Brown House.

"Acceptable," Reinhard said, ever unwilling to actually praise anyone. Dieter chuckled, jabbing his thumb towards the open window.

"You realize you still don't have a typewriter, right?" Amsel said. "You're going to have to go *alllll* the way to the Brown House and lug it *alllll* the way up here."

"Logistical issues," Reinhard said with a shrug, strolling over to his desk and checking the inkwells. "It'll be resolved."

"And if not, it's good exercise, hm?"

"Speaking of exercise," Reinhard said, dropping a pen into the inkwell and gesturing towards the door. "Why don't you march back to the Brown House and ask Hildebrandt for his typewriter since you have nothing better to do?"

"You're joking..."

"That's an order."

"Ugh...you're terrible."

"I can be far worse," Reinhard warned in a voice that was just teasing enough to not give away his true sinisterness. Dieter threw up his hands, shuffling towards the door.

"Please, spare me!" Amsel chuckled before turning to leave. "Oh! Hello, Fräulein Schicklgruber, pardon me!"

Reinhard wasn't even slightly surprised when little Kaia came skipping into the new office, lapping at a lollipop that Viktoria must have given her. The Jewish girl's face bore telltale nail marks from where Victoria had no doubt pinched her cheeks.

"Your landlady's nice, Uncle," Kaia chirped, licking her lollipop. "I went to the Brown House, and they said you were moving here. How come?"

Without missing a beat, Reinhard smirked playfully and replied, "I was trying to get away from you."

"Ouch!" Dieter laughed. "Reinhard, you don't show mercy to anyone, do you?"

"Never. Get moving, Amsel, you'll get less leeway than she does."

"I can imagine. Good day, Fräulein!"

Dieter exited, shutting the office door behind him. Kaia climbed onto one of Reinhard's pathetic, wobbly little office chairs and smiled up at him.

"You should've told me you moved offices!" she said.

"It's not as though you don't know where I live," Reinhard replied, sitting across from Kaia and adjusting the position of his desk a few times. "By the way, you *do* know you're going to have to return to school at some point, right?"

"I'm gonna, but not until the plan's all ready to go so I can stop being anxious 'bout it!" the girl explained, biting down on her lollipop in a way that made Reinhard's teeth tingle. "Did you guys decide to do Operation Chaplin?"

Reinhard nearly winced. The thought of taking the child's sole surviving parent was troublesome, but ultimately, it was for the greater good. Though he was fond of Kaia, he was more than willing to make her an orphan for the sake of saving Europe.

"Your father's still thinking about it."

"What's there to think about? It's a great plan!" Kaia said, pouting and biting down on the candy once more. Reinhard grunted, suppressing a slight twinge of discomfort. He wondered if she would have said the same thing if she knew what the new version of Operation Chaplin would consist of.

"I'm glad you're so modest. We're still plotting out some of the finer details," the Nazi Lieutenant said. The girl finished off her lollipop with one more painful *crunch* and chucked the stick at Reinhard's wastebasket, hooting in delight when it landed inside.

"Is that why you moved offices?" Kaia queried, intentionally making her chair wobble back and forth. "So you could make more plan stuff without anyone spying on you?"

"Smart girl," Reinhard said, earning a grin from the child. There were plenty of benefits besides security and the lack of spies. More space, more silence, and less of a chance that Heinrich Himmler would...

Knock, knock, knock!

"Reinhard!"

Fuck you, you piece of shit, I'm going to put so many bullets in you...

"Come in," Reinhard said pleasantly, through teeth gritted so hard that they threatened to shatter like glass. In walked Heinrich Himmler with a swagger, a cigar dangling from his thin lips, a magazine in one hand and a paper bag in the other.

"I heard you moved offices," Himmler said with a nod of approval, tossing the newspaper onto Reinhard's small desk before smiling up at the portrait of himself. "Good idea. Reduces the chance of any further leaks. Did you see this article? They're calling you the Fascist Cheka."

"Cheka, hm?" mumbled Reinhard, sliding the newspaper towards himself. Without the benefit of foresight, he might have been amused at being compared to Lenin's Cheka state security organization, but knowing just how accurate the article was made him regard the print with a scowl.

"Damn Jew newspapers," Himmler said, putting out his

cigar in the Nazi Lieutenant's ashtray. "Lying pieces of shit..."

"Language," Reinhard scolded, pointing towards Kaia, who had stopped wobbling her chair and had therefore gone unnoticed by the *Reichsführer*. Himmler spun around and greeted Kaia with a bemusedly delighted smile.

"Oh! Dear me, Fräulein Schicklgruber, I didn't see you there, forgive me!" Himmler laughed. "Please don't repeat that word! That's a word for adults only and you might get spanked."

"What word?" Kaia queried sweetly, innocent as a fox in a henhouse. Reinhard smirked. Himmler turned scarlet.

"Ahhhh...errr....well, good that you happened to be here, little one!" the *Reichsführer* demurred clumsily, handing her the little baggie he carried. "I was going to give this to Reinhard to give to you, but this way I can see your face!"

"Oh!" Kaia chirped, peeking into the bag. "Strudel! Thank you!"

"Thank my wife when you meet her. She did the work, even picked the apples!" Himmler replied. "You should come to my farm sometime, Kaia! I think you'd enjoy it, get a sense for what real German life is supposed to be like. Urban living corrupts the soul, you know."

"How?" Kaia asked, perhaps reasonably, which of course led to an unreasonable answer.

"Our ancestors..." (Reinhard barely resisted the urge to strangle Himmler right then.) "They knew how to properly live fulfilling lives in nature. Crowded urban centers, they not only affect your physical health—I remember when I was young and sick, moving away from the city air did me wonders—but it also invites unnatural behavior. Race-mixing, deviancy, all sorts of terrible things. That's why Jews just love cities, you know. Just like rats: they love crowded, dirty places where nobody is self-sufficient. That way they can take advantage."

If Kaia understood a word of what Himmler was saying, she did a marvelous job of pretending that he wasn't a quack. She hummed, nodded, and said, "But not everyone can be a farmer."

"No, certainly not right now!" Himmler laughed. "Not enough land! But that'll change some day."

Reinhard winced. Kaia smiled and tilted her head sideways. "Cities aren't that bad," she chirped. "You meet a lotta different people, and they're nice sometimes!"

She glanced at Reinhard, a silent message. That odd feeling which was somewhere between swelling affection and creeping nausea rose up in Reinhard's chest. He gave her a small smile and a nod to communicate that despite the circumstances, he was quite happy that he had met her.

Kaia turned to Himmler again. "Living on a farm would be lonely."

"Hm…a decent point. I suppose I tend to think that every man should have his solitude," Himmler muttered, stroking his barely existent chin. "But close-knit camaraderie isn't as viable in a sparse environment."

"Also, I like the streetcars!" Kaia squeaked, and that made Himmler chuckle.

"Now *there* I will have to disagree, Fräulein Schicklgruber! Those things are always so filthy and crowded! Full of Jews and thieves! Why, I've had my wallet stolen thrice now!"

"Oh no, that's terrible," Kaia said, and it looked like she was barely suppressing the biggest, proudest smirk in the world.

"Reinhard, make sure to walk Fräulein Schicklgruber home today!" Himmler commanded. "No trams. Wouldn't want *her* to get stolen."

"No trams," Reinhard concurred. Himmler nodded in approval and turned to Kaia, pinching her cheek in farewell.

"Good to see you again, little one! Stop by the Brown House sometime, even if your uncle isn't there! A little spider took up residence in the corner of my office, and I'm doing my best to leave him be and let him snag the flies. I'll feel less nervous if you swing by and tell me if he's the rare poisonous sort."

"There aren't any poisonous species that live in Germany, so unless he escaped the zoo, he should be fine," Kaia assured the *Reichsführer*, earning a sigh of relief from the future mass murderer.

"That's good!" Himmler laughed, mopping his brow with a handkerchief. "I suppose he'll be my personal assistant now."

"Name him Reinhard the Second," suggested Kaia, immediately making Reinhard reconsider his prior disgust at the prospect of killing her.

"Reinhard the Second it is!" Himmler proclaimed. Reinhard the First was desperately looking forward to the day he finally got to murder his boss.

HEYDRICH HAD TOLD HIM TO ACT NORMAL, AND SINCE Adiel Goldstein was not Adolf Hitler, he listened to his potential underling.

He probably could have stayed home if he'd really wanted to. It was midterms, and while an adjunct was proctoring the exam, Adiel was simply standing outside the classroom and collecting portfolios. He probably could have just had another adjunct grab them for him and then swung by later to collect them for grading, but he always liked to offer his students one final "good-luck" before their exams. It would be a little odd if he broke tradition.

"Good luck, Frau Lahner, not that you need it," Adiel said when Elfriede arrived and offered her folder. She gave him a bright grin and skipped into the classroom.

"Hey, you're going to be fine."

A voice that Adiel vaguely recognized drew his attention to the end of the hall, to a student who most certainly did need all the luck he could get. Leon Engel, far younger than the brutal SS man he had glimpsed in Becca's books yesterday, sporting thick black bags weighing down his eyes. Engel must have been tossing and turning all night. Nevertheless, the student smiled as he gave his wife his portfolio and took their three-year-old son out of her arms.

"Norman, wish Papa good luck," Leon crooned. The child that Adiel had once convinced to kill his own mother squeaked something incomprehensible in a sweet little voice that reminded the Professor too much of Kaia when she was tiny. Whatever Norman said must have amused his father because Leon laughed, kissed his son, and then leaned forward and kissed his wife right on the forehead.

In less than a decade, Leon would put a bullet through her skull, and while yesterday that knowledge had filled Adiel with hatred for his least favorite student, he recalled Reinhard's little Christian dictum and felt a wave of nausea wash over him. Awful as Leon was, even he didn't deserve to be put in such a terrible position. Little Norman didn't deserve to be indoctrinated into a cult practically from birth. And Anniska, who had bravely tried to save Jewish children, didn't deserve to die by her own husband's hand.

But she would die, and the Engels would be ripped to shreds, and at the end of the day, it would be Adiel's fault. Because Adiel was as selfish as he had been in that former life. Ever determined to put his wants above all else.

Anniska looked up and offered the Professor a gentle, almost apologetic smile as she took her traitorous son back into her arms and bade her husband farewell.

"Good luck, Herr Engel," Adiel muttered as he plucked the folder from the scowling future wife-killer's hands. Leon grunted in response, giving Adiel a withering scowl and marching into the classroom.

The pile of folders in Adiel's arms suddenly felt unbearably heavy.

WHEN KAIA HAD BEEN TINY, THREE YEARS OLD, SHE HAD forced her father to rewrite *Little Red Riding Hood*, so horrified was she by the ending where the Big Bad Wolf was killed by having his belly cut open and stones placed in his gut. Adiel had resisted at first, asking her why she had such pity for the villain of the fairytale.

Kaia had made several arguments on the Wolf's behalf: he was hungry, and Red should have shared her sweets. At one point in the midst of her defense, however, she had pointed to the image of the Wolf being weighed down by stones and cried, "He doesn't deserve that!"

Adiel kept thinking of that little proclamation. *Deserve.* There was a word he never would have assigned any amount of significance, but to Kaia it had always mattered greatly. Wolves didn't deserve to be tortured no matter how many grannies they ate. Spiders didn't deserve to have their legs plucked off no matter how frightening they seemed. Nazis deserved a chance to save their soul no matter how vile they were.

And then, of course, there was Adiel himself. What did he deserve at the end of the day? On one hand, he hadn't done a thing to deserve losing his entire life, and yet he *had.* He had been given more than he deserved already, and if he wasn't willing to give it all up, then plenty of people would receive a fate that they didn't deserve. Bastards like Engel, heroes like Anniska, and every Jew that wouldn't be able to escape his replacement's wrath.

Adiel took Kaia to synagogue the week after Heydrich proposed the new Operation Chaplin and sat near the playground after services. He watched as Kaia skittered about with the other Jewish children, squealing with glee, a game of tag breaking down all barriers of popularity.

"Hey, Adiel!"

A friendly voice drew the Professor from his ruminations as Chaim Wach, a longtime childhood friend, invited him to come and chat with a few other fathers. Adiel moved from his lonely seat to join the pack of Jews.

"You doing okay?" Chaim asked cheerfully. Adiel laughed and waved a dismissive hand.

"Yeah, you know, just…finals. Tired."

"Ah, I feel that!" another father declared. Saul Finkelstein. He ran the local kosher butchery. He was always very nice. He talked for a little bit about how his new set of twins had been keeping him and his wife up. Adiel wondered what he had done to those twins in his last lifetime. Maybe he'd crushed their skulls like he'd crushed little Avi Libman's. Maybe the horrible Doctor Mengele had gotten his hands on the children and tortured them until death became liberation.

"Adi, are you still going to America at the end of the year?" Chaim queried, and Adiel nodded.

"Yes, ah…you're still going too, yes?" Adiel tried to mask his desperation.

"I am," Chaim confirmed with a chuckle. "Can't say no to that job your father offered. David's not going, though."

Adiel's heart did a backflip. Another friend from his childhood. David Levi had been one of the first people who had welcomed him when he'd been the new boy in class. Adiel had drawn his dog for him. David still had that painting hanging on his wall.

Adiel glanced at his friend. "David?"

David shrugged carelessly. "My roots are here," he said. "And my wife doesn't want to leave her side of the family, and you know my mother-in-law…"

Off David went, complaining about his mother-in-law, which invited cheerful jibes and jokes from the other fathers. A discussion sprung up concerning emigration, and it quickly became clear that the vast majority of the Jews in Adiel's circle intended to stay in their homeland. Familial connections, optimism, patriotism, too many things were tying them to German soil.

Adiel listened to them all chat and laugh, then he glanced at their children leaping about on the playground. He had almost certainly killed them all in his past lifetime. Every one of them, his friends and their children and their wives and in-laws, had been ashes falling on Auschwitz or emaciated bodies in Dachau. It had been his fault then, and it would be his fault again.

Adiel took Kaia home early, pondering the good memories, and then came to a decision: it would hurt, and maybe he didn't deserve it, but none of those children did either.

When Heydrich returned to the Goldstein household, Adiel greeted him with a somber declaration: "I'll do it."

ELEVEN

Obeying Reinhard Heydrich's command to act normal, to pretend like he wasn't going to lose everything in less than two months, was agonizing.

Adiel still had to be a professor. Attend meetings, grade folders, and submit lesson plans since he was ostensibly still going to be employed until the end of January. It would appear too suspicious if he handed in his resignation early and then lingered in Munich for a month, so he did the best he could.

Being a teacher was already exhausting, but when he finally got home, he had to become a student in a horrific subject. Heydrich had scoured every biography about Hitler and studied every newsreel, all in an effort to teach Adiel every tick, every gesture, everything he needed to know to flawlessly impersonate his former self.

Heydrich, maybe unsurprisingly, was an absolutely ruthless instructor. Even if Adiel had been learning something pleasant under his tutelage, it would have been utterly exhausting, and Hitler lessons were anything but pleasant. Pretending to be the monster he had been, even knowing that it was ultimately for a good cause, made Adiel feel like his belly was filled with heavy stones.

But it had to be done, and they had little time. So even though Adiel knew that the end of his lovely life was fast approaching, and even though he wanted nothing more than to spend every second with his precious daughter and beloved father, he couldn't. He had to keep up appearances, and he had to practice becoming Hitler again.

Still, Adiel insisted on taking a break on *Shabbat*, which was nice since it gave him some time to sit with his friends, with the Jews he had been so eager to spend his life with, and remind himself that his sacrifice was more than worth it for their safety. He could spend time with Natan and Kaia and enjoy the time he had left.

And then Heydrich had to go and ruin that.

The Goldsteins had just gotten back from a pleasant synagogue service where Kaia only talked twice, but when they stumbled into their home, they found an uninvited guest perusing Becca's books.

"Herr Reinhard!" squeaked Kaia happily. The Nazi looked up from a notebook he had been scrawling in and a small smile tugged at his lip before he realized he was, for once, in the same room as Natan.

"I apologize," Heydrich said, but Natan didn't give him a moment to explain himself. Stiffening and taking in a deep breath, Natan grabbed his granddaughter's arm.

"Kaia, let's go outside, Bernie must have to go potty," he declared, and it was clear that he was fighting to keep fear and anger out of his voice. Kaia let out a squawk of discontent, but before she could even hope to verbally argue, Natan was yanking her out of the room, then out of the house. Bernie barked happily and skittered after Kaia, wagging his tail.

"I let the dog into the yard," Reinhard muttered quietly. "He nearly had an accident on your piano."

"Ha! *Accident*, sure! Bernie knows what he's doing," chuckled Adiel, hanging up his coat and smiling at the Blond Beast even though he was anything but happy to see him. *One day*, the Professor thought, *just one damn day where I don't have to think about this shit.* His days as Adiel Goldstein were few and precious, and he wanted to have a few moments where he didn't even have to think about Operation Chaplin.

Still, he wasn't about to yell at the potential Butcher of Prague. Adiel smiled at Heydrich and sat down. "How did you get in?"

"Oh. Kaia gave me the house keys. I made a copy," Reinhard explained, the edge of his lip twitching upwards as he reached into his back pocket and jangled his keys. "Don't tell her I told you. She said she'd get in trouble."

"If her grandfather found out," Adiel concurred. "I'll pretend like I'm an idiot. We'll just say you picked the lock. Papa will believe that. Any particular reason you're here on the Sabbath?"

"I know you can't work on Saturday, but I can, and I just got the information about the hotel. Hitler has a nasty habit of switching up things last-minute, so there's a chance he might go back to his apartment at some point, but it's not likely given the Geli Raubal situation."

Adiel nodded, a fresh bout of nausea roiling his guts. That *particular* detail about his old life, the fact that he'd evidently had an affair with his own niece, was still rather hard to swallow. Adiel wasn't exactly glad that the poor girl was dead, but he was grateful that he wouldn't have to deal with that vile aspect of his replacement. If he had vomited upon glimpsing her, well, that would have certainly blown his cover.

"Did you think about my suggestion?" Adiel queried, eager to escape the subject of Geli altogether. "Seeing if he'll invite me over as his former comrade?"

"I have, and it's a bad idea," Heydrich said, slamming his little notebook shut. "Too many risks involved. What if he tells me to kill you to keep his friendship with a Jew under wraps?"

"You think he'd do that?"

"You think he *wouldn't?*" Heydrich scoffed, giving Adiel a patronizing look. Adiel shrugged.

"I don't know," the Professor said, gesturing to the pile of his mother's books. "Adolf protected his mother's Jewish doctor."

Indeed, one of the more surprising facts Reinhard and Adiel had uncovered about the Professor's previous life was the fact that Adolf Hitler had evidently not believed that *all* Jews were worthy of slaughter. He had shown mercy to a mixed-race girl he had befriended, and more interestingly, Adolf had gone out of his way to protect the Jewish Dr. Eduard Bloch, who had tried but ultimately failed to save Adolf's terminally ill mother. Adolf Hitler had called Bloch an *Edeljude*, an honorable Jew. Heydrich had, upon reading about Dr. Bloch, spat that Adiel had been an awful hypocrite in his former life.

"I know he stopped being my friend," Adiel muttered, scratching at his beard, which he was starting to grow out in preparation for the day he donned a toothbrush moustache. "But that doesn't mean he wants me dead."

"Not *yet*. Don't assume you'd be one of his *Edeljuden*," Heydrich advised, spitting the little epithet like it was a curse. "There's too much at stake to trust in your brother's good nature."

"I said the same thing when Kaia suggested recruiting you," Adiel retorted, and that made the icy Blond Beast squirm a bit as he opened his notebook again.

"Hm. A broken watch and all that," Heydrich muttered. "Regardless, we're going to sneak you in. I'll make it look like I was sloppy and didn't check thoroughly enough. Here, I have the floor layout and the guard schedule. Let's go over everything..."

"AHA! FINALLY, KAIA THE LADY THIEF HAS BEEN captured!"

"You can't keep me captive, copper! Psh!"

"Agh, oh no, hidden dagger! Agh, the world's...going...dark..."

"No, you're not gonna die 'cause I didn't hit you lethally! I'm an honorable thief! Heeey, get up, stop being so girly!"

As Natan collapsed into the grass, gritting his teeth, trying to convincingly play dead even as Bernie licked his face, Kaia stood over him. She had donned a paper mask and grabbed a pillowcase filled with "money" (hundreds of Goldstein-Marks, which Kaia had drawn herself.) She poked at her grandfather's side with a small stick, her "hidden dagger," and the old man suddenly grabbed her arm and wrestled her to the ground.

"Haha! Got you! That's what you get for being so noble, Lady Thief!" he cackled. Natan and Kaia ended up wrestling in the grass for a few moments while Bernie desperately tried to stop what he clearly thought was a legitimate brawl. The puppy whined and wriggled his way between the "police officer" and the Lady Thief.

"Truce, truce!" Natan called when wrestling with both his vicious granddaughter and the hysterical dog became too arduous.

"Truces are for girls!" whined Kaia as her grandfather crawled onto the nearest lawn chair.

"*You're* a girl, silly!" Natan chuckled.

"I'm a *lady*."

"*Lady*, right. Ah, looks like Bernie's tuckered out, too…"

Indeed, the dog rolled in the dead leaves covering the Goldsteins' garden for a moment before digging about, making himself a little nest of foliage, and curling up inside.

"I think he's got the right idea," said Natan. "Take five, Kaia!"

"M'kay. I'm gonna set up the next game," Kaia declared, scurrying away and hiding her sack of Goldstein-Marks in a bush on the other side of the property. When she returned, however, she found both her dog and her grandfather fast asleep, snoring practically in unison. Giggling, she decided to let sleeping dogs and Zaidys lie. She took off her mask, tossed her "dagger" aside, and decided to go see how Operation Chaplin was proceeding.

"Any questions?"

"Can I go to the bathroom *now*?"

Reinhard, who had started regretting his career choices the day he had met the Goldsteins, once again found himself wishing he'd become a swimming instructor. At least if he'd been a swimming instructor, he could have responded *no* to that plea without being a complete monster.

Adiel looked as desperate as any six-year-old boy, though, and so Reinhard waved for him to go.

While the Professor retreated to take a bathroom break, Reinhard went through their notes for the thousandth time. If he had a few more months to prepare, he would have felt more confident. Adiel was trying, there was no doubt about that, but there was still something missing. Anyone would be able to take one look at him and realize that he wasn't Hitler, no matter how much he looked like him...

"Hiya, Herr Reinhard!"

A cheerful voice interrupted Reinhard's thoughts. Little Kaia had stumbled into the room, dead leaves clinging to her hair and dress, a wide smile decorating her face.

"You know you don't have to call me *Herr*," Reinhard said as a greeting, offering the child a small smile and making sure that all of the books before him were shut. "If you're going to call me by my first name anyway, it's rather pointless."

He wasn't sure how it was physically possible for Kaia to smile any wider without breaking her cheeks, but somehow she managed. "Okay! Hiya, Reinhard!"

"Where's your grandfather?" Reinhard inquired, trying to hide his nervousness behind a casual tone. Adiel knew that Kaia and the Blond Beast often spoke when they weren't at the Goldsteins' house. The Professor had said he was fine with such interactions but had warned Reinhard not to speak a word to the girl in Natan's presence.

"He fell asleep," Kaia replied, gesturing towards the door to the backyard. "He's old."

That fetched a chuckle from the Blond Beast. "Rude," Reinhard accused, and the girl threw up her hands.

"You're all old!" she cried, and Reinhard let out a small, teasing huff of indignation.

"I am twenty-seven, I am not *old.*"

"To me you are!" Kaia snickered, brushing the leaves from her hair and sneering at him as she shuffled across the room.

"You just love courting danger, don't you?" Reinhard said.

"I'm just bein' honest!" the child giggled. "And I'm not afraid of ya!"

Maybe you should be. Reinhard was frankly a little afraid of himself, all things considered.

Kaia skipped over to her family's piano and idly started stabbing at the keys as children were wont to do. (Reinhard had gotten out of that habit when he was little: one didn't playfully test out tunes in the Heydrich household without incurring his mother's ire.)

"How's Operation Chaplin going?" Kaia queried, running her hands along every key. The piano was in tune, surprisingly enough. Someone in the Goldstein family must have played at least somewhat regularly.

"Classified," Reinhard said with not a small amount of satisfaction. The girl huffed and plopped down on the piano bench.

"Jerk," she muttered. "It's *my* operation."

"It was a very good idea," Reinhard said in a tone so ruthlessly sweet that Goebbels would have given him a medal if he'd heard it. "Thank you for letting me steal it."

"Jeeerk." Kaia played a few more notes, this time more refined, an actual tune, though not one that Reinhard recognized. It sounded distinctly American. Reinhard didn't appreciate jazz very much, degenerate and low-class as it was, but he still knew it well enough that he could pick it out.

"Technically, *you* stole it from Chaplin," Reinhard noted.

"Nah ah, I was *inspired* by Chaplin, that's different."

"Then I was merely *inspired* by you."

"That's not the same thing!" the girl argued, but he saw a small smile form on the side of her lip. Kaia idly tapped a few more jazzy notes on the piano.

Reinhard watched the girl for a moment with amused interest that swiftly became aggravation as she, clearly by habit, started playing *Toselli's Serenade*. The girl realized her mistake before Reinhard could even hope to open his mouth, however. She let out a frightened squeak as though she had stepped on Reinhard's toes and looked at him with wide, apologetic eyes. "Sorry, I forgot—!"

"Don't worry about it," Reinhard assured her in a tone that was gentle enough to even surprise himself. The girl was odd, certainly, but she was undoubtedly one of the sweetest humans that he had ever encountered. Any other soul would have laughed at him for being so bothered by a song. Even Lina had rolled her eyes when he'd switched it off the radio. Little Kaia clearly didn't think less of him for being bothered by it even though she didn't even know why he despised the song so much. She genuinely didn't wish to hurt his feelings.

"I don't suppose you know any other songs," Reinhard said, hoping to make her forget her little mistake. "Anything non-American, maybe something German? Anything but Wagner."

"Why not Wagner?" Kaia queried.

"My father loved Wagner. Wagner, Wagner, Wagner! Have you ever listened to a song one too many times?"

Kaia nodded.

"I've listened to *every* Wagner song too many times."

"Papa likes Wagner!"

That was something Adiel shared with Adolf Hitler. Reinhard hummed. "You don't know any Mozart, by chance?"

"A little! I know…"

Kaia played a few notes of *Für Elise.*

"And, uhm, I can never get this one right, but I really like it. I forget what it's called."

She tried and utterly failed to play Mozart's *Turkish March.* Her cheeks bloomed pink.

"Hang on…" Kaia flung her legs over the bench and focused entirely on the piano, her cherubic face screwed up in an expression of frustrated concentration.

Instinct and arrogance made Reinhard abandon the books and make his way over to the child. Instinct because he had grown up in a music conservatoire and was used to the sound of poorly played music being corrected (usually with a smack on the wrist or upside the head, but obviously he wasn't about to do that to poor Kaia.) Arrogance because *Turkish March* was literal child's play for him, and he did enjoy impressing the girl with hardly any effort.

Reinhard tapped Kaia's shoulder. When she looked up at him with wide, embarrassed eyes, he gestured for her to scooch over and give him space to sit beside her. The girl gave him a smile brighter than the one she had offered when he'd shielded her with his umbrella, and now that he knew what that smile meant, Reinhard felt an odd mixture of affection and guilt take hold of his heart.

"May I?" he asked, gesturing towards her hands. Kaia wiggled her fingers, inviting him to give her orders. Reinhard grabbed her hands and shifted them to the proper keys.

"Just keep tempo for now." Reinhard whipped off his black gloves and set them under the bench, cracking his knuckles and beginning to play. Reinhard wasn't nearly as good a pianist as he was a violinist, but he had a broad range of musical skills. Elisabeth Heydrich had been a piano instructor first and foremost, after all, and she had made sure her son knew her craft. He barely needed to glance at the keys, which meant that he could instead focus on Kaia's dazzled expression.

Those early years of getting smacked upside the head every time he played a note wrong were worth it for the look of admiration he got from little Kaia.

"You don't even need the sheet!" she squeaked. "You're so good!"

That almost made Reinhard hit a wrong note simply because of the little backflip his heart did. Genuine praise was something he thirsted for but rarely received: curt nods from his mother when he performed perfectly, maybe a chuckle from his father, an impressed smile from Lina. And almost always, if it was given, it was part of an exchange. A "good job" for a promise that he would do the family name proud, a note of commendation from Himmler for sniffing out a spy. Unprompted, unconditional, and entirely genuine praise was a rare gift.

"Thank you," Reinhard said. "Can you reach the…? Oh."

He looked under the bench and realized that the pedals were too far away for Kaia's little feet.

"I'm too short for good music!" the girl giggled, and it was a tribute to Reinhard's training as a musician that his performance didn't falter even as he laughed.

Reinhard had never been interested in becoming a music instructor, half because he had never really liked children and half because he particularly didn't like *rich* children. Kaia was a rich child, but it was quite fun to teach her.

Reinhard heard Adiel slip back into the room and spared only a glance at him. The Professor smiled as he watched the two of them perform, offering a nod to Reinhard and carefully sitting back down on the couch.

They finished their little duet and Adiel applauded. Kaia beamed when she realized she and Reinhard had an audience of one. The girl stood up on the bench, giving a deep bow.

"You bow too!" she insisted, and Reinhard, sensing that there would be no getting out of it, rolled his eyes, stood up, and copied her. Adiel chuckled.

"That was excellent!" the Professor proclaimed. It hadn't really been *excellent* since Kaia was so unpracticed, but Reinhard wasn't about to berate her like he was running his father's conservatoire, especially not when she turned to him with her bright blue eyes shimmering. He patted her head twice.

"Excellent," Reinhard said, and Kaia opened her mouth, no doubt to say something very cute that would once again make him feel like a monster for what he would have done to her in different circumstances.

But then a different voice cut in: "Get your fucking hands off of her."

"Papa!" Adiel didn't have time to rise to his feet as Natan stomped towards the piano. Kaia made a move like she was about to leap in between the bristling Holocaust survivor and his potential tormenter.

Reinhard, driven by an oddly sudden and intense instinct that was a bit like what he felt whenever he fenced and dodged an opponent's strike, grabbed the girl and set her on the ground, giving her a small push towards her father. That only angered Natan more, but at the very least it meant that when Natan grabbed Reinhard by the collar and slammed him against the wall, sending the menorah and a few Talmudic tomes tumbling to the floor, Kaia wasn't hurt.

Reinhard's instinct was to push Natan off and maybe beat him into a coma, which would have been easy enough: Natan wasn't short, nor particularly frail for his age, but he certainly wouldn't last a second against an in-shape, six-foot-three Blond Beast.

Of course, Reinhard only needed to glance at the arm that was pinning him to the wall, and more specifically at the faded blue number stitched onto Natan's skin, for him to abandon any notion of engaging in self-defense.

"I wasn't doing anything wrong," Reinhard said, his eyes flitting to Kaia, who was struggling against her father as he held her back. Reinhard could hear whimpering and scratching as Bernie, who had been shut outside, tried fruitlessly to open the door.

"Papa, he was only..." Adiel attempted to argue, but it seemed that Natan was so enraged that he either didn't hear his adopted son or simply didn't care what he said.

"I've been really fucking generous," Natan snarled, releasing the Blond Beast's collar. "I let you into my home, I don't say a word to you, I don't confront you at all..."

"I recognize that, but..."

"Shut up! The one thing I say is that I don't want you going near my granddaughter..."

"Zaidy, he's not—!"

"Kaia, *hush!* Adiel, take her out of here!"

"Papa..."

"*Now!*" The Holocaust survivor's command made the entire manor tremble, and Adiel, who had clearly been trained to follow the fifth commandment, hesitated to leave Reinhard alone with Natan for only a second before he obeyed, dragging the squirming little girl out of the room.

Being alone with one of his victims—not merely a *potential* victim, but someone who bore the scars of Operation Reinhard—was a bit like standing in front of six naval Courts of Honor. Reinhard's habit when he had been young and had incurred the wrath of his mother had been to bow his head, focus on his feet, and brace himself. He diverted to that old survival tactic, grimacing as he forced his eyes to stay pinned on his jackboots.

"Terezin Ghetto," said Natan. Two small words summoned an avalanche of gruesome tales and images. Adiel hadn't felt it necessary to go into deep detail about Natan's personal experiences from the Holocaust, but he had warned Reinhard that Natan's parents and one of his siblings had perished in the Czech ghetto under Hangman-Heydrich's direct supervision. Reinhard braced himself for more details about Natan's family.

That was not, however, what Natan had in mind. "Kaia's a little thief, isn't she?" the survivor hissed. Reinhard sensed that Natan wouldn't like any answer he gave to that question. Staying silent was never the proper response in these situations, however.

"She's not a bad..."

"Isn't she a thieving little Jew?"

Reinhard's wallet suddenly felt heavy. "She's good at stealing things, yes."

"There were a lot of thieving little Jews in Terezin. Little kids. They could slip through the cracks, sneak out and steal some bread. A few of them even stole watches and jewelry. The Bandit of Terezin was the best, we all heard about them. Kaia would have loved them: they stole from SS men and German families. Left little treasures strewn around the ghetto, saved a lot of lives. A real noble thief. Stole from you once, that was the rumor anyway."

"I'm..."

"*Shut up.*" It was clear that as furious as Natan was, he was taking quite a bit of delight in his ability to snap at the man that had once possessed the power to kill him with but a word.

"That was the Bandit, but most of the thieving little Jews weren't as talented as them. They were just little kids, after all. Starving, desperate little kids who just wanted to give some food to their little siblings or their dying parents. I remember really shortly after we got to Terezin, there was this little girl who lived next to us. Playmate of my nephew

Eli. You know the name 'Kaia,' I gave it to Adiel. You know where I got it from?"

Reinhard's boots really needed to be shined. "That girl," he guessed, barely a whisper.

"That girl. You want to know what happened to *that* Kaia? What *you* did?"

He really didn't, and so he said nothing. Natan prodded again, "Well?"

"I can guess..."

"You're such a fucking coward! Coward then, coward now!" spat Natan. "You liked to sit pretty up in Prague and play dress-up with the Czech crown like you were some sort of king. Give Himmler some credit: at least *he* went to the ghettos and the camps and watched what he was doing. You, on the other hand, only ever visited that one little camp for the Black Foxes! Too cowardly to really get down in the muck you were making..."

"I'm not a coward," Reinhard said, letting the slightest edge of defensiveness into his voice, and that fetched a strangled noise from Natan that was half a snarl and half a sob.

"Right! Right! The brave and mighty Reinhard Heydrich, protecting the German people from evil little eight-year-old girls! You and your *noble* SS men sure showed *that* Kaia!"

"I didn't..."

"When *your* men caught her sneaking back into the ghetto with *an apple*, they showed *her* what noble Germans do to thieving little Jews!"

"She..."

"Thieving little Jews get beaten to death!"

"I—!"

"Thieving little Jews get gang-raped!"

Not for the first time, Reinhard felt the urge to vomit on the Goldsteins' carpet.

"And then those same guards got *promoted* for catching that thieving little Jew! Every one of them got a personal commendation from the brave, noble German *hero* Reinhard Heydrich! So you'll just have to *forgive me* if I don't want you anywhere near *my* Kaia, you utter piece of shit!"

"I am *not* like that!" Arguing when he was confronted about his sins had been a mistake when Reinhard was a child, and it was a mistake now. He raised his gaze, indignant and desperate all at once. Natan jabbed a finger in his face.

"Yes, you fucking are! You are the same damn person! Heydrich is Heydrich! Don't even *pretend* to be anything like Adiel! Adiel isn't Adolf Hitler, but you'll *always* be the Butcher of Prague!"

Reinhard's recalcitrance had gotten him into deep trouble at the naval Honor Court, but it was practically instinct: when his honor was questioned, he did not merely bow his head and numbly agree. He argued, and he did so right then.

"You're wrong!" he snapped. "You can't say that I'm the same as the Butcher of Prague and still claim that Adiel's *different!* We're in the same boat! I haven't done anything wrong, and I am not—!"

If Reinhard had maintained the familiar position—*head down, answer like she wants, wait for the hit*—then when Natan finally struck him right in the face with a tight fist, he would have been braced. He probably wouldn't have even felt anything.

Unfortunately for Reinhard Heydrich, Natan caught

him mid-argument, and thus when the Auschwitz survivor's fist connected with the potential Hangman's cheek, he not only managed to split Reinhard's lip, but he knocked him back onto the piano.

There was an awful cacophony as Reinhard braced himself against the keys. When he looked up, he realized that Natan wasn't done with him yet. Reinhard had always thought that the notion of turning the other cheek was utter and complete bullshit, but right then he was prepared to do so. He lifted up his hand to defend his face but had no intention of actually fighting back.

BAM!

"OW!"

"*Kaia!*"

But when Reinhard opened his eyes, he saw a flurry of activity. Little Kaia must have heard all the shouting and, slippery as she was, escaped from her father's grasp. The foolhardy little Jewess had scurried over to Natan, no doubt intending to grab his arm and beg him to stop attacking the Nazi. Natan hadn't even noticed her, however, and so as he pulled back his arm to strike Reinhard again, he elbowed the little girl right in the eye.

All attention immediately flew to the child as she started sobbing and clutching her eye. Bernie's whimpers became frenzied barks upon hearing his favorite human's distress. Natan forgot about Reinhard completely and spun around, slapping a hand over his mouth. Adiel ran into the room and quickly gathered the girl into his arms. Reinhard yelped, "Is she all right?"

Adiel pried Kaia's hand away from her eye and winced, but then looked at Reinhard and nodded. "Black eye, she'll be okay," he said gently. "You should really go. We'll talk later."

"Yes..." Reinhard said, eager for an escape. He quickly grabbed his gloves and jacket, pausing briefly before he ran from the manor like the coward he had been in his former life.

"I'm sorry," he said to all of the Goldsteins at once, his eyes shifting from the injured little girl to his trembling victim.

Natan glanced at Reinhard before the potential Hangman could flee. Two sets of blue eyes met, both wide and worried, before the Blond Beast scurried out into the cold.

"How is she?"

"Well, Bernie wouldn't stop licking her eye and I was worried he'd give her an infection, so I made a little makeshift eyepatch from one of my old ties."

"Ha! She must be happy."

"Extremely. I promised her I'd buy her a real eyepatch tomorrow."

"She'll never take it off."

"No..."

Adiel settled down on the couch, heaving a deep, exhausted sigh. The chaos had ended after Heydrich had left. Adiel had dealt with little Kaia (who was more upset about the fact that her grandfather and Reinhard weren't getting along than she was about the black eye) while Natan had tidied up the sitting room. There was a small splatter of blood staining the piano keys. Reinhard's. Adiel noticed that his father's gaze kept shifting from the Goldsteins' family photos hanging on the wall to the blood-covered keys.

"Go ahead," Natan sighed when his son sat across from him. "Yell at me."

That earned a snort from Adiel. "I don't really think I'm in a position to do that, Papa. All I'll say is..."

Adiel's eyes darted to the pile of Becca's books. One spine bore a picture of Adolf Hitler, offering that scowl Adiel had not yet been able to perfect. His gut writhed.

"Heydrich was right about us being in the same boat."

"Bullshit," was Natan's only argument, and Adiel decided that debating this once more would be fruitless. He reached forward and turned the books so that he was no longer being stared down by his former self.

"You didn't tell me that was where you got Kaia's name," Adiel muttered. Natan grunted, scowling at the little splatter of Heydrich's blood.

"You asked for name suggestions, and I gave you a list," the old man reminded him. "Kaia was just the name you happened to like best. Any other name you picked from that list would have been a dead person too, Adiel. They'd have a similar story."

The Professor nodded once, and then there was a horrific bout of quietness as Adiel stared at a picture of Kaia grinning on her first day of school and Natan kept his gaze fixed on Heydrich's blood.

It was Natan that finally broke the silence. "You didn't tell me what your plan is."

There was a faintly accusatory lilt to the old man's tone. Adiel sighed. "You wouldn't like it."

"I didn't like the last one either."

That wasn't very funny, but Adiel found himself chuckling anyway. Natan snickered too, maybe because dark humor was contagious, or perhaps in an attempt to break the tension.

"Well...don't worry," Adiel said when they stopped laughing and the silence became unbearable once more. "I won't be putting any Kaias in danger this time."

"But you'll be putting yourself in danger." All jocularity was gone from Natan's voice. He turned his gaze to his adopted son, stony and chastising like Adiel was a mischievous nine-year-old once more.

"A bit," Adiel confessed.

"Because you still think that you have to atone for what *he* did." Natan's gaze briefly flitted towards the pile of books.

"Yes, but..." Once more, Adiel clung to Heydrich's lessons and the part of his soul that would always possess Hitler's magnetism. He clasped his hands together, leaned forward, and spoke in a strong, determined tone. "Even putting all of that aside, Papa, I *have* to do it. Even if you're right and I'm not him. If I have a chance to stop it all and don't take it, I'm responsible too. If there's a chance to make sure that no Kaia ever has to suffer like that Kaia from Terezin did, I *have* to take it. Even if it means working with Heydrich."

Even if it means becoming Hitler.

Once more, there was a painful, ponderous silence. Natan stared into his son's eyes and Adiel refused to blink.

"Whatever this plan is, I don't want to be the reason it fails." Natan spoke at last, his voice resigned as he leaned back in his chair and shook his head. "I've been thinking about it for a little while, and I'm going to leave."

All of Adiel's confidence left him. "Leave?"

"For America. Early."

"You weren't supposed to go until…"

"The end of December. But I don't think it's a good idea for me and Heydrich to be in the same country together, don't you agree?"

Adiel did, but at the same time, knowing that he would never be meeting his father in their new American home, he felt a sense of terror take hold of his soul. The desperate terror that he had experienced when he was little, when he would cry when Natan left for work in the morning.

Back then, Adiel had been too young to realize that he would see his father again that very night. But if Natan left early, Adiel would never see him again. He had been prepared for that, to a certain extent, but he had thought that they would all have more time together.

But…he loved his father, and being near Heydrich was obviously painful for Natan. And just as he would rather lose himself than let his old sins repeat, Adiel would rather lose time with his father than force the old man to relive horrific memories of the Holocaust.

Besides, it would be better, safer, if Natan was across the ocean when Operation Chaplin commended. Heaven forbid they failed and Natan paid the price.

"All right," Adiel muttered, fighting to keep a casual tone, to pretend like his plan didn't effectively involve his own suicide.

"And I'll be taking Kaia with me…"

"What? No!" Adiel yelped practically on instinct. To a certain extent, he had been braced to lose his father long before he had agreed to Operation Chaplin, long before he had even learned his true identity. Since Becca's death, he had tried his best to enjoy his time with his father, keenly aware that the old man's days could be numbered.

But Kaia…Adiel was already sacrificing enough time with her. He couldn't give up the few weeks he had until the New Year. And unlike Natan, who was clearly in pain every moment he had to be around Heydrich, Kaia liked the Blond Beast. If anything, she would almost certainly be upset if she was shipped off to America after such an incident.

"Son…"

"I already told you: Kaia won't be involved at all. And we're not even putting the plan into action until January."

"*Son…*"

"Chaim Wach is leaving for America on the 27th of December. I'll send her with him. He and his wife are trust-worthy. Please, Papa, I…I want to celebrate Hannukah with her."

Unspoken were the words *one last time*, but Natan, it seemed, heard them, nonetheless.

"Fine," the old man whispered, biting his lip.

"I won't let Heydrich near her again if you…"

"I said it's fine!" Natan snapped before wincing at his own voice, glancing at the little blood splatter, and whisper-ing, "I don't think he was lying…"

The next day, the Goldsteins went to the zoo, Kaia sporting a new eyepatch. She skipped from the reptile exhibit to the arachnids while pretending to be a pirate. Natan carried her on his shoulders and wouldn't stop apol-ogizing for hitting her eye even though she kept insisting that she was fine. Adiel just tried to be optimistic: he was enjoying himself, at least. He couldn't even remember the last family day they'd had when Becca and Emma were alive. They had left too suddenly, and there had been no time to appreciate what he'd had.

The day after their family outing, Adiel and Kaia saw Natan off outside the airport. The old man gave his granddaughter a particularly tight hug.

"Be good for your papa, all right?"

"Uh huh!"

"And write to me a lot, okay?"

"And I'll draw you pictures!"

"Atta girl. I'll see you for New Year's."

Kaia kissed her grandfather's temple. Her spirits were relatively high, and judging by the way she clung tightly to her father's hand as they bade farewell to Natan, it was likely she had overheard their discussion and was glad that Adiel had convinced Natan to let her stay in Germany a little longer. She almost certainly would have thrown a fit if she'd been forced to abandon her father.

Once Natan had said one final goodbye to Kaia, he turned his attention to Adiel.

"I'll see you in New York," Natan said, his voice trembling. Adiel hated to lie to his father, but he nodded, nonetheless.

"Yes…"

Natan didn't know the full details of Operation Chaplin, but he knew, at minimum, that it could be dangerous. Adiel had confessed to that much. Which meant that they were both keenly aware that this could be their last farewell.

So when they embraced, it was the tightest embrace either had ever offered.

"You're a good man," Natan assured Adiel, who fought to keep himself from breaking down in front of little Kaia.

"And you're a good father," Adiel declared. "The best. Thank you."

"Stay safe, all right?"

"I'll try."

"You know I love you, right?" Adiel felt Natan's body shake with a suppressed sob.

"I do," Adiel assured him in a voice so strong that it even surprised him. "And I love you too."

The last time Adiel Goldstein saw his father, the old man was climbing up the ramp to a plane, pausing to wave at his family, the blue number tattoo that he no longer felt the need to hide standing out against his pale flesh.

Adiel barely saw his father through the tears obscuring his vision, and even though Kaia tried to comfort him by saying that they would see Zaidy again in January, he couldn't force himself to smile and lie to her right then.

TWELVE

Hanukkah,
1931

"Germans, my people..."
"You didn't pause long enough."
"Ugh!"

"Start again."

"From the beginning?!"

"Yes, from the beginning."

Adiel Goldstein had been a truly excellent student: punctual, polite, and always eager to give a speech. But having Reinhard Heydrich as a teacher could drive even the most energetic learner into a state of psychosis. He had a feeling that if not for little Kaia's tempering presence, the Blond Beast would have already made the Professor have a mental breakdown.

Adiel glanced at his two companions. Reinhard sat on one side of the couch, bedecked in his typical uniform which now sported slightly altered markings as he'd recently been promoted to Captain. (Kaia had been far more enthusiastic about that promotion than the Blond Beast: she insisted on keeping her eyepatch on whenever Heydrich came to the manor not because she still needed it, but so that they could both be captains.) Kaia sat on the other side, playing tug-o-war against Bernie with one hand while offering her father an optimistic thumbs-up with the other.

With the duo of captains watching him, Adiel sighed, got back into character, and launched into one of Adolf's speeches. This time, he didn't allow his gaze to glide to the scowling Blond Beast or the beaming little girl. He looked at the window, pretending that the little dots of dew were millions of star-struck Germans watching him, worshiping the man he wasn't, eager to betray all of their Jewish neighbors.

That thought made a fire of anger ignite in Adiel's soul before, by instinct, he remembered his mother's counsel and forced himself to mellow out as he finished the speech. He heard a disappointed huff from the Blond Beast and turned to Heydrich with a groan as he broke character.

"What did I do wrong this time?" Adiel asked. Reinhard was silent for a moment, his wolf-blue eyes shooting straight through the Professor, before he waved one gloved hand and shook his head.

"Nothing specific. There's still just…something missing," Heydrich mumbled. "We'll take a break."

Break! Blessed break! Adiel could use more of them. He collapsed onto the couch and scratched at his beard (which was not the long and impressively flowing type of Becca's father. Adiel could somewhat see why he had never grown it out when he had been a monstrous dictator.) The Professor most certainly looked nothing like Hitler at the moment, but at least he had improved his ability to act like him by quite a bit.

"I think you did great, Papa!" Kaia squeaked cheerfully, releasing Bernie's rope toy, running to her father, and wrapping her arms around him. "You're the best Hitler ever!"

Adiel laughed and kissed her forehead. Heydrich snorted.

"Technically correct," Reinhard said, leaning down and scratching behind Bernie's half-floppy ears as the mutt began pestering the Blond Beast to take Kaia's place in the contest of tug-o-war. "Is something bothering you, Goldstein? Besides, well, in general."

Besides the fact that you're going to lose your daughter in less than a month, was what Reinhard meant to say. Adiel shrugged.

"I had to hand out a few bad grades," Adiel muttered, lifting Kaia onto his lap. "Those never feel good."

More specifically, he'd been forced to give a failing grade to Leon Engel. Adiel had really been hoping that Engel would pull himself together last-minute: he might have disliked the man, but he hated the idea that he had personally set Engel on his dark, destined path. If Operation Chaplin failed, then poor Anniska and Norman...

Nevertheless, Reinhard had expressly commanded Adiel to act normal, and giving out passing grades to clearly inferior students would have been plenty suspicious. Besides, Engel deserved his grades, and there was some talented young person who deserved his spot in the Academy far more than he. It was probably for the best, anyway. Engel had failed out in the other timeline, so maybe the student who filled his spot would have himself become a mad dictator if he hadn't gotten in. Failed artists, it seemed, were rather unfortunately prone towards fascism.

"Plus, it's our first Hanukkah without Papa," Adiel said, gesturing towards the wax-covered, slightly dented menorah sitting on the shelf above the now-clean piano. (Since Natan had left, Reinhard had started giving Kaia short piano lessons during their rare breaks. She had gotten much better and was extremely eager for Reinhard to one day bring his violin to the Goldstein house so they could do a proper duet.)

"Ah, right. I forgot," Reinhard muttered, casting a brief, nervous glance at the menorah before standing up as though the Jewish candelabrum was a bomb that he'd just realized was about to blow. "I'll leave the two of you alone for your holiday."

Before Reinhard could step towards the door, however, Kaia leapt from her father's lap, ripping off her eyepatch so that she could offer a proper sad-puppy look and grabbing the Blond Beast's hand.

"Hey, c'mon, you've gotta stay!" the girl begged. "I wanted to show you my Maccabee book! You'll like it! There's a lotta violence, and there's a guy that gets crushed by an elephant, and..."

Either Reinhard was particularly indulgent, or he was so surprised by the ease and boldness with which little Kaia had grabbed his hand that he was momentarily stunned. He listened to Kaia spoil the entirety of the *Book of Maccabees* without moving.

"...and that's why there's a candelabra, and ours has an elephant on it even though the elephants were the bad guys!" Kaia concluded, and the corner of Reinhard's mouth twitched.

"I see." The Blond Beast knelt down before little Kaia, refusing to wrench his hand from her grasp. "Your father *did* mention that Hanukkah is your version of Christmas."

"Nah ah, no! Christmas is boring, it's just about some guy getting born!" insisted Kaia. "Hanukkah's about war and fighting and *battle elephants!*"

"Well...being honest, that *does* sound like a lot more fun than the Nativity," Reinhard chuckled. "I might have liked being in a Nativity play when I was a boy if there were elephants involved. Regardless, I'm not very comfortable staying for your holiday, *kleine*, but..."

The Nazi Captain pointed towards his rumpled jacket, which rested right under the coatrack. Kaia, realizing right then that their guest hadn't hung up his coat like he normally did, released Heydrich's hand and scurried to the suspicous garment.

She lifted up the black coat and let out a hoot of surprise when she uncovered a gift. It wasn't very carefully wrapped, in fact Reinhard had done little more than tie a bow around it, but Kaia didn't care. She tore the ribbon off and held her Hanukkah gift aloft.

"Ahhhh~! It's a book about spiders!" she yelped, hopping up and down like the hefty tome was made of gold. "*Common Spiders of North and South America!* The pictures are so *pretty!*"

"Took me a while to find a book about spiders that you didn't already own," Reinhard chuckled before an embarrassed blush crept onto his face and he hastily turned to Adiel. "Err, sorry, I peeked at your bookshelves."

"All fine," Adiel assured him. The breach of privacy from the Blond Beast was well worth it for the chance to witness Kaia's clumsy dance of happiness. Bernie, clearly not understanding what was going on but getting energized from all the excess movement, started hopping up and down himself, trying to sniff at the book in Kaia's hands.

"Ahhhh! I love it! Love it, love it, love, love, love!" Kaia squealed, hugging the book to her chest and beaming up at Reinhard as the Blond Beast rose to his feet. "Thank you, thank you! Now you just owe me seven more gifts!"

"What?!" exclaimed Reinhard, and his smile refused to vanish even as he tried for a truly indignant tone.

"Hanukkah's eight days, and I get one present per day, so you owe me seven more!" Kaia grinned cheekily and added, "Also, it has to be a bigger and better gift for every day. That's the rule."

"Greedy little...I am *leaving!*" Reinhard proclaimed, giving the girl a playful little push and grabbing his coat.

"I'm gonna make donuts, though! Stay for a donut!" Kaia begged, to which Reinhard relented, lingering long enough to pretend to enjoy Kaia's poorly made donuts. (Natan's cooking lessons hadn't stuck. "You'd better hope she becomes a biologist or something," Reinhard whispered after sneakily giving the rest of his donut to Bernie. "She'll certainly never be a housewife.") After that, Reinhard bade the Goldsteins farewell and left them to celebrate Hanukkah by themselves.

It was dreadfully ironic that Reinhard Heydrich's presence was missed on Hanukkah, but once he was gone, Kaia's mood noticeably became more somber. That was perhaps a side-effect of the house already feeling far too empty for Kaia's comfort. Hanukkah was typically her favorite of all the holidays: she loved to hear Becca's renditions of Judah Maccabee's incredible exploits. She loved lighting the menorah with her family. She loved defeating

Adiel and Natan in a game of dreidel and winning a pile of coins all for herself.

But Becca wasn't here to talk about Judah Maccabee, only two voices uttered the prayers for the first night, and even though she still enjoyed her dreidel tournament against Adiel and Bernie (with Kaia spinning the little clay top on behalf of her dog) it was clear that she missed her grandparents. The girl kept letting out heavy sighs even as she landed on gimel for the sixth time in a row, earning the whole pot.

"Are you okay, sweetie?" Adiel asked when Kaia didn't burst into her typical feat of gloating glee upon winning at dreidel.

"Yeah, I'm fine!" Kaia insisted in a tone that made it clear she wasn't really *fine* but had nevertheless accepted the status quo. "I'm glad that I got to stay here with you for Hanukkah, but…I do miss Bubbe Becca."

"Me too, Wolfchen."

"I was already kinda sad that she wasn't gonna be here for Hanukkah, and now Zaidy's not here too." Idly, she spun the dreidel once more, sighing morosely when it landed on *shin*, the losing symbol.

"I hate losing…" Kaia muttered, and Adiel was certain that she wasn't talking about dreidel. He reached out and patted her head.

"At least Bernie's here, right?" Adiel said, gesturing to the dog, who was happily gnawing on the bone Kaia had presented to him as a Hannukah present. Reminding the girl of her beloved pet did the trick at least halfway. Kaia brightened, knelt down, and hugged her pet.

"Uh huh! Best Hanukkah gift!" she proclaimed, looking up at her father with an optimistic smile. "And next year it'll be better! We'll all be together, even Uncle Edmund! And maybe after we stop the war, Zaidy will get along better with Reinhard."

Next year. Where would Adiel be next year? Assuming he wasn't dead, probably up on a mountain, in one of Hitler's lairs. Acting his soul out during the day, barely resisting the urge to hurl himself from the top of the Berghof come night. No more dreidel games with Kaia. No way to call her or write to her, and no way to apologize for never getting her another Hanukkah gift.

But of course, Adiel couldn't tell her that. And so he forced a smile onto his face and lied like a true Hitler. "You're absolutely right, Wolfchen. Everything will be better next year."

"Reinhard, have you met with the—? Oh! Kaia, hello! I see your eye is better! I hope that awful little creature who hit you got what he deserved."

"Hiya, Uncle Heinrich!"

Reinhard had strong-armed Kaia into going back to class every once in a while, but he couldn't keep her from playing hooky entirely. Still, he would have been lying if he said that it wasn't always a relief whenever her and Himmler's visits happened to coincide. If Himmler was in a bad mood or raring to ask Reinhard to do some sort of ridiculous seance, little Kaia offered a tremendous distraction. At minimum, she put Himmler in a good mood. He was quite proud of himself for having graduated to "Uncle."

Kaia, for her part, was proud of the fact that she had

stolen seven of Himmler's wallets. She had promised to stop when she hit ten, but Reinhard was relatively sure that she was lying.

Oh well. At the end of the month, she would be all the way in America anyway, probably robbing the Roosevelts.

"She was just leaving, *Reichsführer,*" Reinhard said, straightening out his uniform and offering his boss an unenthusiastic Nazi salute. "I was going to walk her to her father's house and then come back to talk to the men."

"I can get them up to speed. You made everything quite clear in the notes you sent, though you might want to work on your handwriting."

"Hildebrandt wouldn't spare the damn typewriter, blame him," Reinhard argued. *Or pay me more,* he wanted to add, but he decided against it. Something about asking for a raise from the man he was planning on killing in the near future felt wrong even to Reinhard Heydrich.

"At any rate, Reinhard, I wanted to give you this personally," Himmler said, whipping out a small card decorated with Norse runes. A cursory glance revealed it to be an official invitation to Himmler's Yule Day party.

"You'll be there, I hope? And!" Himmler knelt down and ruffled Kaia's curly locks before taking another invitation out of his pocket and offering it to the girl. "This is supposed to be for SS men and their families, but you're practically family yourself, Kaia!"

"Does that mean I get a uniform?" was of course Kaia's response, making both potential mass murderers chuckle.

"No," the *Reichsführer* said. "But it means that if you like, you and your family are more than welcome to attend my party! I'd love to meet your father! I'm sure we'd get along very well."

That statement was either very right or very wrong depending on which version of Adiel that Reinhard chose to think of. Either way, the Blond Beast cut in before Kaia could be a social little moron and RSVP right away.

"We'll have to ask his permission first, sir," Reinhard said. "Me and Lina will be there, though."

"Ah, excellent! I'll finally get an opportunity to do that fertility seance!"

Or maybe not, Reinhard thought, and Kaia only made things worse when she piped up: "What's a fertility seance?"

That question ended up nearly giving Himmler a heart attack, which might have made things easier, all things considered. Maybe instead of convincing Adiel to have Himmler shot somewhere down the line, Reinhard would just have Kaia ask the *Reichsführer* where babies came from.

"H-Have a good day, Fräulein Schicklgruber, and be sure to ask your father about that party! I'd love to see you on Yule Day!"

"Right! Bye bye, Uncle Heinrich!" Kaia waved farewell and skipped down the staircase with Reinhard. The Jewish girl paused to wave at Dieter and Viktoria; Reinhard's landlady was serving cakes and tea to the battalion of SS officers who would be guarding Hitler during his New Year's return to Munich. The Blond Beast barely spared his new underlings a look, instead ushering the girl out of the building.

"Yule is a Viking celebration that they used to do," Kaia said, holding up Himmler's card and launching into a long, cute, and somewhat concerningly detailed diatribe about Vikings and their holidays. By the time she was finished blabbering, she and Reinhard were nearly back at Goldstein manor.

"...and then they would sacrifice a goat!" she concluded with a suspicious amount of enthusiasm. "Are you guys gonna sacrifice a goat?"

"Possibly, or maybe I'll volunteer you," Reinhard teased, which probably wasn't very funny considering the fact that given the choice between killing a goat or killing a Jewish child, most of the SS men who would be attending the party would probably pick the latter. And if they didn't now, they would later.

"I wanna go to the Viking party!" Kaia squeaked, leaping into the air and somehow twirling 360 degrees before landing back on her feet, earning an impressed nod from Reinhard.

"Your father is never going to agree to send you to a party full of SS officers," the Blond Beast noted, and little Kaia's cheerful smile became mischievous.

"Weeeell, you don't have to tell him," she said. "You're gonna be there the whole time, so it'll be fine!"

"Kaia…" Reinhard started to sigh, but the girl suddenly scurried in front of him, blocking his path and forcing him to look into her wide, pleading eyes.

"I already go to your office all the time, so I'm already around SS men all the time!" she argued. "Plus, it's a Viking Party, so they'll all be drunk!"

That earned a snort of amusement from Reinhard, both because of her words and because the visual of Heinrich Himmler downing a horn of mead and drunkenly collapsing was downright hilarious. "Knowing Himmler, I have a feeling that it won't be nearly as exciting as a real Viking celebration."

"If it's boring, then it won't be dangerous!" Kaia argued. Maybe instead of studying spiders, she could try for a law degree.

"If it's boring, why would you want to go?" Reinhard countered.

"I've never been to any kinda party except a Jewish one, so this'll be like seeing Christmas *and* Viking stuff!" Kaia explained, bouncing on the balls of her feet. "Plus, you said your fiancée's gonna be there!"

He had. And since it would be the last opportunity Lina would ever get to meet little Kaia, the prospect was tempting. Reinhard had hoped to introduce the child to his fiancée. If things went poorly, he wanted to be able to show Lina that he'd turned against the Party she loved for a worthy reason. "I suppose she would like you…"

Kaia squirmed a bit in that eagerly anxious way children were wont to when they could sense that they were tantalizingly close to a "yes." She delivered her final argument: "If you take me, then…I'll count that towards the other seven presents you owe me, and you'll only have to get me six!"

Reinhard gave her a scowl.

"Five?" Kaia offered.

"*None.*"

"Deal!"

"I didn't say…oh, all right, fine," Reinhard sighed with a roll of his eyes. "I have a feeling that if I don't take you, you'll just sneak out and wander the streets until you find the party or get yourself killed."

"Probably," giggled Kaia. "You can just pick me up after Papa thinks I've gone to bed on Christmas. Just wait outside the gate."

"Fine. But if your father finds out about this, I'm foisting all the blame onto you. You blackmailed me."

"I did *not!* I *bargained* with you!"

"You…" Reinhard shook his head and once more found himself laughing. "You're unfathomable."

"…AND, ANYWAY, THAT'S WHY I'M HERE."

"More tea, Herr Engel, Herr Amsel?"

"Oh, yes, thank you, Frau Edrich!" Dieter Amsel said with a wide smile, giving the old widow his porcelain cup, which she filled with more lukewarm, over-sweetened tea. Leon Engel refused Viktoria's offer, partially because the tea was bad and partially because his gut was roiling with anger and hatred after talking to Amsel about how he had ended up in the SS.

"I completely sympathize," said Dieter, and Leon smiled and nodded at his new comrade. The two of them had been waiting for either Heydrich or Himmler to come down and brief them on their assignment. An honorable assignment, an assignment to guard Hitler himself. Leon was a bit green for such a task, but since he had been in the SA long before he'd switched to the SS, he was considered trustworthy. Himmler knew that he would obey orders without question and do whatever was necessary to guard Edmund Hitler's life.

Dieter and Leon had bonded right away after a brief conversation between the two had revealed that they were both artists of a sort, Leon favoring traditional painting while Dieter had been an architect before joining the Nazi Cause.

"It's disgraceful how Jews ruin everything that's beautiful," sighed Dieter, shaking his head. "It would be bad enough if they *only* affected our economics, but the fact that they've sunk their fangs into our very culture, *that* is their worst crime. Removing them economically will be easy enough, but their cultural impact will take real work to undo. Even if they all vanished tomorrow, that influence would still remain."

"Agreed," Leon said, smiling a little at the thought of all Jews vanishing tomorrow. What he wouldn't give for that, for every Jew to simply turn into dust. Except Professor Adiel Goldstein. The Jew that had dashed Leon's dreams deserved worse than a sudden bout of nonexistence. Adiel Goldstein needed to suffer.

The day Leon had been kicked out of the Academy, when he'd returned to sweet Anniska who had tried so terribly hard to support him only for the Jews to ruin everything, he had made a promise to himself. *Someday, I'm going to make Goldstein pay...*

"H-Have a good day, Fräulein Schicklgruber, and be sure to ask your father about that party! I'd love to see you on Yule Day!"

"Right! Bye bye, Uncle Heinrich!"

*That voice...*Leon Engel looked up just as two figures, one tall and one tiny, passed by. One was Heydrich, pale-faced but bearing a very subtle smile as he glanced down at a familiar little blonde child.

*That girl...*Leon Engel tilted his head down, letting his visor cap cast a shadow over his face as he pretended to busy himself with his empty teacup. Dieter beamed and waved at the child.

"Goodbye, Fräulein Schicklgruber!" he said. The girl waved at him and a few of the others, several of whom ignorantly smiled and bade farewell to the adorable child.

"Come along, *kleine*," Heydrich said, leading the girl out of the building. As soon as Leon heard the shutting of the front door, he turned to Dieter, forcing a casual smile onto his face.

"Who was that?" he asked, and Dieter chuckled fondly.

"Heydrich's niece. His friend's kid." Dieter jabbed his thumb in the direction of Heydrich's office and said, "She's a sweetheart. You'll love seeing her: she puts Reinhard in a good mood."

The impulsive part of Engel almost blurted the truth right then, but no...no that would be too simple. Too easy. It might even backfire. Breed doubt in hearts of iron.

Later, he decided as Himmler came downstairs with a chipper smile, clapping his hands together and declaring that since Heydrich was chaperoning dear Fräulein Schicklgruber, he would be briefing them on their assignment. Leon listened to every detail with an eager smile.

THIRTEEN

Adiel had once bought Kaia a wooden cutout of a
pirate ship because, as Natan had observed, Adiel
couldn't say no to his daughter. She had named
it *Kaia's Revenge*, inspired by Blackbeard's own *Queen Anne's
Revenge*. Normally, *Kaia's Revenge* simply stood in her room,
occasionally being taken off of its little stand when she felt
the need to carry it around or show it off. When it snowed,
however, that was when *Kaia's Revenge* really earned its keep.

"Beware the Dread Pirate Kaia!" proclaimed the Dread
Pirate Kaia, slashing her wooden sword in the air. One blue
eye was hidden behind her eyepatch, the other gleamed
with pride as she ducked behind her wooden ship, which
stood upright in the foot of snow that covered the Goldsteins' yard and provided a thick white sea for her to
conquer.

"Holding it wrong," Heydrich shouted, not even looking
up from his notebook. He had been willing, at Kaia's insistence, to let Adiel have a break to play with his daughter in

the snow. Reinhard sat on the porch, going over his notes, acting as a spectator.

"Landlubbers don't get to comment!" bellowed Kaia, nevertheless adjusting her thumb and holding her sword the way that Heydrich the champion fencer had shown her previously.

"Aha, merchant ship!" Kaia cried, using a little tube as a telescope and "discovering" Adiel the Dog Merchant, who was struggling to carry their growing hound. Bernie probably wasn't a full-blown purebred German shepherd, but he certainly ate like one.

"Oh no, ugh...Bernie, err, cargo, stop!" yelped Adiel as the dog squirmed happily, wriggling right out of the Professor's arms. The dog landed in the snow and immediately started eating the slush.

"Aha! He's stopped to let his cargo graze!" cackled Kaia, squatting down and grabbing one of the snowballs from the pile of ammunition she had collected. "Surrender now, British merchant!"

"Never!" replied Adiel, and a snowy sea battle commenced. Bernie, utterly in love with eating snow, ignored the volley of snowballs that Kaia and Adiel exchanged. Adiel, whose talent for dodging projectiles had earned him an Iron Cross in two lifetimes, only got hit by Kaia's poorly aimed snowballs once or twice. Bernie was the victim of several bouts of friendly fire from the Dread Pirate Kaia, not that he seemed to care, so obsessed was he with swallowing mouthfuls of snow.

"Agh! We keep hitting the booty! Adjust the cannons!" cried Kaia.

"Take the eyepatch off and you'll have a better aim," Reinhard advised. "It affects your depth perception."

"I *said* landlubbers don't get to comment!" huffed Kaia, ducking behind her ship to avoid a snowball chucked by Adiel and casting a one-eyed glare at the spectator.

"I was in the Navy for nine years," Reinhard noted with a rather childish pout. "I am *not* a landlubber."

"Yeah, well, you got kicked out and now you're a land-lubber! So *shush!*"

Kaia punctuated her rather harsh remark by tossing a snowball at the Blond Beast. While the eyepatch affected her aim enough that she had difficulty hitting the quick-moving target that was Adiel, she managed to strike the stationary SS man right in the face. Heydrich sputtered, but recovered quickly, giving little Kaia a look so murderous that Adiel was momentarily concerned that a single snow-ball had morphed him into his utterly monstrous potential self.

"Oh..." Reinhard said darkly, wiping the snow from his face, shutting his notebook, and standing. "You are *dead.*"

The tide turned against Kaia after that: half because it was two-on-one, half because at one point Bernie got too excited and knocked her ship over, resulting in her dramati-cally proclaiming that the Great Whale Bernie had sunk *Kaia's Revenge.* Adiel and Reinhard all but drowned her in snowballs.

At risk of breaking her little heart, though, Adiel called a draw so they could all go inside and drink some hot cocoa. (Except for Bernie, who got some chicken, and Rein-hard, who opted for brandy instead since he apparently didn't have much of a sweet tooth, the monster.)

Both Kaia and Bernie ended up falling asleep near the fireplace, and after Adiel had picked the girl up and carried her to her room, he returned to the sitting area and found Reinhard flipping through Becca's books.

"She's asleep?" Reinhard said.

"Unconscious. Wore herself out. Hard to do with her."

"Hm. Break's over. We have something important to discuss."

Great. Adiel poured himself a glass of brandy and then sat across from Reinhard again, waving for him to speak.

"We need to decide how we're going to run things once the plan commences," Reinhard said, taking a small sip of his drink before laying out a few notes on the coffee table between them.

"Once I'm Hitler, you mean," Adiel said bitterly, and Reinhard nodded.

"We've planned for the worst already," the Blond Beast noted. "Let's assume the best-case scenario: we pull it off without a hitch. You need to know what to do differently."

Reinhard grabbed a fabric map of Europe, laying it out before them.

"First and foremost," Reinhard declared, tapping the areas of the map representing land taken from Germany by the Allies under the Treaty of Versailles. "Regarding the expansion of the Reich: I think it's vital for us to do every-thing you did in that other timeline. The reclamation of the Rhineland, the *Anschluss* of Austria, we should do all of that without making any changes."

"You just want Germany to have more land," Adiel accused with a chuckle, sipping his brandy and wondering if the burning in his throat was from the drink or his own nerves. Reinhard shrugged.

"Why not?" the Blond Beast said. "I'm still a German nationalist, and just because Nazism was hideously corrupted in this other timeline doesn't mean that German nationalism *itself* is evil. We can strengthen the Fatherland without slaughtering children. That would be a good thing. The Versailles Dictate was completely ridiculous, don't you agree?"

"I personally think that the Great War was *everyone's* fault," answered Adiel, who had never thought very much about the matter: at the end of the war, he had simply been grateful to have his life and his future wife.

"It seems like you don't have very much love for Germany," Heydrich observed, his tone almost accusatory. He was right: Adiel's feelings for the homeland he had killed millions of people for in another life had soured. From hopeful affection to indifference, and now that he knew just how thoroughly Germany despised his people, he all but reciprocated that hatred.

He decided that saying that much to a German nationalist likely wouldn't go over well, however.

"It's more like Germany has never had a lot of love for me," Adiel said. "I was patriotic before the Great War, but even though so many Jews signed up to defend the Fatherland, we got nothing in return except…"

He gestured towards Becca's books. "So, I'd say me and Germany have a bit of a loveless marriage, all things considered."

Heydrich stiffened, nodding slowly. "I didn't mean to imply…"

"My daughter, my father, these are important to me, wherever they are. You don't have children yet, but once you do, you'll agree that they're more important than any flag or chunk of land."

Reinhard let out a small, disbelieving hum. "Regardless,

even taking nationalism out of it, we're going to have a war no matter what. And if we're fighting Stalin, we will need to be prepared. So, in effect, you'll want to do everything almost the same in terms of geopolitics until 1938, when you take the Sudetenland."

"Heydrich, not to be a hypocrite, but if *you're* about to suggest we actually go through with stealing Czech land, that's an awfully bad look from *you*."

The potential Butcher of Prague cleared his throat nervously. "I would argue that the Sudetenland *is* a German area with a German-majority population, but that's beside the point. Whether we keep it or not is immaterial; what *you* need to do is take it and then wait for Neville Chamberlain to drag you to Munich for the peace talks. In this timeline..."

Heydrich tapped one of the books. "You somehow convinced Chamberlain that you would cease your expansion if you were allowed to keep the Sudetenland. This time, we shift things: you will say, quite correctly, that you fear Soviet expansion and have taken action in order to defend yourself from a potential Stalinist onslaught. You will offer to return the Sudetenland and cease expansion if Germany is permitted to join with Great Britain and France in a defensive alliance against Stalin."

"You think they'll go for that?"

"I do. If anything, I think they'll be ecstatic at the idea of a strong ally to fight the Soviets. Frankly, if they were willing to fight *us* on behalf of *Poland* in that other timeline, I think they'll most certainly fight *with* us against their long-time ideological opponent. Even better: if you manage to snag that deal, Stalin may very well panic and choose to attack preemptively, before he's even armed and ready. And if he *doesn't* and tries to stall for time like he did in this alternate timeline with the Molotov-Ribbentrop Pact, well, I already have a blueprint for what to do."

Heydrich held up one book and easily flipped to a page that spoke of Operation Himmler, a false-flag campaign that Hangman-Heydrich had performed to justify Hitler's war on Poland. A rather clever operation, clever as it was wicked: Hangman-Heydrich had sent German soldiers dressed in Polish army uniforms to seize the Gleiwitz radio station and broadcast anti-German messages in Polish. He had even gone so far as to leave murdered concentration camp prisoners strewn around the scene of the crime, bedecked in Polish uniforms to make the supposed attack more convincing. The "attack" on German territory had given Adolf Hitler all the justification he needed to launch his assault on Poland and start the Second World War. If Reinhard needed to, he could certainly pull a similar stunt to start a war before Stalin was prepared.

"Any complaints?" asked Reinhard. Adiel had several.

"I don't like the idea of a war at all," the Professor confessed, his eyes flitting up to a portrait of Emma. "And my wife's ghost will probably haunt me for moving against the Soviet Union."

"You said your wife was a *socialist*," Reinhard noted with a lifted brow. "You're going to be the head of the National *Socialist* Party. And don't tell me she actually *liked* Stalin."

Adiel barely resisted the urge to declare that Reinhard Heydrich of all people didn't have the right to look down on someone else's political opinions. "I know she liked Lenin, hated Trotsky. We didn't talk much about Stalin. Tried to avoid politics with her, keep the peace."

"Peace is all well and good in the hearth, but it *isn't* an option with Stalin," Reinhard said, gesturing to the pile of books before them. "Did you see the pictures of Ukraine? That's happening next year, and we can't do anything about it."

"I know…" Adiel muttered, gazing uneasily at one of Becca's books, which featured an image of the smirking Soviet dictator that the Führer of the Third Reich was eternally destined to battle. "I just wish Kaia could have her way. Run up to the Kremlin and hug the man. Make him 'better.'"

"Hm…" Reinhard squirmed as though he'd just realized there was a rock in his shoe before he shook his head and shoved the map aside. "At any rate, let's move on to internal matters. Obviously, as far as the Jews go, we can hardly change the Party's stance on them without inviting serious trouble. At the same time, we'll try to minimize harm. We can't get away with doing *nothing*, so some segregation is going to have to happen."

"All right…but I'm not taking money from them. And no killing, obviously."

"Obviously. Nevertheless, we should try to get them out, if for no other reason than to keep the peace. It seems that before extermination became their…" Heydrich stopped, took in a deep breath, and corrected himself: "Before extermination became *our* policy we emphasized emigration. We tried to ship them to other nations."

"After stealing all of their possessions and charging them for the *privilege* of becoming refugees," Adiel spat, glancing at the window and thinking of the Mercedes he'd been forced to sell. That had been bad enough. He couldn't imagine being robbed of everything. Robbing his own people of everything.

"Correct," Reinhard said. "Obviously, this time it should be the other way around. Jews should be rewarded for leaving. Maybe we could even work with the Zionist organizations and get them shipped to Palestine. Once we have a treaty with Great Britain, that would likely be simple, and since we won't be an enemy state to the Allies, it will be easier for German Jews to claim refugee status. Plus, if we don't occupy any Allied states, we wouldn't even have to worry about those Jews. France, Belgium, Denmark, they'll all be fine."

"What about the Jews in the East? In the Soviet Union and Poland. Poland has so many Jews, half of my—" Adiel stopped, grimaced, and corrected himself: "Half of *Adolf Hitler's* victims in this other timeline were Polish Jews."

"Nothing to be done," Reinhard sighed, scowling down at his notes. "Hold our noses, focus on the Soviet forces, try to make sure our men don't take matters into their own hands since we won't have an official extermination policy. We can't save everyone."

"Right..." Adiel's shoulders slumped. Once again, he was filled with something akin to survivor's guilt, but far more intense. *There are still going to be some victims. If you had just been a decent soul the first time around...*

"Speaking of our men, we have another problem: the SA."

Heydrich grabbed a book and flipped to a section that described the Nazi Party's 1934 purge of the Brownshirts. "It appears that in this timeline," Reinhard said, "Himmler, Goering, and I convinced you that Ernst Röhm was plotting against you. You gave us permission to kill him and decimate the Brownshirts, and the SS reigned supreme."

"Sounds like something you would do," Adiel noted in a

light tone which he hoped would communicate that he wasn't trying to cast stones. Heydrich didn't take it poorly, however: in fact, he offered a small smirk of pride.

"It does, actually," the Blond Beast boasted. "And frankly, even if it was for selfish reasons, it's still absolutely necessary."

"For a man that doesn't want to be like *that*," Adiel said, jabbing his thumb towards the Butcher of Prague's biography, "you certainly seem to have no problem making some of the same choices he did."

That earned Adiel a real glare from Heydrich, the sort of scowl that had spelled death for any Jew that earned it once upon a time.

"I'm trying to save my nation and preserve the lives of millions of women and children," Heydrich retorted. "That *doesn't* mean you've turned me into some bleeding-heart liberal that's going to give out hugs to every degenerate, communist, criminal, and faggot. Röhm and his ilk are at least three of those four things. The Brownshirts are rowdy and uncontrollable. If you want to get anything done, you can't afford such a rogue element. The SA can't be trusted."

"The SA didn't perpetrate the Holocaust," Adiel argued, crossing his arms, and Heydrich slammed the book shut and tossed it onto the table.

"Correct," the Blond Beast said, placing a hand on his black-uniform clad breast. "The SS perpetrated the Holocaust because *you* ordered it. If you *hadn't*, then the SS wouldn't have acted by itself, and if you explicitly refuse to pursue a policy of extermination, the SS will not do so independently. I can see to that myself. I *can't* make such guarantees of millions of Brownshirts. I'm surprised *you're* so sentimental about eliminating them when I can assure you: even if they didn't perpetrate the Holocaust in that other timeline, they certainly *would have*."

"I'm not sentimental," Adiel declared, leaning forward and shoving the book about the purge of the Brownshirts aside. "The Night of Long Knives can happen thrice for all I care."

It felt odd to dismiss so many lives like that, with but a few words. Had it been so simple and easy as Adolf Hitler? Adiel shivered, but then steeled himself, remembering Leon Engel and his horrible comrades, remembering that day in the park.

Heydrich was right: Adiel was willing to give up his own daughter for a chance at saving Europe, and he wasn't about to risk Jewish lives to save the goons of the SA. They would deserve whatever they got.

"Then it's agreed," Heydrich said with a victorious little smile, the sort he had no doubt sported in the other time-line when Ernst Röhm had been executed. "The SA will go, and the SS will take its place. Then, of course, it will be important for us to make sure that we have complete control over the nation: you'll need to get rid of Himmler, and that will allow me the opportunity to become *Reichs-führer* in his place."

Reinhard leaned back, took a hearty swig from his cup, and declared with a fair amount of optimism, "I'll then ensure that all of your policies are carried out. We can crush Stalin, and then Europe can be at peace with a strong Germany ruled by a kind, merciful Führer. National Socialism can become a positive ideology, and you'll be remembered as Europe's liberator."

"Maybe this time around, I really *will* be the Führer of

a thousand-year Reich," Adiel muttered in a bitterly casual manner.

"Potentially," Heydrich replied with a shrug.

"Assuming you don't try to overthrow me since you're handing yourself quite a bit of power." Adiel spoke in a jesting tone that didn't entirely mask the genuine concern he felt. Reinhard, however, didn't take offense at all: he gave a short bleat of a laugh.

"You think I'm doing all of this to become the Führer?" the Blond Beast chuckled. "That would be rather stupid of me. I'm unpopular, and you won't be once you're Hitler. Nobody would follow me if I tried to usurp you."

"Otherwise you would try?"

"No," Reinhard declared with utter seriousness before he smiled and pointed towards the ceiling. "I wouldn't want to upset Kaia."

"You like Kaia, hm?" Adiel said, his voice softening. Reinhard's eyes flashed with surprise for a moment. The Blond Beast took a contemplative sip of his brandy and then, slowly, he nodded.

"Quite a bit," Heydrich confessed. "She's very odd, but charming in her own way."

"You're good with her," Adiel noted, and that earned another surprised look from the Blond Beast. It shouldn't have been so startling a realization: Reinhard had read about his genocidal exploits, yes, but he must have also read that he was destined to become a devoted father.

"Really?" Reinhard murmured, gazing down at the small amount of brandy left in his cup and swirling it about. He chewed on the inside of his cheek, fidgeted, and then gave a small sigh.

"You know," Reinhard muttered somberly. "When I first

met her, when I saw her at the park, I got an...odd feeling. I'm not even sure I could describe it. Almost nausea, but also...something good? As though she was reminding me of something. She seemed almost...familiar. That feeling's gone away over time, that nausea, but sometimes it does feel like..."

The Blond Beast squirmed again, gnawing on his bottom lip, seemingly searching for the words to describe the strange feeling of familiarity that Kaia Goldstein summoned within him. After a few moments of pondering, however, Reinhard gave up, shrugging as he downed the last of his brandy.

"Well, anyway, I *am* fond of her," the Blond Beast said, pouring himself another drink. "I'm grateful that she believed in me. I know that nobody else would have. *You* wouldn't have."

"No," Adiel confessed, glancing up at a picture of his daughter and smiling gently. "Kaia's special. She always believes the best in everything. Spiders, people. I've always been afraid that she would get in trouble one day because she'd pet a dangerous dog or a snake or something. She scares me, but at the same time, I think that the world would be a much better place if everyone were like her."

"Or we'd all be dead," Reinhard joked. Both laughed, and then there was a dreadful bout of uncomfortable silence.

Reinhard finally broke it, his eyes gliding up to one of Kaia's portraits.

"Actually, I *was* thinking," the Blond Beast muttered. "Despite that...familiar feeling she gave me, I know that can't be the result of some sort of...connection between the timelines. After all, she didn't exist before."

Adiel hated the thought of his daughter not existing, but he hated the thought of her suffering more. "That's true."

"I think that might be why I can...be around her without discomfort. I don't have to look at her and think about what I *did* to her. Only what I *might have* done. It's all hypotheticals. What-ifs. I didn't actually..." Reinhard's gaze shifted to the books.

"I know what you're saying," Adiel muttered. The thought of his daughter going through even a fraction of the agony he had put millions of children through in that other timeline made him feel ill.

"For you, it must be even worse," Reinhard observed. "I don't really like any Jew except for Kaia, but it's personal for you."

"It is," Adiel confessed, finishing off his own drink. "It's like I betrayed everyone I care about. All my friends, my parents, my wife...shit, I hate that I don't know what happened to her, but at the same time, I don't *want* to. It's a little difficult to go to synagogue and be around all of my friends knowing what I did to them."

Perhaps the alcohol was making him a bit too honest because Adiel's gaze flitted to a picture of his father and he blurted, "I hate that Papa isn't here, but I'll admit it's nice to not have to see that number..."

Guilt immediately took hold of the Professor's heart, and he shook his head. "That's awful, though, isn't it? That's an *awful* thing to say..."

"You're human," Reinhard muttered in the tone that he typically reserved for Kaia.

"*Subhuman*," Adiel noted with a small smirk. Reinhard shook his head.

"Well…" the Blond Beast said. "If we want to get technical, you're not. You're not a Jew by race, after all."

"Nice try!" Adiel retorted, wagging his finger at his former underling. "I read the Nuremberg Laws *and* the commentary. 'Belonging to the Jewish religious community is to be generally regarded as such a strong commitment to Judaism that the passing on of the Jewish attitude to the descendants must be expected.'"

"Kaia would count under that," mumbled Reinhard, ticking off his fingers like he was in math class, running calculations in his head. "So, she would be a full Jew because her mother was a blood Jew, and you're a convert. And even if you stopped being a Jew, she would still be considered a full Jew. Hm. Awfully silly, if you think about it. The idea that you become a member of a race because of your parents' *attitude.*"

"Jews aren't a race," Adiel said, somewhat defensively.

"Aren't they?" Reinhard replied, sounding genuinely curious.

"Aren't '*you,*' you mean." Adiel maintained a friendly tone even though he was beginning to feel a bit anxious. It was bad enough that soon he would no longer be a Jew. He despised the notion that he had never been one at all.

"Well, that's the question," Reinhard mused. "I read the Nuremberg Law commentary as well. 'A full-blooded German who converted to Judaism is to be considered as German-blooded after that conversion as before it.' So, Kaia would be regarded as a full-blooded Jew even though she only has one genetically Jewish parent, but you'd still be considered German."

"Absolutely crazy," Adiel sighed. "You mentioned your

co-worker, Amsel, his friends have Jewish blood, and they don't know about it."

"The Kellers."

"They're loyal Germans, complete anti-Semites, and they love Hitler. Yet they'd be counted as Jews and exterminated. But I've been raised as a Jew all my life, and yet I'd still be counted as German and trusted more than them."

"*Trusted*, no. I'm sure *in practice* we probably didn't let people like you waltz through the streets wearing a kippa. At minimum, we would have said you're not a blood Jew, but a German allied to the Jews. Unless you renounced your conversion, I'm sure we would have swept you up too."

"'Conversion,' ha! Is that what it would be for me?"

"If we're being *technical*."

"Not sure how you'd *renounce* circumcision. I'd rather not find out! Either way, though, I wouldn't renounce Judaism."

"You enjoy being a Jew, then?" Now there was a somber sort of inquisitiveness to Reinhard's tone. Adiel supposed that was to be expected: Reinhard Heydrich had been accused many a time in this and the other timeline of having Jewish blood, and that accusation had eternally been a source of torment. Heydrich must have thought it strange that anyone would *want* to be a member of Europe's most despised people.

"Yes, I do," Adiel declared. "I like being a Jew. I like being myself. I don't…"

The alcohol was most certainly affecting him because a sober Adiel Goldstein would have never let a sound that was half-hiccup, half-sob rip from his throat in front of another man. But he did, whimpering like he was a little boy once more. "I don't want to be Hitler."

"Adiel..."

"It's funny, you know," Adiel said, giving a humorless chuckle. "I was thinking before, when I was trying to make myself feel better, that Hitler would have *hated* being me, so it's good to be me..."

Adiel wasn't sure how much sense he was making, but nevertheless, the Blond Beast's sharp features softened as he replied, "I think you're a good person. Take that how you will coming from me, but a truly evil soul wouldn't go through with this."

Heydrich gestured towards the notes in front of them, the plan to destroy Adiel Goldstein. The Professor hummed miserably.

"Maybe not," Adiel muttered. "But maybe this is justice in a way. *Ain takhat ain*, like the Torah says."

"I don't know Hebrew."

"An eye for an eye. None of this would be happening at all if I'd made the right choices the first time around, after all. But in that other life, I chose to tear families apart and erase everything Jewish from the planet. Now I have to erase myself even though I don't want to, and now I get..."

Adiel choked on his words. Tears were making him blind. If Reinhard was gazing upon him with sympathy or disgust, he could no longer tell.

Adiel had refused to let himself break down on the day that Becca died. Even when he had lost Emma, he had only ever cried in private, afraid of frightening Kaia, afraid of appearing weak. But right then, helped along by alcohol and the looming sense that there would be no turning back time again, that these were his last hours as himself, he put his face in his hands and sobbed.

"I'm sorry..." Adiel said, to Reinhard because of his unmanly display of emotions, and to the universe itself. He hoped that perhaps if he let himself cry, the all-powerful entity that insisted all of this misery had to happen would hear him and let him keep this wonderful life that he didn't deserve.

FOURTEEN

December 25th

C hristmas had once been Adiel's second least
favorite holiday right behind Easter. Adolf
Hitler himself had apparently been something
of a Scrooge during the holidays, presumably because
Klara Hitler had died around Christmastime. Adiel, for his
part, had hated the Christian holidays for the same reason
most Jews did: because their gentile neighbors always
decided that days devoted to their Messiah should be celebrated by tormenting "Christ-Killers." Easter had been
worse, of course, but Adiel had gotten plenty of rocks
tossed at him on Christmas, and the synagogue was almost
always defaced on December 25th.

However, Kaia had never shared his hatred for the holiday. At worst, she thought that it was boring, nothing at all
compared to Hanukkah. And this year, it filled her with
excitement, likely because this was the first year that they
had anything resembling a gentile friend to shop for.

And so Kaia dragged Adiel out to the shopping center on the morning of December 25th to buy gifts for the Blond Beast—or at least she insisted that every item she picked out was for the Blond Beast, though Adiel wasn't entirely sure why she thought Heydrich needed a new wallet.

Regardless, Adiel bought her whatever she wanted without question, hounded by the knowledge that Chaim Wach would be coming to collect her on the 27th. Today and tomorrow would be the last days he spent with his daughter. He intended to make them count.

And so they had a lovely father-daughter day, buying presents at the few shops that were open, sampling candy, pausing to play in the snow with Bernie. They went out for dinner, then ice cream, and when they got home and Kaia had finished wrapping up her presents, Adiel told her his adjusted version of the tale of *Little Red Riding Hood*.

He finished the story by describing how Little Red and the Big Bad Wolf became inseparable friends and then kissed Kaia's brow, keenly aware that this would be one of the last goodnights he shared with her.

"Tomorrow we'll do whatever you want, okay?" Adiel said, and Kaia nodded eagerly.

"Uh huh! And then...boom! Operation Chaplin!" she declared, striking a dramatic pose. Adiel laughed hollowly. Naturally, he hadn't told Kaia that he was shipping her to America and would never see her again. She was under the impression that Chaim would be taking her to a secret locale where they would be dropping off Edmund Hitler after they kidnapped him per her original version of Operation Chaplin. She was eagerly looking forward to meeting and saving the soul of a new family member, innocently ignorant of the fact that she was about to lose her father forever.

It was better this way, though. The truth would set in slowly, the sorrow would take its toll, and she would be safely in America with Natan. At the end of the day, Adiel was lucky to have had the little time he'd gotten with her. That was what he kept telling himself, at least.

"I love you, Wolfchen," he said. "Sleep well."

"Night night, Papa!" Kaia chirped before lying down. Bernie curled up at the foot of her bed, and Adiel left them be, trying once more to carve the image of her slumbering smile onto his brain so that when he had nothing else to remember her by, he still had that memory.

KAIA WAITED WITH THE PATIENCE OF A LADY THIEF FOR THE sound of her father's snoring to echo through the manor. When she heard it, the child sprang into action: she changed out of her nightgown and into the white dress she had selected for the Yule Party, slipped on her shoes, grabbed the gifts she had wrapped, and bolted out of the house before poor, exhausted Bernie could even hope to wake up and follow her.

Shivering in the snowy night air, she scurried to the front gate. Reinhard was waiting there, bedecked not in his usual black uniform but in a suit, tie, and coat. He greeted her with a smile as she drew close to the gate, but when she reached the barrier, she realized that in her haste to leave, she'd forgotten her key.

"Help!" Kaia pleaded, clutching onto one iron bar with her free hand. "I'm trapped!"

"Oh, well," Reinhard said with a shrug and a smirk, pretending as though he was going to walk away without her. He let her bellyache for only a moment before he pulled his own key out of his pocket and released her.

"You look nice, but where's your uniform?" Kaia inquired.

"Can't wear it right now. Political action groups are banned. Wouldn't want to get stopped," Reinhard answered, shutting and locking the gate behind her. "You look nice, too, but aren't you cold?"

"Yeah, but the party's inside, right?"

"It is, and we won't have to walk, so you're lucky." Reinhard ushered the girl down the street and gestured to a small, shabby black car parked on the side of the road. Kaia let out a squeal of joy.

"Ahhhh! A car?! You gotta car?!"

"Rented. Have to pick up my fiancée in something nice, and I wouldn't put you on a motorcycle."

"You have a motorcycle?!"

"Had one. Sold it. It'd get stolen in this city. Jump in."

Kaia did so eagerly, clambering into the back of the cheap little car. Reinhard spared a moment to adjust his tie before hopping into the driver's seat.

"I got gifts for some people," Kaia said, dropping all but one package at her feet. "Here, this one's for you! Unwrap it now so I can see your response when you're not doing any acting!"

She handed a clumsily wrapped gift to the Blond Beast, which he accepted with a smile.

"Oh..." Reinhard muttered as he tore the paper away. It

was a notebook—no, he flipped through it and realized that it was a blank music book. The cover sported an image of a sailboat on blue waters with a family of ducks gathered on the shore.

"There were two at the store. There was one with a horse and that one," Kaia explained excitedly. "And I almost got you the horse one because Herr Dieter said you like horse riding, but you also like sailing and water, and we met at the lake with the ducks, so I got you that one! And I already wrote your name in it!"

She had, on the inside flap, with a smiley face and a heart drawn beneath it: *Property of Reinhard*. He had received many gifts in his life. Cigars, fine china, a signed copy of *Mein Kampf*, and watches, so many watches! This was easily the cheapest and most thoughtful gift that he had ever been given.

"I appreciate this. Thank you," Reinhard said. "Though, I actually haven't ever written a song, I've only played them."

"Your papa wrote great music, though, so it's genetic! You'll write something good!"

"I'll try to write something worthy of this very lovely book," Reinhard vowed, setting it on the passenger seat. "Thank you, Kaia."

"Merry Christmas!"

"Happy Yule Day, *kleine*. Himmler will have an aneurysm if you call it Christmas."

"What's an aneurysm?" asked the girl, and the rest of the ride to Lina's hotel consisted of a flustered Reinhard trying to find a child-friendly way to describe what an aneurysm was.

Lina Von Osten was waiting outside, bundled up in a

long, slightly torn coat and sporting a wide smile. She was seven years Reinhard's junior, a very pretty girl with blonde hair tied up in a braided bun, light blue eyes, and an active spirit. When Reinhard leapt out of the car to greet her, she enveloped him in a tight hug and kissed him without shame.

"Child's watching," Reinhard muttered with an embarrassed blush, and indeed, Kaia had her face pressed against the car window. Lina gave a small giggle. Reinhard had, of course, told his fiancée as little about the girl as possible, only saying that he had befriended her father and was teaching the child piano lessons. None of that was a lie. Not *technically*.

"Kaia, Lina. Lina, Kaia," the Blond Beast said as he opened the back door of the car for Lina. Reinhard's fiancée slid into the back and greeted the little girl with a warm smile.

"Hiya!" Kaia squeaked. "I didn't get you a gift 'cause I don't know you, but I'll get ya something next year once I know what'cha like!"

"Oh, you're so cute!" Lina chirped, and Reinhard felt a wave of relief wash over him as the ever-maternal Lina started chatting with the girl about piano lessons and Vikings and Himmler. They got along, thank Heaven. When and if the truth ever came out, Reinhard could almost certainly depend on Lina to understand.

They arrived at the building Himmler had rented out for the party, the interior of which was decorated with an abundance of mistletoe and a huge Christmas tree covered in silver Norse-rune ornaments. They swiftly found that Reinhard had been overly cautious in refusing to wear his uniform. Despite the ban, most of the men were nonetheless bedecked in their SS apparel. Maybe they had all gotten changed in the bathroom.

"Reinhard! I barely recognized you out of uniform!" Dieter Amsel ran forward to greet the new arrivals, kissing Lina's hand and giving a particularly warm smile to Kaia.

"Hi, Happy Yule Christmas Day!" Kaia cried, handing Dieter his little gift. Amsel offered all of the mandatory thank-yous and you-shouldn't-haves before unwrapping the present.

"Oh! How cute!" he declared when he held up her gift: a little figurine of a stable.

"You have those little architectural things..."

"Models," Reinhard supplied.

"Yeah, those!" Kaia giggled. "And you like horse-riding! So...there!"

"I'll put it with the rest of my models as soon as I get home. Thank you, Fräulein Schicklgruber!"

"Ah! Reinhard! And Lina at last! And little Kaia as well! Was your father not able to make it?"

Himmler, who was one of the few SS men that hadn't donned his uniform for the occasion but instead sported a grey suit, scurried over to greet the guests. Kaia almost immediately shoved her gift into the *Reichsführer's* arms.

"Papa got sick! Here, Merry Yule!" she declared. Himmler smiled that gas-chamber smile of his, ruffled Kaia's hair, and unwrapped the little bundle.

"Ah! Just what I needed!" Himmler laughed when he unfurled a little leather wallet decorated with a Norse rune.

"It's one-hundred-percent theft-proof," Kaia assured the *Reichsführer*, and it took all of Reinhard's self-control not to burst into laughter.

"We'll see about that next time I'm on the tram!"

chuckled Himmler, shoving the new wallet into his back pocket. "Ah, but for now, Reinhard: let's give you your gift."

Himmler's gift, cheap as he was, consisted of a promotion: he muttered something about intending to give Reinhard the rank of Major as a wedding day gift, but since Lina and Reinhard wouldn't be getting married until January, it would have to do for Yule Day.

The other guests clustered around Himmler and Heydrich as the former made the latter a Major, but one Nazi in particular stood out: Adiel's least favorite student, Leon Engel, bedecked in his full ceremonial SS uniform, complete with an SS dagger strapped to his side. He had seemingly left his wife and son at home.

Reinhard might have been worried, but he had known for some time that Engel was in the SS, and the young Nazi had never reacted when he saw Kaia visiting the Blond Beast's office. Reinhard was thus certain that the failed art student didn't recognize the girl as Adiel Goldstein's daughter. If he had, he would have surely done something weeks ago, for no one as virulently anti-Semitic as Leon Engel could have possessed the same astute self-control as Reinhard Heydrich when it came to Germans cavorting with Jews.

Engel barely spared the girl a glance as he marched forward to shake Reinhard's hand. "Congratulations, Major!" he said, flashing a friendly smile. "When this ban's lifted, you'll have a new uniform to show off."

"New markings, maybe," Reinhard muttered with a shrug, glancing down at Kaia, who was pouting with disappointment at the fact that Reinhard and she could no longer be captains together.

"Jonas, and Ava too, come on over and meet *Major*

Heydrich!" cried Dieter, drawing Reinhard's attention away from Engel and towards a pair of teenagers. Jonas Amsel politely marched forth to do his father's bidding, dragging his plus-one along. Ah, this must have been the eldest daughter of the Keller family, Jonas' little girlfriend. It seemed that Kaia wasn't the only Jew that Himmler had unwittingly invited to this party.

The teenagers bade hello and congratulations to Major Heydrich, Jonas giving him an energetic handshake, Ava a brusque one before she grabbed her boyfriend's arm and dragged him to the mead table. Reinhard's eyes darted towards Engel, and he wondered what the smirking SS man would say if he realized that he was standing so close to the person who would, if Operation Chaplin failed, arrest his precious wife.

He decided not to dwell on such matters tonight, however. It was Christmas, after all. Or, rather, Yule Day. Yule *Night*.

Whatever it was, the party was surprisingly pleasant. Perhaps because Himmler controlled himself and didn't ask Reinhard to do any sort of seance with Lina. Perhaps because of the decent company: it was very nice to be near Lina again, and watching Kaia dart about with the other children was amusing. There was good food, good drink, and at one point an SS man handed the Blond Beast a violin and had Heydrich perform for the partygoers, which earned him a round of applause and a pair of admiring gazes from both Lina and little Kaia.

Eventually, the partygoers broke off into little groups. Lina scurried off to talk with some of the other women, Kaia flitted after the children her age, and Reinhard found himself standing in a semi-circle with some of the men: Engel, Dieter, and a few others.

"Major Heydrich, your daughter's quite the little dictator," Engel laughed, gesturing to the corner where the children were playing. Kaia was indeed dominating her fellows, proving that the blood of a tyrant was flowing through her veins. She had dubbed herself the captain of a Viking expedition and was barking orders at the little boys, who scrambled to obey like a harem of horse-whipped husbands.

"Not my daughter, daughter of a friend," Reinhard explained with a fond little chuckle.

"Which means he can't be held responsible for her being bossy," Dieter joked. "Her and Ava should have a contest to see who can scare the boys most by the end of the night."

"Keller would win," Reinhard predicted. "Kaia isn't scary, she's *charismatic.*"

And it was quite unfortunate that at that moment, when everyone was looking at little Kaia, nobody noticed a brief flit of motion as Leon dropped something into Reinhard's drink.

KAIA HAD BEEN RUNNING HER SHIP WITH THE RUTHLESSNESS of a Viking Hitler, but even Vikings needed to pee. She placed her first-mate, one of the more competent boys, in charge while she skittered upstairs and dove into the bathroom. As she emerged a moment later, however, she nearly bumped into a man that had been standing right outside.

"It's clean," Kaia assured him, gesturing to the bathroom behind her. He chuckled and knelt down in front of her, his green-blue eyes twinkling.

"Fräulein Schicklgruber, is it?" he said. "Or maybe you'd prefer to go by Fräulein Goldstein."

Kaia was wise enough not to let her fear show on her face, instead raising an eyebrow and fixing the man with a befuddled expression even as her heart palpitated terribly.

But the man shook his head. "Don't worry about it. I'm one of your father's students. Has he ever mentioned me?"

"Uhm...he doesn't really talk about his work much."

"I'm Leon! Your father's one of my favorite teachers. Forgive me, I recognized you from class. I'm surprised you're here! A real lamb in the lion's den. You're safe, right?"

Kaia's tense little body relaxed as she offered Leon Engel a bright smile. "I'm all right!"

"I just saw that you came here with Herr Heydrich, and I was concerned. Does he know that you're...you know..." Leon drew a Star-of-David in the air.

"Yeah, he knows!" Kaia assured him. "It's all right, you don't have to worry, he's good! I guess you're good too!"

"I appreciate that," Leon chuckled. "I'm only in the SS because I need a job. I don't have anything against your type."

"Oh, okay," Kaia said, her smile dampening slightly. "Uhm...hey, listen, you should talk to Reinhard and my papa because they'll wanna show you something. Maybe you can help us!"

"Oh, help you?" crooned Leon. "Well, for now, we should probably just..."

But right then, both Leon and the girl heard a commotion downstairs: a few worried voices and Lina Von Osten yelping her fiancé's name. Kaia, hearing that, let out a small squeak of concern and scurried down the stairs, failing to see the small smirk that quickly flashed across Leon's face.

"Is he all right?" Kaia cried, rushing to Reinhard's side as Lina helped him onto a small couch. A few SS men laughed when they saw the Blond Beast stumble and mumble incoherently.

"Heydrich had too much to drink?" one chuckled. Dieter shook his head, his brow furrowed in concern as he looked down at his boss.

"He only had one drink. He was sober a minute ago," Amsel insisted as Lina placed a hand on her fiancé's forehead.

"Reinhard, don't die!" commanded Kaia, grabbing his arm and giving him a slight shake as a shudder went through his body and he collapsed onto the couch, unconcious.

"Oh dear, is he sick?" Himmler said, hovering nearby. "Maybe we should call a doctor?"

"He doesn't feel warm," Lina whimpered, brushing a hand through her fiancé's blond locks. One SS man who happened to be a medical student bolted over and gave Reinhard a cursory examination. When he couldn't find anything, he suggested taking Heydrich to a hospital.

"Oh, I'll go with him!" Lina said as Amsel volunteered to drive him to the nearest doctor's office.

"Can I go too?" squeaked Kaia, taking a step towards the unconscious SS man as his co-worker and his fiancée struggled to lift him up and carry him outside. Himmler knelt down beside the child, patting her shoulder and shaking his head.

"Reinhard will be just fine, little one!" the *Reichsführer* assured the Jewish girl. "In the meantime, we should get you home. What's your address?"

Before Kaia could even hope to come up with a lie or an excuse, Engel stepped forward. "I can take her home, *Reichsführer*," he said, flashing a smile at the girl. "Me and her father are already acquainted, so it'll be less stressful."

Kaia let out a squeak of agreement that disguised a small sigh of relief. Himmler, ignorant as he was, agreed, commanding Leon to get her home safe and wishing Kaia a happy Yule Day.

"Have a good night, Kaia! Don't worry, your uncle will be just fine!" the *Reichsführer* said. Kaia nodded, though nervousness still made her bite her lip as she said her good-byes to the other guests and took Leon Engel's hand.

Worrying about the Blond Beast's safety far more than her own, Kaia let Leon lead her into the snowy night.

ADIEL GOLDSTEIN WAS A DEEP SLEEPER. THIS WAS, IF HIS mother's books were anything to go by, a genetic trait. Natan had once joked that a bomb could have gone off in their home and he wouldn't have woken up, and Adiel was beginning to realize that probably hadn't really been a joke since as Adolf Hitler, he had literally slept through bombs hitting his bunker.

So he slept right through Bernie's frantic barks as the dog, who had swiftly realized that his mistress was missing, peered out the window and saw two figures approach the front gate.

He slept right through Kaia proudly proclaiming that she had forgotten her key but could pick the lock if Engel just gave her a moment.

He slept peaceably, ignorantly, as Leon Engel watched the girl yank a bobby pin from her hair and contemplated his next move. It likely would have been easy enough to let the girl invite him in, to walk right into the Professor's room and stab him to death as he slept.

Engel could have done that. It would have been easy. Entirely too easy. Professor Goldstein hadn't taken Leon Engel's life, but he and all of his ilk had ruined Germany's future, stolen their dreams, and for that he deserved far worse than a quick death.

And the little Jew girl...well, she was small, but she was already sinking her claws into their very best. Perhaps she didn't deserve to suffer as much as her father did, but she was nevertheless a maggot that would one day become a poisonous monster.

So, Engel considered it an act of mercy when he drew his SS dagger from its sheath and plunged it into her chest, turning on his heel and fleeing just as quickly, leaving the girl to bleed out. A quick death was a kindness, far more than any Jew deserved, and the pain that Adiel Goldstein would experience come morning would be more than enough revenge.

Adiel slept through his daughter's death, but when he awoke, followed Bernie outside, and found her in a pile of scarlet snow with an SS blade buried in her back, his scream woke up the entire neighborhood.

FIFTEEN

Five days had passed since Christmas, and Leon Engel was convinced that he had gotten away with murder.

(*Not murder*, he assured himself again, because Jews weren't human. The little fits of nausea that he still felt when he thought of his sudden, swift, almost instinctual act were repressed over and over by this thought: *not human, not murder.*)

Engel reported for duty at the Brown House the day after Christmas with anxiety burning in his heart, fully expecting to find himself facing a murderous Blond Beast. Heydrich would have no doubt been told that Leon Engel had been the one to escort Kaia home, and once he put two and two together...

But Heydrich was as cold to Engel as he was to every other SS man, no more and no less, the frigid mask never slipping. Maybe that meant he'd snapped out of whatever trance the Goldsteins had put him under. Maybe he had been blackmailed the whole time, and Engel had actually liberated him from the Jews' grasp. Maybe he just hadn't liked the little shit that much. Maybe he hadn't even heard that she was dead.

That was the woefully ironic thing about it all: if Kaia Schicklgruber, friend of Heinrich Himmler, "niece" of Reinhard Heydrich, beloved guest of the SS, had been found dead, then Munich would have been lit ablaze. If Leon hadn't left his SS dagger buried in her back, Himmler would have blamed the communists or the Jews for the poor child's murder, and she would have gone down as a martyr for the Cause.

But Kaia Goldstein received a very small obituary in a Yiddish-language newspaper that nobody at the Brown House read, and so it seemed that they were none the wiser. Himmler even asked Leon if Kaia had gotten home safe, and Leon was tempted to tell him the whole truth, to expose Heydrich right then, but he instead decided not to try his luck. Ideally, he would figure out exactly what Heydrich was planning and then stop him, become a hero to the Cause. But since Heydrich was utterly unreadable and Himmler seemed quite attached to the Jewess, Leon decided to smile, assure Himmler that Kaia was just fine, and wait just a bit longer.

And so, Leon continued on as though nothing had happened, and when he and the rest of his troop were sent, seemingly without Heydrich, to do one final search of the hotel before Hitler's arrival, he thought nothing of it.

"Engel, here, you're with me," Amsel commanded with a chipper smile. "We'll search Room Fifty-Eight one more time. I wanted to ask you about that painting you showed me the other day. I thought it was truly excellent! You really have a flair for drawing buildings. The Führer is the same, you know, have you seen his works?"

Leon followed Amsel, chit-chatting with him about art, then about their respective sons and how Dieter had survived Jonas' toddlerhood. It wasn't until Leon stepped into Room 58 and Dieter locked the door behind him that he realized he'd been trapped, and so easily too.

"I wouldn't bother with the gun. It's full of blanks. And you don't have a dagger."

Leon turned away from Dieter, who quietly blockaded the door, and found himself facing the Blond Beast himself. It seemed that Heydrich had forsworn weapons as well. He had neither a dagger nor a gun at his side. Instead, somewhat bizarrely, the Blond Beast held a pillow under his arm, which he tossed casually onto a chair.

Heydrich was phenomenally good at hiding his anger: even now, with all pretenses gone, he maintained a cold mask that didn't betray whatever he was truly feeling about Engel. His voice offered only the barest lilt of disgust.

"I see..." Leon mumbled, puffing out his chest and squaring his shoulders, like a lone cat surrounded by feral dogs that sought to make itself seem larger and more threatening than it was. "You roped Dieter into this. Maybe blackmailed him. Or are you *both* traitors?"

Dieter's head was bowed, his lips pursed in a thin line. He said nothing, and neither did Reinhard. When the silence became oppressive, Leon broke it with a snarl.

"Either way, you're both pathetic!" he snapped. "You have the ideological fortitude of wet paper, Heydrich! Honestly, I can't believe I once respected you!"

327

"I don't need respect from a man like you," came Heydrich's reply, this time biting. Leon cackled.

"Ah, don't act so high and mighty! That Jew you're such good friends with ruined my life, and that little shit wasn't even a full human! She was already showing all the typical Jew traits! You would have done the same thing!"

"I would never—!"

And Reinhard stopped himself because he would have. He did once.

"I *won't* be like you," Reinhard said instead, his voice a deathly whisper that almost sounded like a plea. "I would rather die."

"Come at me, then," Engel sneered. "That's why you pulled this shit, right? You wanted to avenge your little *niece.*"

"No." And now Heydrich's voice became something else entirely, an ice storm made sound. A shiver went through Engel. Even Dieter winced. "If I wanted to avenge her, Engel, I would do far worse. But I have something I need to do, and if it fails, I don't want to die without knowing that I'll see you in Hell."

With that, the Blond Beast advanced. Engel dove for the nearest potential weapon, a fire poker, but Reinhard had already tackled him before he could even touch it. The two wrestled for a moment, but even though Leon was younger than Reinhard and only a little shorter, he was an art student while Heydrich was an athlete, a former naval cadet. Reinhard easily subdued the SS Private.

"Dieter, pillow!" the Blond Beast commanded, and Dieter scurried away from the door, grabbing the pillow that Reinhard had left on the sofa. At his superior's command, Dieter shoved it beneath Leon's face.

Killing someone via suffocation, Reinhard decided, was entirely unpleasant. Even suffocating a bastard like Leon Engel made him feel ill. Holding Engel down and feeling him writhe and sob and squirm was awful even though he deserved every second of it.

It certainly made Reinhard think worse of his other self, the Reinhard Heydrich that had suffocated millions of people. Maybe if *that* Reinhard Heydrich had been forced to personally smother every Jew that he had wanted to murder, every old man and child, then he would have thought twice about what he was doing. Surely he couldn't have hated any of them as much as he hated Leon Engel right then. Reinhard dearly wished he could have just shoved Engel into a little metal box and let poison gas do the filthy job for him.

But Reinhard didn't have a gas chamber, and the job needed to be done, and so he forced his heart to become hard as iron and did it. And maybe he had done the same thing once upon a time under the impression that *they deserved it*. Maybe Hangman-Heydrich had burned away those weak feelings of disgust the same way he did once he was sure that Engel was dead: with a righteous fire of self-assurance.

Either way, Leon Engel went limp. Reinhard checked his pulse and only let him go once he was certain the man was dead. *There you have it*, the Blond Beast thought, standing up and scowling down at the body. *Your first murder.*

"I'll make sure the hotel's clear, and then we can take the body to the...place," Dieter mumbled, yanking the pillow out from under Engel's face.

Reinhard nodded. Killing Leon Engel would have been easy enough: a gunshot to the head, a slice to the neck.

Suffocation had been unpleasant, but necessary. If it appeared that Leon Engel had died fighting, then when the Nazis found his body, the SS would no doubt blame the communists and the Jews. He would be dead, yes, but he would be a Nazi martyr.

Reinhard would rather die than be forced to worship the memory of Leon Engel like he was Horst Wessel, and so he and Dieter had instead agreed that it would be best if they smothered Engel to death and then dumped his corpse half-naked behind a known hangout for homosexuals. The propaganda outlets would scramble to hide the disgrace of it all, and Engel would be rendered an embarrassing memory for the movement.

It would have been difficult even for Reinhard Heydrich to get away with murder all by himself. Quite fortunately, Dieter Amsel was more than willing to be Reinhard's accomplice.

"I'll handle it all, you can head back and do whatever you need to do," Dieter assured his superior, offering him a brief pat on the shoulder before leaning over Leon's body and spitting directly on the dead SS Private's skull. "Piece of trash!"

Maybe Dieter only said that to appeal to Reinhard— *There, I hate him too, see?*—but then again, maybe he meant it. He had liked little Kaia, and he was seemingly still fond of the Kellers. When Reinhard had, in an effort to rope Dieter into his little scheme, finally told Amsel that the Kellers were blood Jews, Amsel had looked as frightened as he had furious. But when Dieter had vowed to cut them off entirely and Reinhard had encouraged him not to be too hasty, he had been noticeably relieved.

"You'll burn those papers then, right?" Dieter asked for about the trillionth time as he tore the pillowcase off of the soft murder weapon and carried it over to the stove heater. Reinhard nodded.

"You and I will be the only people in Germany who know that the Kellers are Jewish," Reinhard vowed. "As long as what happened in this room never leaves it."

"It won't. I promise," Dieter sighed, fighting with a match for a moment before he managed to light it, toss it into the stove, and then chuck the pillowcase in to be incinerated. He straightened up and wrung his hands.

"I suppose I should just hope that my son's little crush on Avalina dissipates as time goes on," Dieter muttered. "But if it doesn't…"

"If it doesn't, you don't have anything to worry about," Reinhard assured him in the gentlest tone he had ever offered to a subordinate. "Nobody else will know. Every official document will make it seem that they're Aryans."

"*I'll* know," Dieter said, his eyes flitting to a map of Germany that was one Versailles Treaty out of date, several territories too big, now more of a goal for the Nazis than a matter of fact. "They're Jews. They fooled me, they *lied* to me…"

"They almost certainly don't know themselves, Dieter. At least Otto doesn't: he's a National Socialist."

"Maybe it was all a farce…"

"*Dieter.*" Reinhard cut off that line of thought with a tone like a knife made of ice. "I don't have time for conspiratorial bullshit."

"You're right," Dieter sighed, raking a hand through his silvering locks, and visibly trying to make this square peg fit into the round hole that was his worldview. "I suppose it's only natural that some Jews would be perfectly normal if they've interbred with us for centuries. The Kellers and poor little Kaia."

Hearing Kaia's name made Reinhard desperately want to kick Leon Engel's corpse, but he refrained for the sake of their scheme.

"Either way, thank you. I suppose we're bound by secrets now," Dieter declared, offering Heydrich a small smile. "Being honest, you made me very nervous."

"I should still make you nervous," Reinhard said, gesturing with his eyes to the man he had just killed.

"True, but nonetheless, I thought you'd be more…" Dieter's eyes darted to the map again, and he shook his head. "Well. Either way, I'm grateful you were…empathetic. Thank you."

Empathetic was most certainly not a word that Reinhard would have used to describe himself, but right then he was too angry and too exhausted to argue about such minutiae. When Dieter offered a handshake, Reinhard leaned forward, and the two conspirators shook hands above the dead body.

Becca's books tended to ask the question of *why* quite a bit. *Why would someone do this? Why would the world let this happen? Why would anyone look at a little girl and decide that she was less than human?*

Adiel had read his mother's books and been plagued by a different question. *How?*

How did *he* do this? That was a natural question, for once upon a time, Adiel had thought that he knew himself well.

But perhaps just as pressing: how could Edmund do this? Adiel may have been Hitler, but even ignoring that, he *knew* Hitler. Hitler, his doppelgänger, his brother, his replacement. Edmund Hitler had not been a good man, but he hadn't been worse than a demon either.

But then Adiel would remember Edmund Hitler's face. The crookedness of his smile, the way his eyes would cloud over when he clutched at his breast pocket, where he always carried a picture of his mother. Adiel would realize then that Corporal Hitler had been a strained soul. His siblings' deaths, his mother's passing, his father's cruelty, his dashed dreams of being an artist, all of it had piled and piled and stacked and stacked, and when his final lifeline, the glorious war, had ended in defeat, something in Hitler had *broken*.

Adiel had looked at the pictures of his alternate self, at those bright blue eyes, and realized that Adolf Hitler had not been a whole man. There was something missing inside of him, maybe his heart or his soul. Hitler was a moustache and a scowl, yes, but he was also blisteringly hollow, like an oven with nothing inside it but fire.

Something inside Adiel broke when Kaia died. Not the day he found her, or even the day after. Not until long after the little funeral, when he was back in his home, petting Bernie, sitting before a pile of Becca's books. His mother's voice echoed in his ears. *It burns you before it burns them.*

Numbness became something else. Something great and terrible. Something maternal platitudes could no longer contain.

Reinhard Heydrich arrived at the Goldstein household

with news that Leon Engel was dead and disgraced, but his proclamation petered into nothingness when he saw Adiel.

"You..." the Blond Beast said. Adiel was standing before a fireplace filled with books that predicted an awful future. His mother's books and films were smoldering.

Adiel turned to face Reinhard, his frighteningly hypnotic blue eyes reflecting the flames, revealing that he had shaved his beard, leaving only a small tuft of hair beneath his nose.

He looked *exactly* like his brother.

"You're ready," Reinhard said, grim and determined all at once.

CHAIM WACH HAD EXPECTED TO DEPART FOR AMERICA WITH a little girl, a dog, and a note. Instead, after staying behind to comfort a father and bury the girl, he took the dog and the note, made his way to America with only a bit of harassment from the immigration officials, and delivered onto Natan Goldstein the dog, a note, and horrible news.

It wasn't the first time that Natan Goldstein had lost everything. The first time, when his tattoo was fresh, his head was shaved, and his son was his tormenter, he had forced himself to keep going out of both love and hate. Because he still had Becca and he loved her, yes, but also because Adolf Hitler would have wanted him to kill himself, and he had hated Hitler more than he'd hated living.

This time, he screamed and tore at his clothes in grief,

but decided to live, because Adiel Goldstein would want him to, and he loved his son more than he hated living.

SIXTEEN

"**M**ajor Heydrich, is everything ready?"

"Secure, *Reichsführer.*"

"Just making sure. We *are* one man short since...ah...well..." Himmler mopped his forehead with a handkerchief and offered Heydrich a small smile as the Nazi Major journeyed down the spiral staircase, the one and only route to Hitler's suite.

Smuggling Adiel into the room hadn't been as difficult as making sure that no well-meaning maid made an unscheduled trip to the suite and spotted the assassin. Luckily, Operation Chaplin had been successful thus far. Adiel was crouched in Hitler's bedroom, ready to replace his brother.

As long as nobody went upstairs with Hitler, they would be fine. Reinhard would need to stand by the staircase and make sure that Hitler didn't bring any spontaneous guests. It was unlikely he would: Hermann Goering wasn't in Munich, Ernst Röhm was in Hamburg, and Joseph

Goebbels would no doubt be spending the New Year with his new wife Magda.

Eva Braun wouldn't be showing up either even though she was supposed to later in the evening: her invitation had been oh-so-unfortunately lost in the mail, and her phone line had sadly been rendered inoperable. Eva would probably be crying herself to sleep tonight thinking that Hitler had spurned her advances, and maybe Hitler himself wouldn't notice, his mind no doubt being occupied by thoughts of Geli Raubal.

Fortunately, Himmler had no intention of following Hitler up to the suite. "I'm going to go inspect the men downstairs and greet the Führer at the door," the *Reichs-führer* declared. "I hope Goebbels doesn't show up."

Reinhard did too, though not for the same reason as Himmler, at least not entirely. Himmler had once gotten along with the diminutive Nazi propagandist, but Joseph Goebbels the rising star was far too arrogant and abrasive to maintain friendships. Himmler mumbled something about Engel and left Heydrich to guard the staircase.

Reinhard glanced out the window and spotted an unmistakable Mercedes that hastily pulled up to the hotel, and even from the third floor, he could hear Goebbels' distinctive voice. (It was a good voice, the sort of voice that Reinhard would have killed for, the sort of voice that could drive a nation to mass murder.) Given the choice between Magda Goebbels and Edmund Hitler, apparently Joseph Goebbels would rather choose Hitler, worshipful peon that he was.

Footsteps and a steadily loudening series of Heils informed Reinhard that Edmund Hitler was drawing close. In the blink of an eye, there he was, strutting through the archway with a small briefcase in hand and an Iron Cross glistening on his chest, his blue eyes a flaming void.

Goebbels, who, with his short stature, dark hair, ugly appearance, and crippled leg was easily the least Aryan man that Reinhard had ever seen, limped at Hitler's side, blabbering about banners. Adiel's replacement raked a hand through his dark brown hair and looked up at Reinhard as he approached the staircase. Calmly, Reinhard lifted an arm. "Heil, my Führer."

"You're Major Heydrich, yes?" the Führer said. Goebbels glanced at Hitler's suitcase, then at Heydrich, and then he let out an expectant little rumble like Heydrich was an untrained busboy that had failed at his duties.

Edmund Hitler saw this little interaction: Heydrich standing stubbornly rigid, Goebbels looking like he was five seconds away from leaning over to Hitler and whispering about *the help these days.* The Führer rolled his bright blue eyes and shifted his briefcase to the other hand, offering Reinhard a small smile and a handshake.

"Loyal Old Heinrich speaks very highly of you," the Führer said. "I expect you'll do very well."

Hitler most certainly didn't intend for that to be a threat. It didn't sound like a threat: delivered in the genial tone of a boss that was warmly greeting a new secretary. It didn't look like a threat either: Hitler's smile, quite ugly in almost every one of Becca's books, wasn't as off-putting in person. It was easy to see how he fooled everyone, but then again, Reinhard reminded himself, Hitler almost certainly didn't think he *was* fooling anyone. Just as he didn't think that he was threatening Heydrich.

But he was, at least as far as Reinhard was concerned. And so, the Blond Beast shook the Führer's hand and

mumbled a promise to live up to every one of his expecta-
tions, hoping that he would be one of the last men to see
Edmund Hitler alive.

From the corner of his eye, Reinhard saw Goebbels take
a hesitant step forward. No doubt the propagandist wanted
to ask if he could come up with Hitler and continue their
chat, but fortunately, Reinhard had read Goebbels' biogra-
phies and had come prepared.

"Herr Doctor Goebbels!" Reinhard said brightly, stepping between the spiral staircase and the propagandist.
"Might I say, I read your novel *Michael* and it was absolutely
inspiring! I had so many questions to ask, and I would *love*
for you to sign my copy."

Reinhard heard Hitler chuckle as he began to ascend by
himself. Goebbels' oak-brown eyes sparkled. He looked like
a dog that had just been offered a five-pound steak.

"Ah, of course!" the ever-arrogant Nazi novelist cried.
"I'm always willing to discuss literature with discerning
gentlemen!"

It was going to be a long walk to Goebbels' car, but that
would be fine. Reinhard heard the slamming of a door up
above. Now everything was in Adiel Goldstein's hands.

ADIEL KNEW EDMUND HITLER BETTER THAN ANYONE IN THE
Nazi Party did. Not only because he *was* him, not only
because of Becca's books, but because he remembered
when he was Hitler the Comrade.

All appearances aside, Hitler was not a very sociable
man: conversations with him would be long but one-sided,

with Hitler doing most of the talking. He would rant about something for twenty straight minutes. Once he was done, however, Hitler would retreat to his cot to pet his dog, sketch, and recharge. Even a social interaction where he did almost all of the talking seemed to exhaust him.

So, it wasn't surprising that when Hitler entered his suite, he took off his coat and gloves, tossed his briefcase aside without bothering to unpack, and immediately collapsed onto the nearest chair. A day of travel and talking and spewing lies had worn him out so much that he didn't give his new room even a cursory glance, and therefore, he didn't notice a doppelgänger waiting in the shadows.

He didn't, that is, until he opened his eyes and found himself facing said doppelgänger. Hate-filled blue eyes locked with identical, surprised blue eyes. Adiel aimed a gun at the Iron Cross his brother wore on his chest.

Adiel could have just killed his brother right then. Maybe he should have, but something made him speak. He might have been surprised by the sound of his own voice—coarse and harsh and all-Hitler—but he didn't truly care about such trifles anymore.

"Do you know who I am?" Adiel asked his brother. Edmund Hitler, clearly already a bit befuddled by the fact that he was being confronted by his own reflection rendered homicidal, narrowed his eyes and clutched at the thigh of his pants.

"Goldstein?" he guessed. Bitterly, Adiel realized that this was the last time he would ever be referred to by his true name. He nodded proudly.

"That *is* my name, but not the one I was given at birth," Adiel declared, his gaze disdainfully darting over Hitler's shoulder and falling upon a map of Germany that hung proudly from one of the suite's walls. Two swastika banners bordered the map. It was difficult for Adiel to believe that he had once killed millions for something he hated so, *so* much.

"I was born as Adolfus Hitler, your older brother. My parents took me away from our awful family when I was little, so I wouldn't end up like *you*." Adiel let that truth, bitter and yet blessed, hang between them for a moment before his brother scoffed.

"You've lost your wits," Hitler said. "First of all, my mother was *not* awful. Second, all of her children save me and my younger sister died of natural causes."

"That's what they told you," growled Adiel, who hadn't expected Hitler to believe him and didn't really care either way. "And I haven't gone mad, *you've* gone mad! I want to know why. You were never a good man, but you weren't *this*!"

With his free hand, Adiel gestured to Hitler's entire being. His replacement clutched his pant leg even tighter.

"You want to know why I changed my views about your people?" Hitler said, shifting his weight subtly, as though he would have liked nothing more than to accompany his rant with overwrought gestures but knew better than to do so when there was a gun aimed at his skull.

"*Evidence*, Goldstein, I found *evidence* of it all," Hitler declared. "Whereas before it seemed to me that the hatred of your people was entirely based on pointless religious infighting, I've seen *evidence* that it is in fact entirely reasonable. Scientifically minded, rational people have noted the differences between the races and have deduced that the Hebrew race is long-lived and innately parasitic. We stand at the climax of a conflict thousands of years in the making between Western civilization and decedent Judeo-Bolshevism, and I intend to ensure that my people are the victors."

"You and your nonsense speeches!" Adiel snapped, stepping forward, his finger tapping the trigger threateningly. Idly, he realized that if he pulled it, then it would be the second time he shot himself in the head.

"You're just an arrogant, selfish piece of trash that wants to be some sort of brave hero because you're an utter and complete *failure* at everything else!" Adiel continued, his hand trembling, a sob nearly wracking his body. "And you don't care how many innocent children you have to murder! As long as you can prove that *papa* was wrong when he called you *worthless!*"

Hitler seemed taken aback for a moment, but then he shook his head, likely deciding that Adiel was merely making assumptions. Easy enough: it wasn't as though most men his age had loving, gentle fathers. Adiel had been lucky in that regard, getting something that he had never deserved.

"You're entirely off-base, Goldstein," Hitler said. "First and foremost, I'm most certainly not a murderer, I've never killed anyone in my life. Secondly, my movement is entirely moral in its aims. Obviously, in a battle of races, some decent people on both sides will be harmed. I should say, though I doubt you'll believe me, that I *did* intend on contacting you at some point to ensure your safe emigration once I became President since you proved yourself to be a decent Jew in the trenches…"

"Oh, I'm so *honored!*" spat Adiel. "The great humanitarian Ad…*Edmund* Hitler continued to think of a worthless undesirable like me! Every Jew is evil and needs to be killed except the ones *he* knows! Me, and how about Gutmann? How about your mother's doctor?"

"How...?" Hitler muttered, but he must have assumed he'd spoken to Adiel about Dr. Bloch at some point and had simply forgotten the conversation since he shook his head again and proclaimed, "While collective measures are entirely necessary in this struggle and the Jews, most certainly, have not behaved humanely towards their German 'friends' throughout history, I believe it is important to show clemency where it is warranted. Ideally, the few decent Jews that exist would not be harmed at all and would leave, never to interact with the Fatherland ever again, but we all know that real life is not so simple. The price of victory is suffering."

"Just like I said!" Adiel snapped. "You want victory at all costs, and you'll do some token little gestures to spare *your* Jews, to spare *your* feelings! So you can sleep at night and pretend like you're a good person, and all the dead children you leave in your path to 'victory' are just collateral damage or necessary sacrifices!"

"You've spoken of 'children' twice now, but I fail to see why," observed Hitler, and now his determined but calm tone gave way to a smidgeon of umbrage. "It's the Judeo-Bolsheviks that have mercilessly slaughtered children and corrupted those they haven't butchered..."

"Don't give me that shit! One of your *noble* SS men killed my nine-year-old daughter! Stabbed her right in the back and left her to die!"

Adiel realized right then that he hadn't actually said what had happened to Kaia yet: the police hadn't truly cared about the fate of a Jewish child, he'd been too numb to say anything during her funeral, and Reinhard had already known what had happened. Saying it out loud, and to Hitler's face, to *his* face, made it feel horrifically real all of a sudden. It made his heart break all over again.

Hitler's expression softened. "I see..." he muttered. "That's why you've gone mad, why you're doing this..."

Hitler didn't dare move his hands, likely knowing that Adiel would shoot if he even suspected that the Führer would go for his weapon. His eyes, however, flitted down towards his chest, either to his Iron Cross or the pocket which held a picture of his mother, one or the other. Maybe both.

"If that's true, your actions here might be understandable, but they're entirely ineffective and misguided," Hitler proclaimed, looking up, his blue eyes flashing. "If you're under the impression that *I* ordered such an act, you're wrong. I wouldn't do such a thing."

"Yes, you would..." Adiel hissed, feeling like a snake was wrapped around his throat. *Yes, I would.*

"Look, put the gun down and I can help you," the Führer vowed, and it was easy for Adiel to see how Hitler had once been able to lead a nation astray because he wanted to obey. Maybe because he wanted to believe that Hitler, that *he*, was a good person deep down, a Big Bad Wolf that could be saved with a bit of affection like Kaia had wanted. Or maybe because he would still rather die as Adiel Goldstein than live for a second as Adolf Hitler.

"We can conduct an internal investigation into whatever regrettable incident occurred, and if it *was* an SS man, I can assure you that I'll see to it myself he's prosecuted. Believe me, it's in my interest as well. I have no desire for our ranks to be filled with criminals. Our movement is meant to be pure."

"It's *not*...." hissed Adiel, gritting his teeth so hard that he almost tasted little flakes of bone on his tongue. "It's not, and you're a *liar*..."

"Goldstein, old comrade, I beg you to come to your senses. You have my condolences for what happened," Hitler said, his voice soft, genuine. If he was lying, then he was the greatest liar to ever breathe air. "I promise you: I didn't harm your daughter and I never would. Whatever you've been told or whatever you've come to believe, it's entirely wrong. I haven't become a monster. I'm a good man—"

BANG!

"No, you're not!"

BANG!

"*No, you're not!*"

BANG!

"NO! YOU'RE! NOT!"

By the time Adiel ran out of bullets, Edmund Hitler's body was completely unrecognizable. Adiel spared only a moment to catch his breath. If he'd possessed a mirror right then, even he would have been startled by how much he looked like the man he had just murdered: red-faced, wild-eyed, mop of dark hair doused in sweat, splattered with blood.

Adiel could already hear a commotion downstairs, however, and so he hastily stole Hitler's blood-stained Iron Cross, took out Hitler's gun and put it in the corpse's hand, then grabbed his brother's coat and gloves and hastily donned them, hoping that the troop of SS men would be fooled.

"...NOW, THE MINE INCIDENT, ON THE OTHER HAND, WAS truthfully inspired by my old friend Richard Flisges. Now, *he* was a real German..."

"Heydrich! Get in here! The Führer's been attacked!"

Oh, thank God, thought Reinhard Heydrich. Even if Adiel had failed, escaping from Goebbels would be its own reward. Reinhard would happily skip to his own execution if it meant never having to talk to the propagandist about his terrible novel ever again.

The Nazi Major turned on his heel and abandoned the squawking propagandist, rushing into the hotel while Goebbels limped after him.

"Yes, yes, my Führer, I'm terribly sorry..."

"Is this Heydrich boy you kept bragging about a damn soldier or not, Heinrich?!"

Even from the bottom of the spiral staircase, Reinhard heard a deep voice shouting. Worry stabbed at his heart. That sounded like Hitler. That sounded *too much* like Hitler. Had they failed?

He bolted into the suite just in time to steal a glance at a corpse seconds before an SS man tossed a sheet over it: the head was completely gone, blown to bits, and the body was battered with bullets. Standing nearby, flailing his arms, red-faced and ranting, was the killer, sporting a slightly blood-stained coat and an Iron Cross. Himmler was doing his best to calm the hysterical Hitler down.

Hitler...*was* it Hitler? When the man turned to Reinhard and his blue eyes glowed with fire...

"Heydrich, you moron, there was an assassin waiting in

my room! Some damn insane Jew-communist! I was assured of your competence, but it appears I've been misled!"

"I..." Reinhard croaked, his mouth dry, his mind abuzz, searching for something, *anything*, to indicate that he had won.

"I apologize, my Führer," he whispered when he could find nothing.

"My Führer! Are you all right?!" Goebbels shoved his way past Reinhard, and the Blond Beast watched the propagandist carefully. If anyone could have realized that a double was a double, it would have been Goebbels, who probably stared at a photo of Hitler for an hour before sleep every night.

Goebbels didn't hesitate, didn't declare that the person before him wasn't his Messiah. He limped right up to the man with the moustache and the scowl, worry pouring from his brown eyes.

"Hardly!" snapped the Führer. Even if he wasn't Hitler, he was the Führer now. "The Party and the movement are fortunate that I'm not some worthless stuffed-shirt politician who's never fired a gun in his life!"

"Absolutely, my Führer!" cried Goebbels with a simpering smile.

"I'm already exhausted, and yet I can't even depend on my elite *protection* squad to *protect* my life when they've been given *two months* of advanced notice!"

"Positively shameful, my Führer," Goebbels concurred, casting a quick smirk at Himmler, who winced like he was facing a fox in his chicken coop.

"Perhaps next time I should ask *Ernst* to see to my accommodations, Heinrich!" the Führer snapped, whirling about to face Himmler, who bowed like a serf that had just offended his lord.

"As I said, I'm deeply troubled and humiliated, my Führer, but I can assure you that this sort of thing will never happen again!" Himmler said.

"I should hope not! If Heydrich hadn't done decent work in the intelligence wing, I'd have him fired on the spot. As it were: he is to be disciplined, and until further notice his tasks are to be regulated to intelligence matters and *only* intelligence matters! And he should consider that an act of extreme mercy from me given what almost happened!"

"You're so very generous, my Führer," Goebbels chirped, though he must have felt genuine sympathy for his literary "fan" since when he glanced at Reinhard, his smile morphed from one of absolute poison to a somewhat skewed smirk.

"I...thank you, my Führer," Reinhard mumbled.

"Now, assuming you're not blind, start using your intelligence skills to investigate this incident!" commanded the Führer. "I want this Jew's accomplices tracked down!"

"My Führer, we have a new suite set up for you," Dieter Amsel said, poking his head into the room. The Führer gave a curt nod, gesturing for Goebbels to follow so they could discuss how the Nazi press would be spinning this seemingly botched assassination. Goebbels followed at the Führer's heel like a loyal dog, and Reinhard could only watch, deaf to the scolding Himmler gave him, as the Führer marched out the door with an unmistakably Hitlerian gait.

Reinhard Heydrich would never be sure if Operation Chaplin had succeeded or not until the day he died.

THE PRICE OF VICTORY IS SUFFERING. EDMUND HITLER HAD said that, and even though Edmund Hitler had said a lot of bullshit, the man who would never again be known as Adiel Goldstein decided that his brother had been entirely correct about that.

He and Goebbels chatted for about an hour after they arrived in the new room. Soon, however, the stomping of jackboots died down, the sounds of New Year's partygoers echoed about Munich, and the Führer dismissed his herald, commanding him to go spend the first hours of 1932 with his new wife.

"Please sleep well, my Führer," begged Goebbels, offering a cheerful smile and a Nazi salute to the man that had just blown his leader's brains out. Adiel bade Goebbels farewell and found himself alone. Alone and victorious.

Victory felt worse than empty. He now knew what his mother had meant when she'd warned him that *it burns you before it burns them.* She hadn't merely been trying to forestall the creation of a future Hitler. She had been trying to warn Adiel just how thoroughly it would hurt to have a fire permanently housed in his soul. He wondered if it had hurt Adolf Hitler this badly.

He hoped so.

Adiel spared a glance at his new room, which significantly less luxurious than the top-floor suite that was now coated in his brother's blood and brains.

The SS hadn't had time to decorate this smaller room with all of the Nazi fineries, but there was an impressive globe in one corner that reminded Adiel a bit too much of the one from *The Great Dictator* save, of course, for the fact that this globe was entirely solid. He felt its heft when he gave it an idle spin, noticing right away that the Germany on the globe possessed its pre-Versailles borders and was bright blood-red while the rest of the world was a dull shade of grey.

Adiel traced the outline of a nation that in a few years, with his guidance, would extend to almost the entire continent of Europe. Heydrich's adjusted Operation Chaplin did not demand such actions in its second stage, but Adiel did not intend on following the carefully laid out plan Heydrich had made for a powerful, heroic Nazi Germany that would ally with the Western forces against the scourge of Stalinism. No.

There would be no Holocaust under Adiel Goldstein's reign as Führer, but as for every other blunder he had made in his past life, he would make it again and worse. He would invade Russia right before the onset of winter with criminally under-supplied troops. He would start a multi-front war. He would lose the war. Germany would lose the war, Nazism would lose the war. Germany would be utterly decimated, and Nazism would have no place among civilized society.

He would fail, and he would fail gloriously and purposefully, and that act of collective vengeance disguised as arrogant incompetence would be his strike against a nation that had embraced Adolf Hitler and rejected Adiel Goldstein. The movement which had killed little Kaia would be bywords and ashes. He would see to it, and he wouldn't let anything stand in his way.

Because he had been wrong before. There was no

redemption for him or anyone else. Only retribution. Tit for tat. An eye for an eye.

In a way, if this was all the design of a creative but eternally just God, then that God could not have picked a better punishment for Adolf Hitler than this. To hate being himself so much that he wanted nothing more than to destroy everything he had once killed for.

SEVENTEEN

Victory in Europe Day
1945

"Becca, here, hold him while I get a picture!"

"Speak English, Krauts!"

"*Fuck you*, how's that for English?!"

"Ah! Natan! Language!"

"*Language*, Becca, ha! I'm sure he can't even hear me over all this! Avi, can you hear Papa?"

"Hi, Papa!" answered little Avi Libman, neither confirming nor denying that he had heard or understood the curse that his father had flung at that particular xenophobe. The xenophobe himself hadn't even seemed to hear it over the din of people crowding into Times Square to celebrate the end of the latest war to end all wars.

The news of Edmund Hitler's suicide had sent the world into a joyous tizzy. Spontaneous celebrations had broken out everywhere. Becca's sisters had vanished into the throng, no doubt to smooch their American boyfriends. Natan's mother had a crippling fear of crowds, and so she'd opted to stay home. His father was working, his sisters were shepherding little Eli around with his friends, and that left Natan, his wife, and his son by themselves. Natan was fighting with the fancy camera that had been a gift from...

"Need a hand with that?"

"Zaidy Nate!" squealed Avi as an old gentleman broke from the mass of Americans, having found the meet-up spot beneath one particular streamer-decorated lamppost. Natan Goldstein gave Natan Libman a pat on the shoulder. It always felt like touching his younger self should have created a spark, maybe a black hole, but nothing of the sort ever occurred: it was no different from clapping the shoulder of any other young man from synagogue.

Then again, of course, even though he and this bright-eyed young man were technically the same person, they truly weren't. Natan Libman had never lived in a ghetto, had never watched his baby son die, had never raised a monster as his own. Natan Libman was optimistic, only a little bitter about the baseline xenophobia that he and his family faced as well-off refugees saved from the fires of war by the intervention of his wealthy "uncle."

Natan Goldstein had never intended on being part of his younger self's life to this extent: always, the plan had been to be a pen-pal and benefactor to the Libman and the Blum families. To get them to safety and then leave them be. He had assumed that seeing them, knowing them, being their friend, that would be too painful. Seeing himself so happy but not being able to feel it sounded like absolute torture.

Surprisingly, it wasn't. Desperation and sorrow after Kaia's death and Adiel's destruction had driven Natan back to the family he had lost, and they had embraced him with open arms. It was nice: different, of course, but he felt like a part of it rather than an outsider being forced to look in.

"Avi, stop wiggling!" Becca sighed. She offered Natan Goldstein a beautiful smile, and he felt his heart clench up. It wasn't so hard to see himself or his sisters or his parents, but seeing her made him edge towards feeling jealous of Natan Libman because Becca was eternally Becca, Auschwitz or no: always a bright spot. Nevertheless, he'd had a lifetime with his Becca, and so he was able to greet her with platonic warmth that didn't betray his true feelings.

"Zaidy Naaaaaate!" little Avi squealed, and Becca handed her son—*their* son—to the old man. Becca was hard, but Avi was almost too easy. The wiggly little loud-mouth was absolutely nothing like the meek, starved boy that he had known, loved, and mourned. He reminded Natan of Kaia quite a bit, which sometimes hurt, but often instead felt like a blessing, like she somehow lived on in him. When little Avi called him "Zaidy," Natan could even swear that he heard Kaia's voice sometimes.

"How are you, Avi?" Natan asked, kissing the rosy-cheeked toddler to distract himself from the pain in his heart. The boy looked down at the old man's heels and let out a disappointed huff.

"Where's the puppy?" Avi squeaked. Natan felt his heart sink a little, but he chuckled, nonetheless.

"Bernie had to stay home, Avi-*boychik*. You know he's old like me. Walking around would hurt his poor legs."

Avi let out a small squeak of understanding, and Natan

saw Becca purse her lips. She had suggested several times that the poor arthritis-ridden dog would likely need to be put down soon, but Natan insisted that Bernie had a few years left in him. Really, though, he wasn't sure if he'd be able to make that choice when it became utterly necessary. Bernie was the only living link he had to his old family.

Natan decided not to think of that now and focused on his new-old family. "Want me to take the picture?" he asked. "Get all three of you in there."

Natan Libman cheerfully agreed, and Natan Goldstein struggled for a moment to take a picture that wasn't ruined by some photo-bomber tripping into the frame or Avi pulling a face. Luckily, the wealthy Natan Goldstein could afford plenty of film, so he snapped away.

"All right, let me at least *try* it!" cackled the younger Natan, stealing the camera from his older self. "Here, Avi, pose with Zaidy."

Natan the Younger took a few pictures of Avi with Natan the Elder before the old man handed the boy back to his mother. While Becca tried to make the squirming toddler calm down so her husband could snap a picture of her holding him in front of an American flag that dangled from a nearby deli, Natan Goldstein spared a look at the celebrations. Confetti was hurled from skyscrapers, American flags were waved energetically, and the jubilant civilians sang gleefully of the Allied victory.

There was good cause for this celebration. The war in Europe was over. One of the worst wars in world history.

Only Natan Goldstein, however, knew how good they had it as a world, knew how much worse it could have been. The seemingly inevitable ideological war had been awful, horrific, but the death tolls were short by millions.

In a way, Becca had gotten exactly what she had wanted when she'd asked for Adolf Hitler's life. Her family was alive, his family was alive, and since "Edmund Hitler" hadn't pursued a policy of extermination against his racial enemies, millions of Jews were alive.

Hitler had all but neutered the SS in 1938, executing Heinrich Himmler and Reinhard Heydrich right before his disastrous meeting with Neville Chamberlain, ensuring that the Holocaust as Natan had known it never occurred. Concentration camps existed strictly for political prisoners. Emigration was aggressively pursued for the Jews in the occupied territories, and when that became impossible because of Allied interference, they had simply been permitted to live in segregated areas not nearly as terrible as the ghettos that Natan had known.

It had hardly been a comfortable experience for the Jews of Europe, but Natan Goldstein would be the only Jew in the world with an Auschwitz tattoo, and to him, that was more than enough.

With the absence of the death camps, without any such overwhelming acts of evil, perhaps in time Edmund Hitler's reputation would be reexamined. In one-hundred years, perhaps he would be regarded as no more or less evil than Napoleon Bonaparte. Certainly, his name would never become a synonym for the Devil the way *Adolf Hitler* had come to represent evil manifest in Natan's timeline.

For now, however, the beleaguered denizens of Europe and America would not forgive so easily. And so, while they had no idea just how terrible Hitler might have been, they despised him just as thoroughly as they had in Natan's time. Hitler the Warmonger's death was a cause for great cele-bration, and at least for the next few decades, almost nobody would dare to think of Nazism as a redeemable ideology.

And thus, America cheered. Soldiers kissed nurses, trumpets were blown, and newspapers displayed the good news in bold font: **HITLER DEAD.**

One such newspaper fluttered about the partiers' ankles until it came to a stop at Natan's feet. With a lump of sorrow blocking his throat, Natan bent down and picked it up, his gaze shifting from the headline to the picture right beneath it.

There was his son, flawlessly presenting as his worst self. Heiling an army of men who would die for him never knowing just how thoroughly he hated them all.

Officially, Adiel Goldstein had died in the last hours of 1931. Driven to madness when a rogue SS man killed his young daughter, Adiel Goldstein had boldly tried and failed to assassinate Hitler. Anyone who knew of Adiel Goldstein spoke of him with somber, regretful reverence. *Poor man,* they would say. *He tried. It's a shame he didn't succeed.*

For some time, as the Führer continued down his destined path, Natan had mournfully thought that his son had indeed failed. But then changes started happening: the relative ease of Hitler's Jewish emigration policy, the absence of Kristallnacht, the purging of the SS. No reports came out about mass shootings, and it was then that Natan realized what his son had done.

It had taken guesswork because the note that Adiel had sent, his final note, had been frustratingly vague. Filled with paragraphs of praise and declarations of love from the boy that had once been a monster. Adiel hadn't dared to write out his plan for fear that someone would read it. The closest he had come was one paragraph, which

Natan, in moments of weakness, sometimes pulled out and read.

You and Mama took my life before, and now I have to take it back. I despise this, Papa, but it has to be done. Please forgive me for what I do next, and know that in my heart, whatever it seems, I'll be mourning being the man you made me. Know that no matter what I say in the future, I love you dearly. I will always be grateful for the life you gave me.

Natan looked down at the scowling monster in black-and-white. Tears obscured his vision. He despised the thought that his poor son had been forced to play this role for over a decade. Every second of being Hitler must have been agonizing beyond belief for him.

Adiel had died as he had once upon a time: in a bunker, with a gun to his skull and a poison pill in his mouth. Unlike Adolf, he had died alone. Unlike Adolf, who must have regarded the death of Hitler as a tragedy, Adiel had almost certainly chomped down on that cyanide pill with great gusto, relieved to finally be free of the horrid life of Hitler.

Natan Goldstein was so terribly proud of the man that Adiel Goldstein had become.

"Papa…"

"Avi, quit squirming."

"Papa, Zaidy's crying." Avi's tiny voice trembled with concern as he pointed towards Natan Goldstein, prompting Natan Libman, who was holding his precious son and trying to pose for a picture that Becca was taking, to glance at the old man.

An onlooker would have seen the old man clutching the newspaper with both hands, crumpling the historical proclamation and staining it with his tears, and assumed that he was crying tears of joy.

But young Natan Libman, who knew himself well, could only stare at the old man and wonder why such wonderful news was breaking Natan Goldstein's heart.

EPILOGUE

"Hey...hey, we have another one! Erm...are you okay?"

Adolf Hitler could only answer the way he always did: "Of course not."

To be continued in The Hangman's Master

HISTORICAL NOTES

While *Adiel and the Führer* is a work of historical fiction, many of the details concerning its historical characters are not made up.

Regarding Reinhard Heydrich: the information about his dismissal from the Navy is generally correct. Heydrich served for almost a decade in the German Navy, and did indeed propose to his eventual wife Lina Von Osten after a mere three days of courtship. This did, indeed, cause a former girlfriend to have a mental breakdown and report him. The exact details of this affair and the Honor Court hearing that subsequently commenced are subject to controversy, but historians have generally agreed that Heydrich's rude and abrasive behavior before the Honor Court brought about his dishonorable discharge. "Instead of accepting responsibility and settling for a minor punishment, Heydrich insisted that the woman had herself initiated their sexual relationship. He also denied ever having promised her marriage in return, describing their liaison in dismissive terms that annoyed the members of the court."[1] Notably, Heydrich "said it would be dishonorable to marry a girl who had given herself beforehand—even to him."[2] This is what Heydrich references in this novel when he states that he "effectively called his ex-girlfriend a whore in front of the Honor Court."

The details of Heydrich joining the SS—Lina forcing him to go, Himmler cancelling the initial appointment, and Heydrich using British detective novels to outline his plans for the SD—are also accurate.[3] There was confusion during Himmler's interview process because, while Heydrich had been a signals officer ("*Nachrichtenoffizier*") in the German Navy, Himmler mistakenly believed that Heydrich had been an intelligence officer ("*Nachrichtendienst-Offizier.*")[4]

It took several years of service in the SS for Reinhard Heydrich to "grow into it." As noted in the novel, Heydrich had previously considered himself non-political, and he expressed doubts about Nazism to friends as late as 1932.[5] His wife Lina noted that his only concern early on was getting a job and getting married, and he initially cared very little for Nazi ideology.[6]

Heinrich Himmler did indeed have a preference for an agrarian lifestyle—his earlier statement in this novel about leaving the city as a child for the sake of his health is accurate.[7] Himmler received a degree in agriculture in 1922 from the Technical University of Munich.[8] While he most famously attempted (and failed) to raise chickens, at various points he and his wife did also try to grow different crops, including, as stated in this novel, apples.[9]

Himmler did indeed maintain an anti-Christian worldview throughout his reign as chief of the SS, instead favoring a strange "German" flavor of neo-paganism.[10]

Throughout his life, Himmler would carry with him a copy of the *Edda*, a collection of Norse myths, and the *Bhagavad-Gita*, a Hindu holy text.[11] Reportedly, Himmler's more esoteric and supernatural obsessions were a source of argument between him and Reinhard Heydrich. "Once when he [Heydrich] explained to Himmler the nonsense of one of H.'s [Himmler's] speeches, H. [Himmler] said to him: 'You, with your damned logic!'"[12]

Adolf Hitler did indeed have a younger brother named Edmund, who did indeed die of measles when Adolf was eleven.[13] This reportedly affected the young Hitler greatly: "it is certain that there was a dramatic change in Adolf's character during the year following his brother's death...he becomes a morose, self-absorbed, nervous boy."[14]

Adolf Hitler was indeed born directly above a bar called the *Stag*. The *Stag* typically served the residents of Braunau Am Inn while renters such as the Hitlers would live on the upper levels.[15]

Many of the smaller details about Hitler—such as his favorite color being green or his habit of pacing and grabbing the thigh of his pants when nervous—are gleaned from reports of Hitler's servants in *Living with Hitler: Accounts of Hitler's Household Staff*.[16]

The relationship between Adolf Hitler and his niece Geli Raubal is a source of major historical controversy, with some sources claiming that Hitler's feelings towards her were entirely platonic, some stating that Hitler had romantic inclinations towards her that were never acted on, and some decreeing that he and Geli had a sexual relationship.[17] Conspiracy also abounds regarding Geli's death, but it is generally accepted that, after an argument with Adolf Hitler, Geli Raubal committed suicide via a gunshot to the chest on September 18th of 1931. Geli's suicide shook Adolf Hitler greatly: "for weeks Hitler seemed close to a nervous breakdown and repeatedly decided to withdraw from politics."[18] Quite unfortunately. Hitler did not follow through on this.

Notes

HISTORICAL NOTES

1. Gerwarth, R. (2012). *Hitler's Hangman: The Life of Heydrich* (Illustrated). Yale University Press.
2. Dougherty, N., & Lehmann-Haupt, C. (2022). *The Hangman and His Wife: The Life and Death of Reinhard Heydrich*. Knopf.
3. Gerwarth, R. (2012). *Hitler's Hangman: The Life of Heydrich* (Illustrated). Yale University Press.
4. Deschner, G. (1981). *Heydrich: The Pursuit of Total Power*. Orbis.
5. Dougherty, N., & Lehmann-Haupt, C. (2022). *The Hangman and His Wife: The Life and Death of Reinhard Heydrich*. Knopf.
6. *Id.*
7. Himmler, K., & Mitchell, M. (2012). *The Himmler Brothers*. Macmillan Publishers.
8. Longerich, P., Noakes, J., & Sharpe, L. (2012). *Heinrich Himmler: A Life*. Oxford University Press.
9. Himmler, K., Wildt, M., Ph.D., H. T., & Hansen, A. J. (2016). *The Private Heinrich Himmler: Letters of a Mass Murderer* (First U.S. Edition.). St. Martin's Press.
10. FitzGerald, M. (2021). *The Nazis and the Supernatural: The Occult Secrets of Hitler's Evil Empire*. Van Haren Publishing.
11. Kurlander, E. (2017). *Hitler's Monsters: A Supernatural History of the Third Reich*. Amsterdam University Press.
12. Williams, M. (2018). *Heydrich: Dark Shadow of the SS* (1st ed.). Fonthill Media.
13. Toland, J. (1992). *Adolf Hitler: The Definitive Biography* (1st ed.). Anchor.
14. Payne, R. (2014). *The Life and Death Of Adolf Hitler*. Brick Tower Press.
15. Ingber, S. (2019, August 6). *A Long Legal Battle Over Hitler's Birth Home In Austria Ends*. NPR.org. https://www.npr.org/2019/08/06/748588026/a-long-legal-battle-over-hitlers-birth-home-in-austria-ends
16. Krause, W. K., Döhring, H., Plaim, A., Kuch, K., & Moorhouse, R. (2018). *Living with Hitler: Accounts of Hitler's Household Staff*. Greenhill Books.
17. Toland, J. (1992). *Adolf Hitler: The Definitive Biography* (1st ed.). Anchor.
18. Ullrich, V. (2017). *Hitler: Ascent: 1889-1939* (Reprint). Vintage.

A NOTE TO MY READERS...

Thank you for reading *Adiel and the Führer*! If you enjoyed it, please tell your friends. I'd love to hear your thoughts on *Adiel and the Führer*, and reviews help authors a great deal, so I'd be very grateful if you would post a short review on Amazon and/or Goodreads. If you'd like to read more stories like this and get notifications about free and discounted books and short stories, follow me on <u>Twitter</u>, <u>Face-book</u>, <u>Amazon</u>, and sign up for my newsletter at <u>elysehoffman.com</u>! You can also follow me on <u>Bookbub</u>!

Printed in Great Britain
by Amazon

42527704R00208